The Husband Hunt

Books by Jillian Hunter

Fairy Tale
Daring
Delight
Indiscretion
The Husband Hunt

Published by POCKET BOOKS

JILLIAN HUNTER

The Husband Hunt

SONNET BOOKS
New York London Toronto Sydney Singapore

This book is a work of fiction. Names, characters, places and incidents are products of the author's imagination or are used fictitiously. Any resemblance to actual events or locales or persons, living or dead, is entirely coincidental.

An *Original* Publication of POCKET BOOKS

 A Sonnet Book published by
POCKET BOOKS, a division of Simon & Schuster, Inc.
1230 Avenue of the Americas, New York, NY 10020

Front cover illustration by Ben Perini

Printed in the U.S.A.

For my daughter, Jacqueline.
May the Lord bless you forever.

Acknowledgments

Special thanks to my agent, Andrea Cirillo, who is absolutely the best.

Chapter 1

Devon, England
1814

Catriona Grant hoped that the rumors of Viscount Rutleigh's reputation had not been exaggerated; only a man with a tarnished reputation could overlook the life she had led.

There was a ring around the moon on the night she finally reached Rutleigh Hall. She stopped at the edge of the woods and wondered whether this was a sign that she should turn back. For most of her life, she had been chased from fine houses such as this, or else smuggled up the backstairs to the curtained bed of a dying person while her mother worked her healing charms in the candlelight.

From what she had just learned, however, the English lord who owned this estate was not known for welcoming visitors, except for the London ladies who had shared his bed in the past. Apparently, the viscount had run a bit wild in his younger years, but war had tamed him somewhat, and whatever questionable behaviors he now indulged were done so in secret.

She liked the look of his estate, though, an elegant two-story, H-shaped house of sandstone set in its own parkland. The foundations of the ancestral manor had been laid in Elizabethan times of stone quarried from the nearby moor in the deepest roots of which lived His Satanic Majesty. A few local folk believed that the influence of these accursed stones had turned the Rutleigh men into something of demons themselves, dueling, womanizing, gambling, until holy wedlock had put a damper on their dark desires. But in Devon, the devil was thought to have a hand in many things.

All this helpful information about Lord Rutleigh had been imparted to Catriona less than an hour ago over a pint of inferior ale in a local inn by no less reliable a source than the village barmaid.

"He's kindly to his sister, though," the woman had been forced to admit. "Give the devil his due—mercy, my dear, you're not hoping to ask charity of 'im?" she had asked in alarm. "If it's work you want, I say go elsewhere. Better to work in a textile factory than to fall prey to his charms."

Catriona had straightened her slender shoulders. "I am a relative, not a charity case." Actually, it was through his lordship's brother-in-law that she claimed a fragile thread of kinship.

"You—related to that family? Do tell."

Catriona frowned now, recalling how the barmaid had scoffed at her claim of blood relationship to the house. And what was so amusing about herself? she wanted to know. True, she hadn't made a proper toilette in several days, and her cloak was snagged with burrs and briars. And while the gown beneath might not be the height of style, not anything a young lady might admire in good society, it was of quality wool and decently tailored.

"Sir Lionel Deering is my cousin," she had said in a dignified voice.

"Sir Lionel?" There had been an awful pause during which the woman's amusement evolved into an air of pitying astonishment. "But he's been dead for almost three years, dear. Didn't anyone tell you? Sir Lionel was killed in battle."

The floor had seemed to dissolve beneath Catriona's feet. She couldn't have come all this way for nothing; she couldn't have pinned all her hopes on the generosity of a cousin who had died without her ever knowing.

"His wife is still alive, though," the barmaid had added gently, distressed by the young woman's sudden pallor. "That's Lady Deering, the sister I told you about. She has a soft heart, that one, which makes it all the stranger that the viscount is such a difficult man."

Well, it was too late for her to return to Scotland now. She had shamed her brother by running out on the party celebrating her own engagement to a widowed laird in his sixties who had five unruly children. She had also run out of funds and had no means to make the journey back. Her future had hinged on the casual invitation of her late cousin, who had said, "If you should ever need anything, come to Devon."

Now she glanced at the short, raw-boned Scotsman standing beside her, his face as seasoned as a Celtic battle shield. "What do you think?"

"I dinna feel right about this. I think they've been expecting us."

"How could they know we had arrived when they are probably unaware that I even exist?"

"Someone could have warned them," he said mysteriously. "There are those who saw us leave the castle and might remember your connection to your cousin."

"We cannot cower here in the bushes all night."

"We canna walk into a trap," he said firmly, refusing to budge.

"I am not afraid of Lord Rutleigh, Thomas. I expect he isn't nearly as bad as that barmaid exaggerated. At any rate, I am obliged now to introduce myself."

His craggy face softened. "Aye, ye were always the brave one, even from the day we found ye alone on the moor, howling yer wee heart out with the indignity of it all. A lady rescued by ruffians, ye were. Aye, blood shows."

Catriona paused. Somehow, being reminded of that day, of her preadolescent self tumbling out of a tree into a dead bramble bush and having her rough-handed uncle pluck splinters from her bum, did not give her the composure she needed to face the notorious Lord Rutleigh.

"Thomas, I would prefer simply to knock at the door and introduce myself."

"Not until I'm sure there isna a trap about to spring. Fergan's lured the dogs away."

Catriona glanced uneasily around the darkened estate. Fergan was the castle deerhound and her companion on cold lonely nights since she had found him limping on the moor years ago, as lost as she. He was a tough old dog but perhaps not a match against the well-trained mastiffs that patrolled the viscount's grounds for intruders.

"Aye," Thomas said in a low voice, "there's someone watching from the house. I tell ye, they're lying in wait. I feel it in these weary old bones. My blood is all a-tingle with anxiety."

"Not to mention several pints of ale," she said wryly. "Besides, who would have written to warn him we were coming?"

"Yer half-brother, mayhap. The one whose castle ye ran away from. The one who had arranged yer marriage to one ancient laird who is probably having heart seizure at the altar as we speak."

She bit her lip. "Aye, so. But would James be angry enough to have me shot on sight, I ask you?"

"The English do things in queer ways, lassie. Mark my words. We're in hostile territory now."

A flicker of light from the house interrupted their whispered conversation. She looked up at the long gallery windows of the ivy-draped manor house. A man in elegant evening attire had paused to look outside, candlelight emphasizing his powerful frame. She stared up at him in wonder, at his fine muscular figure. Surely his silhouette was deceiving, as exaggerated as the talk of him. Surely he would not appear so arresting on closer inspection.

She brushed a red-gold curl from her face, squinting to see better. "That must be Lady Deering's brother, the viscount."

"How can ye tell?"

"It's a man I saw in the vision." Besides, she added silently, he certainly looked like a man who had seen the more interesting side of life.

"Aye? Well, yer visions I willna argue with. Here." He placed a heavy pistol in her hand. The tips of her fingers went numb with cold fear.

"What is this for?" she whispered in alarm. "I've come here to ask his mercy, not to murder him."

"He's an Englishman, lass. They're unpredictable."

"Be that as it may, I am not going to kill the man."

She glanced up again at the house, disappointed to see that the intriguing male figure had disappeared. She had been fascinated by her glimpse into the world she imagined he inhabited, of duels fought at dawn and glittering ballrooms, of late-night parties and self-indulgent pursuits. It was certainly a contrast to the inelegant life she had led, being shuffled from relatives to boarding schools back to relatives again.

"Oh," she said softly. "He's gone. I thought he sensed we were here."

"Aye, 'tis why I'm worried. I swear to ye, he's watchin' fer someone. Now, I'm headin' around the house to the stables. When I give the signal—"

He wheeled spryly toward the path as the baying of dogs resounded in the oak woods that surrounded the estate. Sometimes Catriona thought that he lived for blood-stirring moments such as this. She, on the other hand, would be very happy to settle down to a more sedate existence.

As she waited for him to return, she closed her eyes, an unspoken plea forming in her heart. *Please, please, just for once, let me find a place to belong.*

The tallest man at the table threw down his hand of cards as unearthly howling rose from the woods that encircled his estate. His lean face registered more annoyance than alarm at the commotion.

"What poor creature have those damn dogs cornered now?" he wondered aloud, lounging back in his chair.

"Not one of our guests on the way home,I hope," the man beside him said. Lanky, fair-haired, light-hearted, he was the antithesis in temperament and appearance of his host, Knight Dennison, Viscount Rutleigh as of last year when his older brother had passed away after a brief illness in India. Having also recently inherited, Wendell Grenville, the Duke of Meacham, was a darling of the *ton* to Knight's devil, an elusive favorite among the marriage-minded mamas and debutante daughters the members of this private house party sought to escape.

"You've wrecked the game now, Knight," grumbled another guest. "I was winning, too." The third man at the table, a portly local squire who dealt in lace, gave a good-natured sigh, folded his hands over his paunch, and promptly fell asleep.

The man he had addressed only grinned boyishly at the complaint and rose to stare out into the night. A cluster of pedunculate oaks enclosed the well-tended grounds, giving way to an overgrown tangle of woods. Beyond the borders of his estate stretched the moor, a misty realm pitted with tors and megalithic boulders.

"The dogs have stopped their infernal barking," he said in relief. "With luck, it was only a badger and not Lord Jennings's carriage they were chasing."

"I hope the badger wasn't hurt," a woman said from the corner.

He glanced down with affection at the brunette sitting below him on a chaise, his younger sister Olivia, who seemed impossibly fragile in her pearl-gray dress of watered silk. The cashmere shawl he'd given her for Christmas did not conceal the prominent bones of her collarbone any better than her skillful application of rice powder hid the hollows of bereavement below her cheekbones. His beloved sibling was wasting away to a wraith before his eyes.

"Did you eat anything for supper, Olivia?" he asked quietly.

"My goodness, yes."

"Two bites of pudding," Wendell said disapprovingly from the card table. "Two tiny bites that would not have nourished a fly."

"I ate the entire bowl," Olivia protested.

She was lying. She glanced away to avoid Knight's perceptive gaze, and he felt a familiar surge of panic and guilt. Almost three years ago, he had watched her husband die on the battlefield, and now he feared he was losing her, too.

She tugged on the cuff of his white cambric shirt. "Do you really think it was just a badger?"

He looked up again at the window. There had been a rash of housebreakings recently among the small circle of wealthy aristocrats who comprised the upper crust of West Briarcombe. The crimes had been executed with a clumsy daring that made Knight suspect at first that a gang of well-heeled youths were taking revenge on their indulgent families. He and Wendell had even laughed at their harmless mischief until a footman at Wendell's ducal estate had been brutally beaten and left for dead.

"Our house is the next logical one to be broken into," Olivia said worriedly.

"It's been three weeks now," he said, using a casual voice to calm her. "Duke got off a good shot at one of them, and his mama pitched a chamberpot on their heads as they escaped down the ladder."

"A full chamberpot, I might add," Wendell said with a grimace. "Quite nasty, that."

Olivia gave a faint shudder. "Your poor mother, Wendell. She says she is never going back to that house, and who can blame her? You mustn't return there, either. Knight and I absolutely forbid it."

"Olivia." Knight knelt down beside her, his dark gray eyes gentle. "We've never been able to get rid of Wendell, have we? He's like a piece of furniture, a portrait on the wall. Furthermore, Smythe and Howard are patrolling the grounds at this very moment, looking like utter fools with their ancient fowling pieces, and would I let anything happen to you?"

She pressed her forefinger against the hard contour of his chin. "And who is going to protect you, my brother who believes himself invincible?"

He smiled, thinking that her eyes looked like huge bruises in her too-thin face. Ever since the day he had returned from Albuera to tell her that Lionel, her husband and Knight's closest friend, was not coming home, she had begun to vanish on him, to disappear by subtle degrees. She pretended to eat to please him. She could not sleep. And he had not even revealed the horrible truth of how Lionel had died, not the swift storybook death of a hero that she believed. Oh, no. Not for nothing had their regiment been called the Die Hards.

"I am perfectly capable of protecting myself," he said in an amused voice. "And I am not going to expire for some time yet."

"We're all going to die sooner or later," the squire remarked cheerfully. He hoisted himself out of his chair, brushing biscuit crumbs from his waistcoat. "With God's grace, I shall not do so on the way home. Good night, all."

"Good night, Melvin," Olivia said, rising to kiss his whiskery cheek.

"Shall I see you in London this year, Knight?" he asked over Olivia's shoulder.

"London," Wendell said, "is losing its appeal by the day. M'friends and I are entirely too bad at remembering all them rules. Society doesn't like that."

"Society likes Knight well enough," Olivia said in defense of the older brother she adored. "At least, the debutantes seemed to, although he didn't like any of them enough to bring one home as a bride, I'm afraid. Like my older brother he seems destined for bachelorhood."

"I hope," Melvin said, shaking his head, "that Knight is not still in love with that awful Arabella."

Wendell rubbed his face to hide a smile. Arabella Minton was the local heiress to whom Knight had been unofficially betrothed since childhood. Everyone knew Knight could have done better in his choice of a bride, but he'd never seemed inclined to look. Arabella knew him in all his moods and did not appear to be the type of woman who, as a wife, would make excessive demands.

As it turned out, Arabella no longer appeared to be his type at all. While Knight was risking his life in the Peninsular campaigns, Arabella had shocked her friends and family by marrying a Devon baron and businessman named Anton Rathbone. No one was surprised at her lack of loyalty to her childhood sweetheart. Arabella was not exactly well liked in West Briarcombe. But Anton, in terms of height, was half the man Knight was and sported twice his girth, which left many people scratching their heads in surprise that she had chosen the rotund Rathbone as her husband.

Wendell pulled a straight face, winking at Olivia. "I

know for a fact that Knight's feelings for her are dead. Burned to a crisp." He glanced at his friend, his wicked grin creeping back. "Ashes of Arabella."

Olivia hesitated before indulging in an uncharacteristic moment of spite. "The Annoying Arabella."

"Excuse me." His handsome face revealing no emotion whatsoever, Knight plucked the brandy decanter from Wendell's hands before his friend could pour another drink. "It is past midnight, time for all badly behaved dukes to be in bed, and my personal life is not open to discussion."

"It still grieves him to talk of her," Olivia said, giving her brother a sympathetic look.

Melvin grunted. "He's—"

The sharp report of a pistol outside the house brought an abrupt end to the conversation. Olivia pulled away from the startled squire, her shawl fluttering to the carpet. Wendell rushed up to the window behind Knight and pushed her out of the way, shielding her with his body.

"Now, that," Knight said quietly, "is a very talented badger indeed."

Chapter

2

❦

Catriona *settled down* in the shrubbery and watched Thomas dart across the lawn, a barrel-chested figure in tattered tartan. She knew it stung his pride to bring her here to England. He resented asking anything of the Sassenachs who had robbed his family of dignity and fortune, but as he himself had admitted:"Yer half brother is drinkin' himself to death and liable to hurt ye in his bad spells. Yer Uncle Diarmid is gone, and these people, English or no, are yer kin, albeit indirectly. They're yer own, Cat. They'll take care of ye. I'm too old to serve ye much longer."

She fumbled on the ground for her portmanteau, spilling its contents in the dirt. A miniature hand-mirror glinted in the moonlight, and she picked it up, recoiling at her silvery reflection.

She had never envisioned making her social debut on English soil looking like such a guttersnipe. But then nothing in her life had ever followed a proper path. She was illegitimate to begin with, a come-by-chance child. Her noble father had died without ever acknowledging her, and she had inherited her hard-working mother's gift, or curse, of prophecy, which tended to make her even more of an outcast.

Not that her gift did her much good. It never came to her when she needed it, such as now when she was anxious to know how her English relatives would receive her. Foretelling the future wasn't a talent a young woman could brag of to attract a beau. In fact, it frightened all but her closest friends away.

"You, Catriona Beatrice Grant," she informed the unsmiling face in the mirror, "are an anomaly of nature, and you look like hell. I wouldn't let you into my fine Rutleigh mansion. I wouldn't even put you in my privy."

She reached down in the dirt for her brush, noticing that there wasn't a single weed in the manicured flower beds. Not one dandelion dared to show its sunny head, which, along with the ring around the moon, Catriona regarded as a portent of bad things to come. If the people who lived on this estate were that particular about their garden, they would certainly not appreciate the more unconventional aspects of her past.

Suddenly, a man appeared on the front lawn with a musket. Had Thomas given the signal? she wondered in horror. Had he been taken hostage by English aristocrats while she stared at her disreputable self in the mirror?

The shrubbery that concealed her parted, and she slowly raised her head, staring up into a musket barrel. "Please don't shoot me," she said in the calmest voice she could manage. "I know my appearance is rather unexpected, but I am Sir Lionel's long-lost cousin from Scotland. We had planned to go to his estate first, but then we learned of his passing, and that I could find her ladyship here. The dogs frightened me, you see, and that was why I deemed it prudent to wait."

She fired the pistol straight into the air to summon Thomas. A few seconds later, he pushed through the bushes to frown at her. "Put down that weapon," he said in an undertone. "The old gardener has only come to help me bring up yer things."

Catriona stared in concern at the elderly man who had stumbled back in the shrubbery, blinking in disbelief. "Well, it's a good thing neither of us shot the other." She frowned at Thomas. "You never gave me the signal."

"Aye, I did. Ye were off in that other world, no doubt, or frettin' with yer damn hair."

She rose to her feet, whispering as she did, "What did you tell them about me?"

Thomas positioned himself in front of her like a bodyguard. His voice was a low growl in her ear. "Not everything. Just enough to ease yer entrée, lass."

"They're going to find out sooner or later," she said worriedly. "You know James will trace me here, if he hasn't already. I could swear we were being followed in Carlisle."

"Perhaps."

"I do not wish to deceive my new relations."

"Just leave everything to me, lass. I got you here safe and sound, did I not?"

"That remains to be seen," she said, staring past him.

Her attention had been diverted by the black-haired

man in evening dress who strode with authority across the lawn. There was arrogance in the set of his broad shoulders, and even though she could not yet see his face, she imagined it to be a study in the unyielding Sassenach nature, a lord who lived to conquer and crush anyone who dared to cross his path. As she had done.

"What the devil has happened here?" he demanded.

She shivered in reaction to the imperious depth of his voice, which he had scarcely raised for effect. It was restrained and wonderful, low-pitched and full of power, like thunder breaking above the moor. Even Thomas seemed to stand in awe.

The gardener said, "It was all a misunderstanding, my lord. No harm done."

"Misunderstanding?" The owner of the impressive voice glanced at Catriona, his tone registering frank suspicion. "I thought you had caught the housebreakers. Did I or did I not hear a shot?"

He had reached her now. He was tall enough that she had to step back to examine his face, and even then she could not decide exactly what lay beneath the composition of shadows and chiseled angles. Perhaps she was better off not knowing. His eyes were iron-gray, cool as mist; the only hint of softness in his features was his wide, sensual mouth, and even that was overpowered by the harsh symmetry of his bone structure.

"Well," he said, circling the silent group with his hands clasped behind his back. "Have we all been struck dumb by lightning? Is anyone going to answer me?"

No one spoke.

Catriona studied Thomas from the corner of her eye, but he, too, seemed to have turned to stone. "It was I," she said at last, her voice insubstantial in the silence. "I shot into the air to summon my servant."

"You—and *who* are *you?*" He turned on his heel to regard her.

Their eyes locked, and for a moment she felt tempted to throw herself at his mercy and tell him the truth. But there wasn't a trace of understanding that she could discern in his unyielding gray eyes, and she was spared the humiliation of such a melodramatic gesture by Thomas, who had finally gathered his wits.

"Look at her carefully, my lord. Do ye no see a resemblance?"

The man stared at her until color mounted in her cheeks.

Her hair was tawny red, abundantly thick and curly, a perfect foil for those soft golden-green eyes and finely drawn features. She smelled faintly of—it was a nice smell, actually—herbs and flowers and earthy things. Her clothes certainly weren't impressive—a blue woolen dress beneath some sort of purple-gray plaid that women probably wore in the north. He might have labeled her an attractive female had she not gazed back at him with that challenging stare that brought out a rather beastly impulse in him to rattle her composure.

"What is the ragamuffin supposed to resemble?" he asked with a dismissive shrug. "And why are there armed intruders in my garden?"

Catriona glanced at the gardener, expecting him to explain exactly what had happened, but he merely hung his head in silence, clearly intimidated by his master's wrath.

"I think that this is a matter for her ladyship's ears alone," Thomas said cryptically.

The man blinked in amazement. "Are you referring to *my* sister?"

"Aye, my lord. Lady Deering, that's who we've come to see."

"Whom," Catriona whispered, nudging him in the side.

Thomas looked blank. "What?"

"*Whom* we've come to see."

"Mercy," he said with a shrug of impatience. "Does it matter?"

The viscount snorted. "I'm not taking either of you anywhere near her ladyship. Besides, you've come too late. The gypsies were here last summer with their lurid claims that they could contact her ladyship's late husband."

Catriona ground her teeth, tempted to inform him that *she* had never had dealings with the netherworld, and she wasn't a gypsy, either. But he didn't look as though he would listen; he was more concerned with protecting his sister, which only made Catriona think of her own miserable half-brother James, who did not give a fig anymore whether anyone lived or died, including himself, and how it was because of him that she was there, standing before a man who made her feel entirely unwelcome.

"Let's go, Thomas," she said, lifting her portmanteau with a weary sigh. "It was a bad idea to come without writing first."

The old man looked at her in bewilderment. "We canna go. We've nowhere to go." He glanced up into the viscount's forbidding face. "Ye canna turn her away."

"Of course I can," Knight said without emotion, and then he glanced at the three servants who were witnessing this unexpected drama. Or, rather, he glanced at two of them; Howard, the young footman, was halfway to the house, presumably to fetch reinforcements for this minor dilemma.

"In that case," Catriona said hesitantly, "you should give this to Lady Deering. It belonged to her husband. He said it would bring me luck. It hasn't."

Knight stood in silence as she removed a brown silk pouch from her cloak. Inside the bag was a heavy gold ring twisted into a knot.

"Take it, and tell her that I'm sorry he died. He was kind to me. I wish I'd known him better."

He raised his gaze to hers, unprepared for the impact of those intelligent eyes in a face that was more piquant than pretty. "Where did you get this?" he demanded, taking it from her hand.

"Lionel gave it to me as a keepsake. He was going off to war."

"Lionel?" He stepped toward her, forcing Thomas off to the side. "I was not aware that he had any truck with the gypsies."

She drew a breath. "And I wasn't aware he had such a difficult brother-in-law." She was painfully earnest as she stood there, setting him down in one breath, asking for hospitality in another. "If I had, I wouldn't have come."

"'Tis her ladyship ye want," the older man reminded her.

Knight glanced down at the ring. He could not remember the exact conversation, but to his regret he *did* recall Lionel mentioning his Scottish blood, the "uncouth" side of the family, and how amusing and endearingly barbaric he'd found their behavior. But this puffball of a female and her shrunken husk of a protector in their fusty plaids, well, it was too much. What was he supposed to do with them? Send them on their way, of course. He was under no obligation to do otherwise.

Except that she had Lionel's eyes, those gentle, knowing, mischievous eyes that Knight could never forget and missed more than he could admit.

"How did you come by the ring?" he asked, his voice expressionless.

"He gave it to me for healing his knee. He said I could use the ring as part of my marriage portion."

"He was my closest friend," Knight said in a clipped voice. "I never heard him mention your name."

"I never heard him mention yours, either," she said indignantly. "And I was his cousin."

"A fact that remains to be proved," he said.

She frowned. "Excuse me?"

He frowned back at her. "The usual manner for a social introduction in these parts is to knock at the door."

She lifted her brow. "And how does one, in these parts, reach the door when one is beset by attack dogs?"

His eyes glittered. "One usually does not pay a social call this late at night."

"What has happened, Knight?" a woman inquired softly behind him.

He glanced over his shoulder in annoyance, slipping the ring into his pocket. Howard had brought reinforcements, all right, but not for Knight's side. Olivia and Wendell had arrived to investigate the disturbance; they had obviously been informed that their lives were not in any imminent danger.

"Go back into the house, Olivia," he said, returning

his attention to the strange pair who had invaded his privacy. "I am handling this matter."

"And not very well, either," he thought he heard the young Scotswoman murmur.

Olivia and Wendell began to angle for a position around him, making a game of it. Irritated by their interference, Knight planted his legs apart to block their way. It didn't deter them for a second. The two of them were incorrigible together, like a pair of children. Sometimes he thought he was the only person in the house who possessed any common sense whatsoever.

"Howard thought our visitors had something to do with Lionel," Olivia said, pausing to draw a breath. She was shivering in her thin silk gown until Wendell gallantly pulled off his jacket to cover her.

"They are not visitors," Knight said succinctly. "They're, well, I don't quite know who they are, or what they want."

Wendell was eyeing the old Scots servant with amused curiosity before his interest turned to the woman. Knight could almost feel his friend's male instincts go on the alert. What, he wondered, did Wendell see beneath that unattractive woolen cloak? Perhaps he needed to take a closer look.

"They hardly look intimidating, Knight," Wendell said under his breath.

Olivia was staring at the young woman's face as if making some sort of connection. "Who are you?" she asked, sounding half wistful, half afraid. And then, as an afterthought, she added politely, "Have we met?"

Catriona bit her lip. "Are you Lady Deering?"

Olivia nodded, throwing a puzzled look at Knight, who merely lifted his broad shoulders in a shrug. "Yes, but who—"

"I am Catriona Beatrice Grant, Lionel's cousin, ma'am. His uncle was the Earl of Roxshire, my father."

"The Earl of Roxshire."

Olivia looked so utterly blank that Knight dared allow himself hope that this entire long-lost relations nonsense would die stillborn before it could go any further.

"There," he said, with such profound satisfaction that everyone glanced around to stare at him. "I thought that they were imposters, carrion trying to feed off the grief of others."

Then Olivia's face broke into a radiant smile—the first genuine smile Knight had seen her give since he came home from battle. "The Earl of Roxshire? From the Borders?"

Catriona's slight shoulders fell in a sigh of relief. "Oh, aye. The same one. Your brother has the ring that Lionel gave me."

"And you are Lionel's Scottish cousin, the moorling he mentioned?" Olivia said in wonder.

Wendell regarded her in friendly delight. "She is family, Olivia. Roxshire's daughter. Isn't that a happy surprise?"

Catriona glanced up, her gaze clashing with Knight's as if she had sensed the suspicious turn of his thoughts. An earl's daughter, indeed. A moorling, whatever that was supposed to mean. She had not made the arduous journey here to strengthen family ties, he thought as he fished the ring from his pocket and handed it to Olivia. The young woman wanted something.

"I wouldn't have come without notifying you beforehand," she explained awkwardly, "but circumstances forced us to leave our home with little preparation."

"What circumstances?" Knight asked, his predator's instincts on the prowl.

Both Olivia and Wendell subjected him to looks that said he was an insensitive oaf for even asking such a question.

"Circumstances can happen to anyone, Knight," Olivia said in undertone, clutching the ring tightly in her hand, "even to a young lady of a gold pedigree."

"She shot a pistol into the air to summon her servant," Knight said in disbelief. "What sort of lady behaves in such a way?"

"A resourceful one, I would think," Wendell said.

"The gardener did approach her with a musket, my lord," Thomas pointed out. "And it was my pistol. I'd asked her to hold it."

"I might not have fired the gun at all," Catriona explained, "except that he startled me as I was brushing my hair, and the pistol rather went off by itself."

"There," Olivia said in triumph. "She was brushing her hair to make a dignified introduction, Knight. Is that ladylike behavior enough for you?" She tucked her arm into the crook of Catriona's elbow, giving a pleased little chuckle. "Come into the house, cousin, and don't let my brother frighten you. He isn't half bad when he's at home."

Catriona stole a glance over her shoulder at him as Olivia led her toward the mansion. He could have sworn she gave him a fleeting smile, but that would be rather dangerous of her, challenging him, and before he could call attention to it, a huge dog came bounding out of the woods, took a flying leap, and knocked him into Wendell.

"Dear God," he said, "where did that come from?"

"'Tis the young lady's," Thomas said, grabbing the panting animal by the scruff of the neck.

"Well, put it in the kennel with the other dogs."

"The young lady willna like that, my lord."

Knight raised his brow. "That's too deuced bad, isn't it? I do not want this beast frightening my household—"

Before he could finish, the deerhound sprang free, or, rather, Thomas released it, pretending to look alarmed as the dog shot between the two young women. Olivia screamed, then started to laugh again. The Scottish female was laughing, too, as the hound jealously nosed Olivia from her side. Thomas hurried after them, clearly not about to abdicate his role as guardian.

Wendell shook his head in amusement. "And so family matters have taken an interesting turn."

"If she is who she claims to be," Knight said, shaking his head.

"Can you doubt it? My God, she has Lionel's eyes, in case you hadn't noticed."

Knight hesitated. "I noticed."

"She'll be good for Olivia, don't you think? It was hard enough for her when she lost the baby, but with Lionel not here to help her accept—"

Knight turned on him. "Do you not find it peculiar that she, an earl's daughter, appears out of the mist dressed like, well, I don't know how to describe her?"

"Reduced circumstances, Knight."

"Maybe, Wendell, but what am I supposed to do with her? What am I to think?"

Chapter
3

They led her into a beautifully appointed drawing room, all blue and rose brocade glowing invitingly in the candlelight. She picked up a glass figurine of Persephone on the table, then wandered to the window, tracing a pattern with her fingertip on the damp pane at the precise moment that Lord Rutleigh entered the room. She edged toward the sofa where his sister sat, surprised by the shimmering excitement that stole over her. She hadn't dreamed that an English lord could be so, well, so dangerously virile.

She pretended not to notice him as he moved toward her, but her senses tingled with shocks of awareness. How wonderful it would be to rule other people with a few well-spoken words. She thought he was going to reproach her for touching the figurine, and she waited, half hoping to hear his voice again. She had stood up to more intimidating men then he, handsome English viscount or not, and she would prefer not to show that his aristocratic hauteur affected her in such an embarrassing way.

Kindness, less common in her life, also affected her. She glanced at Lady Deering and felt a bewildering flood of emotions. The woman was so sincerely sweet and gentle that Cat could not help liking her. Yet grief had begun to wear Olivia to a shadow, and if nothing intervened to save her, she would eventually disappear. Cat could sense her ladyship's spirit hovering between this world and the next, just as her own foolish mother's had lingered before she finally realized that the man she had loved her entire life did not love her. And then Mama was gone, leaving a void that had never been filled.

"What in the devil's name is this?"

His voice. Dark, with a resonance that sent a pleasant chill down her arms. She watched him from beneath her lowered lashes. He was examining the broken heart she had traced on the window, which had begun to drip beads of moisture like pearlets of blood.

"It looks like a window, Knight," Olivia said, giving Cat a sly wink.

"Someone has drawn something," he said in an annoyed voice.

Wendell sprawled out next to Olivia on the sofa. "That's hardly a crime, is it?"

"It's a heart," he said.

Catriona leaned forward. "Well, so it is. Perhaps it's a sign."

"A sign of what?" he asked.

"A sign that you need to wash the windows," Wendell said.

The viscount turned to stare at Cat, and she forced

herself to meet his disapproving look, even though she could feel the power of his presence down to the soles of her feet. It wasn't just that he was big in a physical sense, which he was. But he seemed to have complete command of his surroundings. She felt suddenly vulnerable and insufficient, as if he sensed she was not what she claimed, and she knew then that it was only a matter of time before he stripped her of her secrets. He did not seem to be a man who gave his trust easily.

"Where did you live before you came here?" he asked, pausing to take a chair. His voice might be casual, but he'd laid the question like a steel trap.

Thomas moved up behind her. "With the current Earl of Roxshire, my lord."

"And before that?"

Thomas looked away. "She stayed with her mother's people until the young earl took her into his care."

"Has the young lady suddenly lost her voice?" Knight asked coolly.

"She has not," Catriona said.

"Then please answer my questions."

"I just did," she said.

Olivia frowned in disapproval, leaning back comfortably against Wendell's outstretched arm. "Can your interrogation not wait until tomorrow, Knight? Howard has just brought in refreshments."

He glanced at Catriona, his gaze hooded. "If you prefer."

Olivia motioned her to the sofa. "Here. Sit between Wendell and me. We promise not to subject you to any more questions tonight. Come, let us just enjoy your company. Have a little brandy if you like. How happy we are to meet you."

Cat felt Lord Rutleigh examine her as she obeyed, wedging herself between Lady Deering and the duke, whose aquiline features reminded her of a fairy-tale prince. Och, she must look like a lump of coal amid a pair of diamonds, dirty and drab. She frowned at her scuffed shoes, her big toe practically poking through the worn leather. She'd best not take that brandy. She needed her wits about her to fend off the viscount's interrogation.

Wendell cleared his throat. "I'm not going to bite, you know."

"What?"

He leaned closer to her. "You're as stiff as a statue, my dear. I said that I am not going to bite you."

She looked at Knight, isolated from the others in a huge wingback chair in the corner. "What about him?" she whispered.

"Knight?" Wendell's blue eyes softened. "I cannot say what he will do. He's not quite the same these days, but in all honesty, I can say that I've never seen him bite anyone."

"Would you two kindly stop whispering?" Knight asked dryly. "It gives the impression that one is being talked about."

His sister gave him an admonishing smile. "People do have other matters to discuss besides you."

"No one discusses me much anymore," he said, breaking into a grin. "I have risen above gossip."

"Only because you've never been caught at your misdeeds yet," Wendell said. "Your time will come, I predict. Some journalist will unearth a juicy scandal from your past."

Knight lounged back in the chair, reminding Catriona of a feudal lord with his chiseled face half-shadowed in firelight. "There are only three people who know me well enough to relate the details of my past misadventures. Lionel is one, and he is gone, enjoying a divine adventure of his own, I hope. Olivia is another, but she is the soul of discretion." He paused. "That leaves you, Wendell. Are you threatening to tell?"

The duke laughed. "I would in a minute if it didn't mean implicating myself. There's a certain vicar in Dartmoor who is still out for our blood."

"Lucky for you both that you were wearing masks," Olivia said with an affectionate laugh.

"Only over our faces," Wendell said, sharing another grin with Knight. "The other less identifiable parts were left exposed."

"Oh, Wendell, stop it," Olivia said, hitting his hand. "You'll give her a horrible impression of us."

Catriona felt the tension begin to seep from her coiled nerves at their easy camaraderie. How different this was from her world, from her earliest years of distraught parents with sick children crowding into her mother's cottage for an herbal cure, her life with Uncle Diarmid and his unruly Border raiders, then her most recent years with James, in the castle watching him destroy all he held dear. Aye, she could sense the caring beneath their banter and wished to be part of it. But her tongue was tied in knots. What did she know of witty conversation, she who had never been properly courted by a man? She whose only genuine skill would mark her as an outcast in their glittering society where an ill-chosen remark could ruin a young woman's chance for acceptance?

She looked up in chagrin as she realized that Lord Rutleigh had just spoken to her and was awaiting a reply. He studied her in amusement, his gray eyes mirroring the flames. "I don't suppose you have any secrets, Catriona?" he said, one dark eyebrow lifting in mock suspense.

"Probably none as interesting as yours," she said.

"Leave her alone," Olivia said lightly. "She looks exhausted, and we are rude to keep her up after what must have been a harrowing journey. Come on, Catriona. I shall tuck you into bed myself."

"Come to think of it, I am dead tired. You are very kind, Lady Deering." She rose, eager to escape the perceptive curiosity burning in the viscount's eyes.

"Isn't she?" he murmured, his fingers steepled beneath his strongly molded chin. "Yes, rest, cousin. In the morning, we shall discuss what to do with you."

There was a moment of silence. Then Olivia, who until then had given Cat the impression that she was the epitome of a subservient English lady, turned on her brother like a tigress protecting her cub. "The matter has already been decided, Knight. There is nothing to discuss."

Olivia whisked her upstairs with an astonishing air of determination for one so frail, the deerhound watching from the hall. "We must do something about your wardrobe, Catriona. Oh, I'm sure that heavy plaid is perfectly acceptable in the drawing rooms of a Border estate, but your figure is far too lovely to hide beneath that dull, shapeless wool."

"Not to offend your judgment," Catriona said, "but there isn't much of anything to hide. Uncle Diarmid said I'm as flat as a griddle cake, with the exception of two currants for a chest. So it isn't the wool that's shapeless. It's me."

Olivia turned outside the bedchamber door and

stared at her, her mouth falling open. "This is going to take more work than I thought."

"What is—oh, is this where I'm to sleep?"

She was about to explore the small, darkened chamber when Olivia herded her through another door into a larger room where a coal fire had just been lit. Warm shadows danced on the wallpaper. "That was the antechamber where your maid will sleep."

"My what?"

"Your maid. When we employ one." An experienced woman with a background in current etiquette and fashion, Olivia thought grimly. She was going to have her hands full if Catriona was ever to be ready for a proper season. That the young woman might not care to embark on the social seas did not even occur to her.

"This is your room, Catriona."

"It's perfectly lovely."

Olivia smiled. "It needs a good airing out, I expect."

The room was furnished with a delicate French escritoire, a four-poster rosewood bed, an armoire, and a marble-topped washstand. The chambermaid had already brought up Catriona's small trunk and laid her nightdress on the bed. The air smelled faintly of must and the faded lavender buds that scented the mattress, freshly turned and beaten.

Olivia fingered Cat's threadbare flannel night rail in distaste. "Do you actually wear this?"

Catriona pulled off her buckled shoes and sank backward onto the bed. "Aye. Every night. It keeps the bad dreams away."

"Does it? Well, has it ever been washed?"

"Of course," Catriona said, deeply offended.

"Perhaps we could find a replacement for it. Something prettier to suit you."

"It's embarrassing to admit this, but the fact is, I'm prone to nightmares. Angus and Dugall used to swear up and down that my screaming in the night made their blood run cold. That's vervain sewn in the hem, by the way, not dirt."

Olivia took a deep breath. "Angus and this Dugall—they *slept* with you?"

"Aye. Well, being the only female, I was given the loft. The sounds carried, you ken. The farmhouse was barely bigger than this room, and we all coveted the fire on a winter night."

Olivia felt suddenly faint at the enormity of the task she was about to undertake. "This Angus and Dugall—they were children, then?" she asked hopefully.

Catriona snorted. "Only in terms of mental ability." She sat up, frowning at the look of horror on her champion's face. "I didn't *sleep* with the bastards. My uncle did possess some sense of morality." Though not much, Cat reflected fondly.

"Well, thank God for that." Olivia sat down on the edge of the bed, her brow furrowed in a frown. "How many men shared your home, dear, if I may ask?"

"Ten when I lived with Uncle Diarmid. Twelve or so in James's castle. Retainers, most of those. A damned useless lot, as far as I'm concerned."

Olivia blinked, obviously unable to visualize anyone of the weaker sex living in the midst of this manly congregation. "And your mother did not object?"

"She was dead by then, but when she was alive, no male ever crossed her doorstep except for the fathers bringing in their sick children. My mother never let another man touch her after she bore me."

Olivia was quiet for a moment as if she guessed that there were a few pertinent details missing from this explanation, but she could not figure what they might be. Or perhaps she did not want to know. "When did you meet Lionel, dear?"

Cat leaned back against the fluffy, down-filled pillows; both of them were relieved at the change in subject. "Four years ago, I think. At my brother's castle, the very month I had moved in."

"Would this brother be James?" Olivia asked, her frown deepening. James was the only name she could retrieve from her memory of Lionel's conversation about his Scottish relatives, and she wasn't sure, but it did seem as if there had been a vaguely negative connotation to the name.

"He's the fourth earl now," Cat confided. She struggled modestly beneath the coverlet to change into her nightclothes. "He went off to war about a month or two before Lionel did." She paused, tossing her smock expertly onto the chair. "I'm that sorry he's gone."

Olivia forced a smile and pretended not to notice the undergarment sailing through the air. "But James returned."

"Aye, but he wished that he hadn't. The girl he planned to marry died of fever while he was off fighting for the Sassenachs."

"That is sad." Olivia's face reflected compassion; loss was something she understood too well these days.

"Worse even," Cat said, "was that she died giving birth to the baby he'd put inside her before he left."

Olivia could not speak for a moment. There seemed to be little of life that Lionel's lovely cousin had not witnessed. "What happened to the child?"

"Her parents whisked her away to parts unknown to raise. James searched for months but came back with a broken heart and no daughter to love."

Olivia released a sigh, staring across the room at the fire. "I can imagine. I learned that I was carrying Lionel's baby right after he left, too, but I miscarried in the third month. I am still bereft."

"But you can have other children. In time, I mean."

"Not Lionel's," Olivia said, lowering her gaze. "Oh, goodness, I don't want to start crying now."

"At least you've withstood your grief better than my brother. He's dead drunk all day long, and he berates everyone in sight. He's losing all his lands, too, from gambling and foolish investments."

Olivia compressed her lips. Catriona had definitely been exposed to the darker elements of life. "Then someone needs to take him in hand."

"Aye," Cat said in a heavy voice. "I've tried. 'Tis part of the reason I'm here, to help raise funds to pay off his mortgages before he squanders everything. A horrible man is hoping to buy up the land for bleach fields, and so many people would be put out of their homes if James weakens." What she needed, Catriona had decided, was a rich husband of her own choosing to take affairs in hand.

Olivia had only a vague notion of what Catriona was talking about; she had been so immersed in her own sorrows in recent years that she had lost touch with the rest of the family. "I expect Knight would be able to offer you better advice than I can on the matter, but it does seem a rather ambitious goal for someone in your position to accomplish."

Catriona gave her a level look. "There's little help to be expected from that quarter, then. Your brother did not like me."

"Knight doesn't much like anyone these days," Olivia murmured, "sometimes not even himself."

"And why not?"

"Because—" Olivia started to laugh. "It's none of your business, you sly boots."

"Am I not family?"

"Of course you are. But it's well past midnight, and you look exhausted. We have endless days ahead to talk."

She rose briskly and arranged the green silk coverlet over her charge like the loving mother she ached in her heart to be. The young Scotswoman was a far cry from Lionel's child. In fact, she wasn't a child at all, she was as cynical as she was sweet, and she didn't remind Olivia even remotely of her late husband except for those remarkable eyes, and what else was it? Lionel had possessed a certain gentleness and excitement for life that Catriona seemed to share. She wasn't a replacement for what Olivia had lost. Nothing could bring back the baby she had yearned to hold or the husband she had hoped to spend an entire life with.

"But you are here," she said under her breath, "and I will gladly lay claim to any part of Lionel that I am given."

Catriona half opened her eyes, drifting asleep and wondering what the woman's strange words could mean. "Be careful going down the stairs."

"What?"

Cat's eyes flew open in irritation. Thomas had warned her not to reveal her ability to foretell future events, and she was never sure herself when or how it would happen. But just as she'd begun to relax, she had seen an image of Olivia walking down the stairs and starting to fall.

"Don't go back downstairs yet, Lady Deering. You'll fall if you do."

Olivia's disbelieving look turned to one of delight. "Oh, my heavens. Do you have the Sight—that is what you call it in Scotland, isn't it?" She stepped closer to the bed, regarding Catriona in wonder. "I remember reading something about it in a book, but Lionel never mentioned that it ran in the family, although he always knew when it was going to rain. Do you have visions?"

Catriona sighed and contemplated an evasive answer. Fatigue had made her careless, and now she had ruined her chances for making a decent impression by revealing her fatal flaw. Thomas was right. She had a mouth as big as a gully, and hadn't it gotten her into trouble in boarding school when she had predicted the headmistress would die, and the poor women had expired exactly one week later while reading *Hamlet* to the class?

That unsettling vision had labeled her a social pariah among the few girls who had been willing to overlook Cat's unstable upbringing and inferior wardrobe to befriend her. Troublemaker, they called her. The Border girl with the witchy eyes and queer power. Years later, she was still the same, an outcast but only older.

"It was nothing, Lady Deering. I talk in my sleep. Always have."

Olivia looked unconvinced. "Then go back to sleep, and do stop calling me Lady Deering. I'm Olivia now, and we *are* family. We are also delighted that you have come to stay."

Except for him, Catriona thought. It would be a battle to win his lordship over to her side.

"I suppose I should see that your man is made comfortable for the night," Olivia murmured as she finally moved toward the door. "Sweet dreams, cousin. You are in loving hands. Your hardships are over for the time being."

Catriona made an unintelligible reply that was meant to express both doubt and gratitude. She knew she should tell the woman that Thomas wouldn't remain in this house for even one night, and she should probably sneak downstairs and attempt to talk him into staying before he got himself killed on her behalf by her brother. But her legs wouldn't obey her order to move, and a great weight of darkness pressed down upon her, the welcome oblivion obscuring even the shadow of the tall man who was standing outside her room when his sister opened the door.

"Knight, you startled me half to death," Olivia whispered, ushering him back into the hall. "What on earth are you doing skulking about like that? What do you want?"

"What do you mean, what do I want?" he asked, catching a glimpse of the woman curled up in bed before the door closed. "I intend to ask our uninvited houseguest a few more questions, if you don't mind."

"I *do* mind. She's asleep, and no wonder. Imagine making that journey with only an old man to protect you."

"She seemed to protect herself well enough with that pistol," he pointed out.

They turned to the stairs together, Olivia descending first. "Do you blame her? Oh, Knight, I should never have forgiven myself if we had shot Lionel's cousin."

"I'd have a hard time forgiving her if she had shot one of us."

"Yes, but—oooh—"

She seemed to struggle for balance before sliding down three steps and landing in an inelegant heap in the hall below. "Good heavens, Olivia," he said in alarm, hurrying down to help her. "What happened— why are you grinning like that?" He knelt beside her, his hand arrested in mid-air.

Olivia was shaking her head, not making the least effort to rise from the floor. "It's true, don't you see?"

He gave her a blank look. "Don't I see what?"

"She has the Sight, it really is true. Lionel might even have mentioned it before. Perhaps fortune telling runs in the family, on the Celtic side, of course."

"What does that drivel have to do with you almost breaking your ankle?"

"Cat, Lionel's cousin, warned me only three minutes ago that I would fall down the stairs."

He looked up over his shoulder at the staircase. "Well, what have we here?" He reached back for the battered portmanteau that had caused Olivia's fall. "No wonder she predicted you would have an accident. The little baggage left her baggage right where you were bound to fall over it."

Olivia frowned at him. "She did *not* leave it there. One of the footmen did because she had nothing with her when we went upstairs. She has the Sight, I tell you, and now that I think of it, Lionel did have uncanny intuition for a man. He always knew where I had left my sewing scissors."

"Only because he always sat on them." He hunkered down in front of her and gave her a stare that made her heart stop. "If Lionel had such astounding intuition, why didn't he save himself at Albuera instead of putting us all through the torment of losing him?"

"Oh, Knight." Her face crumpled at the question,

which seemed deliberately cruel and calculated to
bring her down to earth; she had been so immersed in
her own sadness that she kept forgetting he blamed
himself for not bringing Lionel home.

"Have you been drinking?" she demanded. She bal-
anced on her knees to sniff at him. "Oh, you have."

"Stop doing that, Olivia. You're behaving like an
animal. It's annoying." He pulled away. "Smelling me.
We were all drinking earlier, if you recall. We were
having a nice party until the fortune teller dropped
into our midst."

"Well, Wendell liked her, and I respect his judgment. Besides she likes me." She settled back down
onto the stairs.

"What do you mean?"

"Her relationship with her family is troubled, if I
dare exercise a little intuition of my own."

"I just don't know about this, Olivia," he said quietly.
He helped her to her feet, half stumbling over the bag
he'd pulled down the stairs. "Look at this thing, anyway. What does she have in here, a cast-iron stove?"

"Don't go into her belongings, Knight," she said in
horror as he bent to examine the contents of the bag.

"What the devil?" He gave an unpleasant laugh.
"Stones. Stones and dead weeds. Exactly what every
earl's daughter carries to make social calls."

"Stones and weeds?" Olivia said, chagrined despite
herself. "Are you sure?"

"Have a gander." He waved a fragrant dried brown
plant under her nose, its roots dangling like hairy spi-
der legs. "Lovely, isn't it?"

"It's an herb." Olivia sounded relieved. "Perhaps
she brews medicinal teas."

"And the stones?" he said darkly.

"Probably for throwing, which I will start to do myself if you don't get your nasty hands out of her personal effects."

He dropped the polished white pebbles back into the bag with a thud. "There. Good Lord."

"Thank you," she said softly.

He looked up into her eyes. "I'd do anything to bring him back."

"But he's gone, and she is here."

"A hell of a replacement."

"Let me take care of her. Knight, please. Everything will be all right."

Nothing would ever be all right again for either of them, he thought. But tonight was the first time in years that he had actually seen Olivia happy, despite the fact that he and Wendell had dedicated themselves to uplifting her. And if that alleged cousin of Lionel's was responsible for providing a brief diversion for his sister, he would do his best not to interfere.

"Fine. You handle her, but do be careful, Olivia."

"Of what?"

He shrugged his broad shoulders, unprepared to put his qualms into words. Heaven knew he was a suspicious man, and not everyone harbored evil motives. "I don't know. I think she might be hiding something."

"But she can stay?"

"For now, Olivia." His amused gaze strayed to the bag of rocks on the staircase. Bloody hell, she had carried half of Scotland with her. "Only for now."

Chapter
4

❧

*K*night *waited until the house* had settled down for the night before he awakened his secretary. He assauged the guilt he felt for taking action behind Olivia's back by reminding himself that he only had her best interests at heart. She was far too vulnerable and emotional to show sound judgment in personal matters. He and Wendell were almost afraid to leave her alone.

In the first year following Lionel's death, Knight had traveled to London to attend his neglected business affairs. During his absence, Olivia had been beset by a score of those hoping to capitalize on her grief: would-be suitors, solicitors who offered to manage her money for ungodly fees, and, yes, even gypsies who had promised to put her in touch with her beloved Lionel's ghost. Knight had come home to find her half persuaded by all of them.

Recently, he'd convinced himself that Olivia had

even begun to accept Lionel's death, that she was finding peace with her loss, until one night three weeks ago when he'd come upon her in his study, clumsily trying to load his pistol. Not for a second had he believed her shaky excuse that she thought she'd heard a housebreaker and wanted to be prepared. She had meant to kill herself; God knows whether she would have carried through with the act had he not interrupted her. But only then had he truly understood the depths of her despair.

He sat forward at his desk as his secretary took a chair. The middle-aged man looked understandably flustered at being summoned at this late hour. "My lord, something is amiss?"

"I apologize for disturbing your sleep, Simmons, but we have been just taken off guard by an unexpected visitor. A young Scotswoman who claims a distant kinship to my late brother-in-law."

"I was unaware that Sir Lionel had relations other than those I'd notified of his demise, my lord."

Knight settled back in his chair. "Not even on the Scottish side of the family?"

"What Scottish—" The man put on his spectacles. "Oh, yes. I do believe he had relatives in the Border district. I do not recall whether we attempted to notify them."

"That isn't what I care about," Knight said slowly. "I want to know if this woman is a genuine relation or an imposter. She claims to be the Earl of Roxshire's daughter, but she was raised by some old uncle upon her parents' deaths. Her name is Catriona Grant, and she has apparently been living in the castle of the current earl."

"And you would like me to investigate her claims, my lord? Shall I begin by contacting the earl?"

"Yes, but I do not wish my sister to hear a word of this, and you might need help. Contact Daniel Truesdell at the Red Dragon to see if he would like a job. I understand he's offered his services to the Bow Street Runners more than once. On second thought, wait a while before contacting the earl, Simmons." Knight couldn't say what instinct had prompted him to add this amendment.

"I shall begin the investigation in the morning." Simmons leaned forward to rise, his voice hushed. "Do you think she poses a danger to the house, my lord?"

Knight paused. Aside from shooting into the air and dropping a bag of stones on the stairs, he could not in all honesty say that Catriona appeared to be a menace to his household. "Not in the usual sense, but I do believe she might be a threat to my sister's emotional stability."

"A fortune hunter, perhaps?"

"And a fortune teller," Knight said dryly.

The door opened several minutes after Simmons had left. Howard, the young footman, bustled in with an air of intrigue. "It was as you feared, my lord. The old man and the dog have vanished into the vapors. Disappeared, flown the coop, evacuated, departed, es—"

"I understand, Howard," Knight said. "The man has gone." He heaved a deep sigh. "And left Catriona Grant in my care."

At three o'clock that same morning, a horned owl appeared on the oak tree that overlooked Cat's bedroom window. An owl in the park, being a nocturnal hunter, was not an unusual occurrence. But this was the largest one anyone who lived on the estate had ever seen, and the noisiest by far.

The bird set up a loud, mournful hooting that penetrated the deepest dreams. Mrs. Evans, the housekeeper, sat up in bed even before the owl began to hoot. She heard it scratching in the tree and thought the new parlor maid was eloping with that idiot footman Howard, which might not be a bad thing unless it reflected poorly on Mrs. Evans's management of domestic matters.

Olivia heard the hooting and wondered immediately whether owls could communicate with the departed. Wendell heard it and pulled a pillow over his head. Knight, who had just gotten to sleep, swore and asked himself what else to expect that night.

Catriona was the last person in the house to awaken. But then, she was accustomed to sleeping with nature's symphony in the background, storms over the mountains, a merlin crying from the moor, rain battering the stones of the old cottage.

Then someone from the depths of the house shouted, "Shoot the damn thing so we can get back to sleep!"

Cruelty to a helpless creature was more than Catriona could tolerate. She got up and fumbled her way around the unfamiliar furniture, walking twice into the wardrobe before she managed to open the window.

"What do you want, then?" she whispered to the frowning bird that seemed to stare directly into her room. "Are you trying to impart a message from the otherworld?"

She stared past the sleeping park to the edge of the

snarled woods, where gray moths pollinated the evening primroses and night animals stirred, prey and predator. Beyond lay the moor with its high tors towering in the mist. Was someone waiting for her out there? Was it her brother, or the old lecher he insisted she would marry? Was the owl warning her that she must flee again?

For a great part of her youth, she had counted on animals for companionship. Certainly, few children had been allowed to play with *her*, illegitimate daughter of a charmer. Her only friend had been an odious boy named Lamont Montgomery, an apprentice to her estranged Uncle Murdo, who practiced magic in the Border hills. She had pretended not to care that no one else sought her company, and when her mother had found a wounded hawk or even a hedgehog in the woods, there had been solace for her own hurts in helping the creatures heal.

The owl gave vent to a long, melancholy hoot.

"What do you want?" Catriona whispered again.

"A little peace and quiet would be nice," a deep voice drawled from the window several feet to her left.

She turned her head in surprise and felt a shock ripple down her spine, this one leaving a wake of unsettling warmth that confused her. All she could see of the speaker in the misty darkness was a sharp profile and a powerful upper torso, loosely clad in a half-buttoned white cambric shirt.

"What are you doing here at this hour?" she asked, before she realized how absurd the question was.

"I happen to live here."

"I realize that," she retorted. "But why are you not in bed?"

"I *was* in bed."

The sarcasm in his voice was not lost on her. "Are you implying it is my fault that an owl has awakened the entire household?"

She imagined rather than saw the infuriating smirk on his face. "Isn't it?"

Catriona had been accused of far worse things in her life, of causing rain showers during a church service, and crops to fail, even a death once, but this man's casual arrogance seemed absolutely undeserved.

"That is quite unfair. How could I possibly summon an owl out of the ethers?"

"I have no idea," he said, sounding thoroughly annoyed, "and I'm sure I don't care. I just want you to shut the blasted thing up."

She was trying to think of something clever to say to that when another owl fluttered from above the trees and settled down on the same limb as its noisy partner. She blinked in disbelief.

Knight gave an indignant snort and pointed at the tree. "That's exactly what I mean."

"It's your tree," she said incredulously.

"Well, they're certainly not my owls."

"They aren't mine, either."

"They must be Scottish owls," he said, *tsk*-ing under his breath. "No sense of propriety."

"No Scottish owl with an ounce of sense would be caught anywhere near *this* house," she muttered back.

The second owl began to hoot in chorus with the other.

She fixed the pair of them with an impatient frown. "Oh, do be quiet, would you? He thinks that *I'm* what has brought you here."

And both owls, as if spellbound, subsided into the requested silence.

For a moment, the viscount was apparently too startled at this development to speak. Then he gave one of his low, wicked laughs that wreaked havoc on Catriona's nervous system. "Well, well. The owls have obeyed their mistress."

She felt her cheeks flame. "If that's true, let me ask them to—"

A torch flared in the yard below, illuminating the house. Catriona stole a look at Lord Rutleigh's face, the masculine features schooled into a dark mask of amusement. The light must have revealed her face, too. His gaze caught hers, rooting her to the spot with its intensity. She felt her heart quicken, and a flush of a pleasant disconcertment she had never before experienced warmed her from within.

They stared at each other in a mix of reluctant curiosity and mistrust. Catriona knew what she resented about him—he was an autocratic Sassenach who thought himself superior—but she admitted he seemed to have his good qualities, although it puzzled her that she found him so attractive. She shrugged inwardly, reminding herself that she had been rebuffed by his sort most of her life.

He gave an affected yawn as if his interest in the whole affair had waned. "You were saying?"

She drew back into the room, talking to herself in an indignant undertone. "If I did have all the power everyone accuses me of having, I'd command an entire flock of birds to carry certain people to the peak of Ben Nevis and drop them from the sky on their heads."

"I can hear every word you are muttering," he called in amusement from the windowsill.

She stuck her head back outside. "Then it's a good thing you can't read my mind."

"Is that the gratitude I get for taking you into the bosom of the family?"

She knew he was baiting her, she could practically hear Thomas on her shoulder warning her to control that temper, but who could blame her? "I don't want anything to do with your bosom, my lord, opinionated bosom that it would appear to be. You aren't my family, anyway."

"Exactly."

"Lady Deering is."

He leaned forward from the windowsill, a muscle ticking in that elegant jawbone. "That remains to be proven, doesn't it?"

For a moment, her heart ceased to beat in her chest. The naked suspicion on his face stopped it in mid-stroke. "I am not a liar, my lord," she said. Which she wasn't. She had only omitted a pertinent detail here and there.

"And I am not a fool," he said. "Furthermore, I fully intend—"

She was spared the discovery of whatever nasty promise he meant to make by a sudden commotion below their windows. One of the estate servants came sprinting across the lawn with a fowling piece.

"Good God," Knight said, his face darkening in disbelief, "my country estate has been turned into a circus. What in heaven's name are you doing, Howard?"

"Shooting the owls, my lord."

Catriona gasped in horror. "You can't allow it, my lord. Don't let him hurt the innocent wee things."

"Who gave such an order?" Knight demanded of the young man below, ignoring her on purpose.

"Mrs. Evans, my lord."

His eyebrows rose. "This is not the French Revolution, Howard. One's housekeeper does not give orders to attack the local wildlife. Am I understood?"

The footman lowered his musket, looking confused.

Lord Rutleigh vented a sigh, glancing at Catriona from the corner of his eye. "You are only to shoot at the owls if *I* instruct you to do so, Howard. Do you understand that?"

"I think so." The footman waited several moments. "Should I shoot them, then, my lord?"

"Absolutely not!" Catriona could not help herself, even though she felt his lordship stiffen at her interference. "You'll bring bad luck on this household!"

Howard sat down on the ground; the viscount turned his head and fixed Catriona with an ironic stare. "I'd say it was a bit too late for that, wouldn't you?"

She was speechless.

"Think of another way to handle this, Howard," he shouted, "but don't shoot the damn birds. My God, what an evening." He glanced at Catriona. "Well, now what is the matter? You have gotten your way, and we'll all be mad by morning, but at least you and Olivia won't have my head for ordering an owl shoot."

"Thank you, my lord."

"I'm not sure that you are welcome."

"It was the right thing to do," she said.

He grunted. "Was it?"

"Indeed."

"Let us just hope that this is the end of it," he said.

"Well, *I* most certainly hope so," she retorted.

He narrowed his eyes. "It would be nice to get some sleep."

"Wouldn't it?" she muttered.

He ducked back into his room, pulling the window shut with a decisive bang. Catriona shook herself, realizing how chill the night air had become and that the owls had flown off into the night, their message to her, if that was their purpose, delivered to one who could not understand it.

Mrs. Evans had been unable to sleep after the incident with the owls, not even after she reassured herself that Howard and the new parlor maid had not eloped. The normally quiet house was in an uproar, everyone bumping around in his nightwear with a rather festive air and much speculation about what the symphony of raptors could signify.

The new parlor maid, Dorcas, gave a shiver of fear and huddled closer to Howard at the kitchen table. "I wonder what it could mean, those birds hooting like that."

"What it means," the old butler, Aubrey, said with an ominous smile, "it is that someone in this house is going to kick the bucket."

A chorus of gasps met this announcement. Mrs. Evans slapped her towel on the sturdy table for order.

"You are mistaken, Mr. Aubrey," she said with an air of authority; an indisputable mystical awareness ran in her Welsh veins. Much to the chagrin of her staff, the woman was rarely wrong in such matters. All voices stilled in deference to her opinion.

"What it means," she continued in a deep, lilting whisper that conjured the land of daffodils and dragons, "is that a certain female in this house is going to surrender her chastity."

"Well, don't look at me," the young laundress said into the electrified silence that met this prediction.

The coachman grinned at her across the table. "No good in cryin' over milk wot's been spilt, eh?"

"But there were two owls hooting," Howard said. "You can't lose your innocence twice, can you?"

The butler allowed himself the smallest smile. "As my dear mother always said, you are only a virgin once. Unless, of course, you happen to work in certain London brothels, where I understand there are means of extending the number of times—"

"Mr. Aubrey!" the housekeeper said in horror.

"As if an owl can foretell a seduction," Dorcas said, snorting at the idea. "You made that up, Mrs. Evans."

The older woman frowned at her. "I most certainly did not. In my little Welsh village, people still lament the loss of innocence whenever an owl is heard to hoot outside the house."

"I wonder what it means if it's heard hooting inside," Howard said to himself.

"It means that I shall be watching each of you very carefully," Mrs. Evans said in a humorless voice. "No one under my employ is going to surrender her virtue if I can help it. This will be a moral household."

"Why? " Howard asked. "It never was before."

Knight found Olivia and the mysterious relation standing together at the window of the green drawing room the next morning. Their breakfast plates sat virtually untouched at the table. For several moments, he remained in the doorway, enjoying his unguarded scrutiny of the young Scotswoman who was speaking in an animated voice to his sister. An unexpected warmth flushed through his veins as his gaze traveled slowly up and down Catriona's figure.

"And that's a painted lady butterfly," she was explaining, her heavy hair caught back in a ribbon.

"Really?" Olivia sounded as interested as if she were being shown the Crown Jewels. "Is that what it's called? I never even knew it had a name. I just thought it was a pretty garden butterfly."

Catriona looked wistful. "My mother knew the names of every bug and beast within a hundred miles of our home."

"An amateur botanist, was she?" Knight said as he entered the room, ending his lustful examination of his houseguest. He would at least try to be civil in front of his sister.

Catriona pivoted slowly. "I suppose you could call her that."

They studied each other in silence. He had to admit she looked more worthy of her claims to the family clad as she was in one of Olivia's older gowns. It was a morning dress that his sister had not worn since Lionel died. The high-waisted lines of the lemon-yellow silk drew attention to Catriona's slender grace and the well-proportioned curves of her figure. He could see now what Wendell had perceived the night before and felt his male senses stirring in response. In fact, she was quite a lovely young woman, he thought in surprise.

"Oh, look," she said, breaking the strained atmosphere, "that's a grayling, Olivia. They're attracted to the clover."

"Is there any breakfast left?" Knight asked as the two women hurried back to their butterfly watch. Receiving no answer, he turned to the table and frowned at the untouched plate of eggs in front of his sister's chair.

"You eat like a bird, Olivia."

She turned, a smile lighting her face. "Speaking of birds, did you hear those owls last night?"

He glanced up meaningfully at Catriona, feeling that sting of arousal again. Hell, what was the matter with him? "Everyone from here to Dartmoor heard those blessed owls."

Catriona pursed her lips. The brief look he'd given her when he entered the room, meditative and brimming with male sensuality, had made her skin prickle with a rather wicked sensation. "They really were not my birds, you know."

"Of course I know that," he said with a touch of amusement. "No one really has that sort of power over wildlife."

Olivia, intrigued, sat down at the table opposite her brother. "What are we talking about? Have I missed out on a previous conversation?"

"His lordship believed that I summoned those owls to the park to bedevil him," Catriona said, her face remarkably innocent.

He glanced up, his lips tightening. It sounded so absurd, put like that, and yet last night, in the mist, he could have sworn there was a connection. He could have sworn that she had cast a spell over the house. "That isn't exactly what I meant."

Olivia's eyes darkened in distress. There was nothing she hated more than hurting someone's feelings. "Knight, really. Tell me you did not go to our cousin's bedchamber after I gave orders she was not to be disturbed for the night."

"I most certainly did not go to her room."

"He didn't come to my room at all," Catriona said quietly. "He told me off from his window."

Olivia sighed in dismay. "You just could not help yourself, Knight, could you? Not even for one hour."

He grinned. "I simply made a casual remark that the owls might have come from Scotland."

"Because they had no sense of propriety," Catriona murmured. "Just like me."

"Oh, Knight," Olivia said in chagrin, clearly horrified by his behavior. "Must you be so high-handed?"

"Was I being high-handed?" he asked Catriona.

She hesitated. "Well—"

"As if Catriona could possibly attract birds to the house," Olivia said incredulously.

Knight arched his brow. "Is there any toast?" he inquired.

Olivia sighed. "On the sideboard, Knight. Would you like to walk with us in the woods this morning?"

"No," he said. "I would not." He deliberately did not mention Thomas's disappearance. Olivia had been up since dawn, making lists of everything she needed to do to ensure her alleged cousin's social success. It was the first time since losing Lionel that his sister had shown any purpose at all. He put two slices of buttered toast on his plate. "Tell us a little more about your background, Catriona. What did your uncle do for a living?"

He noticed the faint lines of tension around her soft red mouth. "He dealt in cattle," she said vaguely, returning her gaze to the window.

"Cattle," Knight said. "A farmer, was he?"

"Sometimes. Oh, my heavens," she exclaimed in genuine excitement. "Are those black swans swimming on the lake?"

He noticed that a red-gold curl had escaped her

ribbon to curve around the contour of her breast. The rogue in him fought an impulse to touch that wayward strand of hair. "Yes."

"They're lovely."

It was unnerving, she thought, the way he stared at her, the type of questions he asked. Why had she hoped she could ever hide everything from him? Her heart began to pound every time she looked into those stormy eyes, and a weakness spread through her, drawing the strength from her bones. In the daylight, he seemed even more dominant than he had in the garden. More intensely male, and mesmerizing. She had the feeling that if she made the slightest move to escape, he would be on his feet to stop her in an instant. The odd thing was that she felt drawn to these dangerous aspects of his personality and yet threatened by them at the same time.

Knight studied the graceful arch of her back as she leaned closer to the window. Exactly what was it he sensed that lay beneath her charming appearance? What problems could a young woman of her background be hoping to escape? Could she be in trouble? He glanced down at her slender waist, frowning in displeasure at the possibility. Despite himself, he felt a rush of anger that someone might have used her for sexual pleasure and discarded her in such a way. Yet these things happened every day. It was not difficult to imagine a man desiring her. He could not deny her appeal.

"Catriona?"

She hesitated before turning to look at him. Was she frightened—frightened of him or of what he would discover?

"What about your brother?" he asked.

"What about him, my lord?"

"Doesn't he mind that you have come here?"

She paused, her thoughts going back to her last night in the castle, her brother's voice a roar of rage as she confronted him.

"Don't tell me who you will or will not marry after everything I've done for you! You'd be living in a hut if not for me."

She had faced James in front of his retainers, her voice ringing in the silence of the banqueting hall. "I am grateful that you have given me a home, James, but I will not marry a man who is old enough to be my grandfather, and I will not watch you destroy yourself, either."

She'd flinched when he slapped her, the blow knocking her backward into a chair. "Get out of my sight. Go to your room."

"I love you, James."

"Go, damn you. Don't speak to me of love when all I ask is your obedience, a simple favor of respect."

She released her breath, her thoughts slowly returning to the present and all its complications. "No," she said quietly. "I do not think my brother minds that I am here."

Knight glanced shortly at his sister, wondering if she understood what in his questioning had caused Catriona to flinch. Obviously, he was on the right track in pursuing the subject of her past, and if she had something to hide, well, he might even try to help her, though heaven knew why.

He pushed aside his plate, determined to pursue the subject of her guardian's past. He did not acknowledge Olivia's warning looks, but unfortunately even he could not ignore the persistent knocking that sounded at the door.

It was the young footman Howard, who carried

himself into the room with the swagger of a London buck. "There is a man asking to see you, madam."

"A man?" Olivia said, glancing up in surprise. "For me?"

Knight looked around slowly, not at his cheeky footman but at the young woman still standing by the window. She had not turned around at the interruption, although her shoulders had stiffened, almost in a self-defensive stance, and he sensed she was straining to listen without trying to show it.

"Who is this man?" he asked, watching her from the edge of his eye.

Howard blinked, caught in the act of admiring himself in the mirror above the mantel. "What?"

"I asked you who this man was."

"Some silly old coot who went on about being lost, and Sir Lionel and a lady—"

"Lionel?" Olivia came slowly to her feet.

Knight attempted to read the expression on Catriona's face as she glanced back once over her shoulder. He had engaged in only one waterfront spying mission in France several years ago, but he had never forgotten how he'd feared every waking moment that his true identity would be discovered.

He half rose, motioning Howard to the door. "Bring our visitor in here."

Catriona turned back to the window. Knight noticed the quick breath she took, her fingers curling into her palms. He had to admire the way she tried to cover her anxiety.

"In here?" Howard said, smoothing down his sideburns. "A servant, my lord?"

"You didn't mention he was a servant," Olivia said with a frown. "Honestly, Howard."

"Didn't I?"

"Bring the poor man in," Olivia said, "although I daresay if he is seeking employment, he ought to go around to see Mr. Aubrey."

Catriona turned to the door. "I'll leave you alone to—"

"Stay." Knight's voice was so forceful that Howard took a step back.

She crossed her arms over her chest, silent and self-protective as Howard hastened to obey.

Several moments later, a befuddled-looking older man in rumpled livery appeared in the doorway. "Oh, Ames," Olivia said, bursting into a gust of giggles. "You dear old thing."

"Am I in the right house, then?" the gray-haired man asked in confusion, staring around the room.

Knight stole another glance at Catriona. She had lowered her arms to her sides and was so visibly relieved that he felt ashamed of himself for hoping to trap her. "Who the hell is Ames?" he asked without thinking.

Olivia giggled again, pulling a straight face as she recovered. "Aunt Marigold's butler."

Knight looked blank. "Aunt Marigold?"

"Lionel's great-aunt from East Briarcombe," Olivia said, shaking her head. "The sweet old lady with all those wigs. Don't you remember?"

He sighed. "Ah, yes. I'm afraid I do. She was here last Christmas."

"Have you heard of her, Catriona?" Olivia asked as if making an effort to include her in the conversation.

"No, but if you don't mind, I shall take a walk outside while you have your reunion."

Knight settled back in his chair, wondering now if

he would be vindicated. "Perhaps great Aunt Marigold was acquainted with your father, Catriona. Perhaps she will know of you."

"Perhaps she will." Her cool gaze met his, accepting the challenge he had thrown down.

He watched her as she walked toward the door, her slim figure in the gossamer dress as enticing as one of the butterflies she had been admiring earlier. "Call me back in if the lady would like to meet me," she said without looking around.

He got up from the table, feeling Olivia stare at him in chagrin as he turned toward her chair. "What is it you are trying to prove by interrogating her?" she whispered in bewilderment. "You chased her away with your mistrust."

"And I would not be wholly surprised if she did not return," he said without apology. "If my guess is correct, Catriona Grant is about to be unmasked as a fraud."

Chapter
5

⌘

An hour later, Marigold, Lady Ellis, was comfortably ensconced in the green drawing room, a tray of sherry and biscuits set before her. Silver-haired and scatter-brained, she had to be reminded twice that Lionel had died, and once the fact registered, she began to weep softly into her handkerchief. Olivia and Knight sat awkwardly on either side of her, patting her shoulder until her sobs subsided.

Knight had been hoping for a lull in the conversation to question her, and at last it came. "Do you remember Lionel's Scottish uncle, ma'am? The Earl of Roxshire?"

Olivia frowned as if to warn him against spoiling a poignant moment with his suspicions, but he refused to be deterred. It was a stroke of luck that had brought Lady Ellis to them today. Simmons could take weeks to unearth any useful information about

Catriona's background, and in the meantime, well, at least let them know what they were dealing with. Perhaps he was wrong. He would at least be fair.

"The Earl of Roxshire?" The old woman frowned in effort. "I do not—oh, yes, of course. The Border earl. A bit of a scoundrel in his day, like you, Knight, as I recall."

"Do you remember anything about his children, Aunt Marigold?" Olivia asked, leaning forward. "He had—"

Knight cut her off in mid-sentence, determined to get to the truth. "Let her finish. No prompting, please."

"She can hardly be expected to recall the name of every distant cousin in the family," Olivia said crisply.

"I do remember, actually," Marigold said, fingering the pearls at her throat. "The earl had two sons, Rogan, the heir, and James, the young soldier. Rogan died in a riding accident, and James inherited the castle while he was away at war. There were troubles the last I heard. The sweetheart died. I don't know why. I lost contact with the family after Rogan's death."

Knight exhaled slowly, unaware he had even been holding his breath. As he looked up, he caught sight of Catriona outside. She was standing by the garden pond with a cluster of servants gathering around her. He did not know what to feel now that he had been proven right. Hurting his own sister seemed a hollow victory, and there was the unpleasant task now of deciding what must be done.

"Olivia—" he said, searching her face.

She refused to look at him, but her voice sounded a little unsteady as she continued. "That is all, Auntie Marigold? There were no more children? Not a girl—"

"*Olivia*," Knight said.

"A girl?" Lady Ellis's wrinkled face brightened. "Gracious, I forgot all about the young girl. Born on the wrong side of the bed, as they say. Her mother was some sort of soothsayer, and as the story goes, she had come to the earl's aid when he was lost on the moor one night. I reckon they both got more than they bargained for when a baby arrived nine months later."

"She's illegitimate," Knight said in an expressionless voice. "She did lie to us."

Olivia's voice trembled with emotion. "She said she was the earl's daughter. That is not exactly a lie."

"A bastard," he said, shaking his head. "A byblow." But even then, he wondered how much it really mattered. Wendell's own father had left a few illegitimate offspring behind, all of whom were doing quite well in London.

Lady Ellis sat forward. "May I ask what this intriguing little tête-à-tête is all about?"

"You may not," Knight said, his own voice low.

Olivia leaned around Marigold to look at him. "Don't you dare talk to my aunt like that, you narrow-minded man."

"What did become of the girl, anyway?" Lady Ellis asked, her pleasant face concerned. "I thought her uncle had taken her in, but he must be ancient by now."

"He's dead, and she's staying with us," Olivia said firmly.

"Though not for long," Knight added.

Olivia's eyes glittered with purpose. "Just until we find her a decent husband."

"What?" Knight said in disbelief. Where had this diabolical idea come from? "*What?*"

"I planned it last night after I went to bed," she said, staring back at him in undeterred defiance. "I couldn't sleep because of the owls, and I kept thinking of her, and how much I wanted to help her, and what would Lionel do in my place."

"A matchmaking scheme," Lady Ellis said, her ringlets bobbing as she gave a full-bodied chuckle. "How positively delightful."

Knight shook his head, utterly stunned by this. "I am not playing Hunt the Husband for a—a—"

"Her mother was what the Scots called a greenwoman, somewhat of a healer," Olivia explained, completely overriding Knight's sputters of objection. "You did remember well, Auntie Marigold."

"I wonder if she could cure my corns," Lady Ellis said, bending over to examine her feet. "They're killing me."

"Oh, my God." Knight stared at the pair of them in amazement, two spiders spinning an awful web around them in which he was in serious danger of becoming ensnared like a hapless fly.

"I think she has other gifts, too," Olivia whispered. "You know, she predicted I would have a fall down the stairs, and sure enough, a few minutes later, I did."

"You didn't?" Lady Ellis whispered back. "Do you think she could give me a few tips for the next Derby?"

"I had hoped to spend the next months getting her ready for her debut." Olivia gave a long, rueful sigh, and her voice returned to its normal tone. "But now, well, now we shall have to lower our sights and simply do what we can. Not that the details of her birth will destroy her chances for acceptance. But without wealth, hmm, it is going to present a challenge."

Lady Ellis clasped her hands to her ample chest. "I should love to offer my services, as a tribute to Lionel."

Knight stood up, his gaze returning to the window. Nearly every servant in the house was clustered around Catriona now, listening raptly to whatever twaddle she was telling them. And what in God's name were they doing with that bucket?

"She's got Howard draining the pond," he said in a startled voice. "Did you hear me, Olivia?"

"It probably needed draining," she said, not about to be distracted from her discussion of the latest style in female attire and what a stylish debutante would wear that summer.

"She's dropping stones in the water now," he said. "Those weird stones of hers."

Lady Ellis looked up at him in alarm. "I think you ought to go back to London, Knight. The country doesn't seem to agree with you at all."

"Do you know what she's doing?" He gave an incredulous laugh. "She's casting a spell in my very own garden. The little pagan you two silly things plan to launch into society is brewing magic in a bucket."

The two women never even noticed him leave the room. They were too busy discussing the whos and hows of hiring dancing masters and dressmakers to make their Celtic Hecate presentable to the *ton,* lamenting that they could not aspire as far as getting her vouchers for Almack's. They had *purpose,* and heaven help anyone who stood in their way. He strode across the lawn, ignoring Wendell's call from the study window to stop. In less than twenty-four hours, Lionel's cousin had turned the house upside-down. Yes, Olivia needed a distraction, but preferably one in a tamer form who wouldn't transform an ordinary garden tool into a cauldron or bring birds of prey flocking to the house. And call him low-minded, but he still maintained there was more to her than met the eye. If she had not lied, she had not been forthcoming about the nature of her life, either.

Yet was it such a sin, or even her fault, to have been born illegitimate? Even the highest-born families made mistakes, and she was an interesting young lady.

He stood at the outer perimeters of her magic circle, ignored for the second time that day, when he was used to commanding an audience with his mere appearance alone. But Catriona Grant possessed something that he did not. The common folk did not use the word *charmer* for nothing. And so for a few minutes, he allowed himself to be enchanted by her, to see her not with his usual cynicism but with a simple curiosity he rarely indulged.

At first, Catriona feared she was about to have another confrontation, this time with the servants of the house. She had experienced so many throughout her life that she ought to know how to avoid them—whenever one of her mother's love spells failed, and sometimes when they worked all too successfully, or the rare times a patient's condition had worsened after taking one of Mary Grant's herbal potions. She and her mother had fled to the seaside then, though never for more than a few months until the hostility against them died down and Mary could resume her practice in relative safety.

They had always returned to their small house of

unmortared stones on the moor so that the earl would be able to find them, to sweep Mary off her feet and declare his undying love for her. Which he never had because—and it took Catriona years to realize this—he did not want to. All the days of waiting for him to appear, all the nights her mother had watched from the window, for nothing.

But as it turned out, this was not to be another mortifying experience. Catriona had been admiring the water lilies on the pond when the footman Howard hurried by on an errand. Being a sapskull village lad who did not understand his position on the ladder of life, he had spotted Catriona alone and looking vulnerable and had gallantly offered his assistance, asking if she were lost.

Mrs. Evans, peering from behind the curtains of her parlor window, had immediately come outside to make sure Howard did not make a nuisance of himself. The kitchen maids, on a pretense of snipping herbs, had followed. Small dramas such as this enlivened their dreary days.

And so Catriona had been cornered, bravely facing a den of lesser lions, unsure herself what her place was to be in this house.

Mrs. Evans had practically flown across the lawn to interrupt the improper conversation. "Howard! I thought I sent you to the pantry for tea."

He jumped, moving away from Catriona. "And I was on my way, Mrs. Evans, when I noticed Lady Deering's cousin here looking lost."

"And how can she be lost, Howard, when the house is right before her in plain view?"

"I don't know, Mrs. Evans," he said. "But she looked lost to me."

Mrs. Evans cast a curious glance at the young woman and had to admit there was a lost quality about her. Who exactly was she, anyway? Word had already reached the lower echelons that the new arrival might not be all that she claimed. For example, no one had explained whether she was to be addressed as Lady Catriona, as befitting an earl's daughter, or simply as Miss Grant. No one had explained, either, where that old Scotsman had gone with that dog. And what, Mrs. Evans wondered, about those owls last night?

She curtsied, preferring to err on the side of correctness, covertly giving Howard a thump in the ribs. "Forgive him, I beg you. None of us have our wits about us this morning with those owls hooting half the night."

Catriona smiled back at her, apparently unaware that a proper lady would end this conversation on the spot. "Are you Welsh?"

The warmth of that smile might have won Mrs. Evans over for life, but her loyalty lay with the master, and she wasn't about to hand her allegiance to a hanger-on who might be gone in a month. "I am indeed. Hazel Evans is my name."

"Hazel is one of the most sacred trees in Celtic lore," Catriona said. "If one believed in such things, one might assume you had been born with certain supernatural gifts."

Mrs. Evans pressed her work-worn hand against her heart, momentarily at a loss for words. When she spoke, her voice was low with emotion. "Is it that obvious?"

"Only to one who sees beyond the obvious."

The woman stared at her in understanding. "Then you are also—oh, my. Oh, *my.*"

"Do you have a pain in the chest, Mrs. Evans?"

"Nothing that you should worry about. It comes and goes."

Howard made a face. "All over the place. One day it's in her stomach, the next her heart."

"Shall we find out exactly where the trouble is?" Catriona asked.

"Can you do that?" Mrs. Evans said, lowering her hand.

"The stones can," Catriona said confidently. "They are centuries old and very powerful. I shall need a bucket, though."

A bucket was found as Catriona dug through her collection of pebbles at the bottom of her bag. Several more servants had emerged from the house, and Mrs. Evans, kneeling beside Catriona, was too intrigued by the proceedings to pay much attention to the tall man who hid behind the others in the shadows of a leafy tree.

Silence fell as Catriona filled the bucket with pond water and dropped the pebbles one by one to the bottom. She suspected that the viscount wouldn't approve of what she was doing, but she couldn't stop herself. How could she refuse to help someone? She would just have to follow her instincts and face the consequences later, even if those consequences came with steely-gray eyes and a broad-shouldered body that gave her the most delicious goose bumps.

"Well," she said after a moment, "it *isn't* your heart, or your lungs or liver. The problem appears to lie in your stomach."

"My stomach," Mrs. Evans exclaimed. "Why, I haven't eaten a thing all day."

"Except for half a pork pie," Howard said.

"And a few nips of brandy," one of the kitchen maids muttered.

"I believe you might be right," the housekeeper said thoughtfully. "The pain does seem to come after I eat certain foods."

"I shall brew you a tea to help."

"Tell her that the owls last night don't mean we all ought to be wearing chastity belts," Howard blurted out impetuously.

Mrs. Evans shot to her feet and cuffed his ear. "Don't you dare use such filthy talk to a lady, who, if I may hazard a guess, would appreciate the validity of genuine Welsh superstition. Mark my words: when an owl hoots, innocence is lost."

Catriona rose from the ground, the hem of her borrowed gown sopping wet. "That belief is a shade better than what the Romans claimed. In ancient days, it was thought an owl hooting meant someone would die."

"Better death than disgrace," Mrs. Evans said stoutly.

Catriona frowned. "Perhaps, but I fear those owls carried a more personal message for—"

She broke off as her gaze lifted to the tall man leaning against the tree, his hard-planed face amused. Words escaped her as he gave her a slow, admonishing smile. Oh, how much had he heard? And why did those gray eyes of his make her feel as if she'd been caught bare naked, her feelings for him so painfully conflicted?

"It's his lordship," the laundress said under her breath, and before Catriona knew it, the servants had abandoned her, and she was standing alone again at the pond as the English lord took a step toward her.

He whistled through his even white teeth. "What a sight. What a performance."

She did not understood why, but the mockery of this man, with his aristocratic elegance, wounded her more deeply than all the insults of her past combined. "It wasn't a performance," she said, a blush burning her cheekbones. "The stones have power."

"Is that right?"

"They're kelpie stones, some of them. Others have been cast up from Elfland."

"All the way from Elfland? My goodness."

He began to advance on her, forcing her to step back to the water's edge. "Watching that nonsense was almost as interesting as what Aunt Marigold told me about you a few minutes ago."

Catriona's mouth tightened. She considered dumping the bucket on his arrogant head but decided she couldn't reach. "I'm sinking," she whispered.

"What?"

"In the mud. I think—I believe I'm starting to sink."

He looked down quickly and saw immediately that she wasn't exaggerating. In his determination to intimidate her, he had practically walked her into the pond. "Oh, hell," he muttered, wondering what on earth he had hoped to prove.

Try as he might, he could not completely squelch the approval he felt beneath his show of anger. The servants at Rutleigh Hall were like family. He cared for them and did not hold with the current belief that the lower class did not merit kind treatment, although the state of his housekeeper's stomach did seem to be taking kindness a little too far.

He grabbed Catriona by the waist to haul her back

onto the ground, bringing her body flush up against his. For an instant, he was taken aback by the shock of pleasure that he felt, his first instinct to pull her even closer. Touching her did something dangerous to his mind, not to mention his body's flagrant reaction to her tempting curves. The herbal scent of her skin invaded his senses, and he was acutely aware of how still the spring air felt, of a bee buzzing over a patch of mint thyme at the pond's edge. "Look at you," he exclaimed, glancing down in chagrin. "And me. My trousers are covered in mud."

"So they are." She tried to dart around him; she had liked being held in his arms far too much for her own good. "In fact, I'd better run inside to take off this dress before these stains set—"

"Not yet." He caught her free hand and held her still until she slowly revolved to face him. "I know you lied to us, Catriona," he said quietly.

"You do?"

His heavy brows met in a frown. "You're the *illegitimate* daughter of an earl. Roxshire apparently never recognized you."

"I forgot to mention that," she said with a sigh. "It isn't exactly the sort of thing one goes about announcing in public."

He studied her without a trace of emotion on his face. "I suppose that there are worse secrets in the world," he conceded. "Is that why you looked so frightened in the drawing room? Did you sense that your secret was about to be revealed?"

She hesitated. She had come within seconds of bolting when Howard brought word that a strange man was at the door, using Lionel's name as a reference. In her irrational panic, she thought she had been tracked down. It was too easy to imagine James, in his desperation, forcing her into that old man's arms for money, believing he had no choice. Yet for all his callous behavior, her brother was capable of the deepest affection, and she cared for him.

"Well?" Knight's voice coiled around her like a whip, commanding her full attention. He would accept nothing less than her obedience.

He seemed to sense when she was most vulnerable, watching, waiting for her to reveal another weakness, and the female in her was far too quick to respond to his male authority. "The situation of my birth isn't exactly something that I'm proud of," she said after a long pause. "Do you wish me to leave now?"

"My sister wants you to stay," he said in hesitation, sounding none too pleased with the idea himself. A rather insulting smile spread across his face. "She has taken it into her head to find you a husband."

Catriona's cheeks began to burn again. "Why is that so amusing?"

He shrugged. "Well, it's just—"

She squared her shoulders. When had she encountered such arrogance? "Just what?"

"Oh, I don't know." A devilish chuckle escaped him. "Perhaps it's because I don't know too many young maidens on the marriage mart with your particular 'talents.'"

"What exactly do you mean by that?"

"Well, one generally seeks a wife with a stable background and genteel skills, such as embroidering samplers and playing the pianoforte."

"Is that the kind of wife you want?"

He frowned. "I don't want a wife at all."

"And the idea of anyone marrying me is beyond the realm of probability?"

"I suppose more astounding miracles have been performed." He hesitated, his gray eyes twinkling with humor. "Back in biblical times."

She dropped the bucket on his foot. She hadn't meant to, but her fingers had gone numb, and her grip had weakened. When he finally recovered from the pain and stopped cursing, she looked him right in the eye. "I know you aren't going to believe me, but that was an accident."

"Get these rocks off my feet," he shouted, "or both you and the bucket are going into that pond!"

She drew back; he was scaring her now. She knew she ought not to push him any farther, but she wasn't about to retreat until she had made her point. "They're not rocks. They're—"

"Yes. Yes. I heard. Sacred stones from Pixieland." He gave her a nasty smile, bending to pluck a pebble off the toe of his Hessian boot. "Howard's spleen?"

She narrowed her eyes. "It's a heart. Although you probably have to possess one to recognize it."

He tossed a cleft stone into the air and caught it before it hit the ground. "Lungs?"

"No." She smiled archly as he ran his fingers inside the cleft. "Reproductive organs."

His eyes met hers. "I guarantee you'll have your choice of suitors if you season a conversation with a comment like that."

She bent, averting her face, before he could gauge her reaction. "What do you know?" she muttered, too upset to look at him. "I'll give my husband everything he desires, and he won't be mean like you. He'll be kind and gentle, and he won't care if I am a bastard.

He won't make a mockery of the things I believe in. He'll encourage me to help people."

He stared down at her. Damnation, he had offended her, he realized in surprise. Before he could stop himself, he knelt and began to help her collect her stones, grumbling, "Well, my teasing got the better of me, but as I said, you will have to get used to it."

"I've known worse." She glanced up, her eyes brimming with emotion. "Give me back my reproductive organs, and if you make fun of me, well, I'll show you what magic it can do."

He settled back on his haunches, trying not to laugh at the threat as she dropped a handful of stones into the bucket, her nose in the air.

"Careful," he admonished gently, glancing down. "I think you might have just put a dent in Howard's spleen. Or was that another unmentionable organ?"

"Brain," she said, biting her lip against a sudden urge to laugh. "But of course you have to—"

He grinned. "—possess one to be able to recognize it?"

"You wouldn't be the first man not to know his brain from what grows below."

One corner of his mouth curled up in amusement. The conversation was beginning to have a very unexpected arousing effect upon him. He had never met such a disarmingly honest woman before outside his own family, and found this encounter rather invigorating. "I suppose you're an expert on such matters?"

"Well, I certainly cannot claim to have *your* experience." She didn't have any, actually, unless she counted the time Lamont, her wizard-uncle's apprentice, had kissed her while simultaneously dropping a handful of earthworms down her bodice. Not exactly a soul-stirring romance.

He leaned forward, his nose practically touching hers. His voice lowered an octave to a dangerous whisper. He really was going to have to teach her a few things. "I've known you for less than two days. Who in this house is telling tales out of school?"

"I'd cut my tongue out before revealing my sources."

He stood with a frown. "It was Olivia."

She rose, not about to be craning her neck to talk to him. The man's lithe, muscular body made her feel vulnerable and insubstantial. "No."

"Wendell?"

She shook her head.

"Then it has to be Howard."

"It was not."

He stared at her for several moments. "You won't last long in my house if you take every remark to heart. My world is rather ruthless, I'm afraid."

"Hmmm." She turned to go, and before he could stop himself, he caught her by the waist and drew her back toward him. She glanced up, transfixed by the dark promise in his eyes.

"What—"

"Don't ever let a rogue make you cry," he murmured a split second before he lowered his head and kissed her.

She did not resist. Perhaps she was too surprised. He savored the sweet innocence of her lips and felt her hand lift to his shoulder, whether to push him away or hang on for balance he wasn't sure. For a perilous moment, he wanted to take this further, wanted to wield his power to subdue her. The way she arched against him, unaware of her own danger, aroused some dark sexual instinct to master her.

"Oh," she said, her head falling back, the effect of his kiss utter devastation.

He narrowed his eyes to watch her. Tentatively he touched his tongue to hers. Her body shivered against his, giving him all the encouragement he needed to deepen the kiss. He slid his arms down her back to support her, but suddenly his control was slipping away, and it was no longer a game.

No, she thought distantly. Escape wasn't a choice. His strong body molded her to him in an unbreakable hold, not that she possessed the wherewithal to go anywhere. It had happened too fast, and she had to concentrate on breathing, on not allowing her legs to give out on her. When his large hand brushed lightly against her breast, she felt as if her body had caught fire.

"And don't," he added in a low, ironic voice as he drew his mouth from hers, as composed as she was shaken, "let a rogue kiss you, either."

There was barely time to recover. The sound of footsteps on the path to the pond broke the dangerous tension between them, and just as well, too. Catriona had no idea how to react. He had completely flustered her control. She took a shaky breath as he drew back a respectable distance. Her entire body felt achy and flushed with the most unsettling feelings. In fact, she could not remember a time in all her past humiliations when she had been tempted to resort to the supernatural for help. The man had no idea how fortunate he was that she had exercised such remarkable restraint. Or how deeply she regretted that the wonderful kiss had ended.

Chapter
6

✧

Olivia burst upon them like a child finding a hidden treasure in the garden. "Oh, there you are, making friends. I cannot tell you how pleased I am to see you together like this."

Knight straightened, belatedly offering his hand to help Catriona step away from the pond. The fact that she ignored his help seemed completely to escape his sister's notice. Olivia saw what she wanted to see, which was her beloved brother and her beloved husband's cousin caught in a friendly conversation. She would fly into the boughs if she dreamed what sort of conversation they had actually had.

He folded his arms across his chest and let out a loud sigh to express his resignation. He could feel Catriona stealing a look at him from the corner of her eye, and at first he was amused that she was still upset at him. But then he began to wonder if she was afraid that he was going to send her away. Did she even have a home, or was the talk of her half brother in the castle a lie? Certainly, the new earl had not been obligated to take in his father's illegitimate daughter.

He looked down into her face, noting the distress that clouded her features. And then, once again, he glimpsed a shadow of Lionel in her beautiful eyes. It caught him by surprise—a wilder, secretive, female version of the friend he grieved for. And he knew that whatever her flaws, there must be strength of character in her, too, which only enhanced her sensual allure to an alarming degree.

"Is Aunt Marigold gone?" he said, lifting his gaze to Olivia.

"No." She was obviously too excited to sense the storm clouds of emotion that charged the air. In fact, Knight was taken aback by the change in her, her mood brighter than at any time in recent memory. "She's staying the rest of the month to help me plan the party."

"Party?" he said with a frown. "You're giving a party?"

"No, Knight," she replied sweetly. "You are."

He groaned. "I thought we came to the country for peace and quiet. Besides, none of our friends except Wendell is willing to travel this far for a party."

"Not those people," Olivia said. "I'd only hoped to invite the locals. Everyone did like Lionel. Besides, I wouldn't dream of overwhelming Catriona with society yet." If ever, she added silently, noting the disgracefully muddied state of Catriona's attire. And Knight's pantaloons, too. Goodness, what had the pair of them been doing, making mud castles?

Catriona shook her head. "I can't possibly allow you to hold a party in my honor."

"Why not?" Olivia asked.

"Perhaps she prefers a quieter sort of entertainment," Knight said in a pensive voice. "She doesn't exactly share our upbringing."

Olivia refused to be deterred from her mission. "Then we shall serve as her guides. I nearly expired myself the first time I faced the dragonesses of Almack's. Her education must begin today. None of us is getting any younger, and one's prospects do dim with time."

Knight did not know what to say. Only a few days ago, he would have given his right arm to have Olivia so frivolously occupied, alive again. Anything to erase the horror of coming upon her with a pistol in her hand and the realization that her grief had become too much to bear. And now, well, hell, his wish had apparently come true, but with complications he could not possibly have foreseen.

"Fine. Give your little party, Olivia. I suppose there is no harm in it." He should have known that the moment the words left his mouth, fate would step in to bedevil him.

She threw a victorious smile at Catriona. "*Your* party, Knight. It isn't quite appropriate for me to be entertaining in your house."

He released another sigh. "*My* party."

"I think she'll need some new dresses."

"No, really," Catriona said, "all this fuss is quite unnecessary."

Olivia frowned. "All this fuss is *essential*. In fact, I have already sent for the dressmaker. You remember, Knight, the pretty Frenchwoman in the village who likes to flirt with you?"

He felt Catriona turn to stare at him again, one sleek eyebrow raised. The fact that her mouth looked faintly red and swollen from his kiss only aroused him all over again. "I don't remember anything of the kind," he said irritably. "But a dressmaker is getting a bit ahead of ourselves, don't you think? Shouldn't she at least learn how to dance before she makes a debut?"

Catriona tried again to insert her opinion. "But I—"

"A mock debut," Olivia said with a negligent shrug of her shoulders. "Stop being such a stickler for details, Knight. This isn't London. In the country, the rules are rather more relaxed. Anyway, I've already found someone to teach her to dance. And—"

Cat said, "I—"

"His name is Mr. Edwards," Olivia went on. "When I mentioned him, Marigold made the most brilliant suggestion that we find a mock suitor for Catriona's mock debut, someone patient and experienced with women to show her the finer points of our social rituals."

"Seeing as how the men and women in Scotland dance in the raw around a fire before clubbing each other senseless," Catriona thought aloud, highly annoyed that she was being viewed as such an uncivilized creature.

Olivia's face turned bright red. "Oh, my dear. I didn't mean—but *do* you know how to dance a cotillion?"

Catriona gave a shrug. "No, and I don't particularly want to, either."

"And has a man ever paid you court?" Olivia asked even more gently.

She shrugged again, glancing up at Knight as if she defied him to laugh. "A few have."

"But you do wish to find a husband?" he said dryly.

"Aye. On my own terms. Preferably one who is rich, doesn't drink himself into oblivion or spit, and is kind to animals. I miss my dog."

Olivia closed her eyes, trying to hide her chagrin at such an unacceptably frank admission. "Oh, dear. We *do* have our work cut out for us, don't we, Knight?"

"We?" he said in a horrified voice.

She smiled up at him. "As the elder male of the family, her brother being either incapable or unwilling to fulfill that duty, it is your obligation to protect her reputation."

"It is?" he said bleakly.

"It is. After all, you are seven years older than she."

He frowned. "And exactly how am I to do this?"

"Yes, how?" Catriona demanded, looking ready to drop her bucket on his foot again.

Olivia clasped her hands. "By playing the mock suitor in the mock courtship that Aunt Marigold and I just dreamed up in the drawing room. Isn't it the most perfect plan?"

Knight summoned Catriona to his office early the following morning. For several minutes, he did not even acknowledge her, determined to finish the accounts for the local Devon pottery firm in which he, Lionel, and Wendell had invested considerable money and time. A gentleman need not work, but these days Knight enjoyed the challenge of using his mind in a more productive outlet than playing cards or racing his curricle.

He studied her from the edge of his eye as he worked at his desk. She was dressed in a striped mint-green gown, another of Olivia's castoffs, and her heavy mass of hair had been brushed to a coppery sheen. She looked undeniably pretty and almost presentable—until the moment she hiked up her skirt and began to climb the ladder to reach the uppermost row of his bookshelf.

He threw down his pen and stared for several moments at her legs, lithe, with well-defined muscles, no stockings. No shoes. In fact, he was certain she was trying to distract him, and he refused to take the bait. After kissing her senseless yesterday, he ought to do penance. He returned his attention to the figures in the ledger, but in his mind he saw only a shapely female form and felt a deep stirring of sexual attraction that unsettled him, sparking a fantasy of her naked on the ladder—

"Look out!" she cried a split-second before an enormous book tottered off the pile she had gathered and threatened to crash in a cloud of dust directly onto his desk.

He looked up in alarm as she caught the falling volume and vaulted to the floor, her face half hidden behind the heap of dusty books she clutched in her arms. "That was close," she said. "I thought I was going to brain you."

He rose, tugged the books from her arms, and slammed them down onto his desk. "Just what do you think you're doing?"

"Entertaining myself while you ignore me. I'm really sorry about shouting like that. You must have nerves of steel not to have jumped through the roof."

"I was engrossed in my accounts, Miss Grant."

"So I noticed."

"That is my Latin collection you are in the process of disordering. Sit down."

He returned to his desk and studied her in dispassionate silence. He found to his annoyance that his heart was beating harder than usual, and the image of her standing naked on the ladder refused to dissolve. What was it about her that had gotten under his skin? Those eyes of hers again, perhaps, managing to look wounded and dangerous, fierce and entirely female at the same moment. She had a way of intruding on a man's thoughts.

She pursed her lips. "Well."

"What?"

"Did you summon me for any particular purpose, or are we to stare at each other all day?"

His mouth firmed at the reminder that she had addled his thoughts again. It was one thing for him to be distracted by her, another to be caught at it. "After a sleepless night, I have arrived at the conclusion that my sister's welfare must come first in this matter."

She examined him in open admiration as he spoke, half listening. She was quite lost in his velvet rumble of a voice which sent little shivers down her nape. She imagined he could be quite persuasive when he put his mind to it. She wondered what he looked like when he laughed, really laughed from deep inside, and what effect it would have on his strong, angular face. And he was concerned about his sister's welfare, which reminded her sadly of James. She wished someone would care about her like that.

"This is a beautiful library," she said. "I love the smell of books."

He looked faintly bewildered. "What?"

"Lovely collection of literature, sturdy desk." She thumped her bare foot on the floor. "Nice carpet."

He drew a breath. "Have you heard anything that I've been saying?"

She leaned back in her chair. That rich voice had deepened into a growl, and she decided that it would take more than a few compliments to elicit a belly laugh from this man. "Would you mind repeating it?" she asked politely.

"I am not in the habit of repeating myself."

Or of laughing, either, she thought, compressing her lips.

"I was, in fact, delivering a warning to you," he said

She glanced up. "About disordering your books?"

"About upsetting my sister."

Her eyes widened in distress. "Why would I do that?"

"I do not know." His face looked devilishly dark and intense in contrast to his casually knotted white neckcloth. "I don't know what you want, or even who you really are, or why you came here."

"Perhaps you ought to lock away the silverware."

"Why did Thomas leave you here?"

"My brother has been feeling a bit down lately." As in the bottom of an ale barrel.

"Is he coming back to claim you?"

Olivia popped her head around the door before Catriona could answer. "I couldn't resist. How is our first lesson proceeding?"

Catriona stared down at the carpet. "We're having a wonderful time."

"Couldn't be better," Knight said with a total lack of enthusiasm.

"Would either of you care for coffee?" Olivia asked, looking from one to the other.

"Brandy might be preferable," Catriona said in a wry undertone.

Knight lifted his brow at her. "Laudanum is better at numbing the pain."

Olivia stepped into the room, her hands planted on her slim hips, her stride energetic and full of vigor. "Perhaps what I ought to do is find a professor to teach the pair of you proper diction. I cannot understand a single word either of you said."

"Which reminds me," Knight said, swinging his long frame out of the chair to rise. "Did Mrs. Evans locate the nursery primers I asked for? I suppose we need to make sure Catriona can even read a dance card before we launch her out onto the social seas."

"I don't need a nursery primer," Catriona said, looking up indignantly.

"Your father paid for private instruction?" he asked, sounding skeptical that a nobleman would invest that much trouble in a love child.

"No, but I attended—"

"The primers are on the floor behind your desk, Knight." Olivia paused behind Catriona's chair to give her a reassuring pat on the shoulder. "I shall return in a little while. Aunt Marigold is calling me."

Knight straightened, eyeing Catriona askance as he lifted the well-worn books from the floor to his desk. "All right. Let us begin. I do not have all day."

She folded her arms across her chest. "This is an absolute waste of time."

"Probably. But it makes Olivia happy. Look," he said, thumbing through the yellowed pages. "Can you read any of this?"

She sauntered over to the desk, her head barely coming to his powerfully muscled chest.

"Read this," he said. "It's a nursery rhyme."

She glanced down at the book and yawned.

He shook his head. He didn't want to insult her, but perhaps she needed more help than her pride would admit. The Scots he knew had strong wills and stubborn principles. He dug deep inside himself for patience. "All right. Then we shall try something even simpler." He took pen and paper and scribbled several words on the page. "Try this."

She hunched over the paper for what seemed like an eternity, her foot repeatedly hitting the carpet.

"Stop doing that," he said.

She glanced up. "What?"

"That banging with your foot. It annoys me. Good God, can't you read even those basic words?"

"Did I say that I couldn't?"

"Then read them."

"I did."

His face darkened. "To me."

"Don't you know how to read them yourself?" she asked innocently.

"I wrote the damned things, didn't I?"

He straightened. So much for being patient. He was so tempted to bring his hand down on her backside, propped up in the air, that he had to turn away. "Read," he said in an ominous voice. "Before I lose my temper."

"Olivia wouldn't like that."

He put his hand on the nape of her neck. *"Read."*

She tensed, held captive by the pressure of his strong fingers and the disturbing heat of his muscular body pressed against hers. She wondered if he had already forgotten about kissing her. She certainly remembered, every brush of his lips, the heady sensation of being held against that huge body. "All right. All right. Don't fret your bowels into fiddle strings. I'll read."

He lifted his hand away, staring at the vivid imprint of his fingers on her skin. "Oh, good. I can hardly wait."

She stared down at the paper as he stared at her, his gaze drifting down her back and buttocks to her bare feet. She had a certain elemental charm, he admitted silently. Quite a few men would find her combination of spirit, pride, and innocence provocative. Certainly, she had gotten the better of him yesterday, and even now he felt that inexplicable tug of attraction. "Hurry up."

"The . . ."

She glanced over her shoulder at him, apparently seeking approval. He nodded, motioning her to continue. Had anyone touched her before? he wondered. Would all that fire and spirit follow her into a man's bed? "Good. Good. Go on."

"The . . ."

"Yes. You said that." He realized suddenly that her gown would not cling to the cleft of her backside like that unless she had refused to wear a corset, which shouldn't surprise him as the young rebel hadn't bothered with shoes, either. "It was correct, Miss Grant. Do go on."

"The . . . the m—oh, look, there's a crimson-throated warbler in the tree outside."

He began to circle the desk, thinking that at this rate he would be as old as Methuselah before she finished the simple sentence. He also thought that she had sensual allure for such a slender frame and that if no one had claimed her, it would only be a matter of time.

"Never mind the warbler. Kindly continue to read." If that was what one could call it.

"The m—" Her face cleared. "'The man is a pig?'"

He frowned, moving around the desk to reread the paper. "It says, 'The moon is big.'"

"Oh." She shook her head as if she were completely flummoxed. "You know, I wondered for a moment if that might be what it meant, but there isn't any moon, so it didn't make sense."

"There isn't any pig, either, did you consider that? There also isn't an *a* in the sentence."

"Yes, there is."

"No, there isn't."

She held the paper up to the light. "What's this, then?"

He leaned over her shoulder, unprepared for the fire that caught in his blood. Oh, yes, she had a very alluring body indeed, with curves that could fuel quite a few more naughty fantasies. "It's an ink smudge, I expect."

"And this word is supposed to be *big?*"

"It is."

"Hmm. The *b* appears to have a tail on it."

"The ink ran."

She turned, finding herself trapped between his massive body and the heavy mahogany desk. It was not an entirely unpleasant sensation, but it was disconcerting, sending little sparks of awareness throughout her system. "Your penmanship could use a little improvement," she said tactfully.

"It is your reading that should concern you."

He was spared hearing whatever reply she might have given by Olivia's reappearance in the room. Unaware that she had entered troubled waters, his sister sailed right up to the desk in a state of blithe oblivion. He drew back from Catriona, realizing that once again he had actually enjoyed the contact with her.

"Here's the book you asked for earlier, Catriona," Olivia announced. "It's a dusty old thing Lionel used as a doorstop." She dropped a massive gilt-spined book atop the others on the desk, her nose wrinkling in distaste.

"Lionel's Latin book," Knight said in surprise. He glanced at Catriona. "You intended to use this for a doorstop? Wouldn't a bucket of stones work as well?"

The bewitching smile on her face should have forewarned him. Brushing her bright hair behind her ears, she opened the book and in a sweet voice read: *"Ira furor brevis est.* Anger is a brief insanity. Hmm."

There was a moment of utter silence. Then Knight covered his face with one hand to hide his expression.

"Did Lionel write that?" Olivia asked in a puzzled voice. "It doesn't sound like anything he ever said."

"It was Horace," Catriona said quietly, running her fingertips down the book's spine. "My Latin is rather rusty, and I thought his lordship might help refresh my memory. It seems nursery rhymes are more to his taste."

"Well, you certainly can't speak Latin to your suitors," Olivia went on, clearly perplexed at the thought of a debutante spouting ancient philosophy. "You'll have the young men running off in droves. Knight, I thought you were going to instruct her in the art of light conversation. I understood you meant to teach her how to read a dance card."

"Is this better?" Her eyes dancing with mischief, Catriona pushed the paper Knight had scribbled on across the desk.

Olivia picked it up. "'The man is a pig'? What twaddle is this, Knight? Do you want her to sound like a half-wit?"

"There's little fear of that," he retorted, giving Catriona a look of grudging admiration.

"This is not what I had in mind," Olivia said.

"Nor did I," he said, "and since we are both in agreement that it was a bad idea—"

"Marigold and I had intended that you stage a mock courtship." Olivia began to circle the desk, blind to the horrified looks that her brother and Catriona exchanged, each one trying to appear more appalled than the other. "A dignified seduction, if you will."

He held up his hands, backing up to the window. "Not with me. Not a chance. Find another victim."

"Perhaps he doesn't know how," Catriona said, bending over Lionel's book again.

He glanced at her behind, his hand half lifting to give a good swat. "I know how, believe me."

"But Catriona *doesn't*," Olivia said passionately. "Do you, my dear?"

"Do I what?"

Olivia gave her an indulgent smile. "A young woman must be prepared to handle herself with confidence in any situation. Has a young man ever paid you court, for example? Or made an improper advance toward you?"

"Do you mean tried to do the dirty with me?"

Olivia closed her eyes, reeling with shock at the indelicate phrase. "Something of that nature," she said weakly.

"Well," Catriona said, frowning at the memory, "one of the men who worked for my uncle put his hand under my nightdress while I was in bed asleep once. At least, he thought I was asleep. I suppose one could consider that an improper advance."

Knight glanced around, despite his effort to appear unconcerned, his face darkening. "What happened?"

"I was so frightened that I stabbed him with my dirk."

"Did he die?" Olivia whispered.

"Not that first time."

Knight's mouth tightened in disgust. "He tried it again?"

"The very next night."

"And?" Knight demanded, drawn in against his will. "Did you stab him again?"

"No," Catriona said, shaking her head. "My uncle did. He was hiding in my bed, waiting for him. I was huddled in the wardrobe."

Olivia turned gray. "He killed him . . . in front of you?"

"Almost," Catriona said, nodding with satisfaction. "And after that, nobody ever tried to court me again."

"Well," Olivia said after an awkward silence. "Well."

Knight had returned his troubled gaze to the window, disturbed by the depth of his reaction. It took several moments for him to detach himself from the emotional involvement he felt and a curiosity to understand more about her life. What kind of home had she come from? What manner of events had molded her character? And who the hell had possessed the patience to teach her to read Horace?

"Leave us alone for a few minutes, Catriona," he said quietly, his big hands braced on the windowsill. "I wish to speak to my sister alone."

"Was that necessary?" Olivia asked as Catriona slipped out into the hall, her face unnaturally composed.

"Damn it, Olivia." He pivoted, his voice intense. "Did you hear what she just told us? How can you possibly hope to change her?" *And for what?* a cynical voice asked in the back of his mind. *To unleash her on a world that will mock everything she is?*

"All I want is to make her presentable to society."

"I don't think we have enough time left in our lives to do that."

"Nonsense. She's lovely, Knight. Those eyes—"

"The eyes of a lynx and the wild heart of one

beneath her loveliness, too, I'll bet. Dear God, Olivia, there is so much more to her than the obvious."

"Lionel would expect—"

She broke off as the door opened and Wendell looked in, a playful smile on his face. "A party, and I was not asked?"

"Not for at least another two weeks," Olivia said, unable to resist smiling back at him. Wendell never failed to brighten her mood. "I do hope you will not desert us."

He came into the room. "Have I ever missed a party?"

"And how will she ever be presented at Court with her background?" Knight asked Olivia, returning to their previous conversation. Wendell had always been like family, included in the good and the bad of their private lives.

"If we are discussing our Scottish cousin," Wendell interjected, leaning against the door, "Court will not be a problem. I shall be happy to arrange it should the need arise."

"Oh, good," Knight said, throwing him an irate look. "Then you can arrange her marriage, too."

Wendell winked at Olivia. "I might just do that. For Lionel's sake."

"I think we're a long way from planning any nuptials," Olivia said wistfully. "There's her come-out party to plan for next year in London—"

"Considering her background, Olivia," Knight said without any malice in his tone, "I think we both know that London is out of the question. It would not be good for her."

Olivia paused, accepting the truth of what he said with a rueful shrug. "I'm afraid you might be right for once. But she still could make a good marriage with a country squire, with our help. Oh, Knight, please, *please* will you at least teach her to dance? I shall handle the other matters. She is not an entirely hopeless cause."

"I thought you'd hired a dancing master," he said. "What ever happened to that Mr. Garfield who taught you?"

"Garfield?" Wendell said. "Bit old, isn't he?"

"A bit dead," Olivia said. "For five years now. Oh, come on, Knight. I have not yet heard whether young Mr. Edwards will travel here on such short notice to give her instruction."

"No," he said. "She dropped a bucket of stones on my foot." And she tempted him, her sweet body and that Celtic spirit. "I am *not* dancing with her. No."

"Oh, leave him alone," Wendell said. "He's still sulking over losing Arabella to that fudgy old Anton. I'll teach her to dance, Olivia."

She gave him a grateful smile. Sometimes she didn't know what she would do without Wendell, and she felt guilty for keeping him to herself. She wondered why no woman had caught his eye and was surprised at how unhappy the thought of losing him made her feel. And there were moments when he looked at her that she felt . . . no, that was silly, outrageous even. Wendell saw her as a sister, nothing else. She was imagining things if she saw anything else in his friendship.

Chapter

7

✿

From the small bench hidden in the alcove, Catriona listened to the conversation that drifted from the depths of his lordship's study. Who was Arabella, anyway? Was she the reason he discharged such a foul temper like a thunderstorm?

Catriona didn't know, and she wondered why it should mean so much to her. Thomas had been sorely mistaken. There was no peaceful haven for her in England, no escaping the unpalatable facts of who she was or what she had been. She should never have weakened and believed it safe to trust the viscount with the truth. Or let him kiss her, either, although it was probably the most pleasant part of her experience with the English so far.

It was clear to her that she could not stay in this house forever, causing trouble between Olivia and her brother. Her problems were not theirs, beyond their understanding, and she could certainly take care of herself, had done so for more years than not.

She was capable enough. She was not afraid to work, and she was growing troubled at the thought of Thomas handling James by himself, while she remained there, a source of friction to the family. She could scrub floors at an inn or serve as a governess in a small house. She could humble herself and return to the castle if she had to.

She stared out the window at the moors and felt the wildness pull at her heart. She had wanted so badly to belong there. She had wanted to find a place for herself at last, but she was different from other people. Changing her clothes and manners would deceive no one for long.

In the distance, she watched a merlin circle lazily in the air, mesmerized by its beauty. Again she sensed that someone was out there watching her. She felt a powerful tug that was painful to ignore.

Come to me, a voice seemed to beckon from the moor. *Come to me, and find the part of yourself that you have searched for.*

Knight cantered across the moor, not certain if he wanted to find the missing relative or not. The servants had searched the gardens and found no trace of her. Her beloved stones were still under the bed, so she hadn't run off. He should be glad if she had gone, and yet, well, he wasn't. Having taken her under his wing, he would decide when and if she must go.

The thought of her wandering alone wracked his composure. He had chased her away, he realized that. He would be responsible for any harm that befell her. Guiltily, he wondered if she had overheard his conversation with Olivia, if she had heard him express his doubts about her social salvation. What would become of her if he sent her away? It was too easy to imagine some rake snapping her up as his mistress. If she wasn't well born enough to take as a wife, she was more than desirable as a bedmate, the kind of woman any man would eagerly leave his club to visit late at night. Her honest view of life was refreshing, and he suspected she would be a passionate lover.

He scowled at the barren expanse of boulders and gorse that caught the dying rays of the day's light. How far could she go on foot? And why should he bother to find her anyway, to drag her to the ballroom and teach her to *dance*, when she was not ready to be exposed to even crueler standards than those held in his own home? Dear God, she would be laughed out of London if she arrived in such a defenseless state, unwilling to play society's games.

It pained him to admit it, but he liked the way she looked at him, as if he were the most powerful man in the world. He liked how she gave a little shiver whenever he accidentally touched her, although he suspected those fleeting moments of contact weren't all that inadvertent on his part. They were more a symptom of his inexplicable attraction to her.

It would not do, of course, the way she unsettled him at every turn. How was she managing to slip under his guard? For he guarded his emotions very closely these days. Life was uncertain, its pleasures tainted by death and betrayal. His experiences had hardened him. Tender feelings for an exasperating young woman who refused to conform had no place in his world. And yet she made him smile.

"Catrio-na!" He cupped his hands and shouted into the air, startling a merlin from a crag.

Nothing else moved. A faint wind stirred the bell-heather, and as he turned, sighing, he saw a woman's figure emerge at the edge of the woods.

He realized it was not Catriona before he was even halfway to the woods. The woman was taller, her hair a deeper shade of red, her royal-blue riding habit expertly tailored to enhance her generous curves.

"Arabella," he said, his voice unemotional as he dismounted. "What are you doing here?"

She turned awkwardly, a bouquet of bell-heather in her gloved hand. "I have come here every day to work up the courage to visit you and Olivia. Yet every day, when it is dark, I return home, a coward."

What could he say to the woman who had left him for another man when all he felt, after the anger and humiliation, was a deep relief that their lives were no longer entwined? Everyone had expected Knight to marry Arabella—their families, their friends, the local vicar. Their names were carved into the churchyard yew. Perhaps he had taken her for granted, indulged in one flirtation too many while she demanded his total attention. Perhaps he had wanted more from a marriage, the deep love and devotion that his parents had shown each other. His mother and father had fallen in love at first sight and had eloped, never to regret their impulsiveness. He had been dreading the moment when he would meet Arabella again, and now it was upon him and must be dealt with as politely as possible.

"You look well, Arabella."

"So do you." She bit the edge of her lip. "How is Olivia?"

He shrugged. "I worry about her."

"Yes, you must." Another hesitation. "Does she hate me?"

"Olivia? She does not know how to hate. I think she is disappointed."

"And you? Do you hate me?"

"I—"

He glanced around, distracted by the sense of being observed. Nothing disturbed the serenity of their surroundings, except the merlin circling the crag on the moor. Was it the same bird? No. No. There were two of them now, then a third, a fourth. He did not remember seeing so many birds at the time and wondered what had drawn them.

"Have you seen a young woman anywhere?"

Arabella blinked, taken aback. "A woman?"

"Lionel's cousin. I cannot find her."

"Oh, a cousin." She sounded relieved. He wondered if she hoped he would spend the rest of his life missing her.

"Knight?"

A twig snapped somewhere in the woods. "Did you hear that?" he asked, turning his head.

She frowned. Heavens, he was so handsome, so big and masculine. Couldn't he tell that she still desired him? "It's only my horse. What is the matter with you?"

"Oh, I don't know, Arabella. Am I expected to tremble with joy the first time I see the fiancée who jilted me for a fat old baron?"

She gasped. "Anton isn't fat."

"Put the old porker on a slimming regime, have you?"

"Knight!" Her blue eyes glistened with unshed

tears; he remembered that she had always been able to cry on command. "You say the most awful things."

"Did I just hear a snort?"

She put her hands on her hips. "I told you it was my horse. Aren't you the least bit glad to see me?"

He looked her up and down. "Is that a pimple on your chin, Arabella?"

"You—"

Another twig popped. He grabbed Arabella by the wrist and pulled her deeper into the shelter of the woods. She gave a surprised laugh, sounding breathless at his bold gesture. "Where are you taking me? Oh, Knight, Knight, I knew nothing had changed. Did you happen to bring a blanket?"

He glanced down, startled, at her face. "What?"

She brought her hand to her throat and began to unbutton the jacket of her habit, her lips forming an inviting pout. "I might have made a mistake marrying Anton."

An acorn sailed down between them. He took a step backward, watching his former fiancée in disbelief. "What are you doing, Arabella?" he said in a hoarse voice as she tugged her bodice loose.

"Don't you remember how you used to bite my neck?" she asked softly. "Kiss my breasts until I melted? Oh, Knight, my breasts are so lonely, aching for your special touch—"

An acorn hit her on the nose. Her fingers stilled. "Gracious, I think the squirrels are attacking us."

He gritted his teeth and looked up from her half-exposed cleavage to the wryly embarrassed face of the young woman positioned in the crotch of the ancient oak tree, a book in her lap. "When I get my hands on you, I am going to paddle your posterior but good."

Arabella released a giggle of scandalized delight. Knight had always had a penchant for misbehaving in the bedroom. "I probably deserve it."

"Not you, you dimwit," he said without thinking. He pushed around her to reach up into the tree. "*Her.*"

He caught hold of Catriona's ankle as she gave a yelp of panic and threw her arms around a tree limb as an anchor against his strength. It didn't help. One mighty tug, and he'd pulled both her and the book down hard on the ground, towering over her as she sprawled across the mossy roots at his feet.

"I do not like having anyone spy on my private affairs," he said in a furious voice.

She rose to her feet, her face bright pink with embarrassment. "Well, goodness, how did I know you were having 'a private affair' under this very tree?"

His jaw tightened. "A civilized person might have announced her presence."

"I thought I did."

"Knight."

Arabella's voice was strained as if she sensed that theirs was not an ordinary association. "Do you mind telling me what this is all about? Who is this person?"

"Lionel's cousin." He bit out the words. "She wandered away from the house and got lost."

Arabella looked at Catriona with one eyebrow lifted questioningly. "I thought you meant someone much younger."

"No." He stared hard at Catriona, wondering just how much she had heard.

"I didn't wander away, either," Catriona said. "I needed to be alone to think."

"She has Lionel's eyes," Arabella said gently, her anger dissipating at the reminder of a man who had never said a mean word about anyone in his life. "Oh, my. Look at that. It's uncanny."

Knight wasn't sure how he had gotten into this situation. "She doesn't have Lionel's temperament, does she?"

"Well, I shouldn't wonder," Arabella said thoughtfully. "You could have bruised her bones the way you pulled her out of that tree. There isn't much to her. Did he hurt you, my dear?"

Catriona shook her head. "Thank you for asking, ma'am. You're very kind, but I'm perfectly fine. I probably should have told him where I was going."

Arabella cast an appalled look at Knight. "I know I broke your heart, but is that any reason to have become such a brute? This is not typical of your behavior."

Catriona turned to regard him, feigning disbelief. "You mean he wasn't like this before?"

"Get on my horse," he said quietly.

"I think I prefer to walk," Catriona said, starting to edge around his tall, unmoving figure. "I really need the exer—"

"Do as I tell you!" he shouted.

Chapter 8

∾

There was little conversation between them until they were in full view of Rutleigh Hall. Catriona sat awkwardly, telling herself she really shouldn't be enjoying the ride with Knight mounted behind her, his body as imposing as a granite tower. Arabella had offered to follow along, presumably as a chaperone to ensure that he would keep his behavior under control. Never, never, *never*, she said aloud several times, had she seen him engage in such a shocking display of bad temper, and Catriona wondered once if the woman didn't sound the tiniest bit jealous. But surely not of her, she who was no match for Arabella's aristocratic elegance.

Olivia came running across the park moments after she spotted them from the window. The relief on her face was painfully obvious to Knight, and he put his hand on Catriona's shoulder in warning, pinning her to the saddle.

"Not a word to her about Arabella, do you hear?"

"Exactly what do you want me to say?" she asked curiously.

He slid to the ground; reaching up to lift her from the horse, he said, "Nothing. Just hold your tongue. There's no need to elaborate on what you heard eavesdropping."

"I wasn't eavesdropping," she whispered. "I was sitting in a tree minding my own business."

He arched his brow. "Attacking us with acorns."

"It's hardly my fault you staged your seduction under my tree," she said quietly. "I was attempting to thwart a potentially embarrassing situation for us all."

"I wasn't—" He broke off, his handsome face exasperated. "Why did you leave the house, anyway?"

"I went for a walk. I wanted to think." Her breath caught as his big hands closed around her waist. "I honestly didn't think that you would miss me for an hour or two."

"Then kindly inform me the next time. If you want to walk, I'll have someone accompany you."

She repressed a shiver as he swung her down to the ground; the gesture seemed as effortless as if he were plucking a flower. Or rather, in her case, a nettle, she thought, examining her wrinkled skirts and sun-browned arms in distaste. Och, what a sight she was. Not the kind of perfumed, flirtatious lady who could invite a man to bite her neck and touch her breasts as casually as she drew a breath.

He eyed her efforts to restore order to her appearance in amusement. "I want you to know you are bedeviling my life." He lowered his voice. "Furthermore, I wasn't staging a seduction, and if I had been, you should have had the decency not to watch."

"Consider it part of my education. I learned a few choice phrases in that tree today."

His smile was droll. "Arabella is not exactly the sort of woman I suggest you emulate."

"Why?" she asked frankly. "Do you think a man would not want to do such things to me?"

He frowned at the earnestly voiced question, finding it all too easy to imagine a man initiating her into the secrets of sexual pleasure. His entire body flushed at the thought. "This is not a discussion I wish to continue," he said, turning away to escape her unsettling honesty.

"I always imagined that Englishmen were too stodgy to enjoy such things," she said in an undertone.

"To enjoy what?" he said distractedly. He'd been about to help Arabella dismount when Wendell and two grooms had appeared to do the job. He looked around, his face shocked as if he had just realized what Catriona was asking. His dark gaze flickered over her in disbelief. "What did you say?"

"Well, I was just wondering if you felt any peculiar compulsion to bite her neck and make her lonely—"

"Do not say another word," he said in a strangled voice.

She stared up at him in silence, her eyes glimmering with humor.

"And don't look at me in such a way," he added ominously, taking a step toward her.

Olivia bustled up between them, smothering Catriona in a hug of relief. "Thank goodness you're home. You must never let my brother's temper frighten you away again, do you hear me? You are to ignore his angry outbursts as I have learned to do over the years. You did make amends to her, didn't you, Knight?"

"Oh, for God's sake. I found her, didn't I?"

"I'm sure he meant to make amends," Catriona said, her gaze drifting to where Arabella stood, allowing the grooms to brush dust from her habit. "I'm sure it slipped his mind what with other, ahem, matters taking precedence."

"Knight?" Olivia said in a worried voice. She had never really taken to Arabella and absolutely detested the manner in which the woman had betrayed him. "Don't tell me that you and Arabella have made an *arrangement?*"

His chiseled mouth curled into a cold smile. "I met her by chance while I was looking for Catriona. Arabella took it upon herself to escort us home, seeing that I was not in the best of moods."

Catriona glanced away at the penetrating look he gave her, realizing that he was unlike any of the men she had known before. Aye, aside from Thomas, her uncle, and the gentle old minister who had taught her to read, all the males in her life had been loud, immoral louts who cared only for drinking, thieving, and coaxing a girl into bed. Her brother, James, fell somewhere between the two categories, treating her with both kindness and cruelty. But this man, cultured, mature, a master of restraint, made them all seem like young boys playing at life, and even though he tried to hide it, she could sense that his feelings ran deep and strong. No, it hadn't been a mistake to come to him. Her heart had known what her intellect could not understand. Finding this man had been the best thing she had ever done.

*   *   *

Olivia took him aside in the foyer as they entered the house. "What were you thinking?" she whispered. "To meet Arabella alone in the woods? Surely you are not conducting a liaison when she is married to another man?"

"I said it was a chance meeting."

"And you are going to make amends to my cousin?"

He hesitated. "And exactly how am I to do that?"

"I suggest that you spend the evening with her in the ballroom instructing her to dance."

"I thought Wendell offered to help."

"He isn't as good on the dance floor as you," she whispered.

"Of course he is. And what is the infernal hurry, anyway?"

She bit her lower lip. "The hurry is that she just might decide her brother needs her more than we do, and she'll return to her unhappy home. She'll end up marrying a Scotsman, and I shall never see her again."

"All right, Olivia, would that be such a tragedy?"

"I think it might, to me. Don't you care about her in the least?"

"I care about you," he said guardedly. Then he added, without knowing why, "Oh, all right. I am not completely impartial to the minx, though heaven knows why."

Olivia laid her hand gently on his forearm. She really could not remember her brother behaving like this, not even in those first months after coming home from war. What had happened to him? "Then find her and bring her to the ballroom. She's just gone down the hall."

*   *   *

He didn't have to look far to find her. She was sitting quietly in the alcove window seat. Her face was turned toward the window. She took a quick breath but did not look at him. For a moment, he was struck by the thought that Olivia had never looked as, well, sensual in that same dress. His sister had seemed merely frail and inaccessibly elegant wearing it, not in the least enticing to a man's senses. But by some mystery, some alchemy of nature, the gown clung to Catriona like gossamer, giving her the whimsical allure of a displaced wood nymph.

Of course, a man wouldn't notice his sister in such terms, anyway. But he certainly felt a surge of masculine interest in Catriona's curves now, her pose inviting and vulnerable. He experienced a powerful urge to explore the soft body hidden from view, and yet as quickly as the sensation came, he subdued it.

"Catriona." Good. Not a trace of unbridled lust in his voice. No hint that he had contemplated taking her in his arms and kissing her until she begged him for mercy. He sounded quite in control. "Kindly turn around and look at me."

She gave him a quick, curious glance. "Where's your mistress?"

"Lower your voice." He glanced around in embarrassment. Fortunately for them both, the hall was empty. "And she isn't my mistress. She's a happily married woman."

"She certainly didn't look like one," she said wryly.

He lowered himself onto the seat and caught her by the arms so unexpectedly that she gasped, trapped between his powerful thighs. "I think you and I need to have a little talk about the meaning of discretion, young woman."

"What is it you would like to know?"

He wanted to kiss her again; he really did. She was the most attractive and intriguing female he had ever known, and he would have given anything to meet her under different circumstances. "Exactly how much did you hear—or do you *think* you heard?"

"Enough." She eased her arms loose, disconcerted by his overwhelming masculinity. She would die before she showed that being held against him unnerved her. How his single kiss had invaded her dreams and changed the shape of her desires. If nothing else, she refused to be put in a class with all the other women who worshipped at his feet.

"How much?" he demanded, tightening his thigh muscles to prevent her from wriggling away.

"I heard her asking you to make a full-course meal of her neck."

"Olivia is right," he said thoughtfully. "You do need a social education."

"I've learned plenty today, thank you."

"You will not mention a word of this to my sister."

"A word about what?"

"That is much better," he said approvingly.

"I saw nothing," she said, arching her brow.

He smiled. "Good."

"I suppose I didn't hear anything, either."

He nodded. "Excellent."

"You could put me in a torture chamber, and I'd never reveal what I didn't see and hear."

He paused, scratching his chin. "I don't think we need to take it that far."

She drew a breath as their eyes met. The air between them practically crackled with the clash of male-female energy. "I am curious, though," she said, ignoring the shiver that ran down her spine at his inscrutable smile. "Did you want to—"

"What? Bite her neck or—it's none of your affair."

She studied his face. He was so skilled in hiding his deepest feelings that she couldn't begin to fathom what dark thoughts lay beneath his handsome features. "Some men would have obliged her right there against the tree. I have to say that I was impressed by your self-control. I didn't think you had it in you."

"Self-control," he said, setting her away from him with a strangled laugh. "Hmm, yes, I think we ought to change the subject."

"Why? I find it rather interesting."

He stared at her perfectly shaped mouth, the urge to silence her with kisses almost overwhelming. "Then you shouldn't. Or, at least, you shouldn't admit that you do, especially to me."

"Well, you are supposed to be well versed in these matters," she said pragmatically. "Besides, who else can give me advice on personal affairs?"

"Ask Olivia," he said with a frown.

"Has Olivia ever been anyone's mistress?"

"Most certainly not."

"Not even Wendell's?"

"Why on earth would you think that?"

She shook her head. "I'm not sure; there's something in the way they look at each other. Anyway, I don't see any point in asking her opinion on something that would alarm her. Have you considered making Arabella your mistress?"

"No, I have not. Arabella is a recently married woman."

"And recently married women are permitted to take such liberties with other men in English society?"

He gave her a dry look, reluctantly admiring how she cut to the core of the matter. "Under certain circumstances, married men and women have been known to look outside the marriage bed for satisfaction." There. He paused to take a breath. That was tastefully phrased, if a bit pompous for a man in his position to be explaining to someone who would probably leave any suitors in a dead faint with her frank questions. "I suppose things aren't much different between the opposite sexes in Scotland."

"I can't say for certain," she said. "I suppose they are. Still, if *my* husband were to be conducting trysts with someone else under a tree—"

He brought his hand to his face.

"—I might be tempted to stab him through the gullet a half-dozen times with my dirk."

"Don't tell me you've seen that done before," he muttered.

"Aye, by my aunt to my uncle when he betrayed her."

"And he lived afterward?" he asked, lowering his hand.

She nodded. "My aunt was a healer, as was my mother. She forgave him and sewed him back together. He was faithful to her until the day he died of natural causes."

He smiled, shaking his head. "I shouldn't wonder. Now, listen, Catriona, in all seriousness, you simply cannot repeat what you saw from the tree today. I'm sorry now that I even talked to Arabella. If I could erase—"

"*Vestigia nulla retrorsum,*" she said. "Horace has an answer for everything. There's no going back."

"Not Latin again," a voice said in dismay as Olivia

opened the alcove curtain to peer in at them. "There you are. Honestly, Knight, she needn't sound like a professor, you know. Latin is extremely off-putting at a party." She looked directly at Catriona. "Did the pair of you make friends?"

Catriona glanced up at him. "I think so."

Olivia pulled her to her feet. "Then come along, you two. We've got the ballroom lit and Howard and Smythe on the fiddle. Arabella is staying for supper, Knight. Not that I really wanted to ask her, but I suppose it was the only thing to do. I cannot quite bring myself to forgive what she did to you, but, oh, she isn't truly evil."

"Do you think *I* wanted her to stay?" he asked in patent disbelief.

Olivia glanced at Catriona, speaking in a half-whisper. "I just hope you will not yield to temptation now that Arabella has broken the silence between you, but I do believe that your meeting with her was quite innocent. That said, will you escort my cousin to the ballroom?"

He sensed Catriona's eyes on his face and turned unwillingly to stare at her. So, she was inquisitive about love, was she? And he, through no fault of his own, was suddenly expected to satisfy her maiden curiosity. He gave her a smile that warned that he was probably the worst candidate for the job. Because he was actually amused by the situation, because he hadn't figured out how to disentangle himself, he would comply with Olivia's wishes.

But no one had better blame him if the scheme backfired.

It was dark when a small group began to assemble in the ballroom below; the long mullioned windows caught glints of candlelight. Howard, Aubrey, Smythe, and even the estate gardener had been commissioned to form an impromptu band in the gallery above. The ladies of the household were still fussing about upstairs. Olivia had insisted that Catriona change into one of the daringly designed ball gowns that she had worn herself before her bereavement, a diaphanous pale pink creation that framed Cat's willowy curves like the petals on a rosebud. Olivia stared at her in wistful approval; the last time she had worn that gown, she had danced with Lionel, and he had told her she was the most beautiful woman on earth. Oh, to go back to those happier times.

Arabella entered the bedroom while Olivia finished dressing Catriona's hair, a task that proved more daunting than the older woman had expected as the mass of coppery curls resisted every effort to be tamed into a tidy coiffure.

Then, when Catriona was announced presentable—it was, after all, only a rehearsal for the real event—she stood examining herself critically in the mirror.

"I look half-naked. Is there not a warm wool jacket to cover me up? Something essential appears to be missing from this dress."

"You aren't wearing any shoes, for one thing," Olivia said. "I don't suppose you brought any dancing slippers with you from Scotland?"

"I must have left them at home with my tiaras and feathered turbans," Catriona replied, covertly yanking pins from her head while Arabella just as resolutely poked them back into place.

"Here." Olivia's voice was muffled as she made a foray into the depths of her wardrobe. "Wear these."

Catriona stared in chagrin at the dainty leather pumps. "They're far too wee. I'll cramp my toes. You see, I was born flat—"

"One has to suffer for beauty," Arabella said, shoving her down onto a stool.

Catriona endured the other woman's attentions with good grace, studying Arabella's aristocratic features in detail. She could see why the viscount had wanted to marry this creamy-skinned, blue-eyed beauty, but she didn't understand why Arabella had chosen another man in his place. She obviously still desired him, or she wouldn't have made such a fool of herself in the woods.

"I'll make sure the men haven't sneaked off for a brandy," Olivia murmured from the doorway. "Arabella, don't let her leave this room until I call you. She has to learn the meaning of making a dramatic entrance. Social impact is an art."

Arabella glanced up slowly as the door closed. She stepped back to admire the shoes she had forced onto Catriona's feet. "There. They're on. How elegant they look."

"Except that my toes are going to swell up like piggy sausages, and I'll be utterly miserable."

"Well, don't make such a vulgar observation aloud if they do. At least, not to the gentlemen who dance with you." Arabella hesitated a moment, her blue eyes beseeching. "And I do hope you won't say *anything* about the unfortunate incident you witnessed today."

"You mean when you were begging the viscount to touch your lonely breasts?"

The color drained from Arabella's face. "If my husband ever heard that, he'd call Knight out, and Anton would end up dead."

"Why? You're the one who said it. Not his lordship. Seems to me you're the one who should be shot."

Arabella looked as if she might cry. "But you aren't going to tell anyone, are you? Not even Olivia? Oh, please, Catriona. As a favor from one woman to another."

"I can hold my tongue." She paused, tugging a thread from her sleeve. "Why did you marry someone else if you still loved Knight?"

"I don't know if I do love him," Arabella said miserably. "I wanted him to kiss me to see if I still felt the magic. Not that someone of your inexperience would understand, but when a man like Knight kisses you, well, a woman falls to pieces and does anything he asks. It spoils her for anyone else. I didn't want to feel like that forever. I didn't want to be in his power."

"You might have tried your experiment before you wed another," Catriona pointed out, ever practical while at the same time her own natural self-protective instincts were aroused. Until recently, she never would have believed that a man's kiss possessed that much power. But even if what Arabella said was true, how could one hide from a love that all-encompassing?

"I know I was wrong," Arabella said wistfully, "but the trouble was, I was never really certain that Knight *would* marry me. He was always so vague about our future, so detached, and, well, who ever would have thought he'd change?"

"Not me." Catriona shook her head, more puzzled by Arabella's viewpoint than before. "He's been rather a tyrant since the night I met him."

"Promise me," Arabella whispered pleadingly as the door knob turned, giving Catriona's hand a fierce squeeze. "Not a word of this to anyone. I am never going to be caught alone with him again."

The door opened before Catriona could agree; it seemed that everyone was making a fuss over nothing. "They're waiting," Olivia said with a soft giggle of anticipation. "Isn't this exciting?"

"Oh, aye," Catriona said wryly. "I'm completely beside myself."

"Come on, then." Olivia dragged her to the door and into the hall. "Go down the stairs. Slowly. Slowly. No, dear, descend. Don't bounce."

"Float like a cloud," Arabella said, waving her shapely white arms in the air. "Float . . ."

Chapter

9

"*Float like a cloud, my foot.*" Knight shook his head amusedly from the bottom of the stairs, where he and Wendell had been given orders to wait. "Sink like a bloody stone is more apt," he said, grinning. "Here comes the social disaster of the season."

"I heard that," Catriona exclaimed, suddenly afraid that she must look awkward in a gown designed for an evening of sophistication. The sight of him certainly gave her pause. He had changed into a crisp white linen shirt, a waistcoat, and a black evening coat that showed the breadth of his shoulders. Wicked merriment danced in his eyes and then faded; for a moment, she wondered if she'd imagined the glint of approval as his gaze flickered over her.

The arrogant grin that promptly returned to his handsome features reassured her she had. "Lionel's cousin looks very nice, Olivia," he said, clearing his throat. "Now, if we can teach her not to—"

He stopped in mid-sentence as Wendell rudely elbowed around him. "What the blazes are you doing, duke?"

"Shoving aside the throng that has come to admire the Scottish beauty who is taking the *ton* by storm."

Knight made a show of looking around. "Where is she?"

"Let this young lady meet me," Wendell said, "and know there is no other to win her heart."

Catriona laughed in delight. "No other what?"

"No other idiot," Knight said with a wry grin. "Allow me to introduce the Duke of Idiots."

Wendell put his hand to his heart. "'She walks in beauty like the night—'"

Knight raised his voice. "'—to give us all a dreadful fright.' What instrument of torture did those evil women use on your hair, Catriona? You look as if you've just walked through a windstorm."

She tapped her fan down against her wrist. "Do I have your permission to hit him, Olivia? Just once. One wee slap on the noggin."

Olivia stepped between them, attempting to keep a straight face. "You won't have to. I shall do it myself if he does not behave."

"I haven't seen him act this badly in years," Aunt Marigold said thoughtfully as she was helped into the hall by her faithful manservant Ames. "It makes me wonder."

"Whether he has a brain?" Wendell asked, gallantly taking her other arm.

"Knight, kindly come here," Olivia said, motioning to Catriona.

He sighed. "Yes. Fine. My turn to be tortured next."

Catriona tensed as he took her hand, prepared for his next insult. What she did not expect was the sting of pleasure she felt at his strong forearm supporting her. She could not take a step without acknowledging the sheer power of his masculine presence. No wonder he made fun of her. He could probably snap his elegant fingers and summon any woman he wanted. Hadn't Arabella warned her of his dangerous allure? Hadn't she experienced it firsthand and wished for more? Well, perhaps she should have wished for an antidote.

"You *do* look nice," he said in an undertone as they reached the ballroom floor. "I was only teasing before."

She pressed the back of her free hand to her forehead. "Oh, no."

"What is it?"

"I must be feverish. I thought I heard you giving me a compliment."

He smiled down at her. "Lesson number one, brat. You must accept a compliment as if it were your due."

"Well, perhaps if I had more practice in receiving them, I might be able to take your advice."

He drew his hand from her elbow and stared down at her, his gaze disarmingly serious. "I expect you will be sick of compliments before the year is over."

She waited for his familiar mockery to follow, but it never came. Instead, he gave her a fleeting smile and moved into the brightly lit room, leaving her to stare after his impressive figure and wonder what on earth he could be talking about and why her heart ached so.

*   *   *

More aware of her than he dared show, he walked into the ballroom and left her standing at the door. He realized that his behavior seemed rude, but the woman had begun to unsettle him in ways he could not seem to predict or control. One moment, she looked for all the world like a seductive angel; the next, he half expected her to pull out her aunt's dirk and let fly. Or recite Horace. Or cast a spell.

The only thing he could count on was that she would be herself and that, despite himself, he would end up utterly charmed by whatever facet of her character was revealed. Should he have expected less from his best friend's relative? Everyone had loved Lionel. Charm apparently ran in their bloodlines.

Slowly, insidiously, she was changing him. She was altering his perspective, bringing color to the dreary world he had withdrawn from. His rigidity had begun to crumble, and he felt comfortable with her in a way that would have been impossible with anyone else.

He suppressed a chuckle as she walked into the room. Heaven help the man who actually ended up marrying her, and at the thought of some young rogue's hands on her body, clumsily taking her inno- cence, his mood took an unexpected dive. He couldn't think of a single young buck in the whole of England worthy of touching her, and he had no idea where this sudden protective instinct had come from, unless it derived from a sense of obligation to Lionel and Olivia. Once again, he was astonished at the depth of his attraction to a woman who broke every rule in the book. But then, perhaps he was tired of rules. Perhaps it was time to turn rebel, take a chance, and live as his parents and reckless elder brother had lived, by the heart. From the corner of his eye, he watched her stand alone at the wall.

"You look positively brainsick, Knight," Olivia whispered beside him. "Are you going to dance with her or not? Come here, Catriona. My brother is going to be on his best behavior."

Catriona slowly approached, studying Knight in open skepticism. "Are you certain?"

He couldn't help laughing. "Suspicious creature."

Olivia glanced around the room, gesturing to the small group in the corner. To add to the fun, she had recruited the other household servants to form a set. "Ames—over here, if you please, Dorcas—and you, too, Mrs. Evans. We need four couples to complete the square. We'll start with a cotillion. Howard, when Arabella gives the signal, you are to begin playing."

Knight took Catriona's hand, engulfing her small fingers in his strong grip. "May I have the honor of this dance"—he gave her a teasing smile—"brat?"

She raised her chin. "I'd rather dance with the village idiot."

"Ah." He glanced around. "Wendell, she's asking for you."

Olivia gave them a hearty shove forward. "Watch me and Ames, Catriona. Knight, make sure she ends up on the same spot."

"I'll be lucky if she doesn't end up on the floor," he said, grinning. "She probably has two left feet. Of lead."

Catriona politely attempted to pry her hand from his. He impolitely tightened his hold on her slender fingers, chuckling at her efforts. "Wrestling with your partner is *not* a part of the dance," he said.

"Oooh—you infuriate me, you ham-headed lummox."

He grinned. "Poor relations have to endure so much humiliation."

"Aye, especially from the elderly members of the family." She frowned as he released her hand and leaned down to search for something on the floor. "What are you doing?"

"Looking for my false teeth and spectacles. We elders are always misplacing them."

"Oh, very amusing you are. I think I'd have a more gratifying conversation with an ape."

He straightened, the infuriating grin still in place. "But we're stuck with each other for the time being, and there's nothing we can do about it, is there?"

Arabella gave the signal. Howard paused dramatically before he started to play. Aunt Marigold settled into a fan-backed chair by the fire, prepared to point out every misstep.

"Nothing I can do?" Catriona said, walking him into the wall with a mischievous chuckle. "I can put a hex on your private parts, you scapegrace, for a start. We'll see if you laugh then."

He leaned away from her in mock horror. "I can see it now, the belle of the ball spitting out Scottish curses over a bubbling cauldron. What a sensation that will cause. Olivia, prepare the house for an invasion of admirers. Every eligible bachelor in Europe will flock to our door for his own personal curse."

"That's it," Catriona said. "I've run out of patience, and I am giving you the Evil Eye."

"Oh, no," he gasped, clapping his hands to his cheeks. "Anything but that."

"Yes, that." And she closed her left eye, frowning him into the ground with the other as she did her best to look like a prophetess of doom, which was difficult considering she could hardly keep a straight face. "There. Your fate has been sealed, and I'm not undoing it until you apologize. You realize this is a very serious matter. I'm not even sure myself of the ramifications of such a curse. No one has ever provoked me to this point before."

For an instant, he didn't even move. She watched him, her hand to her mouth, remembering her mother warning her that one must never hex, not in anger or in jest. Goodness, what if she had really hurt him? What a pretty kettle of fish that would be.

He glanced up at the ceiling. "Well, here I stand, prepared for the worst. No thunderbolts so far. Nothing is happening. I feel no strange quivering in my innards."

"Just wait. You're not so powerful as you put on," she said, backing away from him. "Your hair will probably turn green during the night, and your toes will wither up like walnuts."

"Only my toes?" he asked, lifting his eyebrow roguishly at her.

"Just wait," she said again with a devilish chuckle that promptly died as she turned and found herself face-to-face with Olivia.

"Is something wrong, dear?" the woman asked. "I realize the steps of the cotillion seem a bit complicated at first, but it really is the—" Olivia frowned, struck by the obvious irreverence in the air. "Are you teasing her again, Knight?"

"Me? I gave her a compliment." His eyes twinkled with mischief. "She returned the favor by putting a curse on my, ahem, my manhood."

"A curse on your—" Olivia blanched. "Oh, really, Catriona. What am I to do with you?"

Catriona turned away, refusing to acknowledge the naughty grin the silly beast gave her when Olivia wasn't looking.

"I am on my best behavior," he said. "Honestly."

Olivia sighed. "Why is it that I cannot believe you? Perhaps we ought to start with a waltz, just to help her over her awkwardness. We'll leave the cotillion until the proper dancing instructor arrives."

"Not a waltz, Olivia," he said, sobering as he stared at the graceful line of Catriona's back. A voice in the back of his mind warned him that was asking for trouble. "Oh, what the hell. Come, cousin Catriona. Ignore my teasing. I cannot help myself."

Something inside him knew that he had made a fatal mistake the moment he turned her resistant body to his. His hand encircled her narrow waist, drawing her closer, and in an instant he felt a quickening in his heart, all the more lethal because he had forgotten the power of purity. The women in his past had never looked at him with such unguarded emotion.

"Truce?" he asked quietly, guiding her away from the others.

She searched his face. She wanted to dislike him; he made her laugh one second and ache to strangle him the next. She had lived among dangerous men long enough to recognize that he posed a threat to her security, although not perhaps in the manner she expected. She had never encountered his dark sophistication before and had no defenses against it. Why should she be any different from the other women who had found him irresistible?

"You should dance with Arabella," she said, her voice catching. "She's not taken her eye off you all evening."

A smile creased his handsome face. "And what a boring, predictable eye she has. Not capable of anything nearly as exciting as a hex on my nether regions."

"She must have been capable of having some effect if you'd planned to marry her," she retorted.

"That seems like a very long time ago," he said.

"Aye, was it?"

"Ancient history."

"Perhaps not to her."

He smiled, his fingers closing around hers with gentle strength that took her off balance. "You know a secret about me. Now I must know another one of yours."

Her heart missed a beat at the intimacy of his smile. Suddenly, she found it hard to catch her breath; it was too tempting to trust him. "Do I look like someone who has secrets, my lord?"

"Everyone has secrets." His deep voice sent a shiver down to her toes. "Tell me yours. So we may be equals, if not friends."

She twisted to put distance between them, her attraction to him alarming. His arm held her in an iron band, drawing her nearer. "And you may use it against me," she said, smiling up at him uncertainly.

"But then perhaps we would be forced to trust each other."

She felt an undefinable emotion, an ache, in the area of her heart. "I think you should stop leaning down to whisper in my ear. Everyone is looking."

"No wonder." He drew her nearer to him. "You are something to look at."

She stumbled a step, her pulse quickening. He paused and glanced down at the floor. "Good God," he exclaimed, "where are your shoes now?"

"I slipped them off for a moment. Your paramour practically forced my feet into them, and they were crushing my wee toes to death."

He halted in his tracks. "She is not my paramour. Stop saying that, or I—I shall be forced to spank you."

"During a waltz?"

"I daresay it can be done," he said gravely, his eyes twinkling. "In your case, it should probably be performed on a regular basis."

She started to laugh. "And you expect me to keep your secret when you say things like that?"

He whirled her toward the corner. "Lower your voice, Miss Grant. Aunt Marigold is all ears."

"The woman loves to gossip."

"I could give her something to talk about," he said thoughtfully.

Catriona gazed up at him, not certain she should trust the boyish smile that lit his sardonic features. "Such as?"

"Such as giving my partner a passionate kiss in the middle of the dance floor."

His gaze met hers in a seductive look that made her heart skip several beats. "During a waltz?" she asked, trying not to sound too hopeful.

"I daresay it can be done," he said, his fingers pressed into the soft flesh of her waist. "In your case, it will probably be attempted on a regular basis."

"Display some exuberance," Aunt Marigold shouted from her chair. "Some *joie de vivre!* The pair of you dance like the dead!"

"For a dead man," he said quietly, his smile an arrow that shot straight to Catriona's heart, "I have never felt more alive than I do at this moment."

The music ended, and the spell was broken.

Catriona could not have remembered a single step she had followed to save her life. She looked up slowly into Knight's face, unsure what she would see, but he had turned away to watch Olivia and Wendell approach. She felt a painful tug at her heart as she stared at his strongly etched profile.

Olivia glanced from Catriona to Knight as if she suspected that something had changed between them. "I trust that the two of you were civil to each other and that the dancing went well."

Knight adjusted the cuffs of his sleeves. "Well enough for our first lesson." He glanced at Catriona, giving her a playful wink. "She'll probably be ready for her come-out sometime in the next century."

Aunt Marigold rose from her chair to offer her analysis of the situation. "That wasn't half bad for a beginner, Catriona. You have a natural grace that will improve with practice. But you, Knight, well, you were as stiff as a pikestaff, and all that stopping and starting. What is the matter with you?"

He smiled politely. "Nothing that five bottles of brandy won't help. Good night, ladies. Wendell, it's your turn to torture Catriona. Keep a firm grip on your heart."

He strolled out on the assembly, wondering suddenly if there were something to the rumors of Scottish witchcraft. Never in his life had he enjoyed being with a woman as he had the one he teased so unmercifully to hide the deeper emotions that she stirred in him.

He heard footsteps running down the hall behind him. He paused at the door to his study, fully expecting his sister to demand an explanation for his abrupt departure.

But it was Catriona, shamelessly barefooted, bearing down on him with a look of determination on her face that warned him he was in for another dose of trouble. Suddenly, it was obvious to him that this sensual young woman was not going to need *his* help finding a husband. Watching her now, her graceful stride, the pale rose gown twining around her lithe legs, he felt a desire for her that was almost self-destructive considering the peculiar aspects of their association.

She was turning his life upside down. How could he explain it? He had enjoyed their encounter in the ballroom. He wanted to learn more about her, layer by layer. Her easy smile, her womanly body, and the outrageous things she said brought out the very best, and worst, in him.

He was the man she had come to for protection. Even before they'd met, something had drawn her here. Yes, he teased her for her beliefs in the supernatural, but even he could not help wondering what power had brought them together. She had needed him, and he needed . . . nothing.

He stared down at her, striving to look unaffected when it was all he could do not to drag her into the study and lock the door behind them. He tortured himself by remembering how her mouth had tasted, by wondering how she would feel beneath him, what sounds she would make when he drove inside her. How his life would change if he claimed all that innocent fire for himself.

"Knight," she said, a little out of breath from trying to catch him before he disappeared. "Wait. I want a word with you."

He drummed his tapered fingers against the door.

She ran the tip of her tongue over her bottom lip, and he felt another bolt of heat destroy his control. "What do you want?" he asked, not doing a thing to put her at ease. "I am not teaching you the pianoforte or spinet—"

"I want to accept the terms of your truce." She gazed up at him with an adorable determination he could not resist. "Please."

Damn her. Just when he was ready to find any excuse to break this absurd attraction. "Oh, fine."

"I will keep your secret. I won't tell anyone about Arabella."

He leaned one shoulder against the door, perversely wanting to punish her for a sin she had no idea she had ever committed. Was it her fault he looked at her and lost his ability to think?

"Perhaps I don't care anymore," he said, frowning at the ceiling. "Perhaps I'm feeling in the mood for a duel. It's been a long time since I shot anyone. Tell the world about me and Arabella if you like." He paused. "Don't forget the part about her lonely breasts."

She frowned. What a difficult man. "I am trying to make amends, my lord."

His gaze traveled over her with an interest that roused her self-defensive impulses, as well as a few rather indecent ones along the way. "Are you?" he asked quietly.

She took a slight step back. "I ought to go back to the ballroom. I left rather abruptly."

He studied her and realized that she had no idea of her own appeal, of how difficult he found it to battle the selfish desire that she aroused in him. His voice was deliberately detached. "A truce under one condition."

She arched a brow. She knew she should not ask. "Which would be?"

"I told you." He pushed away from the door with elegant animal grace. "Tell me a secret."

She hesitated, her eyes locked with his. He did not know what he expected her to say. He had no clue how many skeletons lurked in her past, if any, or what he would do with such information. But he wanted to understand her.

"All right." She took a breath, wondering why she always felt so gauche in his presence. "But you must promise not to laugh."

"I shall not laugh. Go on."

"It is . . ." She would have taken another step away, but he drew her back against the door so that they stood in the shadows, faces almost touching, the heat of their bodies charging the air. A man and a woman on the verge of a moment that might alter them forever.

He was anything but the detached gentleman he appeared to be. The delicate scent of her soap teased his senses, stirred a longing in the depths of his heart. The brush of her soft breasts against his shirtfront made his teeth ache. He flexed his fingers, aching to touch her everywhere, to peel that gown from her body and make her moan in pleasure.

"Shadows are made for sharing secrets," he said, tilting her face to his with his knuckle. "Well?"

"It is . . . that I find you exceedingly handsome," she said in a hesitant voice. "I am drawn to you."

His eyes widened. No, not at all the sort of secret he'd expected, but she had stunned him just the same. "Are you?" he whispered, smiling in delight.

His smile undid her composure. She felt utterly

miserable and mortified that she had admitted such a thing. Of course, a decent young lady would never confess her innermost feelings to a man. A decent lady would certainly not feel this wicked tingling in her blood. "On second thought—"

His kiss destroyed whatever dignity she'd hoped to salvage. She felt his arm slide around her waist like an anchor as the muscles supporting her legs seemed to dissolve. His mouth captured hers so gently at first that she did not understand her danger. But as she twined her arms instinctively around his neck, he kissed her with an urgency that swept her into a shadow world of sensual languor. His tongue dueled with hers as he backed her into the door, and she was his, riveted with need. Just like that. She could barely recall what they had been discussing, but in the back of her mind, she remembered Arabella's confession, that when he kissed a woman, she would do anything he asked. And when he brushed his lower lip across her mouth, she almost fell to her knees. The assault on her senses was too much, the pleasure he offered too enticing.

His face, as he broke the kiss, brought her hurtling back to earth. Surely he would torment her endlessly now. "On second thought—" she began again, a shiver of delayed reaction making its way down her spine.

"Your secret is quite safe with me," he said quietly. "Sealed with a kiss, in fact." There it was, that infuriating glint in his eye again. "And," he added in a whisper, "it was not even interrupted by an acorn attack."

She whirled around, her cheeks stained pink, stopped once to say something, then turned again and hurried down the hall. If she had paused to glance back a second time, she would not have found him laughing at her at all. She would not even have recognized him as the man who teased her without mercy. No, she would have taken one look at the intense longing on his face, and she would have realized that he had just staked his claim.

She was different from any woman he'd ever met. He understood this more clearly by the hour, and by the hour he lost a little ground in his fight against his attraction to her. Where could it lead? He dared not speculate. She was a talisman who had slipped into his heart as if to counteract the spell of cynicism that had taken hold. She was white light to the darkness that had fallen over his house. In a brief time, she had brought laughter back into his life, and hope.

He waited until she had vanished from sight before he turned and noticed the morning post sitting on the hall stand. With all the fuss over finding Catriona, and the ballroom, he had forgotten to read it.

He recognized Simmons's precise handwriting in the candlelight and broke open the seal, waiting for his heart to resume a normal rhythm before he read:

My lord, before I even reached Scotland, I came across some information about your houseguest that may concern you. Due to its confidential nature, I shall return to deliver it in person before proceeding further. You were correct in your suspicion that the young woman is not what she seems.

Yours obediently,
Simmons

Chapter

10

❧

The owls returned to Rutleigh Hall that same night, a chain of predators that hooted across the woods until the entire household was thoroughly unsettled.

Aunt Marigold got out of bed and summoned Ames to her room, stating, "Someone is going to die, that's what the owls are saying, and since you and I are the eldest people in the house, it must be one of us. I shall pray for our souls."

He plumped the pillows behind her head. "I shall make you some calming camomile tea, ma'am."

"Ames," she said in distress, "are you not at all concerned over our imminent demise?"

He glanced toward the window. "Actually, madam, my dear Welsh grandmother believed that a hooting owl meant a woman was going to lose her chastity. It did not portend a death."

"Truly, Ames?"

"She was a veritable fount of wisdom, madam."

She settled back against the pillows. "How interesting. Did you know that *I* am a maiden myself?"

"Then we must guard your virtue." He smiled at her as he went to the door. "I assume it will be safe at least until I fetch that tea."

The owls had not awakened her. Catriona hadn't been able to sleep a wink, anyway, not with her whole body feeling as if she'd been struck by lightning. Every time she closed her eyes, she saw Knight's angular face looming over hers. She had been electrified by that last kiss, and she scolded herself for feeling so hopeful about it when it was obvious that any entanglement with a man like him could only bring heartbreak. But, oh, how wonderful he was. What a beautiful devil.

And it did seem rather ungrateful of her, so disloyal to Olivia, to be falling in love with her rogue of an older brother without first seeking her advice on the matter.

She pulled the pillow over her head as the hooting grew louder, amplified until it seemed to throb against the walls of her room.

"Just go away," she whisper. "Leave me—"

She sat up abruptly and stared at the window. What if the birds had not come as a warning? What if it were not her brother James or her suitor who had followed her here? All of a sudden, it occurred to her that the owls might have been sent to *find* her, not to warn her, their unholy calls summoning their master in the dark. And there was only one person in her world who possessed such power over birds and beasts: Murdo Grant, her estranged uncle on her mother's magical side of the family, the brother who had fought bitterly with Mama over her foolish loyalty to the man she loved until her last breath.

Uncle Murdo, the crafty old wizard who lived in the Border hills with his young apprentice, Lamont, a scrawny orphan boy who had troubled Catriona's earliest years with his tricks and malicious mischief. Hadn't Lamont trained a raven when he was eleven, teaching it to recite crude verses outside Catriona's window? Murdo used birds as magical messengers. Lamont used them to play pranks.

She slid to the floor and hunted under the bed for the bag she'd hidden. She couldn't imagine what Murdo would want from her, unless it was the Earth stone he'd stolen from her mother, which Cat's mother had stolen back to pass down to her daughter.

The red-veined stone was believed to be one of four that had belonged to the infamous Scottish magician Michael Scot. Catriona was not convinced that the stone possessed any healing properties, but she was starting to believe that whatever power it owned might be drawing Murdo to her like a magnet.

And where Murdo went, or so Mama had claimed, unhappiness was sure to follow.

She dug the plaid-wrapped bundle out of her portmanteau, said a quick prayer, and threw her old plaid on over her nightrail. The stone had suddenly taken on an evil aspect that she felt obligated to remove from the house.

His lordship had no idea what sort of secrets lurked in her past, but with any luck, she'd be burying one while he was still in bed before it could bring him misfortune. After tonight, she had decided that her feelings for him had changed, or perhaps what she felt had just come into focus. She was not going to let any harm come near his house.

Did she actually think that she could go for a walk at this hour? Knight leaned across the desk where he had been sitting in a semi-trance for the past two hours, thinking about how to handle the situation with Lionel's desirable cousin. Mulling over that mysterious note from Simmons and wondering why it didn't matter more. He hadn't bothered going to bed. No, he had been hoping to get drunk in the library, thereby bypassing the need to come to any decision, when the army of night birds descended on the woods.

If it hadn't been for the damned orchestra of owls, he probably would have been pleasantly foxed by now, but as bad luck would have it, he was completely awake. And he looked out the window just in time to see the cloaked figure edging across the lawn into the woods. He leaned forward, bringing his feet to the floor.

She was carrying her bag.

The owls were going wild, hooting more loudly to proclaim her presence in their territory.

Where would she go in the middle of the night? Had his kiss frightened her away? She had kissed him back, hadn't she? A stirring of doubt darkened his mood. The odd thing was, he knew exactly how she felt. It was a terrifying experience to feel your heart being stolen when you least expected it. At his age, you would think he'd have become immune, and yet, as he had noted earlier, she was different from the other young ladies he had kissed into a swoon. He couldn't expect her to take to the couch with her hand lifted to her brow.

Still, he couldn't believe that she would leave like this after they had made such a to-do about their truce. But then, perhaps he had underestimated his effect on her. Perhaps that kiss in the doorway had undermined her composure as deeply as it had his.

He sprang out of his chair, his eyes dark with determination. He was sorry if he had driven her away, but at the same time, she had to understand that he expected her to follow certain rules of civilized behavior. Even if his own conduct to this point had been anything but.

Catriona buried the stone with her bare hands under a blasted oak in the event that she might need to find it again. The fluttering of the owls above rattled her nerves. So did the stone; it seemed to pulse and glow in the earth. She couldn't understand why her mother had treasured such an odd thing, anyway, because now that she looked at it closely, the stone seemed to resemble a human heart.

Her own heart nearly burst with terror when she heard footsteps behind her and the crash of bushes being broken as a man burst into the clearing. For a frightening instant, she thought that Murdo had found her. But the intruder was bigger and much better-looking than her elderly uncle. Every particle of her being tingled in response to his presence, his long, muscular legs planted apart, the lines of his face taut with emotion.

"What the hell do you think you are doing?" he shouted at her.

The owls grew ominously silent.

She rose to face him. He was fascinating and truly terrible in his outburst. And handsome, even with his thick black hair disheveled and his shirt not tucked into his trousers. She couldn't imagine what she had done to make him so angry, though. They had just made a truce a few short hours ago. Hadn't he kissed her and left her drifting on a cloud of bliss and tender dreams?

She frowned at him. Her cloud was rapidly deflating, sending her crashing back down to earth.

"How could you do this to me?" he roared.

She shivered beneath her cloak and searched her memory. Did mental problems run in Lionel's family? But then, he wasn't actually related to Lionel except by Olivia's marriage. Heaven only knew what brain aberrations had affected his lordship's bloodlines.

"Don't you care at all what Olivia would think?" he yelled at her.

"About what?" she said in consternation, ducking behind a tree.

He strode toward her. "How do you think she would feel if she found you gone without a word in the morning?"

"I had every intention of returning to the house, my lord."

"Did you?" He looked down at her closely for the longest time, then let loose a strain of the foulest curses she had ever heard. "You're wearing a night rail. A night rail, for God's sake. What is the meaning of this?"

"I do have my cloak on over it," she said in annoyance. And she certainly hadn't expected to meet anyone else there at that time of night.

He snorted insultingly. "How far did you think you could run in a nightgown? Ha."

"I wasn't running anywhere, you big idiot."

He waggled his finger under her nose. "I saw you

from the window. You were running with"—he glanced around and saw her bag beneath the oak—"with *that*. You would have broken Olivia's heart without a thought."

She set her jaw. "I was definitely not running away. I was running an errand." She sniffed delicately and then made a face. "Oh, brandy. I should have known."

He walked her backward, almost to the blasted oak where she had hidden the stone. She didn't want to step on the burial spot; to do so seemed a sacrilege.

"What sort of errand?" he asked in an intimidating voice.

She cast an uneasy glance around the clearing. She was a step from where the stone lay, but she couldn't decide which was the greater threat, a stone with supernatural powers or this man who had seemingly lost his mind.

She decided to take her chances on the Earth stone. She stepped back to where she had buried it.

Instantly, the woods burst into sound. Owls were hooting, fluttering across the treetops, and a small animal came scurrying out of the underbrush. A sharp pain shot through the soles of her feet into her spine.

"Oh!" she cried, doubling over. "Oh, oh, oh. Now look what you've made me do."

Knight stared around him in bemusement. "What is it now?" Had she stubbed her toe on the tree trunk? What had happened?

She pulled away from him and hobbled over to a mossy crop of rocks, where she collapsed in a heap. He followed her, a menacing shadow that she pretended to ignore.

"I want an answer, Catriona. What are you doing

here this time of night? Stop pretending to be hurt. I never touched you."

"I went for a walk. Do I have to account for every moment of my life to you?"

"As long as you live in my house, yes. Were—" A shocking thought occurred to him. He knelt and grabbed her by the arms, scanning her face. "Were you meeting someone?"

"What?"

"Were you meeting one of my servants?"

Her lips tightened. "What an insult. Apologize, please."

"Wendell." His face darkened. "Did the rogue ask you to meet him here?"

"Aye," she said crossly. "Can't you see his carriage behind that tree? We were just about to elope when you found us. I was so swept away with passion that I didn't remember to change my clothes."

He sighed, realizing how irrational he must sound and that, knowing as much of Catriona as he did, she was probably telling the truth. "All right. I admit it was a stupid thing to ask, but you can hardly blame me for wondering what you were doing."

"Not everyone has a lover waiting in the woods," she muttered.

One dark eyebrow lifted at that. "Indeed. And not everyone runs about in their nightclothes, either. Explain yourself this instant."

"Why? You'd only make fun of me again."

"Not if you had a reasonable explanation."

"You wouldn't understand."

"I might."

She raised her head. "I was *not* meeting anyone, and I most assuredly wasn't running away." She paused, peering around his shoulder to where the stone lay. "I was burying something, if you must know."

"I hesitate to ask, but reassure me—it wasn't a dead body, was it?"

"Don't tempt me," she said darkly.

"Did this have to do with one of your magic spells?" he said, muffling a chuckle. "Have you taken my toenail clippings while I slept?"

She hid her face in her hands. "You're never going to believe me. Why do I bother?"

"This will upset Olivia, you know. Well-bred young women don't sneak about on missions of sorcery in the woods."

She lowered her hands in dismay. "I did it for Olivia, you dunderhead."

"What?"

"So that the evil wouldn't come near the house."

"What evil? What nonsense are you talking about? What did you bury, Catriona?"

"A stone."

"A—oh, Lord."

"A very *special* stone."

"Aren't they all?" He glanced around. "It wasn't one of Howard's organs, was it?"

"Most certainly not."

"That's a relief. For Howard, I mean."

"I don't think you're taking this seriously."

He snorted. "You can say that again."

She looked into his gray, mirthful eyes. "There are more things on heaven and earth than our minds will ever know. This particular stone belonged to a powerful wizard who was said to have stolen it from Saint Bride and her nine vestal virgins."

"Nine of them—all in the same place?" He suppressed a smile. "And here I was worried you'd run away because I kissed you earlier."

She tossed her head, feeling her heart begin to race. "It would take more than that to scare me off. It was only a kiss."

He narrowed his eyes. "Was it?"

"Aye." She peered at him more closely. "Wasn't it?"

"Actually, I thought it was rather more." He gave her a beguiling smile. "It excited me," he said quietly. "Did you really forget what you felt?"

She shook her head, afraid he could hear her heart pounding in her chest. "Are you teasing me again?"

He lowered his voice. "I would like"—he put both his hands around her shoulders and drew her down hard against his muscular body—"to be the man you wanted to meet tonight."

Before she could react, he was kissing her again, devastating her with a sensual skill that sent tendrils of fire deep into the pit of her stomach, into her loins. She moaned as he caught her face in his hands, the scent of brandy on his breath warming her cheek, the desire in his eyes demanding that she yield to him. She slid forward, unbalanced, boneless, against the strong plane of his chest. His arms locked around her waist, and she lost the ability to breathe at the contact of that powerful body cradling hers, her bottom resting behind his hard thighs. His kisses drugged her, weakened her, melted her bones.

Suddenly, it seemed to her as if the entire world had gone still. Either that, or the rush of blood to her brain had drowned out all other sound. There was nothing but him in that moment, nothing but his mouth devouring hers, stealing her breath, her body a hot flush of sensations. His virility rendered her helpless. She barely protested when his hand brushed her breast, when his hips lifted into her, steel against the vulnerable softness of her body. He had set her blood on fire, and she would never be the same.

He broke off, giving her the illusion that she was safe. Then he anchored his fingers in her hair and brought his mouth down on hers again, harder now, hungrier. She was trembling in his arms, beyond resistance, and he knew that with a little persuasion, he could take delight in her body. Hell, he was going to hammer her into the ground if he didn't get hold of himself. But she felt so good, soft and submissive, her body molding to his. Every male instinct urged him to make her his mate. He thrust upward, into her, releasing a groan as her back arched in response. Untutored, untamed, she was more than he could resist, and he wanted to teach her everything he knew about sensuality.

He brushed his lips across her throat, burying his face between her breasts. "This is a hell of a time to discover I have a conscience," he muttered.

"You had a conscience today when you met Arabella," she pointed out.

He closed his eyes. He was too aware of her body, her every curve, her breasts, her belly, the warm hollow between her thighs that he was aching to explore. "That was entirely different. My conscience didn't stop me as much as my lack of desire."

"Do you desire me?" she asked softly.

For a moment he, couldn't move, his brain and body screaming the answer. He wanted to push her beneath him and take her down the dark channels of his desire. He wanted to nail her to that tree and thrust until neither of them could walk. She wasn't wearing anything under that nightgown. He could be inside her in a matter of seconds, but she would be shattered afterward, and the thought of hurting her was more than he could bear. He liked this cousin of Lionel's, liked her far more than he should.

"Do you desire me?" she asked again, her soft voice stirring the nerve endings on his neck.

"You have no idea," he said curtly. He stood without warning, drawing her to her feet. "And with any luck, you never will. Olivia means to find you a perfect husband. This does not qualify as helping the situation."

She didn't move away from him at first; she was pinned to the spot by the suppressed need that darkened his eyes as he stared down at her. Goose bumps prickled a path of forewarning down the surface of her forearms. His hands tightened briefly around her waist, holding her against him so she could feel the hard ridge between his legs.

"Catriona," he said, before bending his head to kiss her on the cheek. "There. Be quiet going back to the house."

"I liked your kisses," she said quietly. "They make me feel, well, I can't even describe it."

He closed his eyes for several moments, a shard of lust piercing the remnants of his control. "Get your bag. Now."

He felt her edge around him where he stood, seemingly unperturbed as he allowed her to escape when already, in his mind, he had taken her a dozen times. Had it only been that morning that he'd been criticizing *her* behavior? Twice in one day, now, he had let a rogue's instinct cloud his judgment. Well, at least he'd gotten himself under control. At least it wasn't too late to repair whatever damage he'd done by kissing her.

He motioned her to walk ahead of him. "Run into the house first. Just in case anyone is watching."

"But—" The stark emotion in his voice gave her pause. A wiser young woman would not have admitted she liked what had happened between them. Deception was another skill she would never learn.

"Go, Catriona, before I make things worse between us. Go, or so help me God, I'll have you on the ground, and Saint Bride will have one fewer virgin to watch over."

She shrugged and whirled around, her eyes briefly meeting his. He trailed behind her, a raw feeling inside him. He had never been caught in a woman's power before, at least not to the degree that he couldn't predict his own behavior. He didn't particularly enjoy the feeling, but it wasn't too late to put an end to it. He—

He stopped, the hairs on his nape tingling. Either he had not been paying attention, or the woods seemed different from when he'd arrived. Had he noticed the toadstools glowing? Was that owl in the branches above, the only one left from the unholy raptor orchestra, *following* them?

If he had turned around, he might have noticed the earth pulsing beneath the blasted oak, the humus trembling as if it contained a human heart. He might have known he was wrong. He might have remembered the warnings of his father that he had laughed at in his reckless youth, that once love took hold of you, that was the end of reasonable behavior.

It was already too late.

*　　*　　*

He saw Catriona hurry up the steps to the house before he followed. Engrossed in watching her, he failed to notice his sister standing in the doorway, tapping her fingers impatiently on the door; if he'd seen her, he would have sneaked in through the servant's entrance to avoid an embarrassing scene. Instead, he walked right into the core of the erupting volcano.

"Well, Lord Rutleigh, isn't this a surprise?" Olivia said in a crisp voice. "Did you two enjoy yourselves?"

He paused. "Not exactly."

"In her nightclothes, Knight!" she burst out. "Of all the scandalous—you're both hopeless, you do realize that. Completely hopeless."

He nodded.

"Are you trying to ruin her?"

He sat down on the steps, not helping the matter by grinning in response. "Ruin her? Hell, I was trying—"

She grabbed Catriona by the hand, dragged her forward, and slammed the door on him. The door of his own house, mind you. Put out like a dog that couldn't behave.

He could hear Catriona being escorted down the hall, saving her own skin with a skill he had to admire. "It was all my fault, Olivia. He was worried when he saw me outside. On my honor."

"Then why were you outside in the first place?" Olivia shouted.

"I was trying to get those awful owls away from the house."

Then another woman's voice. Lord protect him, it was Aunt Marigold, ancient but on the alert. "What? What? They went for a walk, in their nightclothes?

Odd. I thought Knight slept in the nude like his father . . ."

He stared out into the night, venting a sigh. The taste of her still lingered on his lips. His neck tingled where she had clasped him with her hands, sending a warmth deep into a place in his heart that hadn't been touched in a long, long time. In the morning, he would double his efforts to avoid her. He would redefine the boundaries between them, reluctant guardian to recalcitrant charge. He would establish emotional distance—

He looked up as a great horned owl descended in the branches of the tree that faced her window. *Her* window. Within moments, he heard the treetops beyond rustle with the arrival of other birds. Predators. Creatures of the dark. Secret messengers—of whom?

What did they want with her?

He sprang to his feet, ran down the steps, and collected a handful of gravel from the drive to throw at the tree. Whatever she thought she'd done in the woods to discourage them hadn't worked.

"Go away!" he shouted, flinging another handful into the air. "This is my house. Those are my trees, and she's my—"

He glanced at her darkened window. "—problem."

He lowered his hand, letting the gravel fall to the ground. The trees were empty, the woods suddenly silent. In fact, the only sign of life on the estate came from Catriona's window, where she stood watching his peculiar behavior with Olivia and Aunt Marigold, protectors of her virtue, on either side.

Chapter

11

❦

The widowed French seamstress who had set up shop in the village of West Briarcombe arrived early the next morning. Claudette Malraux knew that rumors abounded about her past, whispers that she was really a countess in exile or even a royal refugee. She allowed the rumors to circulate, sometimes even secretly encouraging them. Such tidbits of scandal helped business, and business had been dismally slow of late except for the usual funerals.

Lady Deering had indicated that this summons involved some sort of personal emergency, which was just the sort of situation Claudette needed to revive her own sluggish spirits. For a time, she had even thought she might have a chance of becoming Viscount Rutleigh's mistress. Surely she had not imagined the sexual interest in his eyes when she had seen him at his pottery factory last winter.

He had been jilted by that insipid moron Arabella Minton for her boring husband, Anton, who was probably as exciting in the bedroom as a Latin mass. Knight had seemed ripe for a love affair, vulnerable, and not linked to any female in particular, and Claudette had waited patiently for him to visit her. But he never had, and this morning, when she passed him in the hall, her hopes suffered a fatal blow when he barely seemed to recognize her.

"Lord Rutleigh," she had said in the deeply accented voice that appealed to a great many Englishmen. "I have not seen you for some time. I trust you are well."

For the most insulting instant, he had seemed not even to remember her, and when he did, there was a decided lack of male interest in his eyes. "My sister has need of your services, madam," he said rather absentmindedly. "It is good of you to come on such short notice. You do remember how to find her room?"

She sighed in disappointment. How formal, how cold, a clear delineation between the two classes, and she knew from that nitwit Arabella Minton's indiscreet tongue that the viscount was a man of insatiable passion. According to his past amour, there was nothing formal about him in bed; he was an inventive and energetic lover, which could only mean one thing.

He had found another love interest. Claudette shook her head resignedly as she hurried up the stairs to Lady Deering's chambers, which she had not visited since before Sir Lionel's funeral to measure Olivia for her dreary widow's weeds. Someone else had caught his eye. Another woman was satisfying his needs. At this rate, Claudette would end up marrying a nobody like that impertinent footman Howard who had tried to pinch her bottom in the hallway. No, she would rather make her own way in the world than lower herself to wedding an underling. Before escaping France, her mercantile parents had been arranging her marriage to the distant cousin of a duke with connections across the Continent.

She knocked on the door, sighing again as it was opened. Lord Rutleigh could be a generous man, as was evidenced by his treatment of his sister, who had her own modest estate but chose to live here. Her gaze went straight to Olivia sitting on the bed. Shocked, Claudette saw the impact of the woman's prolonged grief. Once vivacious and youthful, Olivia had allowed her alluring curves to go to skin and bones, and she looked years older than her actual age.

"Thank goodness you've come," Olivia said, springing off the bed.

"I can see I am needed," Claudette agreed as she mentally rolled up her sleeves for a good day's work. There was enough money to be had here that she could overlook her own neglected love life for the time being.

Olivia smiled ruefully at the younger woman sitting at the dressing table. "She needs help, and rather badly, I'm afraid."

Claudette had not noticed the other woman before, nor had she spotted the baroness leaning against the wardrobe, her face haughty and unfriendly. Their eyes met in mutual dislike, and then Claudette returned her attention to the young woman in dishabille who sat sifting halfheartedly through a jewel box, her bright hair a mass of lustrous waves down to her hips.

"Her, *madame?*" Claudette said with a sniff of disdain. "You want me to help this—person?"

"Please," Olivia said, the word almost a prayer. "Work your magic on her, Claudette. We are quite desperate. She has no wardrobe of her own."

Claudette compressed her lips as the younger woman turned to examine her. Was it possible? Was *this* who had captured Knight's heart, this wild-looking thing who lifted her head with a disinterested sigh?

All right, Claudette thought. Her client had an angel's face and a body to match, and she wasn't as young as Claudette had first assumed, either. And those eyes—there was character there, emotion, and a surprising intelligence with a spark of she-devil to match Knight's wickedness. She could see what had attracted him, although the female had absolutely no sense of style. But those eyes, *la,* this one had lived a life despite her tender years. Claudette forbore an impulse to cross herself, as if in the presence of the supernatural. So this was her rival, she thought again. A woman unaware of her own beauty, and Claudette was expected to polish this raw stone into a diamond?

She squared her shoulders. *Eh, bien.* She was a professional. She could do it. "I do not know, *madame.* So much work."

"Name your price," Olivia said.

"Her hair is impossible," Claudette announced. "It spoils any hope of subtlety."

Catriona did not look at all offended. Rather, she gave a vigorous nod of agreement. "You should see it after it's washed. My head is a bramble bush."

"We'll have to pull it to the back," Arabella said, joining the conversation. "Or have it styled *à la Grecque.* She has the facial structure for shorter hair."

Claudette arched her brow, although privately she agreed with the assessment. She could not stand Arabella. She never paid her bills on time and always bought the most inferior muslin. "I have it on good authority that long hair will be the rage again soon. We'll do something with flowers or a beaded cap."

"Can you do something in two weeks or so?" Olivia asked. "An evening dress, at least. I want to introduce her to the local gentry. I have someone special in mind for her to meet."

"Meet for what?" Claudette said absently, narrowing her eyes to picture her client in French gauze that would wrap around those curves like a dream.

"To marry, of course," Arabella snapped. "Why else would we go to all this trouble?"

Claudette's eyes widened. Was the young woman *enceinte?* Had that devil Knight impregnated her, and was he hoping now to marry her off to some unsuspecting fool before his seed started to show? She frowned. Oh, men. She would have to allow for an expanding waistline in planning a wardrobe.

"I suppose lilac gauze would be best," Olivia said.

Claudette shook her head. "Sea-green, I'm thinking, shot with gold thread to rival those eyes. And we want to expose as much bosom as we can." She eyed Catriona closely. "Well, at least the illusion of a bosom."

Knight needed to escape from the house before his attraction to Catriona deepened into something far more dangerous. He couldn't concentrate on balancing accounts and choosing designs with her picking flowers outside his window or sneaking past his desk to steal another book from the shelf. And he couldn't bring himself to participate with any degree of enthusiasm in her hunt for a suitable husband when the sight of her brought too many unsuitable things to his mind. He was positive there wasn't a man in the whole of West Briarcombe he could approve to court her.

Still, what a wife she would make, warm, supportive, with a mind of her own and a body to haunt a man's dreams. He had known the moment he met her that she was trouble, but with his blinding arrogance, he had never believed himself vulnerable to her appeal. He couldn't guess who would possess the strength, energy, and good fortune to marry her. If he were—he blocked the tantalizing thought before it could take root.

He tried to bury himself in business affairs. He intended to invest himself, both energy and wealth, in the local pottery firm. He liked the fact that he could visit it at will; he liked the idea of speculating in a product he could actually hold in his hands. Creating art seemed like the perfect antidote to the destructions of war he had witnessed. Crude earthenware could be dipped in pale clay to conceal the dark flaws beneath. Or it could be decorated by *sgraffito* to enhance its appeal, remarked to fit a standard form of beauty. A piece of clay could be molded to one's ideals, unlike a human being. Unlike Catriona Grant, whose character had been shaped by mysterious forces indeed.

A knock distracted him. "There is someone who wishes to see you, my lord," Howard said from the doorway.

Knight glanced up. He wondered if the visitor might be Simmons, two days early, and he was sorry now he'd sent the man on a fool's errand because he needed him to go to Bristol on business. He couldn't imagine that Catriona harbored any darker secrets in her past than her illegitimacy, and Olivia was right. Her background didn't matter, anyway. She was Lionel's cousin, and having accepted her into the family, Knight would stand beside her no matter what she had been or done. To hell with what anyone thought.

"It's not Simmons?" he said.

"Oh, no, my lord," Howard said. "I know Simmons. It's the old jeweler from Clover Hill."

"Jeweler? Did I send for a jeweler?"

"I dunno, my lord. But he's brought more pearls with 'im than a bleedin' oyster bed."

"What do I want with—" Knight turned, his nostrils narrowing in distaste. "What is that unpleasant odor?"

"Vetiver, my lord. I bought some at market last month and thought I'd give it a try. To please the ladies, you know."

Knight raised his eyebrow. "No, actually, I don't, but I will pass along a bit of advice on the subject. Unless you wish these particular 'ladies' to pass out in droves at your feet, you will not drown yourself in scent. You have enough on to boil an ox."

"Shall I call Lady Deering down to see the jeweler, my lord?"

"Lady Deering? He asked for my sister?"

Howard scratched his head. "He asked for her first, then he asked for you as you would be the one paying the bill. I took it upon myself to escort him to the entrance lobby."

"I shall take care of this," Knight said in exasperation, rising from his desk. "Where is she, anyway?"

"Upstairs, with that saucy little French—" Howard flattened himself against the door to allow his lordship passage. "Do you require my assistance, my lord?"

"No point in stinking up the entire house, Howard," Knight retorted. "Go to the kitchen and have a good wash."

The jeweler caught sight of Knight in the hall as he attempted to make a covert dash for the stairs. "Ah, Lord Rutleigh. I've done the very best I could on such short notice, bearing in mind your message that expense was no object—"

"I said that, did I?" Knight said grimly, taking the stairs two at a time. "Olivia!" he bellowed.

He heard female voices coming from the bedchamber, chattering, scolding, a curse here and there. Olivia had never demonstrated a sense of economy, not once in her life. If he didn't curb her extravagance, this simple country party would impoverish the both of them.

"Olivia." He opened the door without knocking. "I would like a word—"

The four women appeared to be too engrossed in some wardrobe witchery even to notice him. In fact, he hadn't put two and two together himself when that rather bold-eyed seamstress had appeared at the house early that morning. More money, he thought. And now a jeweler. Good heavens.

He stared into the room. More money spent to dress Catriona so that some clumsy-fingered fool like Anton could undress her on their wedding night and deflower her, so another man could kiss her and take pleasure in her unspoiled spirit. His eyes darkened in displeasure at the prospect.

"Olivia."

His voice cut into the feminine conversation like a saber. Olivia and Claudette, kneeling on the floor, glanced up at him with quick looks of resentment for invading their territory. Arabella, on the bed, looked away in embarrassment, a blush stealing across her cheeks.

The object of all their attention stood in the middle of the floor, draped in a scandalously immodest shell-pink sheath. She looked like a statue, a very unhappy statue, of some legendary maiden turned to stone by a vengeful goddess.

The deepest of Knight's instincts urged him to bring the young lady back to life in the most basic of ways.

He frowned at her reflection in the mirror, his gaze wandering up and down her willowy form. He could see her soft breasts straining against the silk, the dusky outline of her nipples, the hollow of her belly . . . and one naked foot tapping a hole into the floor.

"Well, Knight," Olivia said, putting down a tape measure. "Is there a fire in the house that you have interrupted us in such a manner?"

Finding Catriona in that revealing thing had made his mind unravel. He was perfectly aware that women dressed provocatively in public, but not one he was supposed to be watching over—what *had* he wanted, anyway?

"I do not think that Lionel would like his cousin wearing that to a dance," he said after a long hesitation. "Nor do I wish to be fending off improper advances on her behalf all evening."

"Did you come all the way upstairs to deliver that

commentary, or was there another purpose?" Olivia asked, frowning in exasperation.

"I happen to think that her dress is a little indelicate for a country dance," he said forcefully, afraid that he had not made his point.

"It's a chemise and an underskirt!" the four women shouted at him in unison.

"As if he didn't know," Arabella said amusedly under her breath. "As if he had not removed his share of them in his day."

"Of course I knew," he said, giving a cough. "Just make sure she wears something over them to the dance."

"Exactly what is it that you wanted?" Catriona asked.

"I—oh, yes. The jeweler waiting downstairs. What am I to do with him?"

"I'll take care of this," Arabella said with a sigh.

Olivia frowned. "Why are you being so helpful all of a sudden, Arabella? Why are you even here?"

Arabella whispered, "Isn't it obvious? I want to make amends for what I've done. I handled the situation rather badly, and I—I'm afraid Knight might end up hurting Anton."

"What are you whispering about?" Knight demanded.

"The jeweler," Olivia answered, giving Arabella a searching look. "Go ahead, then. Pick something suitable but in good taste."

"Pick something that doesn't impoverish me," Knight said. "Olivia, that goes for you, too."

Olivia pitched a pincushion in the direction of his head. He ducked, snickering behind the door, and heard Catriona release an unearthly shriek of protest.

Claudette narrowed her eyes in annoyance. "Ooh! I've just stuck *mademoiselle* with a pin because of all this distraction."

"Right in *mademoiselle's* rear, too," Catriona said indignantly.

Knight couldn't help it. He popped his head around the door, his gaze going straight to her injured seat. Male animal that he was, he took a moment to admire the curvaceous rise of her rump before remembering himself.

"He's laughing at me again," Catriona said, catching a glimpse of his grinning face in the mirror. "Make him go away."

"Leave, Knight," Olivia said. "Or I shall be taking her uncle's dirk to you myself."

"Ah, the infamous dirk," he said as she sprang up to close the door on his face. "Does it really exist?"

He backed out into the hall, but as the door slammed, his grin began to fade. Wendell had been hounding him to go to Cornwall for a few weeks to consider purchasing more clay pits for another pottery firm. Knight had a few friends in Penzance, and he could easily divert himself for a week or two. Olivia seemed to be happily occupied for the time being.

It had suddenly occurred to him that he might not enjoy watching the local gentry make utter fools of themselves over the newest morsel on the marriage mart.

In fact, he did not think he could tolerate it.

Simmons arrived late that same night. Knight had managed to put the note the secretary had written him out of his mind until now. Everyone else had retired hours earlier, but he had stayed awake, staring through his study window at the woods. Not for a long time, not since the first months after returning from Albuera as he recovered from a bayonet injury to his shoulder, had he felt this sense of edginess in his own home. As if something were watching and waiting in the benign surroundings of his boyhood. The ladies of the manor were safely in their rooms, reading in bed, brushing their hair, doing the frivolous little things that females did before they could relax. He knew because he had checked—a ritual he had never indulged in until the recent rash of housebreakings had threatened the security of the sleepy village.

He'd stood in the hall outside Catriona's room, listening to the faint sounds she made, paper rustling, sheets drawn back, a shoe dropped to the floor. He had considered knocking, propriety ignored, to remind her again that the miscreants in the neighborhood had not been caught. But it was only an excuse, he knew that. He stared at her door as if he could see her inside, safe in her bed while he waged a battle with himself that would terrify her if she knew how she tempted him, how deep his desire for her ran.

Now he sat in his study, unable to work or read. When he heard a carriage on the road beyond the estate and heard footsteps in the drive, he was not alarmed. He was relieved.

At last. Something tangible to break this strange pall of tension. A distraction that would prevent him from prowling like a wolf outside a young woman's door.

"My lord," Simmons said as Knight brought him into the house. "I am glad to find you awake. By good luck, I met Lord Darnley at the Three Mermaids Inn. Recognizing me as your man, he allowed me to ride in his private coach almost to your door."

"Sit down by the fire," Knight said. "Here. Have a brandy. You surely have not been to Scotland and back in this short time?"

"Indeed not, my lord. However, after our talk, I was prompted by instinct to contact a former friend who had lived in the Border district where the Earl of Roxshire held his original seat. My friend knew enough of the young lady's history that I thought it imperative to contact you before I continued my investigation."

"Is this friend reliable?"

"I should think so. A retired vicar, an Oxford man, well traveled in his day."

"And?"

"She *is* the earl's daughter, my lord, but born out of wedlock."

Knight put down his glass. "Yes. I know that."

"Her mother was what the Scots call a green-woman. She lived with the girl on the moor until her premature death. Apparently, she drew her last breath under the illusion that Roxshire meant to marry her. As it happened, he had already died the year before."

"And Catriona went to live with this rough-mannered old uncle she mentioned? Diarmid Grant?"

"Five years later."

He felt an unpleasant prickle at the back of his neck. "Who took care of Catriona until then?"

"For three years or so, it seems that the child took care of herself," Simmons said. "She managed to deceive the few who cared to ask into believing that her mother was merely ill, bedridden, at the time. The girl left charms on the doorsteps at night and was repaid with food in the same manner when those charms worked. A minister of the kirk found her alone at her mother's grave one night and guessed the truth. It was he who told my friend of the girl's plight."

"Child, you called her," Knight said, his face troubled, aspects of her personality falling into place. "How old was she?"

"Nine when her mother died. Twelve, I suppose, when the minister took her briefly into his care."

"How does a nine-year-old girl live alone, Simmons?" he asked in disbelief. "How could she survive?"

"Countless children are homeless in this world," Simmons said. "It breaks the heart to see it happen."

"It should *not* have happened," Knight said fiercely. "She is Lionel's cousin. Her father should have made provisions."

"It appears he did for a time, but as is so often the case, when he married and his first legitimate child was born, a son, he lost interest. Then another son came along."

"Her brother James," Knight said, frowning. "The one she defends. I suppose it is not an uncommon story."

Simmons took a long sip of brandy. "I'm afraid there is more, which is why I was compelled to warn you about her, my lord."

Knight smiled, surprised to find himself inclined to protect the woman he had hoped to unmask. "I know that her aunt stabbed her uncle. In the gullet, I believe."

"And did you know that her uncle was a common farmer, a man who enhanced his livelihood by stealing cattle from his neighbors? His father was an ardent Jacobite rebel from the Highlands who was publicly executed for treason. The uncle inherited his rebel tendencies."

"That is no stain on her soul."

"Diarmid Grant was accused of murdering a man in cold blood. The girl was in the house at the time. For several years, she lived under his influence—she could hardly emerge from such an atmosphere unscathed."

Was it only a week or so ago that Knight would have paid a fortune to unearth such damaging testimony against her? "She quotes Latin, Simmons. She has learned to read and write from someone. Was it from this minister you mentioned?"

"I do not know. At some point, it is not clear when, there was another uncle who attempted to take her under his wing, some mysterious character who dabbled in the black arts. God only knows what would have become of her if the young earl had not gotten her into a boarding school and brought her to his castle for a proper upbringing."

"James again, the—" Knight turned slowly as he noticed the other man's expression of alarm. Catriona stood in the doorway, wearing one of Olivia's old lace dressing robes that clung to the delicate lines of her body. She stared at him, her face so white and wounded that Knight rose unconsciously from his chair.

"Thank you, Simmons," he said in a soft voice. "That will be all."

"Yes, my lord." The man rose to leave. "Shall I discuss the matter with Lady Deering?"

"That will not be necessary." Knight's eyes never left Catriona's stricken face. "I will handle the matter."

"Come in," he said the moment Simmons had left the room. "Sit down beside me, Catriona."

"I could leave the house now, before Olivia wakes up," she said awkwardly. "I could stay in the village until morning. I don't mind. I'll understand if you wish me gone. I never intended to bring you trouble."

He was furious at himself that she had discovered what he'd done. "You will *not* leave this house. I thought I had made my feelings clear."

"Aye." She took a breath, venturing into the room. "But that was before he came and told you."

"It is impolite for a proper young lady to eavesdrop."

Her gaze held his, brimming with the pain of betrayal. "I think that after what you just heard, we both know I will never be a proper lady. You can dress me in beautiful clothes. You can hammer social niceties into my head, but deep inside, where it counts, I am unacceptable."

"Then it was all true?"

She gave a vague shrug, suddenly looking older than before. "More or less. Will you thank Olivia for all—"

"Sit in that chair," he growled, grasping her elbow to practically push her small form into it. "Did I not give you an order to stay here?"

"Well, yes, but—"

"Then obey it." He hesitated. God, she looked so fragile and—bloody self-assured. "Did your uncle really murder a man? The truth now, Catriona. I am on your side this time. Did he?"

"No."

"Good." He took a sip of brandy, but his relief was short-lived as she managed to shock him yet again.

"He murdered three of them. Two before I was born."

He almost choked. "And this did not seen barbaric to you?"

"'Twas in self-defense," she said patiently. "Is there a difference between killing a man to protect yourself and a duel, then?"

"A duel at least confers an illusion of civility," he said, taking the chair opposite hers. Nine years old. He couldn't stop thinking about it, shaken by the image of a younger Catriona struggling alone on the moor. Had she buried her mother's body by herself? She must have. God help her. That she managed any degree of gentility was a wonder, and he was suddenly, unexpectedly, grateful for this imperfect brother of hers who had rescued her from a fate Knight could not envision.

He sat forward suddenly. "You haven't killed anyone, have you?"

"Not yet." She smiled at him. "Although recently there have been a few moments when the thought tempted me."

He had finished his brandy. He needed the whole bottle to handle this. "We can't act in haste. We have to decide what to do."

"About what?"

"About your family's history of homicide."

"There's not much we *can* do, is there? After all, the men he murdered have been dead for years. No one can bring them back."

"Catriona, I don't think you understand me."

"I usually don't."

He frowned. "What I am talking about is your reputation. Your uncle's penchant for killing is hardly an attractive asset to a future husband. I think the wisest course might be to leave the matter buried in the past."

"And who's the one who went digging it up?" she exclaimed. "I didn't advertise the facts of my life in *The Morning Post*. You're the one who sent that old man to expose me."

He rubbed his forehead. She had the most powerful talent for getting to the heart of an issue, of unsettling him. "Yes. But you can't say I didn't have cause."

"What cause?" she asked. "It's not as if I attacked you with my dirk."

"No," he said slowly.

"Or stole the Rutleigh emeralds."

"But you did shoot a pistol on my estate the night of your arrival."

"Aye, but not *at* anyone."

"Well, I'd never heard of you. I thought I knew Lionel well."

"Poor Lionel," she murmured. "I've made a muddle of his name, haven't I?"

"I don't know what to do with you."

"Are you going to tell Olivia?"

"Absolutely not. She has been in her element since you arrived. There is no point in distressing her. Besides, it wouldn't change how she feels." *How either of us feels,* he thought. Oh, no, if anything, the dangerous knot of his attraction to her had only tightened, his heart imprisoned at the center.

She exhaled, visibly relieved. "Then I won't tell her about you, either."

"Excuse me?"

"The Acorn Affair. Arabella. A hot poker to the soles of my feet couldn't loosen my tongue. On my honor, my lord. I owe you that much."

"Once again, there is a world of difference between that trifling affair and the matter we just discussed." He gave her a droll look, trying not to imagine the delicious body concealed beneath her ruffled muslin nightdress. "What are you doing out of bed, anyway?"

"I heard horses on the moor. I was hoping Thomas had decided to come back."

"Well, he hasn't, and Aunt Marigold will roast me alive if she catches me with you again this late at night."

"At least you're not in your nightclothes."

"I never was in my nightclothes, Catriona. Now, kindly go to bed before we find ourselves in serious trouble. I have many things to think about."

She smiled, making no effort to leave. The firelight accentuated the intriguing contours of his face, edging his features with an elemental beauty that made her shiver with forbidden excitement. She could study him forever. She could sit at his knees and wait for his kisses to weaken her and fill her with that wonderful confusion.

He stared back at her; it was starting again, the desire deeper than anything he had ever known. The urge to take her into his arms and lower her to the floor, to lie beside her in the firelight and initiate her into the secrets of love. He took a breath against the temptation.

"I know I will regret asking this, but your smile is a warning. What is going on now in that sly mind of yours?"

"I was wondering whether I should probably remove that hex," she said teasingly. "My uncle always told my mother you should not hex unless you meant it."

"The uncle who—"

"No. Not him. This other one is actually worse."

"I don't think I want to know the details, Catriona." He crossed his hands behind his head, unconsciously stretching the tension from his knotted muscles. "Has he killed anyone?"

"Not on purpose," she said, watching his wide shoulders lift and relax, the power beneath that casual gesture making her shiver.

"Not—never mind." He decided he did not care to pursue that subject tonight. No, he had enough startling information to digest for the time being. She was sweet, and she was strong. But what did he do with her now? She was curled into the chair in a vulnerable pose that brought out the devil in him. The candlelight caught the streaks of fire-gold in her hair. Had he ever felt this comfortable talking to a woman? Had he ever cared about one to this degree?

"Do not fall asleep in that chair," he said sternly, leaning forward to shake her arm. "I am not carrying you upstairs to have Aunt Marigold lecture me on my lack of morals. Go to bed."

She stirred, sliding her feet to the floor. His forehead creased in a frown of concern as he watched her walk to the door, where she hesitated, her own face averted.

"Did your spy say anything else about my scandalous past?" she asked.

For three years or so, it seems that the child took care of herself. . . . The girl left charms on the doorsteps. . . . He could barely control the anger he felt toward the men in her life who had failed her, her father, her brother James. The childhood of rejection and loneliness she must have endured made him want to shield her from further pain. He admired her courage and compassion, even when she dared to defy him. He understood now.

"No," he said, glancing back into the fire, his gray eyes reflective. "Nothing else."

"Oh, good."

"Are there any more secrets I should know?" he asked guardedly.

A door opened upstairs, and Olivia called down softly into the hall. "Who is it? Knight, is that you?"

Catriona gave him a wry look, then slipped out of the room. For several moments, he stayed in his chair when it was all he could do not to follow her, to hold her, to comfort her against memories he could hardly imagine. It had not escaped his notice that she had managed to avoid an answer, but for tonight he had learned enough about her. His cruel curiosity had been satisfied, and now, instead of using the secret details of her past against her as a weapon, he found that he was filled with an overwhelming impulse to protect her. And to make her his own.

Chapter

12

❦

The two years she had spent at boarding school in Edinburgh had softened the unfinished edges of Catriona's character. Or so Olivia and Aunt Marigold decided as the days preceding the party sped by. She would perhaps collapse in the structured world of London. For example, Catriona could not remember a thing about the code of calling cards, the significance of a crease in the lower left corner to indicate sorrow. Nor did she appear to understand the language of flowers, for all her botanical skills.

"A young lady," Olivia explained, "must refuse a bouquet of Spanish jasmine from a suitor because it signifies sensuality."

"But I love jasmine," Catriona said, "and I don't see how—"

"Nor should she accept one of tuberose, which is an invitation to dangerous pleasures."

Still, for a country event, Catriona would have to do.

She could manage a conversation, with supervision. She could dance extremely well, after intense instruction from the demanding young dance master Mr. Edwards. She already knew the proper utensils to use during dinner, the correct form of address for her guests.

But what she did not know was why Knight seemed to be avoiding her ever since their conversation in his study. Was he ashamed of her? Had Simmons's revelation about her life shocked him? He had not struck her as a man who was easily shocked. And yet, except for the few times she had caught him watching her, he had managed to place a polite distance between them, making her heart ache for a moment alone with him.

She woke up on the morning of Olivia's party and knew in her bones that something awful was going to happen. She'd heard the owls again the night before, not near the house but deep in the woods. She wished now she had thrown that accursed stone to the bottom of a lake.

She stared across the room at the wall and felt a flush of foreboding work its way through her body. Her toes and the tips of her ears were starting to tingle. An aura of wavy lines danced across the wardrobe where Claudette's hurried creation hung, a pale aquamarine silk ball dress that shimmered in the light.

The face of the shepherdess on the flocked wallpaper had taken on a menacing leer.

"No," she whispered, turning her head. "Please, not today."

A familiar masculine shout broke the silence of the house, bringing Catriona back to herself. "Who the blazes moved my boots?"

She gave a shiver of pleasure at the power in his voice and glanced guiltily at the black boots that sat by the door. She had found an armload of natural treasures in the garden only yesterday: smooth white pebbles, a clump of cinquefoil, and a few black swan's feathers. She had only borrowed his boots to transport her loot upstairs.

"Your boots are probably being blackened in the kitchen," Olivia said calmly from the bottom of the staircase. "Please do not shout, Knight. I would like Catriona to be well rested for the ball."

"I would like my boots," he muttered, and their voices faded away only to be replaced by the thunderous vibration of him stomping up the stairs.

"I do not call that walking quietly, Knight," Olivia admonished from somewhere below him.

He grunted. "If I find out that Howard has borrowed them again to go courting, I swear I shall scalp him."

With a sigh, Catriona bolted from the bed and hastily pulled on a wrapper. She emptied her treasures onto the bed, opened the door, and carried the boots to the top of the stairs.

"Here are the missing boots, my lord. I'm the one who borrowed them, not Howard."

"You wore my brother's boots?" Olivia said, clearly startled. "How unladylike."

"I wasn't wearing—oh, never mind." She thrust the boots at Knight's chest. "Here."

She steeled herself for one of his teasing responses, which would be welcome after too many days of his hurtful detachment. Instead, he put his free hand to her forehead, frowning in concern.

"You look flushed," he said, the boots forgotten under his arm. "Are you ill?"

She shivered at the firm pressure of his palm on her forehead. She wanted to lean against him and hide, but the threat that she felt didn't come from outside. It came from a place within herself too dark to explain.

"It fell behind the hallstand," she said.

Knight pulled his hand away, puzzled by the remark. "What did you say?"

"What fell behind the hallstand?" Olivia inquired behind them. "What are we talking about now?"

A bedchamber door down the hall opened slowly. Aunt Marigold poked her head out like a tortoise, her pleasant face perplexed. "Has anyone seen my ivory fan? I can't seem to find it anywhere."

Knight and Olivia looked at each other. "Could it have fallen behind the hallstand?" Olivia asked in an uncertain voice.

Aunt Marigold came out into the hall, looking regal in her gold-tasseled nightrail. "That is exactly what must have happened. I left it there last night while the maid was dusting."

Olivia gave Catriona a strained smile. "How observant you are. I was going to let you sleep another hour, but now that you're up, you may as well spend some time with young Mr. Edwards in the ballroom. He should have been here by now."

"He won't be coming," Catriona said, shaking her head in dismay.

The young dancing master had given her four days of grueling instruction during which she had hexed him a half-dozen times and made him break down in tears, declaring her beyond hope. Yet on their final day, when he wept, it was because she had danced with such poise and grace that he proclaimed her perfection.

"Just do not hex any young gentlemen," he begged privately as they parted. "At least, not aloud."

"What do you mean, he's not coming?" Olivia said, aghast. "Knight, did Mr. Edwards send you word last night?"

Knight frowned, obviously not following the conversation. "There are stones at the bottoms of my boots. Why is this?"

"Mr. Edwards is going to trip over a shovel in the garden and break his ankle," Catriona said to no one in particular.

Olivia's smile faded. "What fanciful talk. How could you possibly know such a thing?"

She sighed, the coldness starting to numb her. "I just do."

Olivia put her hand to her mouth. "It's one of your visions, isn't it? Oh, what dreadful timing. Come back into the bedroom, and let us review everything you are to remember for the party."

Knight caught Olivia's arm. "Perhaps she isn't ready for this."

"She's more than old enough, Knight, and we have all agreed that a proper season is out of the question."

He glanced at Catriona. "She doesn't look up to this. I think something might be wrong."

"It's nerves," Olivia said in an undertone. "Besides, this isn't a formal ball. It's a simple affair in your house. What could possibly happen to her here tonight?"

Catriona slipped back into her room as they spoke, looking so lost in her thoughts that Knight fought the impulse to follow her. What could happen tonight? Any man with an ounce of mating instinct would meet her and be instantly captivated. Worse, she could meet some charming rogue and lose her heart to him, under Knight's own nose. He would watch another man flatter her and make her laugh, and then offer his insincere congratulations, encourage a courtship that would turn his heart to stone.

Which was as it should be. He planned to go to Cornwall at the end of the week on business, anyway. In fact, he would go right now and suggest that Wendell accompany him, if they hadn't both promised to see the party through. And if he knew where Wendell was hiding. Along with his boots, Wendell, the permanent houseguest, had been missing all morning.

Catriona's voice, like a disembodied ghost, floated out from behind her door. "You'll find him in the kitchen, sampling the gooseberry tarts."

And so it went all day. Catriona warned Mrs. Evans to watch her custard, and Mrs. Evans retorted that never in her life had she scorched a trifle. But then, at the last second, a cat jumped onto the sink, and Mrs. Evans went to chase it out. When she returned to the stove, only moments later, the custard had caught.

One minute Catriona's body burned with strange sensations, the next she felt as if icicles were prickling her skin. She paced. She drew shallow breaths. She soaked in scented water with rose oil, but the tension continued to coil her nerves as it always did before a vision. The seeing came in small degrees, flashes of things she did not understand.

Olivia reassured her that this reaction was perfectly normal. Every young woman felt so before her first dance. And Catriona sat in misery, unwilling to explain that she had attended dances before. True, they had been mere country dances on the village green, and once even a ceremonial dance in her brother's castle.

They had not been elaborate affairs, but she remembered the flush of excitement, the thrill of being admired, the agony of hoping a young man would choose her as a partner.

But she never breathed a word of her distress to Olivia, who was the kindest human being she had ever met. Tonight meant so much to the woman, and Catriona could not bring herself to warn her dear mentor that she would probably end up bringing disgrace to the family.

But perhaps she would be lucky for once—perhaps she could hold her tongue and the threat would pass. Perhaps if she bottled up the visions and didn't let them out, they would dissipate and go away forever.

She ran to the bedchamber window and peered outside at the twilight woods. No owls, thank heaven. But then the house was lit up with so many lanterns that it blazed like a bonfire, and, yes, the mass of gray clouds that had appeared above the estate that morning had not moved an inch.

A storm was about to break over her social debut.

Olivia burst into the room an hour later, her cheeks flushed. "What? Not even a candle lit, and why are you gazing out that window? Hurry up, Cat, there are carriages already coming up the road. Oh, goodness, where did I put that jeweler's box?"

It was downstairs in Knight's study, but Catriona didn't say so, or how she knew. She was doing her best to pretend everything was normal.

"Sit down at the dressing table," Olivia said, her diamond pendant glittering in the dark. Louise is coming to help with your hair." Her voice dropped on a troubled note. "And, by the way, you were wrong. Mr. Edwards did not break his ankle."

"He didn't?" Relief spread across Catriona's face. Oh, to be wrong, for once.

"He broke his leg."

They stared at each other in the mirror, and Catriona wanted to warn Olivia that this was only the beginning, but the door opened, and Louise, Olivia's maid, bustled in with a tray of cosmetics and personal accessories, exclaiming about the lack of proper light.

The two women set to work with an unflappable concentration that even Catriona's sighing and wiggling on the stool could not break. Olivia wanted this evening to be a success more than anything she had wanted in a long time. As a tribute to Lionel, she would do everything in her power to find his unconventional little cousin a good husband, and she had the perfect man in mind, a suitor no one had considered before. One who shared a similar background to Catriona's and who could accept her endearing flaws.

Knight stood transfixed in the upstairs hallway as he saw her leave her room. The underskirt of the pale silk dress shimmered like an ocean wave, aqua, turquoise-blue, with pearl undertones and hints of golden thread. The high-waisted creation accentuated her graceful curves in a way that made him want to shield her from public view and keep her for his private pleasure.

"Well," he said, stepping out of the shadows, "now I believe in miracles."

She smiled, basking in his approval. The sight of him always uplifted her heart, even if, more often than not, he provoked her to tears. "Then I pass inspection?"

"Let me see." He took her gloved hands and twirled her around, a peculiar emotion tightening his throat. "No stones, weeds, or other noticeable weapons. Are we wearing our shoes?"

"We are."

"Then heaven help the young men whose hearts you will break tonight." His gaze drifted over her delightful form, and he thought, *including mine.*

While he held her hand, Catriona did not feel afraid. The warmth and male vitality that flowed from him seemed to keep the darkness inside her at bay. If he would stay beside her, his presence protective, then perhaps the evening would not be ruined.

"Don't leave me," she whispered impulsively.

"What?" His handsome face looked startled in the candlelight. She was mortified. She had said the wrong thing. She always said the wrong thing. "I'll be downstairs, Catriona."

"I meant in the ballroom. Don't leave me alone if no one asks me to dance. I will die of shame after all the trouble everyone has gone to."

He grinned. "It's only a dance, Catriona."

"Aye." That was what he thought.

Olivia prodded her in the back as she hung back in the middle of the stairs. "Come along. Arabella and Anton are already here, and I can hear the musicians in the gallery."

Catriona's fingertips turned to ice as she looked down the stairs. This was all for her, and what had she done to deserve it? In a few hours, the guests would be whispering about the Scottish debutante who had revealed herself to be an aberration of nature.

"Do relax, dear." Olivia smiled warmly at her, wanting to banish her fears. "These are my friends and neighbors."

"But if I embarrass you—"

"No one will remember a tiny social gaffe next year."

But they'll remember tonight, Catriona thought, shivering lightly. *They will talk of it for years to come.*

Olivia pried her away from the balustrade. "I broke the heel of my slipper at my first dance and bumped an elderly countess into a potted palm."

I should be so fortunate, Catriona thought, half listening as Olivia launched into a barrage of last-minute advice.

"Don't forget. If Lord Salisbury shows up, you are not to stare at the birthmark on his nose. One pretends to ignore physical infirmities."

"But I *am* to ask Lady Salisbury about her gout?"

"Well, yes. Actually, you won't have a choice. It's all she talks about, anyway."

From below drifted a delicate blend of aromas. Beeswax and vinegar, the garlands of spring flowers strung in the hallways—hyacinths, sweet peas, freesia, and narcissus looped with strong vines of ivy. In the kitchen, Mrs. Evans and her girls put the finishing touches on tiny French pastries and prepared gallons of thirst-quenching lemonade for the punch bowls.

"You're with family," Olivia said as they reached the bottom of the staircase. "Knight and I won't let anything happen to you."

She nodded, biting her lip. But the instant she walked into the ballroom, she forgot every word of wisdom, every warning that Olivia and Arabella and Aunt Marigold had drummed into her head. She smiled politely throughout the introductions. She couldn't have remembered a single name or face to save her life.

She was aware of only one thing in her misery: Knight standing with a knot of male friends in the corner. Knight, whose head lifted the instant she appeared in the doorway. Knight, strong and safe, dark and dangerous to her heart.

He was so devastatingly handsome in his black evening clothes that she caught her breath. Even in Claudette's artful gown, she felt like a serving girl in the presence of a storybook prince. He gave her a private smile, and she didn't even notice the young men already gathering around her, hoping to catch her interest, surprised that Lionel's young cousin was such a refreshing beauty. All Cat knew was that at the sight of *him*, a heady warmth stole through her veins, temporarily thawing the tension she felt.

But the very moment he turned away, the coldness crept back. She stared blankly at the line of male guests whom Wendell and Olivia were attempting to introduce.

"This is Sir Evan Lucas, dear."

"Sir Evan." Catriona gave the solemn-looking young man a smile, but the instant he took her hand, she felt the awareness start, the knowing, and her secret self came to the surface. "You're in the cavalry, sir?"

He looked surprised, then flattered. "Not yet. My father just purchased a commission. I guess my mother must have told Wendell. It was to be a secret."

Another man claimed her hand. And while he

quite rudely stared at her breasts, Catriona experienced a vision of him in a church, a pregnant bride
gazing up at him adoringly. She saw the newlyweds
moving into a dark mansion.

"Congratulations on your impending nuptials," she
said coolly.

He lifted his startled gaze from her neckline. "How
did you—" He squeezed her fingers. "But the wedding
isn't set until the end of the month." He lowered his
voice and grinned. "Who knows how I might spend
my time between now and then?"

"Perhaps you might clear the cobwebs from the
nursery for the child you're expecting," she said
tartly, tugging her hand from his possessive grasp.

His mouth opened in amazed consternation. "She
promised me, she swore, no one else knew."

And on it went. Like Pandora's box, once the lid had
been opened, Catriona found it difficult to stem the
flow of visions that sprang into her mind, the impres-
sions and uninvited glimpses into the future. Usually,
her foresight served to help people avoid troubles. She
had learned early in life that they brought more good
than harm to others. But not to her.

Within a half-hour, the puzzled young men had
put their fingers on the culprit responsible for spilling
their most guarded secrets: it had to be Madame
Malraux, Claudette, the crafty little dressmaker. Who
else had access to bedroom gossip?

Olivia took Catriona aside for a few moments
before the opening set. "Is everything all right, dear?"

Catriona stared at her. She had finally realized that
the more emotionally attached she became to a person, the less able she was to see into his or her future.
Which was just as well. She would hate to know that

something horrible was going to happen to anyone as sweet as Olivia.

"Take my hand, Olivia."

"Are you still nervous, dear? The dance is about—"

"Just take my hand."

Looking faintly alarmed, Olivia did as she was asked. "I can't hold your hand on the dance floor."

Catriona breathed a sigh of relief. "Nothing. I see nothing."

"Are you all right?" Olivia asked again.

"I think so. At least for now."

Olivia glanced around until she spotted Knight and Wendell standing together at the door. At her faint nod, the two men converged on Catriona like royal guards escorting a princess.

Wendell reached her first, claiming the honor of the opening dance, and he stayed with her a second time. He grinned at the cluster of disappointed young admirers who had rushed to her side.

"You're quite the success," he said just before the complicated steps of the dance separated them.

When they were rejoined, she whispered, "The evening isn't over yet. Give me time."

"Why so morose?" He studied her downcast face in concern. "Is it Knight? Has the beast been ignoring you?"

She was too far away to answer.

Wendell glanced around, his gaze amused. Actually, Knight wasn't ignoring Catriona at all. He seemed to be watching her to the point of being rude to his other guests. In fact, before the second dance even ended, he was practically snatching her from Wendell's arm.

"Where are your manners?" Wendell called after him in mock annoyance. "I had only begun to charm her."

Knight grinned rudely over his shoulder as he led her away. "I was rescuing her. She looked bored to tears."

Catriona felt his fingers tighten around hers. If he would hold her hand all night, she wouldn't be afraid—well, at least not of what others might think. With Knight, there were definitely other fears to face.

The dance was a minuet. She couldn't help noticing that the other men present looked slightly silly following the delicate movements. But Knight's muscular body moved with a natural grace that did nothing to diminish the power beneath.

"Are you having a good time?" he said as her head brushed the hard wall of his shoulder.

A shiver of forbidden sweetness rushed through her. "I've never been so miserable in my entire life," she admitted.

"Then no one has stolen your heart yet tonight?"

She looked up into his face, feeling the sensual warmth of his voice wrap itself around her. He was teasing her, but the dark glint in his gaze said something else, and wasn't he holding her a moment longer than was proper? Surely he did not smile at other women like that. Oh, please, let her be the only one.

The dance ended. Neither of them made a move until Wendell forced his way between them.

"I sense trouble brewing between you two again," he said, grabbing Catriona's hand. "Don't either of you dare start any of that nonsense tonight. You promised Olivia you would behave, which reminds me, that's her godmother over there in the corner with Marigold. She wants to meet you, Cat. Come along, and show off your manners."

"Aren't you coming?" she called back to Knight, feeling suddenly cold again.

"No. I'm getting a drink. Let me know if anyone would like a lemonade."

The moment he turned from her, she knew disaster was near. Her toes and ears started to tingle. The figures on the ceiling fresco of King Arthur and his knights seemed to scowl down at her, forbidding and unfriendly. The air grew chill. She pulled her hand from Wendell's.

"I really want Knight to come with me."

He looked at her in amusement. "Knight will be back in a moment. What is the matter with you? You've charmed everyone here like Cleopatra reborn, not a single mistake or misstep to your name. Lady Bennett is the sweetest old woman in the world. You will adore each other."

There was a metallic taste in her mouth. Her toes had gone totally numb. She felt weightless as Wendell led her toward the two elderly women sitting against the wall. She heard him make the introductions, but his voice had a faraway echo that rang in her ears. She even managed a curtsy, but she couldn't draw a breath.

"So lovely," Lady Bennett murmured. "And I do see a resemblance to our dear Lionel in those eyes. How sad he is not here. How tragic."

The two white-haired women sitting before her became a blur; the music of the band faded into the background. As if in a distant mirror, she could see Lady Bennett walking with her cane down a dark corridor, up a flight of marble stairs to her room.

Catriona's heart began to race with sick anticipation. The vision crystallized so that she could see other figures behind the closed door. One was gagged and bound across the bed. The two others wore masks. The tallest man held a knife.

The vision seemed so real. The sash window had been forced open, and a shattered ormolu clock lay in pieces on the floor. One o'clock. The two intruders had been drinking and making crude jokes, waiting for their victim. The door opened. They fell still, and a knife flashed in the dark.

Catriona blinked, aware that the frail old lady had risen with difficulty from her chair. "And now that I have met you," the woman said, "I will go home. At my age, it is never wise to retire after midnight. Visit me soon, young woman. I have a lovely necklace I should like Lionel's cousin to wear."

"Please." Catriona's throat ached as she struggled to make herself understood. Aunt Marigold and Wendell gave her a strange warning look, but she was past caring. She was what she was, a social outcast, a product of illicit love and Celtic magic. "Don't go, Lady Bennett."

"Why, you sweet child. No one has pleaded for my company in years. But that is my footman by the door, and the poor fellow can barely keep his eyes open as it is."

Catriona grasped the woman's hand. "You can't go home tonight, don't you understand? They're waiting to kill you."

The music had stopped, and an expectant hush fell over the ballroom as one by one the guests noticed the small drama unfold. The young men who had rushed to Catriona's side to beg a dance drew back, watching her in amused fascination.

"Are they having an argument?" someone asked in a loud whisper.

Catriona heard nothing but the pounding of blood in her ears. She was oblivious to the scandal she was creating, the stunned attention of her audience.

"Who wants to kill me?" the older woman asked slowly, searching Catriona's anguished face.

"I don't know *who* they are, only that they are evil. They're wearing masks to hide their faces."

"But I don't have any enemies," the woman said in bewilderment.

Catriona shook her head, realizing that nothing she said would convince Lady Bennett of her danger.

"She's suffering a hallucination," a young woman behind them whispered. "The poor Grant girl must be mad."

"No wonder Olivia wants to be rid of her."

Lady Bennett looked around in embarrassment. "I think I should leave now. Perhaps a breath of fresh air would do you some good, my dear."

"I am not mad," Catriona said in a forceful voice. "If you go into that house tonight, you will not see tomorrow."

The elderly woman paled, then motioned to her footman, who stood staring raptly at Catriona for several moments after Lady Bennett had left the room. "Does her window overlook a carriage house?" she asked him softly.

He nodded, rooted to the spot.

"You will find one of her ladyship's servants beaten and hidden under a blanket," she said rapidly. "If help is summoned soon, he will not bleed to death."

He sucked in his breath. "I've felt that someone was watching the house in the past week or so, but no one pays a footman any attention."

"Don't let her go into that house tonight," she begged quietly. "Do anything you can."

"I'll think of some way to stop her, miss. I swear to you."

A pair of strong arms drew her away from the door. "Not even my powers of persuasion will be able to explain this one away," Wendell said in an under-tone. "Olivia is waving to you from the terrace. You are going to walk outside, smiling on the way as if none of this ever happened. In fact, I'm not sure *what* just happened, but I know it was not good, and Olivia will be utterly crushed when word of this reaches her."

She stared up at him, tears blurring her eyes. "You don't understand."

"No. I don't. Now, make your escape. Everyone is staring at you, sweetheart. I need to think of some excuse to satisfy their morbid curiosity. That wasn't the kind of spectacle one encounters at every country party."

She bit her lip. "Please, Wendell. Please listen to me—"

"Not now," he said fiercely, glancing around in chagrin. "I am going to let Knight handle this, what-ever *it* is."

She resisted as he dragged her to the door, but he was stronger, refusing to let her go. The footman was her only hope, and she told herself that she had to trust him. He cared for his mistress and would keep his promise to protect her.

Chapter
13

❧

*K*night *had needed a drink* to keep from ruining Olivia's party. All he could think about during that last dance was how badly he wanted to be alone with Catriona again, how it had been torture to avoid her the past few days. He felt like assaulting every young fool who flirted with her. He hadn't dreamed it would be this painful to watch other men fall under her spell, to witness the idiots he had known most of his life fight for the honor of bringing her a chair. How would he react if one of the young bucks turned *her* head, or touched her? To his chagrin, he felt his body tightening in anger, the mere thought of such an offense heating his blood.

He had managed to keep her in his line of vision until Arabella's husband, Anton, Baron Frampton, interrupted him.

"You're looking well, Knight. Nice of you to invite us."

Knight glanced around, his expression mildly amused. "I didn't invite you. Olivia did."

Anton's plump face went pale. "You aren't going to kill me, are you?"

Knight's gaze cut across the dance floor. Where had she gone? Ah, there she was with Wendell and Lady Bennett. Safe enough from the young wolves for now. His broad shoulders relaxed.

"I say, you aren't still angry at me, are you?" Anton asked in an anxious voice.

He turned again, arching his brow. Anton looked as if his cravat were choking him to death. "Why should I be angry at you?"

Anton cheeks reddened. "Well, I married Arabella."

"Yes. So I heard. Congratulations."

"Then we're friends?" Anton's voice quavered in relief.

"Absolutely." Knight clapped him on the shoulder. "In fact, I've been meaning to talk to you about investing in a new venture. Clay—"

Some sort of commotion had arisen on the other side of the room. Catriona appeared to be in the center of it, which didn't surprise Knight in the least. But Wendell and Aunt Marigold were at her side, and Lady Bennett looked as if she were leaving in a huff. As long as it didn't involve a man, Knight wasn't particularly concerned. Catriona wouldn't be Catriona if she'd gotten through the entire evening without causing a minor uproar.

Anton tapped him on the elbow. "How much do you need?"

Knight glanced down briefly. "For what?"

"The business venture. Count me in."

"Good. What do you say we discuss it tomorrow?"

He didn't hear Anton's reply. He was too distracted by the sight of Catriona running across the dance floor, the suddenly silent assembly parting to let her through. Well, now. He stepped forward, wondering what had sparked this behavior. Where did she think she was going in such a hurry? Why had she torn her dance card from her wrist and thrown it on the floor?

He pushed Anton out of the way only to find Arabella blocking his path. "What happened?" she asked anxiously.

"I don't know. I'm going after Catriona to find out."

Arabella frowned, lifting her hand to adjust the plumes in her headdress. "I meant between you and Anton. Have you set a date for the duel?"

Anton gave an overloud laugh. "That's all in the past now, Bella. Knight and I are going into business together, aren't we?"

Knight didn't answer; he'd noticed that the French doors to the terrace were open and that Catriona had disappeared.

"Where did she go?" he demanded, not caring that several guests turned to stare.

Arabella sighed. "She's out on the terrace with Olivia."

"She's with Olivia?" He stopped in his tracks, telling himself he had read too much into her escape. "Are you sure?"

"Yes. With Olivia and some late arrival she was expecting. My goodness, Knight, Catriona will never survive a single night with you hovering over her like a thundercloud."

"Who is this late arrival?" he asked. He sensed that there was more to it than that, an undercurrent of conspiracy he did not like.

Arabella shrugged. "Some old friend, that's all I know. Olivia was very secretive about it. Oh, look, here's Wendell coming now. Perhaps he can enlighten us."

*   *   *

It was over. Catriona released her breath as she reached the doors to the terrace. She stood for a moment in the evening air, allowing it to soothe her, and she felt relief wash over her in waves as she recognized Olivia outside talking to a stranger. Olivia turned, giving her a warm smile of recognition, which meant she had absolutely no idea of what had just happened in the ballroom. There would be rejection for Catriona when Olivia found out, of course. Rejection and hours of lonely humiliation.

But for now, Catriona took refuge in the woman's acceptance, and without a thought for the tall man with a rugged profile who stood beside Olivia, she rushed down the terrace steps to join her.

"Oh, good, Howard gave you my message," Olivia said, clasping Catriona's hand. "There is someone here who is dying to meet you."

"What message?" Catriona asked; she was praying that she would be allowed a few moments of peace before someone told Olivia what had just occurred at her perfectly orchestrated ball.

"Never mind," Olivia said. "Sir Alistair, this is Catriona, Lionel's cousin. Catriona, I want you to meet a neighbor and a fellow Scotsman, Sir Alistair Stone. Alistair lost his wife the same year Lionel died, and, understandably, he is a most difficult man to bring out of his house. Like you, Catriona, he shuns most social events and prefers the solitude of his garden."

"Oh," Catriona said, suddenly feeling faint, as if the evening's disaster had just begun to take its toll. "How . . . pleasant for him."

Olivia frowned as Catriona stepped into the lantern light, her face drained of color. "You look positively exhausted," she exclaimed. "You must have danced a hole in your slippers."

"*Exhausted* is not perhaps the word," Sir Alistair said pensively. "She looks more like a deer that has been cornered by a pack of hounds. I know I always feel so at these parties."

Catriona looked up as if noticing him for the first time, surprised to discover he was a handsome man, older then she'd thought, with dark, perceptive eyes and glints of silver at his temples.

"Sir Alistair is from Dundee, Cat," Olivia said quickly, as if afraid that her protégée would commit some atrocious social blunder if given half a chance. "Perhaps it's near your brother's castle."

"No," she answered succinctly, glancing over her shoulder into the ballroom. "Not anywhere near."

"Is something wrong, my dear?" he asked kindly.

Olivia's smile was strained, concealing her sudden anxiety. She would murder Knight with her bare hands if he'd misbehaved again. "She's just a little overwhelmed—"

"I ruined everything," Catriona said, no longer able to keep the humiliation inside her. "Your godmother hates me and probably will never set foot in this house again." She covered her face with her hands, her voice unsteady. "In fact, if my vision was right, she won't set foot anywhere ever again."

"Vision?" Olivia turned white, hoping against hope that Sir Alistair had not caught the word.

Unfortunately, he had. His manners might not be the most refined, but his powers of observation were acute. "You have the Sight, do you?" he asked, sounding intrigued.

Catriona lowered her hands to stare at him. Who

was this stranger, anyway, who reminded her of how homesick she was? "I should never have left Scotland," she said in misery. "I'm sorry you went to all this trouble, Olivia. You were right when you said I was hopeless. Everyone is talking about me, and your godmother—" She stopped, shivering as she remembered the vision which was slowly beginning to recede like a dream.

"Is the woman truly in danger?" Sir Alistair asked. He didn't mock her at all but seemed genuinely to accept what she had said.

She nodded. "She didn't believe me. I think her footman might have but she did not."

He glanced at Olivia. "Perhaps I ought to take a ride over to Lady Bennett's estate later on, just to be sure. It's a half-mile from my home."

Olivia hesitated. This was certainly not a complication she had foreseen. "No. I want you to enjoy yourself, Alistair. I'll have Howard and Smythe go. I'm afraid I have come to learn that Catriona's visions must be heeded."

"They'll have to hurry to be of help," Catriona said, her eyes distressed.

"I'll go this instant," Olivia said.

Sir Alistair smiled at Catriona. "Do you want me to take you back into the ballroom? The sight of me is usually enough to keep most people at bay, gossips included."

She hesitated. She realized he was a veritable giant of a man, capable of keeping his word. And good-looking enough, except that his fatherly manner reminded her of Thomas, adding to her sense of homesickness, but it was Knight she wished for. "I'm never facing them again."

"Yes, you are," Olivia said firmly. "You will sit through dinner with a smile on your face even if it kills you. Alistair, walk her around the garden while I run inside. I trust you will keep her out of trouble until I've sent Howard and Smythe on their way."

"Tell them to hurry," Catriona called after her.

Knight had been on his way to the terrace when Aunt Marigold intercepted him. A few other guests had wandered outside, but he couldn't see a sign of Cat or his sister. Curbing his impatience, he lent the older woman his arm for support, but his attention was not on their conversation.

"Take me to the terrace for some air, Knight. No. Fetch me a drink. After that scene, my nerves need fortification. I shan't sleep all night now, not knowing whether Frances is murdered in her bed. I imagine Catriona's gone into hiding—an awful way to launch oneself, and Frances is such a dreadful gossip. Not that she'll do much talking if she's dead. I'd have listened to young Cat if it were me. The Scots have uncanny foresight."

Knight looked down into her worried face. He couldn't make a word of sense of what she'd said. "Why would Cat go into hiding?"

"She'll have to get herself under control before she has a proper come-out. But maybe Olivia's right. Maybe that time will never arrive."

"Aunt Marigold, answer me. Why would she have to hide?"

"To escape the scandal broth, you jackanapes. Where have *you* been all the evening?"

He gritted his teeth. "I thought she was supposed to be on the terrace with Olivia."

"The terrace?" Her face brightened. "Of course. I

forgot in all the commotion about Olivia's little secret."

"What little secret?"

"Are you shouting at me, young man?"

He swallowed a curse. "What secret, Aunt Marigold?"

"The man. The Scotsman Olivia is hoping will toss the handkerchief. It's true he isn't a peer, but he has pots of money." She retreated a step. "Knight, are you all right? You've gone quite queer in the face."

"I am going to hang you up on the chandelier if you don't give me a straight answer, Marigold. There isn't a Scotsman in sight. Who are you talking about?"

She compressed her lips. "Not until you apologize."

"Hell's bells!" he roared. "I apologize."

"Everyone is looking at us now," she said in a haughty voice. "As if there hasn't been enough trouble stirred for the evening."

He glanced around the dance floor, frowning back at the guests who stared at them. "Lady Ellis, I apologize from the bottom of my heart for threatening to hang you from the chandelier."

"And for raising your voice."

"Yes. Yes. For that, too." He grabbed her hand and propelled her toward the doors to the terrace. "Now, who is this mysterious suitor? There isn't a Scotsman in this room."

"Not those twiddlepoops, Knight. And you are right. *Mysterious* is the word for him, now that I think of it. What does he do all day in that house? Count his money? Talk to his dead wife's shade? There's never a light in the window when one passes by. Not a soul stirring behind the gates, and the brambles have grown neck-high . . ."

Then, suddenly, he knew who she meant. He'd forgotten the man even existed, but she could only be talking about Sir Alistair Stone. Made a fortune in woolen imports. Lost his wife the same year Lionel died, and no one had seen him socially since. Knight had passed him once or twice on the moor road to Arabella's home and suspected he kept a mistress in the village on the sly to satisfy his sexual needs. They had spoken only once when they had met by chance at a bank. Alistair had asked about investing in the pottery works, and Knight had invited him to the house for a business meeting.

Sir Alistair had never come, until tonight. The man lived like a virtual hermit, and Olivia must have painted a very seductive picture of Catriona to lure him out of his seclusion.

"Where are you going now?" Aunt Marigold asked in consternation as he pushed around her.

"Onto the terrace. It appears that my party has moved outside, and I wasn't invited."

She caught his sleeve. "Not yet," she whispered. "Olivia's scheme was to give the two of them a few moments alone together. Let us hope Sir Alistair is too charmed by Catriona to care—"

He wrenched his arm free.

"Don't you understand what I am saying, Knight? If you go out there right now, you might interrupt a tender moment."

"I understand all too well," he said, the look on his face so ferocious that she could only put her hand against the wall, trembling with the realization that the scandal in the ballroom was nothing compared with what was about to ensue outside.

Chapter

14

⚮

$\mathcal{H}$e *strode out onto the terrace*, ignoring the few guests outside who called for him to join their conversation. The austere look on his angular features discouraged further invitations. It was generally assumed he had just learned of his Scottish ward's "prediction" and that he was hunting her down to discipline her in private. None of the guests gave Catriona's vision any credence. No one wanted to think of murder during such a pleasant party. A small crowd converged in anticipation, speculating on how long it would be before Knight sent Miss Grant back to Scotland. But nobody in West Briarcombe dared ask Viscount Rutleigh anything of a private nature, especially not in the last few years since he had returned from the war.

"I wouldn't like to be in her slippers when he gets a hold of her," one young man remarked from the steps, where he leaned against the statue of a sleeping lion.

A woman, watching Knight's powerful figure disappear into the darkness of the garden, sighed. "I would. Isn't it time he took a wife?"

"Arabella told the parson that Knight was still in love with her. The rogue's heart was broken by her marriage."

"Well, he didn't dance with her once all night," the woman said with a sniff. "Or look at her much, for that matter. I don't think he has a broken heart at all. I think Arabella has a swollen head."

"Perhaps his Miss Grant is a witch, after all," another man murmured. "His clay pits are producing ten times the others in the area."

Knight had heard them discussing him and didn't give a damn. The anger inside him had burned away the last vestiges of his tolerance for social niceties. He would insult, if not pummel, the first person who blocked his path. And if his instincts proved correct, if Sir Alistair was reacting to Catriona the way any red-blooded male would do in a similar situation—

He stopped, allowing his emotions to subside only long enough to take stock of his surroundings. The woods lay in darkness, undisturbed. There were no sounds from the distant lakeside where Knight had staged one or two classic seductions himself. But that was an eternity ago. The faces of those long-ago lovers had faded, the promises made forgotten. Life had become so much more complicated and unpredictable.

The soft echo of feminine laughter from the stables felt like a knife thrust to the core of his heart. He stood, paralyzed by the tantalizing sound. He saw the door left slightly ajar. He could imagine Alistair easing that provocative gown off her shoulders, coaxing her down onto the straw, taking selfish pleasure in her body. Alistair, who visited whores in secret. A fellow Scotsman commissioned to seduce Catriona by Knight's own sister.

He could have strangled Olivia with his bare hands for doing this, and if Cat lost her innocence on a filthy stable floor, he *would* murder Alistair, society and sister be damned. He should never have allowed Olivia's scheme to go this far, and had he guessed she'd had a covert romance in mind, he would have thwarted her in her tracks.

He had worked himself into an insensible rage by the time he reached the stables. At first, as he stood outside, he heard only the nickering of the horses within, and it was not only anger but irrational jealously that consumed him, a torment beyond bearing. He wondered if he was too late. He didn't think he could stand to see her with someone else, to watch her respond to another man as she had to him. The pain was worse than he had imagined, rocking him to the marrow.

Then he heard them talking, and he released his breath at the relief that flooded him. It seemed he had misread the situation in his own obsession. He had assumed that Alistair would be tempted by her, too.

"Go ahead," the Scotsman said with a deep laugh. "Rub his neck. He won't mind. I bought him last year in Ireland. I'll wager you have a gentle touch."

"Oh," she murmured. "He's so soft for a big beast."

"He likes you," Alistair said in a low voice that raised the hackles on Knight's neck. "And what male of any species would not?"

She sighed. "Oh, I can think of one in particular who doesn't seem to like me very much."

"Then the man's a fool. I, for one, find you completely irresistible, and I tell you in all honesty, I did not expect to feel this way. I thought Olivia had exaggerated our compatibility."

Knight stepped into the stables as she cocked her head, Alistair moving forward to wedge her against the thoroughbred's shoulders. "Sir Alistair?" she whispered, her voice amused but uncertain. "What are you doing?"

He put his hand over hers, stopping the motion of her fingers on the horse's neck. "You and I both know what Olivia had in mind for us."

"No. I didn't know." The spirit had returned to her voice. Knight couldn't see her face at all. "I didn't even know you existed until—oh, I can't stop worrying about Lady Bennett. Do you think that footman took me seriously?"

"The woman will be fine," Sir Alistair said gently.

He placed his hands around her shoulders and drew her against him. "Sir Alistair, this isn't proper," she whispered in polite disapproval.

"Proper?" he said. "Aye, and are we not a more passionate breed than those Sassenachs in that house with their formalities and fancy calling cards? A true man leaves a mark in a more memorable way."

He dipped his head to kiss her. Knight could still not see her expression to gauge her reaction, but her resistance, if she resisted at all, was far too belated for his liking, and that moment of uncertainty, not knowing what she felt, was anguish for him.

"Sir Alistair?" he said behind them, his jaw clenched.

The older man stiffened, seeming more annoyed than embarrassed that he'd been caught seducing an innocent in a stable. "What do you want?" he said gruffly, glancing around.

"Just to leave my calling card. On your face. Here." And Knight deftly maneuvered Catriona around the horse with his left hand as he punched the man squarely beneath the chin, propelling him back several feet into an empty stall.

Sir Alistair fell hard against a bale of straw, looking stunned by the attack. Before he could even rise to retaliate, Knight kicked the door shut and turned his attention to Catriona, who was staring up at him in total astonishment.

"And what did he do to deserve that?" she demanded, looking so vulnerable in the darkness that he wanted to kiss her himself and remove every trace of the other man.

"He kissed you."

She put her hands on her hips. "Aye, and so did—"

There were footsteps outside before she could finish, the creaking of hinges as the door opened. Wendell and Olivia walked into the stable, the same expression of disbelief mirrored on their faces at the scene they had happened upon. Knight barely spared them a glance. He had a more important problem on his hands.

"Oh, that's the limit," he said in a furious undertone, his arm resting on a stall door, his pose deceptively relaxed when every muscle in his body was wound like a spring. That the hoyden found no wrong in Sir Alistair kissing her. That she could stand there looking so innocent and desirable. "Why didn't you faint or cry for help like any other decent young lady would have done?" he fairly shouted at her.

"He didn't do anything to hurt me, Knight," she said softly.

He didn't have a response to that. That kiss had certainly hurt *him*. "Oh, get up off the damn floor, Stone," he said, kicking the door back open so hard that it shook the stall. "I only hit you once."

The man levered himself up on his elbow. "Was that what it was?" he added wryly. "I thought Catriona had clobbered me with a hammer."

"Perhaps she should have," Knight said, his anger refueled at the man's casual use of her Christian name. "Get up off the floor so that I can hit you again."

"There are more civilized ways to handle this," Wendell remarked behind him, sounding amused.

"A duel?" Alistair struggled to his feet, his gaze going from Knight to Catriona. "What a lovely grace note to a young woman's debut."

Knight glanced at her from the corner of his eye, gratified to see that her composure was finally crumbling. "And taking advantage of her was meant to enhance her reputation, I suppose? You might want to explain that to me, Stone."

Alistair straightened the tails of his rumpled evening coat. "What happened in here is a private matter," he said in a cautious voice.

Catriona pulled lightly on Knight's arm. "It was nothing. Please stop doing this. I hate it. You're behaving like my brother."

He pushed her hand away. "He was seducing you in a stable. It wasn't nothing. Damn it, I know what I saw."

"I was trying to court her," Alistair said slowly. "At least, until you charged in here like the Boar of Erymanthus."

That did it for Knight. Courting her, was he? Well, no one had asked his opinion on the matter. No one had sought his advice, and he wasn't having any more of it. He pulled off his jacket and tossed it to Wendell. "I don't feel like waiting for a duel. I'd prefer to kill you now and sleep well tonight."

Sir Alistair removed his watch from his vest pocket. "I may have a few years on you, but I've not lost a fight yet."

"Don't you dare hurt each other on my account," Catriona said in genuine horror.

"Get outside," Knight said, not looking at her, all his attention focused on the man whom he could have cheerfully pummeled into the ground. "I'll deal with you after I'm done here."

Olivia pushed her way between the two men, holding a pitchfork to Knight's chest. "You *are* done, do you hear me?"

"Put that pitchfork back, Olivia" he said as he stared down at the prongs pointed at his chest. "You look bloody ridiculous."

She refused to move, beyond caring if she did appear ridiculous. "I don't know what you think you saw, but whenever it was, it *never* happened. Does everyone here understand me? I have enough of a scandal broth in the ballroom to handle, what with Catriona flying off into that vision like one of *Macbeth's* witches."

"Well, really," Catriona said. "Comparing me to an old crone."

"Be quiet, Catriona," Olivia said. "No one wants to marry a notorious woman, which, accidentally or not, seems to be the path you have chosen to follow. Still, you are family, and no one will denounce you in my presence."

Catriona sighed at that but said nothing, not even when Knight glanced at her with one eyebrow raised as if to say she deserved the set-down. Assessing the icy anger in his gaze, she decided she could have handled the situation better alone. Men always made a mess of their private affairs.

"Knight," she said, but his attention was drawn to the other man with deadly intensity; her voice did not seem to penetrate his anger.

"Perhaps it would be better to finish this on the moor," he said to Alistair in an uninflected voice. "Are you with me, Wendell?"

She heard Olivia draw a breath, sending a look of panicked appeal to Wendell, who betrayed no reaction beyond a brief nod of assent to Knight. Cat understood immediately what the unspoken communication meant, she who had lived among the rough men of the Borders, cattle thieves and seasoned soldiers who taught their sons to fight at the slightest insult. The moor. A meeting place for a duel, desolate, the cry of crows a counterpoint to the gunfire that erupted in the mist.

"You will *not* shed blood in my name," she said in a low voice that cut through the wall of tense silence.

"You might have thought of that before you allowed yourself to be caught in this situation," Wendell said.

Olivia whirled on him. "I was the one who asked Alistair to keep Catriona outside until she had calmed herself, although this is hardly what I had in mind. Therefore, I am as much at fault as Alistair. Do you want to duel with me, too, Knight?"

"That is ludicrous," he said.

"If you continue this," she said, "I shall pack my

bags and be gone by morning. To Holland, and I shall never return."

This announcement brought another awkward silence, during which Wendell gently wrested the pitchfork from her hands. "Holland, Olivia?"

Sir Alistair released a sigh. "I am the cause of this consternation. I lost my head. I suppose it is what comes of living alone too long with no one to please but myself. Olivia. Catriona. I offer my deepest apologies." He glanced at Knight. "Does that satisfy your honor, my lord?"

Knight said nothing.

"There," Olivia said, closing her eyes for a moment. "It is over, and all is well. There is to be no more talk of dueling or brawling like two drunken misfits in a barn. Everyone can stroll back inside for dinner and behave as if we were the best of friends."

Knight did not relax his rigid stance.

"Excellent advice, Olivia," Sir Alistair said, his expression rueful. "But I, however, will take my leave. I've no wish to be the source of further trouble at your table. I'm afraid your brother is not amenable to forgiving my lapse in manners, and perhaps I will serve you best by returning to my solitude."

Olivia looked clearly uncomfortable. "Perhaps that is for the best after all."

Sir Alistair glanced wryly at the man who stood before him like a belligerent warlord, waiting for the slightest opportunity to take revenge. "Aye, I believe it is."

Catriona gazed down at her soup in silent misery, feeling the curious stares of the other guests like pinpricks in her skin. Well, now everyone hated her, even Olivia, who was the last person she had wanted to disappoint. Cat hadn't cared about the party at all, but she had cared about pleasing Knight and Olivia. She had cared about Knight more than she should, giving him the power to hurt her, and so far no one had heard a word from Howard and Smythe.

The only kind looks she had received since the hour of social ostracism had come from the servants' hall. Mrs. Evans had taken her aside and squeezed her hand. "There, there," the kindly Welshwoman had whispered. "We who have been chosen as special ambassadors of the supernatural understand your agony. Be brave, dear. Our rewards shall come in due time. If not in this world, then the next."

But staring around the dining room, Catriona felt only a lingering embarrassment and soul-deep weariness from her ordeal—that and the occasional jolt of frigid anger from Knight when he deigned to look at her at all. Still, he hadn't laughed at her vision when Olivia had explained what had happened. He had even offered to ride to Lady Bennett's himself until he realized that Olivia had sent the servants to investigate.

Lord, by the look of him, his cold glare gripping her heart, he would *never* let her live down her encounter with Sir Alistair.

She stared at her soup bowl and reflected briefly on Sir Alistair's stolen kiss. It had been . . . well, nothing. She had felt absolutely nothing except a faint discomfort where his chin had grazed her cheek; there was a bit of stubble he'd missed shaving that had scratched her.

Yet when Knight had kissed her, she had felt everything, giddiness, warm blushes, a garden of butterflies in her stomach, too much, really, for one young woman to handle. In a rush of emotion, she remembered how much she enjoyed being held in those powerful arms, the firm possession of his lips on hers. Could that be what Arabella had meant? Was it dangerous to lose your heart to a man who reduced you to such a state? It was certainly unsettling to lose control over your emotions, and, oh, she wanted it back. She didn't want to feel this poignant agony any longer.

She frowned, peeking around the floral centerpiece for another glimpse of him. Judging by the frown carved on his handsome face, kissing her was certainly the last thing on his mind. Clearly, she had ruined everything between them, but was she actually to blame?

And the worst was yet to come.

Lady Bennett had surely reached her estate by now. In her mind's eye, Cat could see the elderly noblewoman mounting the stairs one at a time, terror awaiting her. The image promptly dissolved as a servant whisked away her untasted soup, *tsk*-ing in concern under his breath at her lack of appetite. She could only pray that Lady Bennett's footman had taken the warning to heart.

At the first chance, Cat decided she would plead a pounding headache and escape to her room where no one could glare at her. She would go into hiding for a hundred years until the emotional wounds of this evening became a scar. Unless, of course, Knight and Olivia demanded that she leave in the morning. It seemed likely neither of them would be able to forgive her, and certainly no one would forget in a hurry.

And the worst was yet to come. The vision was yet to unfold.

Knight pushed away the plate of poached salmon in parsley sauce and refused the tender duckling that Mrs. Evans had made especially for him. He could see the misery on Catriona's downcast face and reminded himself that she deserved it. He hadn't talked to her once since Sir Alistair rode away but had grabbed her hand and half dragged her back to the house, Olivia admonishing him to be gentle every step of the way. Gentle? Gentle? If the Scottish hellion wanted forgiveness, if she thought he would laugh this off lightly, she was wrong. He wanted to punish her. He wanted her to ache inside as he did.

She had wounded him. She had brought out something so painful and savage in his nature that he hadn't been able to control his own actions. He was appalled at his capacity to go from a pleasant mood to barbarity in a matter of moments.

Yes, he realized it wasn't her fault that Stone had kissed her, but she needn't have behaved so blithely about the matter of her potential disgrace. And what would have happened if Knight had not arrived at precisely that critical moment, he wanted to know? Or perhaps he didn't.

It was quite one thing to find that Catriona melted in his embrace like a snowflake and quite another to catch his little snowflake melting in the arms of someone else. Well, not exactly melting. Knight would be fair even if he was furious. In retrospect, she had appeared to be rallying a rather ineffective protest.

Protest or not, the whole situation had put him in a thoroughly foul temper. He was going to wait a half hour for the servants to return, and if they did not, he would ride over to Lady Bennett's himself to check on her. Not that he believed in visions, but Catriona and Olivia certainly did. In the meantime, he felt like drinking an entire bottle of brandy—no, actually, he felt like hitting Reginald Witt over the head with one.

The Honorable Half-Wit, as he was known to his friends, was either unaware of the scandal over Lady Bennett or uncaring, as he made an utter ass of himself to attract Catriona's attention across the table. Obviously smitten, he plinked a melody with his spoon on a row of wine goblets, until he caught Knight glowering at him. At that smoldering look from his moody host, Reggie shrank down in his chair like a chastened schoolboy.

"Are you quite done playing with that damn spoon?" Knight demanded.

"Um. Yes. Yes, I am," Reggie mumbled, grinning like a satyr.

"Good," Knight said, not grinning at all. "Don't do it again."

His voice carried across the table, earning a sigh of disapproval from Olivia's pursed lips. He raised his brow at her, refusing to be cowed. A rebellion was brewing inside him. He just might grab Reggie by the neck and put his idiotic face in that plate of mashed potatoes.

"Would you like to make a toast, Knight?" she said with a forced smile. Then she added in an undertone, "Nothing untoward, if you don't mind. We have guests."

"Do we?" His smile was lethal. "I hadn't noticed."

His gaze swept past her to Catriona. Her fey beauty drew his eyes like a magnet. It apparently affected half the other men at the table the same way. Knight lounged back in his chair, mentally murdering them one by one. Instead of looking wilted by her disgrace, she appeared only more adorable, the distress on her delicate face appealing to the male instinct to protect.

"A toast?" Olivia asked him guardedly. "Or shall I ask Wendell to do the honor?"

An excited hush fell over the table. Aubrey, standing at the sideboard, put a finger to his lips to still the footmen at the sideboard. The guests regarded Knight in expectant silence, some still hoping for a dramatic finale to an unforgettable evening. For an instant, he and Catriona locked gazes, but instead of the hurt appeal on her face, he saw her in another man's arms. Then he raised his glass, his urbane voice betraying none of the turmoil that was tearing his heart into shreds.

"To Anton and Arabella. Long may the newlyweds enjoy their marital bliss."

A few speculative looks were exchanged, mainly by the females in attendance. Was Knight expressing his forgiveness for Arabella's betrayal, or did he truly not care? The popular vote decided on the latter. Nobody approved of what Arabella had done to him, anyway, and it wasn't like Knight to nurse a lonely heart with so many other eligible women waiting in the wings to win his affection.

Reggie raised his glass; glancing wistfully at Catriona, he shouted with a complete lack of tact, "To the marriage knot!"

Knight looked at Wendell. Both men broke into roguish grins. Then, as they had at countless similar affairs in the past, they said in unison: "The marriage noose, you mean."

*   *   *

Disaster struck over the dessert course. Mrs. Evans had prepared a strawberry trifle in the shape of a swan and tiered trays of petit fours and glazed plum tarts to tempt the appetite. But as the footmen milled about the table, serving the treats, the sound of men shouting on the terrace brought Knight out of his chair.

Before Wendell could join him, everyone had turned to stare at the figure who suddenly appeared at the French doors. Howard, his face white with fright, glanced around the room in genuine bewilderment. The poor man looked so shaken that Olivia could hardly scold him for forgetting his place.

"What is it, Howard?"

Knight grasped him by the arm and guided him back down the steps into the garden. Of course, by then it was too late. The guests had caught the scent of another scandal; truly, it was a memorable evening in the annals of dining in Devon.

Catriona stood at the forefront of the gathering crowd, her small body buffeted by the others, guilt and resignation on her face. "What did you do now?" Knight asked her quietly, resenting the instinct that rose again to protect her. For the first time, the edges of his anger began to crumble, replaced by concern.

She couldn't speak, motioning to Howard.

"Well, what is it, man?" Knight said, and suddenly he remembered that earlier affair, Cat's prediction, Howard and Smythe sent to Lady Bennett's estate. "Dear God," he said disbelievingly. "Don't tell me that the woman was killed."

Howard shook his head, his voice trembling. "No, my lord, but only because her footman persuaded the coachman not to drive her ladyship home. They left her at the parson's cottage and sneaked back to the house to make sure all was well."

"Oh," Catriona said in a rush of relief so profound that her bones turned to water.

"But all wasn't well," Howard went on, horrified by the memory. "Her butler was bound and gagged on her bed, and the housebreakers were lying in wait. I ought not to tell you what the footman found in the coachhouse, not in mixed company, my lord."

"What happened to the housebreakers?" Wendell asked, placing himself like a bodyguard between Catriona and the other guests on the uppermost step. Knight threw him a grateful look. She looked like a glass figurine in that flimsy dress, as if she would shatter if anyone so much as touched her.

Howard shuddered. "The parson's son had brought reinforcements from the village. They caught one of them on the moor. The other shot himself in the—"

No one as much as drew a breath in the silence that followed. By now, there wasn't a single person in the house who hadn't caught wind of the shocking news. A man was dead, a criminal by his own hand; two others were injured. One was Lady Bennett's stable boy, who had been stabbed while trying to defend the estate. Another man, a middle-aged groom well liked in the neighborhood, had been beaten so heartlessly that it would be a miracle if he lived through the night.

And the beautiful Scotswoman who stood on the terrace steps, like a young Greek goddess, had known. No one could decide quite what to make of her. Should she be regarded as a heroine or a social pariah? Then Reggie ran inside and brought her back a fringed shawl, wrapping it around her shivering form until Knight pushed through the gathering and elbowed him aside.

"I'll take care of her," he said firmly.

Reggie squared his shoulders, aware that everyone was watching him. "Well, I—"

Knight looked right through him, raising his voice to address the cluster of spellbound guests. "We have coffee and brandy in the blue room for those of you who wish a beverage before you leave. Under the circumstances, I think most of you would prefer to be home with your families."

Catriona made a covert move toward the steps. He clamped his hands down on her shoulders, his grip like steel as he nodded pleasantly to the departing guests. "Meet me in my study in an hour," he said under his breath. "Do you understand?"

She swallowed hard. "Are you going to kill me?"

"You'll have to wait to find out, won't you?"

Chapter

15

❧

She vowed a hundred times that she would not go. Who was he to summon her like a serving girl? She simply would not go. He would have to drag her kicking and screaming down the stairs. But seventy minutes later, she found herself standing in the doorway of his study, drawn by a power deeper than she could deny. She should have known, that night when she saw the ring around the moon, not to take that first step into his world. But then, as now, she couldn't stop herself.

For several moments, she wavered, watching him write at his desk. His neckcloth and black evening coat had been carelessly hung over the back of his chair. The breadth of his shoulders was the first thing she noticed, as she had on the night they met. But now she curled her fingers at her sides, stifling the temptation to throw herself into his muscular arms and seek sanctuary in his strength. Oh, she hated the delicious torment he made her feel.

He glanced up at the clock on the mantelpiece, then looked at her directly, his gaze distant. "You're late. Sit down."

She took a couch in the corner, still clutching the shawl that Reggie had brought her earlier. My, his voice was unfriendly. No sanctuary in those strong arms tonight. She cleared her throat. "Is Olivia in bed?" she asked in an attempt at light conversation.

"Yes. With a severe headache, which is not surprising, is it?"

She pursed her lips. Well, light conversation did not seem to be in the cards for her, either. She sank down lower in the chair and closed her eyes, sheer exhaustion from the night's events taking its toll. But at least Lady Bennett was alive. Oh, thank God—

His voice snapped her out of her reverie. "So, tell me, did you like it?"

She opened her eyes, heart leaping into her throat, to see him standing over her, his broad frame blocking out the candlelight. The emotion on his face unnerved her. She struggled to answer. "The ball? Well." What could she say? She had detested every second, every dance except for the few with him. No debutante had ever made such a spectacle of herself, but after all the trouble and expense he and Olivia had gone to, surely such ingratitude would be a slap in the face. "Yes. It was a beautiful ball—"

His voice lashed her feeble response into ribbons. "I meant Sir Alistair's kiss. Did you like it?"

She was stunned into another brief silence. Was this the source of his wretched mood? After all that had happened afterward, she had almost forgotten that unpleasant scene in the stables. "I don't know whether I liked it," she admitted honestly, adjusting her skirts. "You attacked him before I had a chance to form a fair opinion."

He sat down beside her, his muscular thighs brushing hers. "Oh?"

She shrank away from the black anger in his eyes. "Well, I—"

He claimed her ripe mouth in a kiss that was designed to be her undoing. It was. The moment his lips touched hers, she was his, body and soul, and the skill he wielded to dominate her was more than her shaky emotions could handle. In a breathless whisper, she blurted out, "If you mean to prove a point—"

"Be quiet, Catriona. I am too busy for idle chatter."

By "too busy" she supposed he meant that he was deftly unhooking her gown, tugging at the ties of her chemise, rendering her shaking and helpless in his arms. A shiver shot through her as cool air brushed her naked breasts, the tender tips of her nipples hardening in response to his sensual regard.

"Look at you," he said mockingly, forcing her back against the chaise. "Half naked in my arms. What a wanton young woman you are. I could swive you on a stable floor, couldn't I?"

His crude words sent a chill of anger mixed with anticipation down her spine. "Knight—"

"I'm sorry," he said with an utter lack of conviction. "Is it my fault that I am insane at the thought of anyone else touching you? You've made me wild with wanting you."

"I thought you hated me," she whispered, her voice catching.

He hesitated; the last thing he had wished to do

was admit the depth of his feelings. He intended to take his revenge in words, but, as usual, she broke through his reserve with the openness that made her so vulnerable. And hadn't the humiliation she suffered been enough? Hadn't the time come for him to face her with *his* own truth?

He knew now that he loved her, that beneath the boiling desire, the emotional unrest, he cared for her so deeply he could not deny it. Perhaps he should have fought against it, but fighting the truth was not his way. He had found the love of his life, and he wouldn't let her go. He would possess her and protect her, no matter what it took.

"Hate you?" His gaze disarmed her with its unmasked emotion. "I lose a piece of my heart every time you walk into a room."

She stared at him, relief bringing tears to her eyes. "You aren't going to ask me to do the proper thing and leave?"

"On the contrary." He leaned forward to kiss the trembling corners of her mouth. "I'm going to ask you to do a very improper thing with me."

His gaze was heavy-lidded and hypnotic, awakening all her senses. Her body ached for his touch. Her breathing faltered as she felt a flush of arousal warm her skin.

She glanced at the door, whispering, "Are you certain about this? Olivia and Aunt Marigold will murder us if they find out."

"They'll find out sooner or later," he said, his smile full of devilish intentions. "If anything good comes of tonight, it is that I cannot keep what I feel for you a secret."

Then his hands were around her shoulders, in her

hair, strong, persuasive, lifting her to him. He pushed the sleeves on her gown down as he kissed her. She tried to cover her breasts, but he shook his head, his eyes burning with need. He wanted to see her body. He held her still beneath him with his muscular weight. She gave a soft whimper, then fell still, her eyes closing. He smiled, pleased at her submission, and trailed his fingers down the arch of her throat to her breasts.

"You are mine," he whispered in a dark voice that made her shiver again.

"I—"

"You will never, ever, let another man touch you, do you understand?"

His fingers plucked at her distended nipples with a sensuality that rendered her powerless. His hard body burned against hers, radiating heat and male aggression. She felt small and defenseless, incapable of doing a single thing to stop him. Not that she wanted to. She gazed up into his intense face through her eyelashes. Pure lust smoldered in the depths of his dark eyes. She was utterly lost in him.

He nuzzled her neck and shoulders, taking small bites here and there that left her feeling lightheaded; certainly, she knew that this was not ladylike behavior. But only for a moment, a few kisses—would it hurt? She needed to be held after the evening's turmoil, but, oh, what if she didn't stop him? And he was jealous; this big, handsome tyrant was enraged because another man had kissed her, even though she couldn't remember that other man's face, or even his name.

He buried his face between her milky white breasts, his big hands holding her as if he would never release her. Her scent reminded him of wild roses, he thought as he flicked his tongue back and forth between her sensitive pink nipples, intent on reducing her to raw sensation. She moaned, pushing herself against him for more. She looked innocent and flagrantly erotic at the same time. He closed his eyes, a shudder rocking his large frame.

"We can't do this here," he said roughly. "Jesus, I am such a bastard."

She made an incoherent noise, captured in all those indescribably wicked sensations that he knew so well how to evoke. As he drew her nipple between his teeth, tugging gently, she gripped the arms of the chaise for anchorage.

He looked up into her eyes, the pupils dilated with desire. "Don't breathe a word of this to Olivia. Let me be the one to tell her."

"She already knows you're a bastard, Knight. I heard her telling Wendell so when they were checking the ballroom this morning."

"Thank you," he said wryly. "Actually, I meant that I should be the one to break the news to her about our engagement."

"Our what?" she said, sitting up in shock, her hand at her throat.

He cupped her astonished face in his hands and kissed her into silence.

"Do I take that as a yes?" he asked, his thumb stroking her cheek.

Mischief danced in her eyes. "Well, I would have to ask permission from the master of the manor. Just as a courtesy—"

She found herself deposited on the Axminster carpet before she could finish, his body nailing hers to the floor. She stared up into his dark, unfathomable eyes and shivered, conquered by his potent masculinity. The weight of his thighs smothered her lower body in waves of pleasurable sensation. The desire smoldering in the depths of his eyes seemed to draw the strength from her body.

"What happened?" she whispered with a dazed smile.

He laughed. Sprawled out like that on the carpet, she looked alluring and disoriented, like a fairy who had fallen out of the sky. How careful he would have to be not to damage this dainty creature. He stared at her creamy white breasts and imagined her body writhing beneath his. But to deflower her on the floor—almighty God, if he did not walk away now, he would tear that dress into shreds with his teeth.

"I have to get you out of here," he said hoarsely.

"Why?" she asked, sounding more disappointed than anything.

"Because—oh, hell."

He pushed her filmy skirts up to her waist, all the colors of the ocean wrapped around her sensuous curves like a ribbon that held an enticing gift. What a sweet handful of woman. What a temptress and, oh, God, the treasure buried deep beneath her thighs, the enticing scent of woman that drifted to him. He wanted to sink his shaft into that softness and pump her all night. He stroked his fingers against her soft flesh. She arched in surprise. She was so tight and slick that his heart began to pound.

"Oh," she said, her back curling into a bow, her gaze on his hard face. She knew perfectly well in theory what a man and a woman did in the mating act, but this, well, no wonder no one had ever explained the finer details. She closed her eyes, awash in embarrassment at her body's animal instinct. It was all she could do not to thrust against his hand, to push down deeper and soothe the ache he had awakened. She begin to move, restless, encouraged by the groan he gave into her hair as he held her. Unconsciously, she held his forearm for reassurance.

His elegant fingers touched her in feathery strokes, over and over, dipping deep inside the most private recesses of her body. Knight watched her opening to him in wonder, her inhibitions shed as he seduced her without mercy. What if he had married Arabella and missed Catriona? The thought of everything she had gone through made him determined that she would have a secure life, that nothing would ever hurt her again. "You have the sweetest body," he whispered. "I want every piece of it for myself."

His belly tightened with a hunger he could not deny as he studied the sensuous curves of her small body. The thought of Alistair touching her reawakened the rage and jealousy he had fought to subdue. She was his. He would kill to keep her. He alone would show her sexual pleasure beyond anything she could imagine. Even now, she quivered at his most casual touch.

He plundered her mouth with kisses that left her gasping. He rubbed his thick shaft against her until they were both moaning in frustration. With a fierce growl, he pulled her up onto his lap so that she was straddling his thigh, her legs sprawled open like a wanton as he pressed his finger all the way inside her tight passage. He broke out into a sweat as he imagined thrusting into that wet, pink sheath.

"Only me, Catriona," he whispered.

She sighed, too engrossed in what he was doing to

respond. She felt hot and aching; her shoulders sagged forward as shocks of pleasure began to spread across her belly. Before he brought her to her peak, her body convulsing, she felt his hand firmly grip her bottom and heard a curse, accompanied by the rending of silk, the painstaking stitches of Claudette's hardworking assistants coming apart. Her underskirt had been torn; she saw that much as she lifted her head in hazy curiosity to look.

"Oh, hell," he said, his breath uneven, his eyes black with lust. "I'll buy you another, but you're not wearing anything this provocative again for anyone but me."

"It doesn't look as if I shall be wearing this again in any hurry, either," she whispered, biting her lip.

"I can't believe I did that to you," he muttered.

He lifted her off the floor, his harsh face inscrutable. He should have known she would tempt him beyond mercy. He should have known that he couldn't touch her sweet flesh and expect to walk away unaffected. He ached to his marrow, drawing on every last remnant of his restraint. How was he supposed to keep his hands off her after this? Nothing would satisfy him until he had her in his bed. His gaze wandered over her, marking every inch of her as his own. She looked tousled and sexy and wanton, and he wanted to take her in every way known to man.

"I adore you, Catriona Beatrice Grant," he said gruffly, "you who nearly shot my gardener the first night I found you hiding in my garden."

"And I thought you were, well, perfect."

He smiled. "Far from that."

"Yes." She gave him a wicked grin. "I found that out, too."

"Brat," he said with affection.

"Brute," she said.

"Twit."

"Tyrant."

He paused. "Scottish sorceress."

"English scoundrel."

He looked up at the ceiling. "Umm. Interesting combination. Think of the children a Celtic sorceress and a stuffy scoundrel would produce."

"If I'm given permission to marry him," she said. "My unofficial guardian might refuse."

"I shall talk to this guardian of yours tonight. Man to man, as they say."

"He can be very difficult."

He took her chin in his hands. "And very persuasive, *and* he will do anything to have you."

"Will he?" she whispered.

"Just watch him." He narrowed his eyes at her, striving to look serious. Speaking as your unofficial guardian, I strongly advise you to accept his proposal."

"Do you?"

"Oh, yes. I hear he's quite a catch. Wealthy and quite devoted once he gives his heart, which is a rarity in itself. I wouldn't let this opportunity go by, young lady."

Catriona pretended to give the matter deep consideration. "But gossip has it that he plans to take Lady Frampton back into his bed the moment her husband isn't looking. They were spotted together in the woods by a reliable source."

"And I have it on good authority that his affair with Arabella is dead. It was more a matter of convenience, anyway. Childhood association and all that. Their parents had pushed the match from their cradle days."

"Really? Well, I happen to suspect there was a little more to it than that."

He kissed her until her head began to swim again; finally, he drew away, his face a mask of agony as he pulled her gown back over her shoulders. "Are you all right, Knight?" she asked curiously.

"Nothing that sitting in a tub of ice water for seven hours or so won't cure." He turned her resolutely toward the door. "Are you ready for what could possibly be the most dangerous mission of our lives?"

"That is hardly an encouraging way to view our prospective marriage."

He grunted. "I wasn't talking about our marriage. I was talking about sneaking you upstairs without being caught. The three Gorgons are on guard."

"Gorgons?"

"Yes. My sister, Aunt Marigold, and Mrs. Evans. Olivia is afraid that you might try to run back to your brother after what happened tonight. Unless we fetch a ladder, we shall have to cross enemy lines to smuggle you safely into your room."

She grinned. "Oh, honestly."

He circled her, arms folded across his chest. "This is a serious matter. The passageway to your room runs past Olivia's and Aunt Marigold's doors. I thought it was foolish of my sister to place you next to me. I realize now it was a crafty act of strategy on her part. She can hear every creak of my door. That is, if we get that far."

"Perhaps we ought to go separately," she suggested. "So as not to arouse suspicion if we're seen."

"What? Where is your sense of adventure?"

She sighed. "I believe it has been quite exhausted for one evening."

"Do you have any idea what will happen if the Gorgons catch us?"

"Well—"

He gripped her hand and dragged her to the door. "We shall be shot on the spot, or transported to Botany Bay, or, worse, lashed to death by my dear sister's tongue."

She hung back, her amusement fading. "Oh, Knight. She already thinks ill of me. I don't want to upset her."

"This is no time to get the cold shivers."

"But—"

She swallowed a giggle as he pushed her out into the darkened hallway. No sooner were they halfway to the stairs than Howard came marching by with a tray of dirty dishes. They ducked into the alcove. A few seconds later, a pair of kitchen maids walked past them, one of whom was sneaking a glass of champagne left over from the party.

"Spies on a midnight intelligence mission," Knight whispered in her ear. "Trained killers, by the look of them. Ah, here comes the grand master."

Catriona bit the inside of her cheek to keep from laughing as Mrs. Evans waddled around the corner, humming a Welsh hymn.

"Do not be deceived by her gentle appearance," he said quietly. "I have it on good advice that the woman is an expert at torture. You should see what she does to a roast chicken on a rack."

"Oh, really."

He raised his brow at her. "You doubt the word of a man who is risking life and limb to see you safely to your base?"

"I doubt—"

"*Now.*"

They launched themselves pell-mell at the staircase, holding hands, a split-second before Mr. Aubrey appeared in the hall. When Catriona rose up on her knees to peer around, Knight put his hand on her bottom to push her back down on the stairs.

"I say," the butler said, scratching his head. "What bleedin' moron opened the door to his lordship's study? It was shut a minute ago."

Catriona grinned over her shoulder at Knight, mouthing, "Careless of you."

He shrugged. "I told you we were working against brilliant minds. These trained professionals miss nothing."

"God's truth," Aubrey muttered. "Look at this lying here on the floor. Am I a lady's maid?" And he bent, creaking at the knees, to retrieve the shawl that Catriona had dropped in her mad dash to the stairs.

"Right." Knight patted her on the backside. "He's gone, and now comes the most hazardous part of the mission. Getting you past the Gorgons."

She swallowed. "You're exaggerating. Surely they would believe us if we explained that we were only talking in your study."

"It would have to have been quite a conversation to explain the state of your dress."

A becoming blush tinted her cheeks. "Yes. That's quite true, so I suppose that the sooner I get into my room, the better. Are you ready?"

He leaned back against the balustrade, admiring her in the moonlight that filtered through the landing windows. "A fallen angel," he murmured, sitting forward to kiss her gently. "Well, half fallen, anyway, and if you don't escape right now, I cannot promise to behave. Go on. Please go."

Her golden-green eyes widened. "Aren't you coming?"

His eyes glittered with devilish lights. "It would only make it look worse if you were caught in my company."

"Oh, you scoundrel. You coward."

He gave a wicked chuckle. "I'll stay here and listen for the sounds of their doors opening. Olivia's has a distinctive squeak."

"Have you done this sort of thing before?"

"Never." He paused. "I'll whistle to warn you."

"Oh, thanks very much."

He crossed his arms behind his head. "You might try tiptoeing to your room. Olivia is a light sleeper."

Snatching her skirts out from beneath him, she rose to ascend the rest of the stairs. He grinned to himself as he watched her flit like a sprite down the darkened hallway, but he didn't bother waiting to make sure that she reached her room. It was enough to confront Olivia in the morning with news of their engagement.

He couldn't even imagine her reaction. Tears of joy, a tantrum? Whatever, her response would involve more emotional turmoil than he could face tonight. He—

He sat up as the woods surrounding the estate began to throb with the unholy hooting of owls. He was so distracted he did not even notice that Catriona had reached her room, nor did he hear the tell-tale squeaking of Olivia's door, as his sister peered out into the hall.

Olivia closed the door and began to pace in the dark, talking to the spirit of her dead husband as was her habit when she was depressed. "Look at her, sneaking back upstairs from heaven only knows what escapade again. Hasn't the girl had enough misadventure for one night? For a lifetime? Well, what would you do with her? She's your flesh and blood. Oh, I know, Lionel. You would have made a joke of it, said the right thing, and turned the whole disaster into a triumph."

She dropped down onto the bed in a dispirited heap. "I love her none the less for her flaws. Isn't that what you always said? One must accept the good with the bad where family is concerned. But, Lionel, what she needs is a husband, and the sooner the better."

Somewhere outside, an owl hooted. Olivia glanced at the window. "Does that mean you disagree? Well, if so, you had best come right out and tell me what to do. If you have the perfect bridegroom in mind, I should very much appreciate your bringing him to my attention. After Knight's show of indignation tonight, poor Alistair is unlikely ever to show his face in public again, let alone ask for her hand. Still, I suppose all hope is not dead. She did vindicate herself in the end."

Chapter

16

❧

The hour of reckoning had come. There was no way that Knight could sit at the table the next morning with Olivia and Marigold without sharing the good news. Fortunately, the two women appeared to be in a jovial mood. Far too jovial, he realized suspiciously, as he sat down to his usual breakfast of coffee, buttered toast, and the newspaper that Aubrey had ironed for him. One didn't need Catriona's powers of prophecy to foretell that the pair of them were brewing up trouble in their tea cups.

Where is Catriona?" he asked as he waited for Smythe to finish pouring the coffee.

Olivia gave him such a bright smile that he blinked. "The little princess is sleeping in late after all the excitement."

"The little *princess?*" he said, a triangle of toast halfway to his mouth.

"What an evening," Marigold exclaimed. She dropped an enormous spoonful of clotted cream onto her currant scone. "I shall never forget it."

"I doubt that anyone will," Knight muttered, picking up the newspaper. Had they guessed? Had they been eavesdropping last night? Their amiability was simply too, well, too abnormal to believe. He pretended to read the latest report on businesses that had recently gone bankrupt.

"You look a little tired yourself this morning," Olivia said in such a sweet voice that he began to wonder if another spirit had taken possession of her body. "Mrs. Evans suggested you bathe your knuckles in witch hazel and comfrey to reduce the bruising. That was quite a blow you dealt Alistair last night."

"My knuckles are fine," he said. "In fact—"

He broke off at the sound of hoofbeats in the driveway, followed by the persistent banging of the brass knocker on the door. "Who the blazes is calling at this hour?"

Marigold grinned at him over her tea cup. "Probably another visitor for our sleeping heroine."

"I hope whoever it is hasn't brought more flowers." Olivia glanced around at the salver on the sideboard, upon which sat a collection of nosegays and calling cards. Everything had changed overnight, she thought in delight. Suddenly, Cat had suitors. Had Olivia's plea to Lionel worked? "You should see the drawing room. It looks like Papa's old hothouse. Oh, Knight, do you remember the year he grew an orange, and it was so sour, but we all pretended to enjoy it because no one could bear to hurt his feelings?"

"I'm going to marry her," he said.

"You ought to put those violets in water, Olivia," Marigold said. "They're starting to wilt. Nothing sadder than a drooping posy."

Olivia sighed, folding her hands under her chin. "Alistair sent her white roses. I think he grew them himself. They have the most delicious fragrance. I almost laid them outside her door so that she would see them first thing—"

"I want to marry her." Knight raised his voice, refusing to be ignored.

There was dead silence at the table. Smythe threw him a startled look before reassuming his usual bland expression. Aunt Marigold swallowed her bite of scone, at a loss for words. Olivia slowly unfolded her fingers and leaned forward.

"Catriona?"

"No, Olivia, the housekeeper." He frowned at her. "Who else but Catriona?"

"No." She shook her head, rising from her chair. "No. Absolutely not."

"What do you mean, no? You are not her mother, and she isn't a minor."

"No, Knight. I want a stable husband for her." She came up beside him. "I do not know exactly how to tell you this—it's the most noble thing in the world for you to offer her marriage. But you aren't the man for her. She is sweet and vivacious. You are—"

"—jaded and intense," Aunt Marigold said, finding her voice.

Knight's frown deepened. "Do you think that I would mistreat her?"

"You are not even aware of the hearts you have broken," Olivia said ruefully. "Oh, Knight, so many girls have cried on my shoulder over you."

"Well, I never hurt any of them on purpose."

"Exactly," she said. "I know why you are doing this."

"Do you?"

She nodded, touching his arm. "To save me. You are actually willing to sacrifice your bachelorhood for me. I am deeply touched."

He shrugged off her hand. "Apparently, in the head. And marrying Catriona has nothing to do with you. She accepted my proposal last night after the party."

"Did you compromise her?" Aunt Marigold demanded.

"Kindly mind your own business," he said.

Olivia pursed her lips. "When I suggested that you and Catriona become friends, a seduction was the farthest thing from my mind."

"This is just not the cheese, young sir," Aunt Marigold said, in high dudgeon from being told off. "In my day, a man knew when to keep his tallywag in his trousers."

Knight arched his brow. "Where my 'tallywag' does or does not wander is not a subject I care to discuss with my best friend's aging aunt."

"It is not a subject I care to discuss at all," Olivia said in distress. "But, oh, you haven't disgraced her, have you? I shall die on the spot if you say you have. It will spoil everything."

"I think it will solve a great deal," he said impatiently. "You wanted a husband for her. You have one."

"More than one, as it turns out," Marigold said with a sly chuckle.

Knight shot her a look. "What?"

Olivia picked up the nosegay of violets. "Reggie's father came this morning asking permission for his son to marry her. Of course, I put him off. Reggie was a last resort at best. I thought we could take our chances at another party or two before giving him an answer."

Knight got up from the table. "What do you mean by 'more than one,' Marigold?"

"Sir Alistair." The woman took such a long sip of tea that Knight was tempted to give her artificial ringlets a good yank. "He sent three dozen white roses and a formal marriage proposal, along with an apology for his misbehavior last night." She gave Knight a pointed look. "Some men know when to ask forgiveness for their rudeness."

"That isn't all he's asking for," Knight said, his tone ominous. "I should have killed the old buzzard when I had the chance."

Olivia's face went white. "Don't you dare start that nonsense again. He's hardly old, he only has five years on you, and he grew the white roses himself. Isn't that romantic?"

"I am all atwitter with admiration," Knight said stonily.

"Well, atwitter or not," Olivia said, "you cannot marry Lionel's cousin. You have been her unofficial guardian—what would people think?"

He shrugged. "I don't particularly care. Lord Newbury married his parlor maid. I haven't seen any-one snub her at church."

"You never go to church." Olivia gave him a wan smile. "I do understand why you're doing this."

"I doubt it."

"You're doing it for Lionel," she said gently.

"Because you came home and he didn't. But don't you realize that he wouldn't have wanted it any other way? That was the kind of silly fool my husband was."

He turned to the window. "People do not discuss this sort of thing, Olivia."

"Then perhaps they should," Aunt Marigold said, straightening her wig.

He looked at her over his shoulder. "You think it's perfectly fine to discuss tallywags at the table. I tell you, I don't hear such low talk at my club."

"Oh, ho. Since when did you become the prude—"

The three of them glanced around at the hesitant figure in the doorway. "Is it safe to show my face, or am I still exiled in scandal?" Catriona asked softly. She glanced at the posies on the sideboard as she took her place at the table. "Where did all those come from?"

Her gaze lifted to Knight. He gave her a small, private smile. She smiled back, her expression asking, *Did you tell them about us?* He nodded. She glanced around the table, biting her lip. Heaven above, but Olivia and Aunt Marigold looked like a pair of mean tabbies chasing away a tomcat. Why in the world weren't they as delighted as she about the impending nuptials? Wasn't this what everyone had wanted?

"I'm starving," she said, sighing at the raw desire in Knight's eyes. She felt a blush heat the nape of her neck. If he didn't stop looking at her like that, the other two women were going to know they were wildly attracted to each—oh, what did it matter now, anyway?

"The flowers are from your suitors," Olivia announced with such enthusiasm that Smythe almost dropped his towel. "Did you hear me, Catriona? I said *suitors.*"

Knight frowned at her. "I think the entire household heard you, woman."

Olivia placed her hands on Cat's shoulders, the gesture overtly protective. "I don't think you understood me, Catriona. Both Reggie and Sir Alistair have expressed an interest in marrying you."

Catriona smiled at Knight. He looked so outraged at the mention of the two other men that she wanted to throw her arms around his neck and smother him in kisses. When she'd awakened that morning, she had been in such a wonderful mood she could hardly contain her happiness. All vestiges of the previous evening's vision had disappeared into the mists of her memory. Gone. The only thing she could think of was marrying him, of the happy future ahead.

Olivia gave her a little shake. "Did you hear me?"

Catriona started. "Excuse me. I must have been woolgathering. Did you say something?"

"I most certainly did," Olivia said.

Knight was grinning now, too. The pair of them were behaving like two adolescents in the throes of their first infatuation. If the matter had not held such dire consequences for Catriona's future, Olivia might have been amused. It wasn't that she didn't adore her brother, but he wasn't meant for someone as inexperienced as Catriona, who clearly worshipped the ground he stalked upon. Not for nothing had Knight earned that rakehell reputation, and Olivia took it as her duty to protect Lionel's cousin from heartbreak even if it meant offending his best friend. Anyway, Sir Alistair was too perfect a match to pass up—wealthy, stable, a neighbor, which meant that Olivia could dote on their children, and he was obviously a man who knew what he wanted, with the maturity to indulge a younger wife.

"Sir Alistair sent you three dozen white roses," she said meaningfully.

Catriona giggled in reaction to Knight's black scowl of disapproval. "Whatever for?"

"Why do you think?" Olivia said in astonishment. "The man is courting you. You obviously made quite a good impression."

"I don't see how," Catriona said, holding in another giggle.

"Neither do I," Aunt Marigold added in a forthright manner. "Unless it was the dowry Knight so generously offered to sweeten the deal."

"The dowry that I—"

Olivia interrupted him. "If Lionel were alive, he would certainly contribute to the marriage portion."

"Oh, for God's sake," he said. "Stop bringing Lionel's name into the conversation. And I never offered to do any such thing, Olivia."

"Well, you should have."

"She doesn't need a dowry." He winked at Catriona. "Especially if I have to pay it to myself."

Howard appeared at the door, wearing a freshly pressed jacket. Recovered from last night's fright, he was ready to accept accolades for the part he had played in saving Lady Bennett. "Excuse me," he said, "but Miss Grant has just received a gift of a half-dozen gooseberry pies. Mrs. Evans would like to know if she should serve them up now or wait until luncheon."

"I don't care about pies right now," Olivia said in exasperation. "Tell her to give some to the staff if she likes."

Knight snorted. "What sort of suitor proposes with a gooseberry pie?"

Marigold glanced at him. "I'd have to agree with

you on that point. It does give the brain a jolt to picture Alistair in an apron."

"Oh, the pies did not come from Sir Alistair,"
Howard said quickly. "Lady Bennett's housekeeper
sent them over as a thank-you to Miss Grant."

"In that case," Knight said, "I shall have a piece.
In honor of our Miss Grant." He moved to the chair
directly opposite her, not caring what anyone thought.
"Did I tell you how uncommonly beautiful you are,
Miss Grant? And by the way, I thought about
you all night long. You almost had a late-night visitor."

"Oh, honestly, Knight," Olivia said, scandalized to
her toenails. "Behave yourself in front of the servants."

Howard's eyes widened. "It's quite all right,
ma'am."

"It is not all right—" She gasped in horror as
Knight reached across the table to take Catriona's
hand. "There will be no touching at the breakfast
table!"

His eyes narrowed as Catriona's fingers curled into
his palm. Reprobate that he was, he could too vividly
imagine her delicate touch on other parts of his body.
No way was he waiting for the honeymoon, not with
those other men drawn like drones to her sweetness.

"Are you engaged for the evening, Miss Grant?" he
asked in a seductive undertone.

Her teeth caught the edge of her lower lip. It was
an unconsciously sensual gesture that forced him to
swallow a groan of sheer frustration. "I don't believe
I am, actually."

"Here." Desperate to dampen the growing heat
between the two of them, Olivia brought the salver to

the table and placed it, with flowers and notes, right under Catriona's nose. "If you have so much spare time on your hands, you might begin by acknowledging these. Howard, stop gaping, and fetch her some writing materials."

Before Howard could obey, a clatter of hoofbeats came from outside the house as a curricle parked in the drive. Moments later, a gig arrived bearing Baron Frampton and Arabella. More carriage wheels rumbled in the distance over the stone bridge to the estate.

"My goodness," Olivia exclaimed, "we have guests. I'm sure I didn't invite them. Did you, Marigold?"

Aunt Marigold put down her cup. "At this hour of the morning? I most certainly did not. I shall have to change my wig. I expect they've come to see Catriona. What you and I perceived last night as a scandal has obviously converted itself into a success."

Knight drew his hand away from Catriona's, a wry expression on his face. "Then I expect they'll have to settle for me. Miss Grant is not receiving callers today."

Catriona sat alone at the table, her face as white as a snowdrop at the commotion in the entrance lobby. It took several moments for her to realize what was happening. She could have told Knight that there was no reason for him to be jealous, if she had managed to gather her own stunned wits. The crowd of people on his front steps had not come to ask her hand in marriage or to befriend her. They had come to seek supernatural help. Why had she thought the English aristocracy would be any different from the Scots when it came to wondering what the future held?

She eyed the closed door beside the fireplace. It led into a passageway around the house to the servants' hall, a possible means of escape if the need arose.

"*Psst.* Miss Grant."

Smythe, standing motionless at the sideboard, suddenly came to life. Oh, no, she thought. She recognized that eager look in his eye. It boded ill.

He scooted around the table on the pretense of refilling her cup. She knew exactly what he was about to ask of her. She didn't need mystical help to predict this unfortunate part of human nature. How could she have forgotten? In the excitement of the previous evening, she had managed to ignore what invariably followed in the aftermath of one of her visions, the human curiosity, the desire to use Catriona's foresight to satisfy personal needs.

Glancing out into the hall, Smythe said quietly, "Miss Grant, I know it is an imposition, but as you have shown yourself to be the heart of kindness, I was wondering if you could use your powers—"

She covered her face with her hands, peeping at him through her fingers as he continued.

"—to help me make a decision. I've taken all my savings to place a bet on the races, and I was wondering if you might advise me on which horse is liable to win."

By mid-afternoon her reputation as a soothsayer had spread to the outer fringes of West Briarcombe. The village chandler sent her a box of beeswax candles with a written plea for a personal interview on the matter of his only son, missing at sea. Lord Beckwith wanted to know if he should invest in tea caddies. Another letter arrived from a "Sir Somebody" asking that Catriona put her powers to work to deter-mine if the child his young wife carried was the product of an adulterous affair.

If the child was his, Catriona was instructed to wave a white sheet from her window at nine o'clock the next morning. In the unhappy event that "Sir S" had not sired the thing, any red article of clothing could be used to convey the bad news.

Catriona did not want to disappoint anyone, but she could not make predictions on command. She never knew herself when a vision would come. The horrible things affected her so profoundly, she wished they would just go away.

By four o'clock, she had also received two more marriage proposals, which left Olivia agonizing over what must be done. It was clear to her that Cat needed to be married without delay, not only to defuse this infatuation between her and Knight but also to restore peace to the estate. Despite the fact that Knight and Catriona seemed hell-bent on marriage, Olivia was not yet ready to accept defeat.

"Perhaps Sir Alistair is too old for her," she confided in Marigold over tea. "And he never leaves his house."

"Except to visit the whores," Wendell said without thinking.

Olivia's and Marigold's heads lifted in unison like a hydra's. "What did you say?" Olivia asked in a choked voice.

"Whores," Marigold said, frowning at her. "My goodness, Olivia, a man does have certain physical needs, or have you forgotten? At least we know he is capable of fulfilling his marital obligations. Catriona will desire children."

Olivia put her pen to her lips. "Wendell, you

referred to these 'relationships' in the plural. How many of these women does he keep?"

"Two, I think." He scratched his knee with his riding quirt. "Perhaps more. I don't know as he actually keeps them. I was under the impression that he paid them random visits when growing roses did not provide enough stimulation."

Two of these women, perhaps more? Surely not at the same time. Olivia was appalled at the thought. One mistress for a lonely man was conceivable, but not a bacchanalian orgy. She could not possibly entrust Catriona to such a man.

"Oh," she said, frowning at Wendell. "I do not believe you. How would you know whether Sir Alistair visits these women?"

He tossed the quirt into the air and caught it. "I have said enough."

Marigold looked at Olivia. "Oftentimes the quiet ones are the worst. And there is something a little off about a man who spends his spare hours growing flowers."

Olivia lowered her pen and surreptitiously drew a line through Sir Alistair's name. Two women, indeed. At the same time. Unwholesome man. "I thought he was such a perfect match."

Wendell smiled at her. "We never know what secrets a man harbors in his heart, do we?"

She sighed. "I suppose not." And she completely missed the message in his eyes, the devotion there that he could no longer hide. Wendell had always been part of their lives. She assumed it was his friendship to Lionel and Knight that kept him there, practically a member of the family, when he had such vast resources at his disposal.

In fact, until recently, she'd never asked herself why he was not off in London with a mistress of his own. Heaven knew there was hardly a more eligible, attractive man in England, and if she weren't a widow, she might have yearned for him herself. But only in secret, of course.

"We shall work on you next," she said offhandedly. "We shall find a wife for Wendell."

"God forbid." He flicked the riding quirt across the sofa. "That will be the day."

Chapter

17

❧

To those who darkened his door in the following week in the hope of asking Catriona Grant what the future held for them, Knight had the same rude reply: "The future holds a viscount with an intolerance for fools and a monumental temper. Go away."

He resented being unable to spend time alone with his fiancée; nobody had thwarted Knight's plans to such a frustrating degree since childhood. Nobody would stop him from having the woman he wanted, that was a fact. In view of Olivia's attitude, however, and Catriona's sudden blaze to fame, he decided that their marriage could not wait. He wanted to take care of her. He wanted to spend time with her on his own terms.

His behavior had become a bit of an embarrassment. It wasn't enough to share hot looks with her across the room. He was consumed with the seduction of his future wife, and all the complications that such a conquest, in one's own house with not only an aging aunt but also a moral-minded sister and house-keeper looking on, entailed. Sneaking about might add a certain spice to his encounters with his be-trothed, but he and Catriona had been caught in fla-grante delicto by the servants so many times that nei-ther of them could look Mrs. Evans in the eye.

"I don't think she believed you when you told her you had dropped your quizzing glass down my cleav-age, Knight."

"Probably not." He grinned. "Especially since I've never been known to use one in my life."

She shook her head. "And I'm not sure, when she found me sitting on your lap in the study, that she was quite convinced we were conjugating French verbs."

"That's a shame." His eyes twinkled with unholy humor. "Because I have quite a few more French lessons planned for you in the near future."

He simply could not keep his hands off her for three minutes straight. He kissed her behind the drawing-room door. He followed her down the stairs and through the garden. He touched her every chance that was afforded him. His gaze followed her, claimed her, and he didn't care who knew it, because it was only a matter of time before she became his wife.

By the end of the week, he had memorized the curves of her body through layers of muslin and lace. He had learned which precise spot to nibble on her shoulder to make her shiver uncontrollably. He had found the tiny mole on her hip, the scar on her left ankle. When he caught her on the way upstairs to change for dinner, he murmured, "Meet me in the summerhouse after everyone else has gone to bed."

"What for?" she whispered, aware that Wendell and Olivia were watching them from below.

He caught her hand. "So I can have you to myself."

"Oh, really, Knight, I—" He rubbed his thumb across the tender flesh of her palm. My goodness, what had she been about to say? She literally trembled in her shoes at the sight of him, aroused to the point of walking into chairs, wrestling at night with the bedsheets, every nerve ending on edge. Oh, the wicked things he did to her with his mouth and hands, the promises he whispered in her ear that set her blood on fire.

He leaned into her, his huge body forcing her against the cast-iron balustrade. She gave a helpless giggle. "Are you quite mad? Wendell and Olivia are *watching* us."

He bent his head and slid his hands around her waist. "Is that a fact? Do you know that your skin is as delicious as Devon cream? No, you are mistaken—Wendell is distracting Olivia to allow me this necessary indulgence. I require touching you as other men need air. Observe him if you don't believe me. He's turned her away from us, and tonight when we are finally alone, he will be distracting her again."

"What?" Shocked and aching with desire at the same time, she peered over his shoulder to discover that Wendell had indeed gently guided Olivia back down the hall. "Oh, how humiliating," she whispered. "Don't tell me he *knows* what you are planning to do."

He raised his head and stared at her, his look unapologetic and amused. "It isn't exactly a secret. I think he feels sorry for me, if you must know."

"Has he done this sort of thing for you before?" she asked in annoyance. "Made himself a distraction, I mean."

"Never to this degree." He kissed her lightly on the lips. "Never when my very heart was at stake."

"Our lives will be at stake if Olivia finds out," she said pragmatically. "How does he plan to distract her?"

"Duke has his charms."

"Yes, I've noticed."

His eyes narrowed. "Is that right?"

"Are you jealous of him, too?" she asked in an incredulous voice.

"My dear," he said gravely, "I am jealous of that numbskull Howard when he hands you your gloves. Catriona, please. I cannot bear this. I want to be with you tonight."

Her stomach gave a nervous flutter. "In the summerhouse?"

"We will elope tomorrow night, after Wendell and I finish amending our plans for the clay pits."

"Elope?" Her heart began to pound at the thought. "But why?"

"I want to meet this brother of yours," he said, drawing away at the sound of footsteps in the hall below. "If I am to bail him out of his gambling woes, I suppose I am obliged at least to counsel him on avoiding future trouble. And my parents eloped. They loved each other devotedly until death. We'll get married on the way to Scotland without all the bother and delays of a wedding here."

A warm flush shimmered over her. She could not possibly have heard him correctly, but it would be good to make amends with James before she devoted herself to her happy new life, even though there would be a few embarrassing moments. She was going to have to explain to Knight about the awful fight she'd had with James over her refusal to marry that old man. "My brother is an irresponsible rogue," she said quietly. "You will never see a shilling of your investment even if he manages to save his estates."

"Did I give the impression that I cared a fig about my returns? There is something I want from this transaction that is far more valuable than money."

"And what would that be?" Olivia said, suddenly standing two steps below him, her eyes bright with disapproval.

He glanced past her at Wendell, who shrugged apologetically as if to say he had tried his best to restrain her. "Do *you* want something, Olivia?" Knight asked her coolly.

"Yes, actually, I was hoping to use the stairs. I do believe it's the only way to reach our rooms so that Catriona and I can dress for the evening." She reached around Knight to take Catriona's hand. "The pair of you may carry on this scintillating conversation at dinner."

"This is my house, Olivia," he said. "I reckon I should be able to chat with anyone where and when I choose."

Olivia looked around to make sure that none of the servants was in earshot before she said, "But we all know that you were engaging in so much more than a 'chat,' don't we?"

Catriona lowered her eyes, fighting the impulse to laugh. "I shall see you at dinner, my lord," she murmured, moving past him.

And afterward, he thought, his gaze glittering with desire as she disappeared from sight.

*   *   *

At ten o'clock that same evening, after an uneventful dinner, a door creaked open upstairs. Olivia
tensed, glancing from the doorway of Knight's study
to the grandfather clock in the hall beyond. The
creaking from above was only Marigold, taking on
her nightly watch of the bedchambers, which meant
that Mrs. Evans should be beginning to patrol the garden right about now.

A half-minute later, the shadow of a masculine figure appeared in the lower reaches of the hallway and
headed for the study. Olivia bolted from the doorway
and made a mad dash for her brother's desk. Ought she
to hide and catch the pair of them in the act? Gracious,
no. That would be too vulgar by half, but all of a sudden there wasn't much choice. She would have to
crouch under the desk and hope to confront Knight
before Catriona sneaked downstairs to meet him.

Except that it wasn't Knight who appeared in the
doorway.

"Wendell?" she whispered, crawling out from
beneath the desk, her voice low with embarrassment.

"Olivia?" he said as she stood to face him in the
dying firelight.

She stared into his aristocratic face and felt a small
flutter of confusion as he closed the door behind him.
"What are you doing here?" she whispered.

"Knight had asked me earlier to review the books
for the firm." He leaned one shoulder back against the
door. "Why are you here? Under his desk, of all
places?"

"I came to look for a book," she said lamely.

She stared at him, completely caught off guard by
the sudden flurry of feelings that assailed her. How

remarkable that her gangly, boyish neighbor had grown into such a good-looking man. She really did need to find him a respectable wife. Obviously not Catriona, and—oh, no. Did she hear voices outside, or was that the wind in the treetops? She'd noticed another breeze tonight in the garden.

She moved toward the door, unsettled that she had allowed him to distract her.

"Did you find one?" he asked.

"One what?" she said blankly.

He took her hand, pushing away from the door. "I'll help you look, although there isn't a great deal of a titillating nature to choose from. How does *Business Failures in the West Country* sound? A little dull for bedtime literature, if you ask me."

She was startled by the sensual heaviness of his hand on her wrist. What was he doing? Was he trying to disarm her? She glanced around in alarm. "It must be this room," she thought aloud. "Something in the furnishings must put ideas of a romantic nature into a man's mind."

Wendell stroked the sensitive underside of her wrist with his thumb. "My dear Olivia, what are you talking about?"

"Are you—" She swallowed, falling silent as he gently turned her toward him. From the dark warren of outbuildings behind the house, a dog barked. "So, that's what this is all about," she said, narrowing her eyes. "You are part of Knight's rotten little plan to distract his sister. I should have known—the pair of you will never change."

"Olivia." His blue eyes were aflame with amusement as he lowered his mouth to hers, silencing her with a kiss. "Knight has absolutely nothing to do with this."

And it was true.

*   *   *

Knight turned away from the dusty brocade couch the instant he saw Catriona appear in the archway to the summerhouse. He had forgotten the impromptu picnics held there years ago, the evenings spent with brandy and friends in the pleasant shadows of the garden. In fact, the place had not been disturbed in ages—there was a wheelbarrow in the corner heaped with dead bluebells, a shovel against a flowerpot, a bottle of old cognac tucked in the cushions of the couch.

The past came back to him in a poignant rush of images. Olivia had been picking bluebells in the garden the day he'd come home. He remembered her flushed face beneath her bonnet. He'd asked her there to deliver the news about Lionel, which the family had kept secret until Knight's return. None of them had used the summerhouse since, and the ghosts of who they had been might have broken his heart had Catriona Grant not arrived at that moment to heal it.

The bittersweet memories dissolved as he studied her; ivy leaves framed her graceful form, and her hair flowed over her shoulders in wanton disarray. Utterly unaware of the effect she had on him, she frowned and bent to pluck a twig from between her bare toes.

"Shoes, brat?" he said in a mild reproach. Nothing in his voice gave away his irrational fear that she might not show up for their naughty rendezvous. Nothing in his manner revealed how much he hated being away from her. "Civilized people in these parts do wear them, you know."

"Not when they're trying to sneak past Aunt Marigold and Mrs. Evans," she retorted. "Do you know your housekeeper actually has a telescope? I swear, she almost spotted me on the bridge. One would think I had just escaped from the Tower of London."

"Well," he said as he drew her up the stairs and into his arms, "I wouldn't mind keeping you in a tower myself, now that you mention it."

He kissed her then, and he kept kissing her, until her halfhearted protests that this really wasn't right turned into sighs of surrender. He ran his hands down the arch of her back to her bottom, pulling her against the support of his hard thighs.

"Nothing underneath." His breath caressed her cheek. "Very nice."

"I didn't have time," she whispered, her face turning pink. "Not with Olivia popping into my room every five seconds to make certain I hadn't disappeared. I think she was on patrol in your study."

His eyes burned down into hers. "I think I am going to die of wanting you."

She smiled mischievously. "Of course you won't."

"I will. Listen." He took her hand and placed it against his chest. She could feel the wild beating of his heart through his shirt, his muscles contracting at her touch. "Before you distract me further, let me tell you about our elopement," he said, his voice suddenly solemn. "I want you to meet me here tomorrow night at eleven. I'll have a carriage waiting at the edge of the woods. We would have escaped tonight except that Wendell and I still haven't agreed on our plans for Cornwall."

"But shouldn't we tell Olivia?"

He turned her toward the couch. "The purpose of an elopement is to elude one's relatives."

She frowned, sinking down onto the musty cushions. "She has her heart set on a formal wedding."

"And I have my heart set on you." He sat down next to her. "I simply will not tolerate my sister parading suitors in my house for the purpose of stealing the woman I love. What if one of them catches your eye?"

"My guardian would never have it." She gave him a demure smile that turned his blood molten. "He's an absolute beast."

"A beast who absolutely loves you. You really should listen to his advice."

"Well, he's warned me about men like you, too," she whispered. "About rakes who lure young women into summerhouses and the wicked things they do."

He slipped his hand around her back and deftly began to unhook her gown. He tugged the puffed sleeves off her shoulders, exposing her perfectly shaped breasts to his warm regard. "Obviously, you have decided to find out the truth for yourself."

A breeze fluttered through the ivy-entwined columns that enclosed them, and she gave a little shiver, not as much from the cool air as from the sensual purpose in his eyes. She crossed her arms over her naked breasts, her mouth suddenly dry, her entire being vulnerable to his demands.

"Don't." His deep voice sent a shiver down to her toes. "I want to look at you."

She sat frozen against the faded brocade couch as he gently drew her hands into her lap. "Catriona." His voice sounded uneven. "You have a beautiful little body, but I think your guardian might have been right."

She shuddered as he brushed his jaw against her bare shoulder. "How?"

"There is still too much of the rakehell in me to resist you."

"Why were you so horrible to me when I first came here?"

He laughed ruefully. "I must have known from the very first moment that you would be the one. No man likes to admit that the woman exists who can bring him to his knees."

"And the marriage noose?" she asked mischievously.

He laughed again. "My neck is yours. And"—he slid even closer, urging her back against the worn cushions, her small hands pressed to his chest—"so is my heart."

"Is it?"

"For always, Catriona."

For a moment, she couldn't speak, remembering all her fears on the night they had met, and how, deep inside, she had wanted to be his even then. And, yes, it was indeed a thing to be feared, this losing all of oneself to another. Yet there had been no other choice for her on that night. Nor was there now.

He lowered his mouth to her breasts, darting his tongue back and forth across her pink nipples until she felt faint with pleasure. She closed her eyes with a dreamy sigh as he pressed her deeper into the couch. She managed only a perfunctory murmur of protest when she felt his hand sliding beneath her skirt, his palm cool against her skin. His strong fingers circled the sensitive underside of her knee. Shocks of decadent sensation tingled along her nerve endings, and her muscles began to relax at his masterful touch.

"You deserve better than a few stolen moments in a musty summerhouse," he said wistfully. "I wish you were in my bed, where I could take my time to do this."

His fingers brushed the damp hollow between her legs, played with the soft flesh there that ached for him. She gripped his wrist and moaned, uncertain whether she could stand this much pleasure. "Is the rakehell suffering a pang of conscience?" she teased him.

He leaned down to kiss her. "Actually, it's a pang of the most painful lust he has ever known. I don't think I can move—do you know I am dying to be inside you?"

"What does it feel like?" she whispered.

He groaned against her mouth. "Are you torturing me on purpose?"

She pushed up on her elbows and began kissing him back. "Is it all right if I do this?" she asked softly.

For several moments, he did not move, except for the shudder of lust that moved down his shoulders and into his spine. But her sweet, demanding kisses destroyed him, not that when it came to her he was a pillar of strength to begin with. He hesitated for only a second, his jaw clenched, before he lifted his free hand impatiently to unbutton his shirt. His pantaloons followed, and then, reaching for a sheet from the top of the couch to cover them, he pressed his naked body to hers. The bliss of forbidden flesh-to-flesh contact burned away the final vestiges of his restraint.

In a few days, she would be his wife, but he didn't think he could wait to take physical possession. He had never felt such a primal need to mate, to leave his mark, and deep beneath the urgings of nature was the fear of losing her, the fear that as mysteriously as she had come into his life, healing his heart, she would disappear.

But he was going to ensure that Catriona did not just pass through his life. He meant to make her a permanent fixture, the mother of his children, matriarch of the family, the woman beneath whose portrait future generations of Rutleighs would pause to remark, "She never wore shoes, they say, and she slept with magical stones under the bed."

He touched her face in a gentle caress and nudged her legs apart with his knee. For an interval, he could do nothing but stare at her. Her body was female perfection, ripe curves and intriguing hollows, and he felt a momentary reluctance at bringing her pain; it promptly dissolved as she shifted restlessly beneath him.

"What are you thinking?" she whispered, rubbing her face against his hand.

"Let me show you." His breath came in hoarse exhalations as he brought his head to her breasts, sucking hard at her nipples. She arched against him and slid back into his arms with a shiver of submission. He wrapped his fist in her hair and sank down beside her, caressing the curves of her hip and belly before lowering his hand to her sex, spreading her open with his fingers.

Another shiver rocked her. He looked so intense. The feelings that burgeoned inside her were too much to bear. "Knight—"

"Shhh. I don't like to be interrupted when I'm making love."

He flexed his shoulders, reaching around with his left arm to make sure the sheet was secure. Catriona stole a look at his powerful body and swallowed a gasp at the sight. A current of unadulterated pleasure shot down deep into her belly. He was so beautiful, his body firmly muscled and blatantly male. Lying beneath all that restrained strength was the most exhilarating sensation in the world.

She raised her face to his. "What if someone sees us?"

He grunted. "With this sheet bumping up and down, I suppose we'll be mistaken for a restless spirit." Not that anything could stop him when he was so close. He curled his hands under her soft white bottom and lifted her against him. She was a natural seductress, to be sure, but he had to teach her a thing or two about the timing of her conversations. "Lift your legs around my back, and hold on tight. Oh, sweetheart, you have no idea how good you feel."

She had only the vaguest idea what to expect, and his first thrust, the deep stroke of his penis into her most tender tissue, took her by surprise. She tightened her muscles, but he did not stop except to reposition himself and thrust deeper, until she felt herself yield, the sensation causing her to gasp. Somewhere in her dazed state, she drew a breath, feeling him shower kisses on her face and throat as he muttered that he hadn't meant to hurt her.

"It's just that I can't—"

"Don't worry." She arched into him as she whispered the words. No, she wouldn't go back in time for anything. She wouldn't take away this moment even as their bodies strained together, even as he battered at her until she thought she would shatter. Then, just when she told herself that she could relax a little, he braced both his arms beneath her and rammed upward with all his might, driving the very breath from her body.

"I love you," he said, his hands gripping her hips as he impaled her. "I love you, and now I have exactly what I want."

She did shatter then; she broke apart into the most blissful state of being she had ever known. The pleasure that rippled through her belly was almost unbearable, so intense she could not be sure her heart was still beating. Then she felt him climax, warmth flooded her womb, and she could only sigh, bereft of words to describe what it meant to belong to him, to feel cherished for the first time in her life. Who would have thought this man with the forbidding cast-iron features capable of such tenderness?

She breathed another sigh into his neck as he snuggled down beside her, one muscular leg anchored over her hip as if to remind her that her place in the world was at his side.

"Oh, Knight." She whispered his name against his shoulder, savoring the musky scent of his skin. "Do you think, um, should we at least get dressed?"

"No." He locked his arms around her waist. "I'm never moving from this couch again. This is heaven."

"Except—oh, goodness!" She struggled into an upright position. "We have an audience, in those trees—"

Catriona had never seen a man move so fast in her life. One moment, she was being cuddled by a strong male body; the next, that body was hopping around into a pair of pantaloons and buttoning its shirt in a blur of panicked motion that made her dizzy to watch. She pulled the sheet over her head to muffle her giggles.

He yanked the sheet down to her shoulders, his hard-planed face stark white with anger. "Where is he? Jesus God, I'll kill the bastard."

She put her hand to her mouth as another giggle threatened to escape. "Who?"

"The man—or woman—who was watching us." He ran his hand through his crisp dark hair and looked around in annoyance. "And pull your dress up," he added in a furious undertone. "It's bad enough for me to be caught with my bare arse poking out from a sheet, but I won't have anyone ogling my bride-to-be's charms."

She grinned in delight, her giggles erupting into the tranquility of the night. "It was only an owl! An *owl* took flight over the treetops, and I first thought— oh, Knight, if you could have seen how ridiculous you—"

"An owl?" He glanced out disgustedly into the trees. "Oh, for God's sake, why didn't you say so in the first place?"

"As if I had the chance." She wiped a tear of mirth from the corner of her eye. "I suppose that charming little act came from some past experience of being caught by an irate husband?"

He scowled at her. "Actually, I was imagining Marigold on reconnaissance in the rosebushes. Can you imagine the old battleaxe's reaction if she found us in the altogether?"

She laughed again. "Especially if she saw you bobbing up and down like a puppet on a string."

"Bobbing?"

"Well, that thing—" Her eyes glittered with irrepressible mischief. "What did she call it, anyway, a tallypole?"

"Wag," he said after a brief startled silence as he wondered how this particular part of his anatomy had become the topic of family conversation. "A tally*wag.*

And the word *bobbing* makes it sound even more undignified. Where is that damn owl, anyway? Are you sure it was even there?"

"Of course I'm sure." She stared out into the woods, her mood suddenly subdued. "And I can't help thinking that those birds are going to bring me trouble," she added in a worried voice.

He turned abruptly and swore. "It looks as if you might be right about that."

"What?"

"About the trouble." He reached down and deftly rehooked her gown. "My sister is heading straight this way. Pull down your skirt."

She sprang from the couch, hiding behind his large frame. "Oh, goodness. I gave her my word I'd stay in my room tonight. How are we going to explain being together in the dark?"

"We aren't. Do you think you can make it back to the house by yourself if I distract her?"

"Of course I can." She came out from behind him. "Will you be able to manage her alone?"

He kissed her on the tip of her nose. "I think so. However, if I do not appear by breakfast tomorrow, you shall know where to look for my body."

She bit her lip. "Perhaps I should stay to defend you."

"And face a three-hour lecture into the wee hours on our immoral behavior?"

"You're right. Defend yourself."

She backed away, then paused on the steps of the summerhouse to blow him a kiss. He grinned and watched her disappear into the trees that encircled them. He was going to have to find a plausible excuse, and fast, to explain to Olivia his presence in a place he had avoided for almost three years now.

*   *   *

Murdo Grant sat in the woods, absorbing the healing powers of the ancient trees. A large owl fluttered down onto a branch above. Murdo smiled. Ah, yes. To those who could perceive, the birds served as messengers of the otherworld. Murdo and his cocky apprentice, Lamont, had been able to keep track of Catriona's whereabouts by sending their winged friends to find her. And now Murdo must simply wait for *her* to find *him*.

The moment approached. He had already touched her mind on several occasions, made her sense his existence. In fact, he could feel her mischievous presence nearby, her youthful energy clashing with his calm wisdom.

Come to me, Catriona. I am your own. We are both healers. The world does not understand us.

He ached to see her again, to reconcile, to guide her into her powers. Above all, he wanted to make sure she did not follow in her tragic mother's footsteps.

He smiled. She was coming.

Chapter
18

❦

*C*atriona *was congratulating herself* on skirting the summerhouse undetected when she spotted Mrs. Evans standing guard on the bridge. Now, how was she supposed to get back into her room without Olivia seeing her? She glanced up as a blur of light from the house caught her eye. Oh, wonderful. Wendell was in the bedroom window, waving a candle like a French spy warning away a ship from the cliffs of Dover, which meant that Marigold must be on guard in the hallway. This did present a problem.

She had no choice but to retreat into the woods until the coast was clear. She glanced back over her shoulder at the summerhouse. There was something unfair about having to go into hiding after such a heart-stirring experience.

She hugged herself as the breeze scattered the leaves around her feet. She was shivering with sheer happiness, instead of shame at her complete ruination. She felt so alive she could run across the moor in the moonlight like a young pagan. She was his.

Voices drifted from the summerhouse. She retreated impulsively into the sheltering womb of the woods. She wasn't afraid of nature, not even at night. It was only people who had ever hurt her. Animals merely wanted to be left alone, to obey their instincts.

She stopped in her tracks and stared through the trees, the nerves at the base of her spine prickling.

Across the clearing sat a tidy heap of dirt beneath the very tree where she had buried the Earth stone. No squirrel had kicked up that mound of soil, nor had a woodland creature left the footprints that led away toward the moor.

She took a deep breath and forced herself to walk forward. She didn't want to discover anything that would ruin her lighthearted mood. Just for once, she wanted to pretend she was like any other ordinary young woman. She peered down into the gaping hole, then plunged her hand into the soft earth. It was as she'd feared. The stone was gone.

Uncle Murdo had found her.

Knight lounged back awkwardly on the couch, his long legs dangling over the walnut-inlaid arm. He felt too contented, too hopeful, too damn pleased with himself to resent Olivia's interference. After all, they both loved Catriona and wanted the best for her— a good marriage, a secure future. And in that future, Knight would have plenty of opportunities to enjoy his young wife's passionate nature. He sighed deeply, remembering the scent of her, female musk and herbs, remembering the precise moment when he had embedded himself inside her. God help him, his heart had actually stopped beating, and he had almost climaxed like a young boy on his first sexual adventure.

Olivia pushed his feet to the floor in an angry swoop. "Where is she, you scoundrel?"

He sat up, so caught up in his erotic memory that her actual arrival had surprised him. "Who?"

"Don't treat me like a ninnyhammer, Knight." She was practically panting with fury, her hands on her slender hips. "I am not one of your buffle-headed women. I know that smile of yours and what it means. Where have you hidden her?"

He grinned. "Buffle-headed women?"

She pulled the sheet from the couch. Heavens above, he thought in amazement. Was she expecting to find Catriona cowering beneath it? The wheelbarrow came next. His eyebrows rose as he watched her slowly touch a stalk of withered bluebell, turning it between her fingers.

"Olivia," he said gently.

She turned, her eyes meeting his. She had to be remembering that day, he thought, as he put his feet to the floor. She had to be remembering the moment he'd told her Lionel was not coming home. All of a sudden, he stood and wanted to put his arms around her, as he had done then, to promise her that he would take care of her, that she would never have to be alone.

"You sneak," she said. "You—you tallywag waver."

His eyes widened. "What did you call me?"

She threw the withered stalk of bluebell at him. "Don't give me that wounded air, lounging in your lair like a big tiger who's just made a tasty snack of a mongoose. You ought to be ashamed. Just tell me where she is. Where have you put her, you monster of immorality?"

He blinked, unable to believe his ears. He had expected her to cry, to crumple, to relive the day she'd learned she was a widow, not to insult and assault him with dead flowers. This was such a wonderful surprise, the best evidence of her healing, that he broke into a smile.

She gave a little shriek of disgust. "And you have the gall to actually grin about your conquest!"

He sobered as she looked around for something more effective to throw at him than a bluebell. "If you don't tell me where she is right now—"

He ducked the musty cushion she hurled at him. "She's probably fast asleep in her room, unless all the commotion you are making has disturbed her. Look— there's a light in her window right now. Shame on *you*, Olivia, for waking her up."

Another cushion came hurtling at his head. He backed around the wheelbarrow, throwing his leg over the summerhouse railing to escape into the garden. He didn't like the way she was looking at that rusty shovel.

"The light in her window is Wendell, you idiot, as if you didn't know," she said. "As if this tryst weren't planned, and him taking your side. And she isn't in her room, because I checked. She left a rolled-up blanket and one of Aunt Marigold's wigs under the bedcovers to fool me."

He chuckled softly. "Check again, Olivia," he said, confident that his resourceful Catriona would have made it back upstairs by now. "I think you are mistaken."

He jumped down into the garden as she grabbed the

shovel and rushed the railing. "That's right," she shouted at him. "Run, you rogue. Run with your tail between your legs. You can't hide from me forever. If I don't catch you tonight, I will at the breakfast table tomorrow."

Catriona spun about in the direction of the summerhouse, staring through the trees. "Oh, my. What was that?"

The short red-haired man who had been waiting patiently for her stepped away from the tree that had concealed him. "I believe it was the sound of some heavy object being thrown in anger."

She swallowed over the lump of anxiety in her throat and turned to face the uncle whom her mother had banished from their lives when Catriona was a child. The reason for the breach between brother and sister had remained a mystery in her mind, some dark family secret not to be discussed, an "adult" matter. Catriona had always suspected the estrangement had evolved over her father, but whatever the reason, Uncle Murdo had become a forbidden topic of conversation in the house.

An irate female voice shouted a string of insults into the night. The actual words were muffled by the time they penetrated the woods; the meaning was clear enough.

Catriona shook her head in distress. "That's Olivia and Knight," she said distractedly. "I should have stayed to help him."

"But you sensed me calling to you," Murdo said in satisfaction. "You knew I would come, didn't you?"

She turned to examine him more closely. He had settled down like a garden gnome on the boulder she had passed a few moments ago. His red beard reached to his chest, and his tartan jacket and trousers seemed too large for his frail-boned frame.

"You're short," she said in surprise. "I always pictured you as a giant."

"You are hardly a Titan yourself," he said wryly.

"And you have red hair."

His bushy red eyebrows met in a frown. "You look just like your mother."

"Thank you."

"You sound like her, too."

"Oh." She clasped her hands behind her back, not coming any closer to him but not running away, as she wished to, either. She had to admit to being curious about this branch of the family, which had caused so much havoc in her bloodlines. There were questions she was dying to ask him, too, such as, "Am I going to have these horrible visions all my life?" "Why don't butterflies live longer?" "What did you and Mama quarrel over?" And "How do you make those birds of prey do your bidding?"

"What have you done with my mother's stone?" she asked simply.

He stepped closer, his triangular face level with hers. "I am returning it to its rightful place."

"Then give it back. It belongs to me."

"Long ago, one of your ancestresses and a powerful wizard named Michael Scot stole the stone from a holy well, and it was eventually passed down to your mother. Until the stone is returned to its home, you are destined to know unhappiness. We must go to the well together."

She studied his face, the keen hazel eyes and sharp features. "How do I know you won't take the stone for yourself?"

"If it was the stone I wanted, I would be gone."

She felt another strange prickle steal down her spine. "Then go."

"I came for you. Your old playmate Lamont wants to see you."

She recoiled a step, aware of wings fluttering in the trees above them. "I am not going anywhere. I'm engaged."

He glanced past her to the house, his face wistful. "Following right in your mother's foolish footsteps, believing in a man, a Sassenach, who will break your heart. 'Tis the curse, Catriona. End it now."

"He loves me," she said slowly, as if to convince herself.

"That is just what your mother said about the earl. And yet, if I have not misinterpreted the situation, this man you defend has persuaded you to conduct a clandestine affair with him. That is what you are doing out at this hour?"

A clandestine affair. She almost laughed, but how could she possibly explain the vigilance of Olivia and Aunt Marigold, their determination to marry her off? Oh, how could she explain that Knight's own sister was the reason for all the secrecy, and not any dark, twisted motive on his part?

"This is different, Uncle Murdo."

He sighed sadly. "She thought so, too."

"You don't understand. I am part of their family."

"You are my family, Catriona Grant, and I have come to claim you."

"Well, you certainly waited long enough to admit that fact." She narrowed her eyes. "Where were you all those years Mama and I struggled to survive?"

He shook his head. "Your mother banished me

from your home for speaking the truth about your father. She laughed in my face when I offered to find a more suitable mate for her. I merely stated the obvious: the earl used her and had no desire to claim you as his daughter."

The words hurt, so bluntly spoken, stung her in some vulnerable place inside, but perhaps not as much as they might have months ago. No, she was growing stronger. The world would not end because her father hadn't loved her. At one time, to admit that would have caused her more pain than she could bear.

"It's too late for us, Uncle Murdo," she said, backing away another step. "Aside from the people here, the only person alive who ever cared for me is James. So even if my father did not love Mama, there was some good in him, to have raised a son like James."

His mouth twisted in a scornful smile. "James, a useless specimen of manhood if I have ever seen one."

"Have you visited him?" she asked in surprise.

"Doubtless the useless fool does not even remember our meeting," he said. "I went to his castle in search of you, only to find him half dead, weeping like a bairn over a bottle for the money he had lost."

"He promised me he would stop," she said, flooded with guilt that she had not been there to help.

"Then his promises are as worthless as those his father made," Murdo said bitterly. "But look at you," he said, his face softening. "A beautiful young woman who need not worry about such things. 'Tis a marriage we should be planning."

"I have made my own choice, Uncle Murdo."

"A poor one, no doubt."

"I love him."

"Him?" He scowled. "A Sassenach noble, arrogant and handsome, I suppose?"

She grinned helplessly. "Oh, aye. He is both."

He drew himself erect. "I can take you into the presence of kings and queens in foreign lands."

Part of her was a little tempted, to explore the secret side of her self. "He's taught me the waltz and the minuet."

He looked scornful. "The dances I would teach you are of the divine, of mastering the elements."

"It's too late, Uncle Murdo." On impulse, she went up to him and kissed his bearded cheek; he smelled pleasantly of mint and rosemary. "They need me, you see," she whispered ruefully. "And I need them, too. I think I've finally found where I belong. Don't spoil it for me."

She had just reached the garden when an image began to take shape in her mind. She didn't think it was a typical vision. There was none of the usual physical manifestations, no tingling or disorientation. But suddenly the impression of a young girl in distress touched her thoughts, jolted her. Something about the girl's features stopped her in her tracks. She closed her eyes, concentrating, willing the connection not to fade.

James, she realized in astonishment. The girl was his mirror likeness—what she was seeing must be her own lost niece, Gaela, the daughter who had been stolen from James by her grandparents. The girl appeared to be in trouble. She was standing at—oh, dear God, it was a grave. She was crying, resisting the angry man who tried to take her away. And Cat could hear her young, heartrending voice.

"Why did they die? I don't want to go with you. I want my papa."

The image started to dissolve. Frantic, Cat willed herself to focus on the smallest detail. The girl was dragged from the graveyard, thrown into a dog cart, driven down a winding street. A tavern with the sign of a red stag. The sound of a waterfall. A crossroads with a stone cross marked—

Nothing. Blank. Gone.

Cat closed her eyes and shivered, feeling helpless and frightened for the girl.

Several minutes later, she returned to the house.

She drew back against the balustrade as a tall figure materialized from the shadows to interrupt her escape upstairs. "Don't make a sound," Knight whispered, gathering her in his arms. "The Gorgons are definitely on to us."

She laid her head on his chest, her heart beating hard. For a moment, she had been afraid that Uncle Murdo had somehow gotten into the house before her. But this was Knight, her protector and, as of tonight, lover. Her anxiety fled, replaced by the sheer happiness she always felt with him. "I thought Olivia might have murdered you," she whispered. "I heard her shouting."

"I was worried when you didn't come back to the house," he said quietly. "Where were you, anyway? Not off dropping stones in the pond to cure Howard's headache?"

"Am I forbidden to do so?"

"Not at all." He broke into a grin. "Drop to your heart's delight. I was really afraid that Alistair might have been lurking in the woods, waiting to abduct the innocent young maiden."

"Except that he's too late."

"Hmm. It's a shame, isn't it?" He pulled her closer, locking his arms around her waist. "Poor fellow has dreadful timing. Perhaps I ought to send him a polite note, just to let him know you're mine."

She felt a flush of heat go through her where their bodies touched. "That isn't a very polite look on your face, though. It's—predatory."

He threaded his long fingers through her hair. "You'd better get used to it, Lady Rutleigh. I'm not sharing you with anyone." His heavy-lidded gaze moved over her, not missing the worry on her face. "But you never did answer me. Where have you been while I was almost murdered by my own sister?"

"Where was I?" she repeated.

"That's what I said."

"Where could I have gone?"

"That is a good question." He arched his brow. "Now, answer it."

She glanced away. Knight's eyes narrowed at her faint hesitation, but he waited patiently for a reply. Where would she have gone? he wondered. What trouble could she possibly have gotten into in such a brief time? Lord, was this what love did to a man's state of mind?

"I had to hide in the woods," she said slowly. "Mrs. Evans was posted on the bridge. Is everyone asleep?"

He relaxed slightly. Going to drastic lengths to avoid his housekeeper made perfect sense. "Marigold is snoring fitfully outside your door," he said. "Wendell said he practically had to climb over her to remove the rope you left dangling from the window."

"What about Olivia?" she whispered.

"My sister exhausted herself trying to kill me with a shovel."

"Oh, dear." So that was the crash she and Murdo had heard in the woods. "I don't think I want to hear the details."

"No doubt you will, anyway, at the breakfast table." He started to laugh, thinking how absurd it was for Olivia to try to stop him. "She called me a monster of immorality."

She bit her lip, looking horrified. "You didn't tell her that we—"

"I didn't say a word to her." His hands moved down her back to her bottom, gripping her gently. It was going to take more than family or any earthly force to keep him away from Catriona. "I don't think I fooled her, though. I am so desperately in love with you that I can't hide it. Damnation, I don't *want* to hide it," he said huskily. "Come upstairs to my room. I want more of you tonight."

"Your room?" she whispered, already melting at the thought.

He brushed his jaw against her cheek. "She can throw another shovel at me in the morning if she likes. Sleeping with you is worth it. Come on."

He drew her back, catching her hands in his. She looked at his large figure and shivered, dangerously tempted. Arabella was right; Catriona knew she was completely in his power.

"No," she whispered. "Not again tonight."

He gave a low, devilish laugh. "Yes. Please."

"No. Oh." Her gasp evolved into a helpless giggle as he swung her over his powerful shoulder only to lower her slowly back to the floor.

"Um, perhaps you're right," he said in a strained undertone.

"Right about what?" she whispered in confusion.

He cleared his throat again. "Perhaps this isn't the best time to read those Shakespearean sonnets."

"Shakespearean sonnets? Knight, have you lost your wig? I—oh." She looked around his huge frame to see Mrs. Evans at the bottom of the stairs, arms folded disapprovingly across her chest. "Yes, I see exactly what you mean."

He carefully edged away from Catriona, whispering, "She must have been assigned the graveyard watch."

"Graveyard is right," she whispered, giggling helplessly. "She looks as if she wants to put you in one."

"May I bring you something, my lord?" the housekeeper asked in a crisp tone.

He cleared his throat. "We, ah, we were looking for something to read. In bed."

"Alone," Catriona added, frowning up at him. "I mean, later. After we read together. But not in bed."

Knight rolled his eyes. "Could you dig that grave any deeper, darling?"

"I only meant that we aren't going to read together. In bed, that is."

"I always read in bed," Knight said, leaning back against the railing to enjoy this.

Catriona wanted to pinch him, the unprincipled rogue. "Not with me."

His smile was diabolical. "Not yet."

"May I suggest the Bible as a source of moral inspiration?" Mrs. Evans asked dryly.

He stared down at the housekeeper, his look clearly drawing the line between servant and employer. "And may I suggest that everyone mind his own business where my morals are concerned?"

"Your morals are quite clearly beyond redemption," Olivia said from the darkened landing above. "Catriona's are not, or at least I assume so." She gave the sash of her dressing robe a firm yank. "Come upstairs, young lady. We shall discuss your behavior in the morning."

Knight winked at Catriona. "It seems as if our discussion on the sonnets will have to wait until tomorrow, too. Shame. I was so looking forward to it."

She sighed, lifting her skirt to obey Olivia's summons. But as she turned from Knight, the gust of violent wind that rattled the panels of the front door caused her to freeze in her tracks.

The dances I would teach you are of the divine, of mastering the elements.

Oh, of all things. Was that queer old uncle of hers trying to prove a point, or was the wind only a coincidence? After all, there *had* been a breeze earlier in the evening. She was on pins and needles now, half expecting her meddlesome relative to come bursting into the entrance hall at any moment, worrying about James's daughter, if that was who she had seen. What good did it do to know the girl was in trouble if no one could find her? Where could she be?

"That's quite a strong wind," Olivia exclaimed, rubbing her arms. "Hurry up, Catriona. You'll catch a chill, you in that thin dress and no shoes again."

She nodded, pausing as Knight stepped down beside her, to whisper boldly in her ear, "I just wanted to tell you that I'm sorry your first time had to be in the summerhouse. I didn't plan it—well, I hoped it would happen—and I also wanted to tell you, in case I didn't make it clear before, that I love you."

She glanced up, staring into his eyes as an enormous clap of thunder resounded above the roof.

Olivia jumped back a step. "What on earth was *that?*"

Catriona compressed her lips, gazing up past Knight's face to the ceiling. *No, Uncle Murdo,* she thought angrily. *Go away. You will not impress me with your owls and loud noises. This is where I belong, not on some windswept hill casting spells with an awful old man.*

"Storm by morning," Mrs. Evans predicted, domestic matters apparently taking precedence over internal affairs. "I'd best have the gardener cover my seedlings before they're blown away." She turned, then paused to glance up at Catriona. "Sutherland," she said, right out of the blue.

"Sutherland?" Catriona said slowly. For some reason, the distant look on the housekeeper's face sent a shiver down her shoulders. "What do you mean?"

Mrs. Evans sounded embarrassed. "Sutherland is in Scotland, isn't it?"

Cat nodded. "Yes, but not where I came—"

"Oh, never mind," the housekeeper said, her cheeks red. "The name just popped into my head, but never mind. 'Tis the Welsh in me again. I'm sure it means nothing."

"Sutherland is in a rather remote area of Scotland," Knight said, watching Catriona's face. "Do you know someone there?"

"I don't think so," she said, shivering again. Could Gaela possibly be in Sutherland? Could Mrs. Evans have received the message that Catriona was straining to hear?

"Enough of this nonsense," Olivia said. "Upstairs, Catriona. Now."

Chapter

19

〜

For a few moments after she awakened the next morning, Catriona lay in bed savoring her precious memories of the night before. Aside from the tenderness between her thighs and a general glow of well-being, she really noted no difference in her body; she hadn't sprouted wings or anything, but oh, how lightheaded and hopeful she felt, what rapture to be in love and to be loved in return by her wicked English viscount.

Everything was perfect, romantic, exciting. She had packed a bag for their elopement and had hidden it at the back of the wardrobe. The journey to Devon from the Borders, so grim and arduous with Thomas, suddenly took on heart-stirring possibilities in the reverse. Sleeping in a remote hillside inn with Knight seemed more like an adventure than an ordeal. What did discomforts such as lumpy mattresses and wrinkled sheets matter when one woke up in those protective arms? How grand to show him off to James, who, if he were not too angry or drunk to recognize her, would be grateful for Knight's financial help. She only wished she knew what that troubling glimpse of James's daughter meant, and if Mrs. Evans's comment about Sutherland was inspired. If the girl could be found, James might have a reason to live again. It gave her hope.

And then she remembered Murdo and that nonsense about the stone's curse and his mention of her childhood nemesis Lamont Montgomery. Well, the stone wasn't in her possession anymore so how could it hurt her? Let Murdo drop it back into the well if that was where it belonged.

She dressed in a demure primrose-yellow muslin day gown and practically floated downstairs. She really ought to wipe the grin off her face and look suitably repentant for Olivia's sake before she confronted her at breakfast. Where was everybody, anyway? The house seemed unnaturally quiet—

And then she knew. She sensed the troublemaker's presence in the house.

Uncle Murdo had come.

She walked woodenly to the blue formal drawing room, her heart lodged in her throat. The door was partially open, and she slipped inside to see Murdo seated in the corner, Aunt Marigold pouring him tea. Knight was standing by the window, his face drawn in deep lines of displeasure. Olivia, perched beside Wendell on the sofa, looked up at Cat in distress, as if to say, *Well, this is the final straw. Even I cannot undo the sort of trouble you are facing now. He is your uncle. I am only a distant cousin-in-law.*

"This—this *person* claims you are his niece,

Catriona," she said in a bewildered tone. "He has just informed us that he's come to take you home."

Knight stared at his beloved, one dark eyebrow raised in amused speculation. Well, at least he wasn't angry, but the almost imperceptible, helpless shake of his head told her that he was perfectly willing to let her handle this little mess by herself. It wasn't fair, she thought. How was she to know a relative she had assumed dead would reappear to cause problems at the happiest time in her life?

She pretended to study Murdo in great astonishment, widening her eyes at his warm smile. "There must be a misunderstanding," she said. "I have never seen this man before in my life." And then, in an inaudible whisper, not wishing to be caught in another lie, she added, "Well, at least not since I was six years old."

Knight watched the scene unfold with an air of resignation from the window. While he felt like scolding his betrothed for withholding yet another secret, he was too deeply in love with her to let the matter come between them. So this was what, or, rather, who had unsettled her last night, and could he blame her for not sharing such a peculiar uncle with the world?

He couldn't decide what to make of Murdo himself, with his slightly pointy ears and scraggly silver-red beard. He resembled some sort of domesticated gnome, a brownie in threadbare tartan who might at any moment leap up from his chair and disappear into the mist.

"Her mother and I had a falling out over her foolish infatuation with a nobleman," Murdo was saying, with a meaningful look at Knight in case he was dense to draw the parallel.

Knight frowned. A suitor he could toss out on his ear. An insulting uncle was another matter entirely.

"It was ever so much more than a falling out," Catriona said, settling stiffly into a chair, "and her love for him was more than infatuation."

"A love that was never returned," Murdo said. "My dear sister wasted her precious life on that scoundrel. He never visited once after the day he ruined her."

"How would you know?" Catriona asked, sitting forward to glare at him.

Knight came up behind her chair, placing his hand on her shoulder like an anchor. He did not want this man upsetting her with reminders of what could not be changed. "What part of Scotland are you from?" he asked conversationally.

Murdo hesitated. "Our family is originally from the Highlands, sir, but I have recently returned to Peebles."

Aunt Marigold covertly adjusted her wig before passing Murdo a plate of raspberry tartlets. "Is that anywhere near Aberdeen?" she asked. "I have an old friend there myself."

"No, madam," he answered, gracing her efforts at kindness with a brief smile, "but I hear it is a charming city, and so, that a friend of yours should settle there is no surprise to me."

"Hmm. Yes. Yes, well." She took a bite of her tart to divert attention from a blush, nodding intently as if he were the most fascinating visitor she had ever entertained. What a shame the unpleasant matter of Catriona's father came between them, this earl who bore a distant relationship to Lionel, thereby also connecting Marigold to his behavior. But then, every family suffered its black sheep. One only had to take a look at Knight, for example, with his taciturn manner and amorous nature, to realize that fact.

"I suppose that one has no choice but to forgive in such circumstances," she said, her blush deepening as she realized she had spoken her innermost thoughts out loud. "Family entanglements are so complicated, aren't they?"

"Indeed they are." Murdo smiled at her again before directing a frown at his wayward niece. "But the point I wish to emphasize is that young people these days think they know better than their elders. Times may have changed, but human nature has not."

"How true," Marigold said.

Catriona heaved a loud sigh, earning a scowl of mild rebuke from Marigold. "What is true," she said, "is that I am no longer a child, a fact my uncle has obviously forgotten. But then, having spent the last decade or so pretending that my mother and I did not exist, his lack of attention should not surprise me."

Knight gave her shoulder a reassuring squeeze. "She is of a legal age to marry without consent. In Scotland, I believe, this would not be an issue."

Murdo shot him a look. "I believe it would. There is more to a marriage than legal consent."

"Indeed there is," Knight said heartily, wondering what this was leading to. He tried to catch Wendell's eye, to gauge his friend's reaction to the situation, but Duke, he realized with a sting of shock, had not stopped staring at Olivia all morning. In fact, now that Knight thought about it, his old friend always seemed to be staring at her these days.

He straightened his shoulders. Could it be? Wendell and his sister? He didn't know whether to knock Duke's head off or shake his hand. Olivia? The victim of Wendell's boyhood pranks, imprisoned in the Meacham manor attic with a skeleton, its skull backlit with one of the old duchess's beeswax candles? Some chance of a love match there. Olivia and Wendell knew each other too well. Olivia was three years older than him. Wendell had loved Lionel, too.

But what *had* Wendell been doing the night before while he was supposed to be diverting Olivia? Knight's eyebrows drew into a scowl of brotherly concern.

Olivia's cultured voice, a quaver of uncertainty beneath the coolness, entered the conversation. "Of course, you are absolutely right about the matter of marriage, which is why, not knowing Catriona could count on your assistance, Marigold and I took it upon ourselves to find her a suitable husband."

Murdo glanced disapprovingly at Knight. "Him?"

Olivia's lips tightened. "That depends on whom you ask. Actually, there are a few other local candidates, two of whom must be given serious consideration."

"You have obviously gone to great trouble on my niece's account—"

"My sister has wasted her time," Knight interjected, "not to mention my money."

"It was all quite unnecessary," Murdo said. "I have already found the perfect match for Catriona, a young man more than equal to her . . . talents. In fact, before her mother and I quarreled, we privately agreed that he would be a desirable mate."

"Who the devil are you talking about?" Catriona

asked, held in place only by Knight's hand on her shoulder. "I don't remember any of this—this mating business."

"Well, of course not," Murdo said. "You were only a bairn, and Lamont was nine—"

"Lamont? Lamont Montgomery?" This time, she did fly off the chair, shock draining her cheeks of color. "That awful, that wicked—"

"So you do remember him," Murdo said in approval.

"He set the village kirk on fire," she exclaimed. "Everyone talked about it for years afterward."

Murdo smiled fondly at the memory. "That was a long time ago, before Lamont had his abilities under control. He's quite a success now. Besides, a lightning rod hit the kirk, or so the story went."

"And what was Lamont doing on the church roof during the sermon?" Catriona asked.

Marigold pursed her lips. "My, you seem to remember this young man quite well yourself. I don't suppose he has a title?"

"Not in this world," Murdo said enigmatically.

Knight folded his arms over his chest and said, rather rudely, "Well, if he was that interested in marrying her, you'd think he would come in person at least to renew her acquaintance, if not to propose himself."

Murdo glanced up at him. "Did I forget to mention that we traveled from Scotland together? Lamont had to stop for some business at Annan, but he should arrive here by dinner tonight."

"By dinner tonight," Wendell said, smiling across the room at Knight. "What do you think of that? The Husband Hunt has yielded some rather interesting quarry."

What Knight thought of this controversial figure from Catriona's past could hardly be expressed in polite company. But whoever Lamont was, he was certainly not going to interfere with the elopement, which reminded Knight that *he* had no business standing there with plans to be made before the journey north.

"Excuse me," he said to the room in general. "Wendell and I have some business matters to discuss. We'll be in the study should anyone require our company."

"Oh, your study," Olivia said, not quite catching herself before Knight saw her sneak a look at Wendell and blush.

So he was right. Something had gone on between the two of them. While he and Catriona had been making passionate love in the summerhouse last night, Wendell and Olivia had been in the study—doing what?

Catriona threw him an annoyed look as he left the room, no doubt wondering why he was abandoning her to this social torture. He gave her a beguiling smile from the door, then mouthed, "Tonight."

"I bet you'd forgotten that the manufacturing chemist from Bristol is due to arrive on Friday," Wendell said as they walked down the hall to the study.

"No," Knight said. "I hadn't forgotten."

"Well, I'm not sure I should be the one to interview him," Wendell said, pausing outside the door. "After all, you're the one with the scientific mind. At least, until recently."

Knight looked at him. "Shall we take this conversation inside my study? I believe you feel quite comfortable there."

"What is that supposed to mean?" Wendell asked.

"I don't know." Knight brushed past him. "Why don't you tell me?"

Wendell followed him into the room, looking perplexed. "Someone clearly did not have a good night's sleep. I think we'll all be glad when you get married and settle down. What do you want me to do while you're gone?"

Knight removed a leather portfolio from his desk drawer, deliberately not looking up. "Everything the chemist needs to know about the porcelain works is in these papers. Take him for a tour, if you like, ask his opinion on whether it's worth digging for china clay. As far as other matters, well, it's obvious you know how to keep yourself occupied."

Wendell sat down on the couch. "What?"

"How long have you been in love with my sister?"

Wendell paused. "Probably since I was seven. Why?"

"Oh, I don't know," Knight said wryly. "Just curious, I suppose. Not that it's any of my business—you didn't seduce her in here last night, did you?"

"I wouldn't tell you if I did."

Their eyes met across the desk. "I don't suppose you'll tell me how she took it, either," Knight said after a long silence. "Or am I the only one who didn't know?"

Wendell shifted his shoulders back against the chair and stared up at the ceiling. "I don't think she knew how to take it. In fact, I've probably shocked her. But"—he glanced down at his friend—"it's all your fault, anyway."

"My fault?" Knight said, his large hands folded in a tight knot over the portfolio. "Kindly explain that remark."

"Well." Wendell sighed. "It was all the romance in the air, the way you and Catriona stole glances at each other at the dance, and sneaking out to the summerhouse. No one is going to be surprised if, nine months from now, there's a bouncing baby in the family cradle for the proud parents to gush over. It made me sad and envious. And impatient. I'm twenty-seven next month."

"Olivia and Wendell." Knight broke into a devilish grin. "You poor fool."

"Do you think Lionel would mind?" Wendell asked anxiously.

"I can't see that Lionel has much of a say in the matter." Knight tapped his fingers against the portfolio. "It's Olivia you have to convince."

"What about you?"

"What do I have to do with it?"

"That's exactly what I mean," Wendell said. "Before you met Catriona, we wouldn't have gotten two minutes into this conversation before you killed me for touching your sister."

"You touched her?" Knight sat forward, frowning.

"What do you think?"

"I think that you would be good for each other," Knight said carefully. "I do wish, however, that you had waited until after I was married to—there aren't going to be *two* babies to gush over nine months hence, I hope."

Wendell stared up at the ceiling again. "The crew of the *Zephyr* have been notified of your arrival. What time do you want my carriage to meet you in the woods?"

"At eleven o'clock, if possible."

"Olivia will be upset," Wendell murmured.

"Then you may console her."

Wendell smiled.

Lamont Montgomery sat at the dining table in the baronial manor house where he was an honored guest, but his attention wandered. Word of his supernatural talents had reached certain social circles, and he was often invited to these private parties in the hope that he would "perform." On occasion, he did.

He could throw his shadow to confound an enemy. He could enchant animals and raise a marvelous storm. But he had not yet perfected the art of shapeshifting, even though Murdo counseled him that such skill would come with time.

A frown darkened Lamont's arrogantly chiseled face. He was impatient. Why should someone of his abilities have to wait? He did not want to increase his power for evil's sake, but neither did he wish to become some silly old wizard whose primary calling was curing warts.

He needed the Earth stone. He ached to know the power that had made Michael Scot a legend. He ached to harness the elements for the sheer exhilaration of it.

Murdo wanted him to marry his runaway niece.

Lamont cast an uninterested glance at the young ladies seated around him, their figures ripe in dampened gowns. Their pretty faces and vain chatter made him wonder if there even existed a woman in this world who could capture his heart. He smiled at the memory of Catriona, a beauty with a mind and power of her own. He wondered if time had changed her as much as it had him. Would she prove to be the mate he sought?

He rose from the table, ignoring the petulant pleas that he stay and entertain his host. Could he walk through walls? a young woman begged. Could he remove Lady Beatrice's garter without touching her? an older man asked slyly.

"Perhaps another time," he said with a polite smile. He moved toward the door, then paused, narrowing his eyes. With no apparent effort at all, without moving a muscle, he concentrated and extinguished every candle in the room, leaving the guests in a smoky haze of awestruck silence.

He was already outside when his startled audience broke into applause. He had tarried long enough, avoiding the inevitable. It was time to renew his stormy relationship with Catriona Grant.

Chapter
20

❧

*K*night and Catriona made a point of ignoring each other for the rest of the day. It was not difficult with Murdo and Marigold overshadowing their every move. But the plans had already been laid; enlisting Howard as an ally, Knight had managed to stash their luggage in Wendell's carriage for the journey to the coast, although he had to admit it seemed rather extreme, two grown people eloping to escape their family's interference.

"Seems like a lot of bother when a special license would have done the trick," Howard remarked on their way back to the house. And then, as if realizing he had once again overstepped his bounds, he added, "Of course, it all has a very romantic air about it, my lord. A duke's carriage waiting in the woods to whisk you—"

"Just don't get any ideas about running off with

the parlor maid while I'm gone," Knight said as they paused at the edge of the estate.

He stopped to examine the house, wondering how it would weather a growing family. When he returned, he would be married, entering a new phase of life. Would there really be children playing fairies and Robin Hood in the garden a few years hence? Everyone grew old, but not everyone had the good fortune to find love, and even those who did sometimes lost it. Take Lionel and Olivia. Would Lionel mind if she married their childhood friend, or did it even matter? Would *he* want Catriona to remarry or remain a widow forever in the event he died before her?

He wasn't sure how he felt about Olivia marrying Wendell. It certainly changed the casual path they had been following. He and Duke would become brothers-in-law, uncles, fathers. Solid and settled-down husbands who stood by the fireplace and doled out advice they had never taken in their lives. But at the end of those lives, there would be a family to mourn their passing, a clan forged of entanglements, celebrations, and heartaches, though, he hoped, not too many.

He liked the thought of being surrounded by loved ones and friends, as long as he and his viscountess did not have to sneak off to the summerhouse to be alone. Which made him wonder if this wouldn't be a good time to add another wing where Marigold could stay when she wasn't visiting Olivia and Wendell. The woman was getting too old to live by herself. And there was Catriona's half brother James to consider. He might come to winter here.

"There's the old dragon Mrs. E now." Howard's voice brought him out of his reverie. "Hide behind the hedge, my lord, before she sees us and asks what we were doing in the woods."

Knight reached out and pulled the young man back into the open by the scruff of his neck. "I am not hiding from my housekeeper on my own estate, do you hear me? The situation is absurd. Can an Englishman no longer take a walk in the woods these days without falling under suspicion? One would think that the little dictator himself had infiltrated Devon."

"Oh, no," Howard cried, practically hopping up and down. "There's Miss Grant, coming this way, and Mrs. E is ploughing a path straight toward us."

"Howard," Knight said in a stern voice, "get a hold of yourself this instant."

Howard shook his head. "But Mrs. E is going to guess, don't you see, my lord? She's going to ask us why we were in the woods together, and then she'll find the carriage, and—"

"Just keep walking, and let me answer the questions," Knight said sharply, nudging the man toward the bridge. "And for pity's sake, Howard, open your eyes. Mrs. Evans is not the firing squad."

"No," Howard muttered. "The firing squad is fast and kind. Mrs. E is death by slow torture."

Mrs. Evans stopped at the foot of the bridge, breathless and clearly out of sorts. "There. I've found you at last, my lord. Mr. Aubrey said you were in the study, and then Smythe said he'd seen you in the stables, and—"

Knight clasped his hands behind his back. "May I help you, Mrs. Evans?"

She frowned briefly at Howard before replying. "It's about the dinner party tonight, my lord."

Knight hesitated. From the corner of his eye, he could see Catriona flitting around the summerhouse like a pale yellow butterfly. The sight of her completely diverted him, especially when he remembered exactly what they had done on that musty couch the previous evening and would be doing for countless enjoyable years to come.

She glanced up and gave him a negligent little wave that drove him wild. Even from there, she tempted him, teased him with that self-conscious smile and that languid way she had of moving. Boys chased butterflies but rarely caught them. He wanted her on that couch again; he wanted to be inside her and feel her legs wrapped around his waist, squeezing the life from him.

"—and seeing that they are both Scottish," Mrs. Evans said, "I had thought it would be nice to start off with pheasant soup."

Knight looked down at her. "What?"

"Our guests, my lord. Miss Grant's uncle and the young man he is expecting."

Knight stole another look at his intended as she sauntered past the summerhouse. Why wasn't she upstairs resting for the journey? Oh, well, he supposed she could sleep in the carriage on the way. At least the weather was mild, last night's peculiar winds had abated, and they should not be delayed.

"For dessert, my lord?" Mrs. Evans raised her voice. "What would you like for dessert?"

Knight smiled at Catriona. She lowered her gaze demurely and knelt to pick up something from the path. What had she found now? "Not another stone," he thought aloud. Her trunk already weighed a ton.

He gazed around, catching the grin that crept

across Howard's face. Mrs. Evans, however, looked as
if she might cry.

"I had no idea you were that tired of my scones,
my lord," she said, her manner prickly and defensive.
"I only made them so often because they're what
Miss Grant fancies, but of course even *I* would not
dream of serving them at a dinner party."

"I did not say scone, Mrs. Evans, I said stone. As in
'Not another stone.' Oh, never mind."

"I had thought to make a trifle," Mrs. Evans said.
Her lower lip had begun to tremble. "That is, if it
meets your approval."

"That would be very nice, I'm sure," he said placat-
ingly. "The world loves your trifles." Now, where had
Catriona got off to? And why wasn't she sitting in the
drawing room with her long-lost uncle? On second
thought, perhaps he didn't want her in Murdo's company, not if the man was hoping to marry her off to
some childhood prankster. Such boys, as Knight
knew from personal experience, often turned into
strong-willed adults.

"Strawberry creme or rum sponge, my lord?" Mrs.
Evans asked him.

"Either one would be wonderful." What did he
care about dinner? Did he really want to be digesting
a trifle in the middle of his elopement?

"Perhaps I should ask Miss Grant's opinion," Mrs.
Evans said. "She might have an idea of what dishes
her uncle would like."

"Ask her," Knight said, looking around with a frown.
"If you can find where she has disappeared to, that is."

With all the undercurrents of tension and conspiracy in the air, Catriona thought it was a miracle that

dinner proved to be such an uneventful affair. Still, every time a door opened in the house, every time a spoon was dropped, conversation stopped, followed by a swell of expectant silence.

Was the enigmatic Scotsman from Miss Grant's past here yet? Everyone seemed to wonder when the young man would arrive. Uncle Murdo had enhanced Lamont's character and personal charm to such a degree that even Cat felt the faintest prickle of curiosity about him. But only the faintest, mind you. Whenever Lamont's name was mentioned, Knight's eyes darkened dangerously, and he regarded her with a lordly arrogance that warned her she belonged only to him.

But the mysterious Lamont Montgomery never put in an appearance, and she told herself that she ought to be glad. That boy had been nothing but trouble from the moment he was born, a changeling child, some believed, and if he was offering to marry her, it was only because he had been blackmailed into it, or could he possibly covet the Earth stone for himself? Could this all be a devious plan on his part to take it from Murdo? She hoped that the mean-spirited troublemaker had decided to abandon this silly idea of a match between them. Just the same, a tiny part of her would have liked to reject him face-to-face. The humiliations he had dealt her in her tender years still rankled. He had teased her horribly, and she wanted to flaunt her newfound love under his nose.

"The pheasant soup was nice," Olivia said vaguely into the uncomfortable void of silence at the table.

"It was salty," Marigold said, dabbing her lips with a napkin. "Wasn't it, Murdo?"

He glanced at the door before answering her. "If it

was, I did not notice. The company at this table was too engrossing."

What poppycock, Catriona thought. They were as talkative as a party of mummies. Everyone was pretending that her engagement to Knight had never happened. She stood on impulse. "Well, if no one minds, I'm off to bed."

"To bed?" Olivia said, shocked as if Cat had just announced she were going to the local pub for a pint. "It's early yet. And Mrs. Evans has made her famous trifle in honor of your uncle."

"Perhaps you ought to eat," Knight suggested in that bossy manner of his that made her blood tingle. A shiver of longing shot through her as she caught his gaze. Of course, she ought to eat because they would be traveling for days, sustained only by passion and awful tavern fare. And in another month, they would sit at this same table as man and wife. He would have the right to tell her what to do, not that he'd been shy in this aspect before, except for the unpredictable part of herself that even she could not control.

They would dine together every night by candlelight like civilized people, and then they would go upstairs and make very uncivilized love in the dark. Her stomach coiled into knots of anticipation at the thought. Goodness, if these sorts of thoughts continued, she would be attacking him across the table. He made her absolutely melt with desire.

"Eat something," he said again, giving her a meaningful look.

"Perhaps she isn't hungry," Olivia said in a tense voice that indicated she knew something inappropriate was in the air. "Why should she eat if she doesn't have an appetite? It's unladylike."

He leaned forward on his elbows, his dark eyes narrowing. The candlelight played up the chiseled elegance of his features, and in the gilded shadows his shoulders seemed double their usual impressive breadth. "Mrs. Evans went to a great deal of trouble over this dinner, and I say we ought to express our appreciation by eating the damn thing."

Olivia flushed. "And since when have you ever cared about hurting *anyone's* feelings, I ask, especially a housekeeper's?"

Catriona sighed in resignation. "All right. I shall eat if you two are going to argue over it."

"Trifle," Mrs. Evans announced brightly from the door as Aubrey marched to the table bearing a tray. "Should I serve—"

The housekeeper gave a small shriek of startlement as the French doors to the terrace blew open, admitting a gust of wind. "Oh, goodness," she exclaimed as the candle flames of the candelabra danced and flickered in the playful breeze. "There's that storm I predicted on its way."

Murdo chuckled dryly, sitting back in his chair. "Dear lady, that is not a mere storm coming. That is only Lamont letting us know he is a little late."

Chapter
21

⚬⚬

Catriona made a furtive escape to the stables two hours later. Good heavens, it had grown chilly outside, and this on the spring evening of her elopement. Did the wind portend an unfavorable outcome? Wrapping her pelisse around her more tightly, she settled down on a bale of hay to watch Knight and Wendell, who were apparently engaged in a friendly argument at the opposite end of the dark, empty stall.

Every time she looked at her future husband, she just wanted to smile and throw her arms around him out of utter happiness. He didn't appear very happy himself at the moment, however. In fact, he was so engrossed in his conversation that he hadn't even noticed she had sneaked into the stables.

"And I swear to you that the bloody ladder was against the paddock fence before dawn this morning," Wendell said in an irate voice. "I nearly broke my back dragging it in the dark around the garden."

"Well, I didn't want it in the paddock," Knight said. "I'm not eloping with a horse. Anyway, it isn't that heavy."

Wendell looked insulted. "It's heavy enough that a woman couldn't have moved it."

"No," Knight said. "But three of them could." And both men paused, presumably trying to picture Olivia, Marigold, and Mrs. Evans meddling in their plans.

"Why do you need a ladder, anyway?" Catriona asked behind them.

The two men turned to stare at her; although Wendell was a handsome devil, a golden young god of the *ton*, it was Knight's dark beauty, the intensity in his eyes, that grabbed hold of her vulnerable heart. She spent several moments admiring the way his black greatcoat and pantaloons emphasized his manly build. He affected her now no less profoundly than he had the first time he had stared her down with all his aristocratic hauteur.

She slid to her feet. "What is it?"

Wendell grinned. "So much for abducting your betrothed, Romeo."

"Oh." Catriona felt a frisson of pleasure race down her spine. Knight had meant to make it a genuine steal-the-woman-from-the-tower elopement. "Do you want me to sneak back into my room? I didn't mean to spoil your plans."

He only smiled. "How did you get down here without rousing the Gorgons, anyway?"

"I used the stairs. Everyone seemed to be asleep."

There was a loud bang behind the stables, followed by a great trembling through the walls that disturbed the horses in their stalls. "What was that?" Wendell asked in alarm. "Surely not the wind again."

"We've found the ladder, my lord," Howard announced triumphantly a few seconds later from the door. "The ladies had hidden it in the maze, but Smythe spotted it from an upstairs window. Clever, ain't we?"

Knight shook his head. "Clever and extremely loud. If all that banging around did not draw attention and awaken the household, then nothing will." He smiled again at Catriona. "Are you ready to go?"

"Yes. Oh." She ran back to the bale of hay and retrieved her bag, that smile of his making her almost forget what she was doing. "Now I am."

He nodded and took the bag from her hand, his fingers closing around hers. She gave a sigh of pleasure. His touch always ignited her female senses.

"Damn it," he said, looking down at her slender fingers. "I've forgotten the ring. I left it on the dressing table."

"Shall I fetch it for you, my lord?" Howard asked.

Knight hesitated. He could just imagine Howard tramping up the stairs and into his room with all the discretion of a baby elephant. "I'll fetch it."

"No," Wendell said. "Let me. Holmes is waiting for you in the woods."

"Do you want me to go?" Catriona asked. "I don't mind. I'm good at pinching things."

A burst of wind blew beneath the stable door and sent a handful of straw flying around them. Knight pulled her closer to him, the gesture instinctual and protective.

"What an exciting night for a runaway marriage," Wendell exclaimed. "At this rate, you'll be blown halfway to Scotland."

"I'll buy you a ring in Carlisle," Knight said quietly to Catriona. "A windstorm isn't going to stop us."

"The house looks awfully quiet," Wendell observed as they paused several minutes later at the edge of the darkened estate.

Knight glanced up at the darkened windows. "Too quiet. I don't trust it."

Wendell shook his friend's hand, then turned to give Catriona a fierce hug. "As Horace said, although probably under different circumstances, *Tempus abire tibi est*. The time has come for you to depart. Take care of yourselves."

Knight nodded distractedly, taking Catriona's hand to turn her toward the woods where the cloaked figures of his sister and Marigold stood, their faces white and anxious.

"I knew it," he said in utter disgust as Olivia rushed up to him, Marigold following more slowly. "I never could go anywhere without Olivia tagging along. It's a miracle she didn't enlist in the army."

"Thank goodness I caught you in time," Olivia said, taking a deep breath. She bumped against him with the enormous basket she carried in her slender arms.

He raked his hand through his hair. "Look, we were just out enjoying the evening—"

"Stop it," she said. "I know perfectly well what you were doing. I've known since last night. Howard is incapable of keeping a secret."

"Then what are you doing here?" he shouted. "Is it possible to take two steps on this estate without my behavior being censured?"

She blinked, falling back a step. "Well, really, I only wanted to give my blessing on your elopement."

Wendell grinned. "Except, darling, I don't think it qualifies as an elopement with a family blessing. That's the whole point."

"In that case, I don't suppose you want the picnic hamper, either, that Mrs. Evans packed," she said meekly.

Catriona's face softened. "Of course we want it, otherwise we'll probably starve." She glanced around, struck by a sudden realization. "If our elopement was that obvious to everyone, then where is Uncle Murdo?"

Olivia smiled gratefully at Wendell as he wrestled the hamper from her grasp, offering to take it to his carriage. "I think he went to bed. Didn't he, Marigold?"

The older woman nodded. "Yes, and he will be very upset when he learns that you youngsters set off for Scotland without so much as a by-your-leave."

Catriona looked through the trees at the house. It seemed rather suspicious that Murdo had given up his cause that easily, but perhaps he realized that the breach between them just couldn't be easily mended. For some reason, it saddened her. She might not be quite ready to forgive him, but he was family, a part of her past.

She felt a rush of tenderness as she saw Knight enfold Olivia in a hard, awkward hug, then bend his tall frame to kiss Marigold on the cheek. "Now, you two Gorgons behave yourselves while we're gone," he said with gruff affection. "And you, Olivia, don't go feeling so sorry for Sir Alistair that you start inviting him to the house, or he'll be sending you roses next, and I really will have to kill him."

She nodded, tears in her eyes. "I only wanted you

to be happy. A summer wedding would have been nice, but an elopement, oh, as if you were some fortune hunter chasing after an heiress. I could die of embarrassment."

"Except that I don't have a shilling to my name," Catriona said soberly, then turned back to Olivia. "It's not that I'm ungrateful, but James has been weighing on my mind lately, and I think he might need me. I have a hunch where his daughter Gaela is being kept. I want to see them together."

"Then be careful," Olivia whispered.

Knight looked up, his dark face reflective as Wendell reappeared from the road. "Perhaps you will have that summer wedding, Olivia."

She shook her head. "I'm done with matchmaking, thank you very much. Look what a mess I've made."

Wendell glanced from Knight to Olivia. "Well, is everyone made up?"

"I was never angry at anyone to begin with," Catriona said.

Knight stared down at his sister. "Nor I. Well, not really."

"I was never angry," Olivia exclaimed. "I only wanted to see Catriona married to a decent man." She smiled reluctantly at Knight. "Which she will be, in a very indecent way."

Wendell raised his brow. "They won't be married at all if they don't leave soon. There's the devil's own wind blowing down from the moor, fiercer than anything I can remember. Holmes is having a time controlling the horses."

"Then go now if you must," Olivia said, embracing Catriona in such a tearful hug one would think they'd never see each other again. "And for heaven's sake, send word from the yacht that you've made it across the Channel. I don't like you sailing off in a storm."

"Go before your uncle awakens," Marigold said. "I shall have a terrible time as it is, looking the dear man in the face when he learns I did nothing to stop you."

Catriona resisted the urge to glance back at the house. She was too afraid that she would see Murdo's face in the window. Instead, she concentrated on the blissful feeling that enveloped her as Knight took her arm and told his aunt, "Just tell him you couldn't stop us. It's the truth, anyway. I am marrying his niece if I have to walk through fire to do—"

"Oh, good heavens!" Olivia said with a muffled shriek; the wind had just torn loose the uppermost branch of a hazel tree and sent it flying across the garden beyond.

"Now we really have to go," Knight said firmly, his hand gripping Catriona's. "And, trust me, I will not let anything happen to my woman."

Catriona could only smile, feeling protected—and refusing to believe that the strange windstorm had anything to do with her elopement.

The carriage sped over ancient bridges and careened around hillocks and fields of tidy apple orchards. The wind seemed to chase them as they squeezed down stone-walled lanes, disturbing the ghost moths that haunted the hedgerows. Holmes swore at the top of his voice from the driver's box that they would be blown to Scotland once he reached the open landscape of the moor.

A few minutes before midnight, they passed through the sleeping village of West Briarcombe. Catriona frowned when she saw the blacksmith working at his forge outside the smithy. Red-hot sparks flew from his anvil into the night, and there was something disturbingly familiar about his black-caped form. He half turned as he heard the carriage pass and . . . waved?

She sat up, her breathing arrested. "Knight, did you see that? Isn't it a bit late for a smithy to be banging away like that? And he waved at me. He *waved.*"

He leaned over her shoulder. "I don't see a blessed thing."

"We're past him now," she said, staring back at the rows of thatched cottages that receded into the distance.

"Yes. Almost to the graveyard," he said conversationally, lifting the hair from her nape to blow into her ear. "Hold your breath."

She started to laugh, only to subside into silence at the sight of several ethereal figures floating around the gravestones in some ghastly spectral dance. She pressed her face closer to the window, disbelieving.

"You're shivering," Knight murmured, biting gently at her shoulder. "Cold or excited?"

"Tell me you don't see ghosts dancing around the graves," she whispered.

He glanced up in amusement. "Figments of the mist. That's a bucket swinging over the well, not a ghost."

"Except that there isn't any mist," she said half to herself. "There's a wind. No mist. Something strange is in the air." Or *someone* strange. Surely Lamont did not possess such powers.

Knight brought both his hands to her shoulders. "I have the sovereign cure for nerves," he said in a deep voice, his muscular thigh pressing against hers.

She blinked. "What?"

"Take off your dress, and I'll show you."

"Take off—in the carriage?" she asked, her voice catching on a scandalized laugh.

He pulled off his heavy black coat. "We're going to give it a good try."

"You aren't serious—"

"Do you prefer the summerhouse?" he asked, unbuttoning his shirt. His broad chest bare, he drew her dress and loosened chemise down to her waist.

"I prefer"—she turned to find herself captive in his arms, his eyes dark with sensual intent as he studied her half-naked form—"you," she said, the word almost a whisper. "And I don't care where."

A slow grin spread across his face. "You look very fetching in that dress, by the way, and even better out of it."

He kissed her slowly, then moved his hand under her silk skirt to stroke the skin of her inner thigh. "Oh, my," he said against her mouth, his cool fingers touching the warm hollow of her womanhood, tangling in the curls there. "I've found what I was looking for."

"You really are a wicked man, Knight." She gave another breathless shiver as he began to kiss the aroused tips of her breasts. "And don't tell me you've never done this before in a carriage."

"I haven't." His fingers slid deep inside her slick heat. The invasion into her most sensitive flesh, coupled with his mouth at her breasts, forced a groan from her throat. "But I intend to, at least a dozen times before we reach the coast."

"Rake," she whispered, closing her eyes in erotic surrender.

"One who has apparently been reformed."

"I don't think so," she murmured, her body arching.

His dark eyes gleamed with enjoyment as she writhed against his hand. "But who could blame me for not being able to resist you?"

She laughed softly, loving him so much that her heart ached. "Oh, I can think of quite a few people."

He pretended to frown. "Yes, so can I, now that you mention it." He paused to press his finger so deep inside her that she gasped. "Of course, they'll never know unless you tell."

"Or unless Holmes unexpectedly decides to stop," she said, biting her lip against the sweet pain he inflicted.

"Holmes," he said, taking a moment to watch the pleasure on her face, "is used to this sort of thing. Duke is hardly a saint, either, if the truth be told."

"But he is in love," she whispered.

"Aren't we all?"

He leaned forward to kiss her trembling mouth. With a sigh of sublime pleasure, she locked her arms around his shoulders to anchor herself against his hard body, against the skillful play of his fingers below. It was the strangest feeling, the carriage hurtling across the heath almost as if the driver had surrendered control of the vehicle, while the man she loved seduced her without an inkling of shame. She twined her fingers in the crisp black hair that curled around his neck. Oh, she could die like this, in his arms. Several blurry minutes of pleasure passed before she even realized he had removed his pantaloons and was spreading her legs apart with his bare knee.

"How did you undress like that?" she asked in amazement, struggling to look over his huge shoulder. The dark, confined space seemed to enhance the animal power of his body. All she could see was his muscular back and sinewy buttocks.

"With some great difficulty," he said as he kissed her back into a sensual daze. "I think Holmes is trying to set a personal record for hitting every hole on the heath."

"That wind is wickedly cold," she whispered.

He threw his coat around them, cocooning their bodies in warm wool. "There," he said. "Is that better?"

"I meant that Holmes might be cold," she whispered.

"Well, I'm not crawling up to the driver's box *au naturel* to offer him my coat, if that's what you're thinking."

"I wasn't thinking at all," she said shyly, running her hand down his broad chest. "I was . . . well, enjoying. You are quite magnificent."

"Am I?"

He closed his eyes as her fingers trailed lower, teasing the head of his shaft until he caught her hand in his, and he drew back on his knees to enter her. "Open your legs all the way," he ordered her quietly.

"Knight, what if we slide off the seat?"

He eased his hands under her bare bottom to lift her to him. The tip of his penis pressed upward, and she caught her breath as he surged into her, his eyes gleaming with satisfaction. "There. Now you aren't going anywhere."

"Unless we both fall on the floor in a most undignified manner."

He gave her a smile as she closed her eyes, impaled on his rod. "In which case, I shall be so deep inside you that neither of us will care."

"You are everything I have ever wanted," she whispered breathlessly.

"You are more than I ever wanted." His smile faded, replaced by a look of somber realization. "I love you, Catriona."

She drew another breath as he braced one foot on the floor to pummel into her, gripping her hips so tightly that at first she could not move except to shiver. Then, slowly, she began to ride him, raising herself to absorb the powerful thrusting of his body as the tension inside her mounted. And when it broke, she heard him groan her name and felt his large body convulse in climax while outside the carriage the wind howled into the night as if in lament for what they had done.

Chapter

22

❧

She fell asleep with her head cushioned on his hard shoulder a few minutes after they dressed. Every so often, he would have to shift his weight to collect the damn stones of hers that kept sliding around the coach.

"Thank you," she murmured in a drowsy voice. "I'm thinking now that I made a mistake not going with my uncle to the holy well."

He wrapped his arm around her. The temperature had dropped inside the carriage. "It wasn't a mistake."

"Except for the curse on your progeny."

He glanced down at her, eyebrows raised. "I wasn't aware that I had any. At least, not yet."

He stared outside as the coach sped over the windswept heath. "The last time I came here was with Lionel and Duke hunting grouse," he said with a rueful smile as he remembered the three of them clambering over mossy rocks to chase one elusive bird in particular.

"And Lionel lost his footing and fell into a pool with his gun," Catriona said quietly, her eyes still closed.

He glanced at her. She looked so charmingly disheveled that he wanted to tumble her again. "I'd completely forgotten. Did he tell you, or did Wendell?"

"Neither." She buried her face in the firm hollow of his shoulder. "I just saw it in my mind."

"Toss a shilling in the hat!" he said in a theatrical voice, unable to resist teasing her. "She sees the past as well as the future."

"It's the present I'd be worried about if I were you," she said grumpily. "You're two seconds away from being clouted on the head."

"I will never mock your abilities again," he said solemnly.

She looked up at him. "Promise? Really, really promise?"

A horrible smile spread across his face. "No."

"Oh, you—you miscreant."

She curled up into a ball while he struggled not to laugh. "This takes getting used to. Give it time, Cat."

"What for? You're only going to get worse with age." Her forehead wrinkled in a frown. "And my visions are never going to stop, either, if that stone isn't returned to the holy well, or at least that's what Uncle Murdo said."

"Who can believe such a thing?" Knight asked her, smiling at the very notion. "He was probably only trying to lure you into the arms of this Lamar."

"Lamont." She sighed. "My mother always said that boy was trouble."

"Did you like him?"

"Well, when he wasn't tormenting me or showing off, he could actually be pleasant company."

"How pleasant?"

"Not as pleasant as you. I think Uncle Murdo had high hopes for turning Lamont into a healer, but it never happened. Lamont and I stuck together because we were both outcasts, that's all."

He grunted. "It's a good thing for him that Lamar didn't come to my house. I doubt he would have appreciated the welcome I had in mind."

"The same sort of welcome that you gave Sir Alistair in the stables?"

"Precisely," he said.

"Then you're right. He wouldn't have appreciated—"

At that moment, the carriage veered off the road to avoid a monstrous boulder that Holmes apparently had not noticed. His curses rang into the night as he struggled to bring the four frightened horses around. The vehicle slowed, and with a frown, Knight jumped outside to assess the situation.

"I'm sorry, my lord," Holmes said, standing in the middle of the moonlit road with a baffled expression.

The wind blew the tails of Knight's coat up around his back. "What happened?"

"I don't rightly know. I swear that this bloody rock was not in the road a few moments ago."

Knight glanced around. There were no hills within walking distance, only an ancient tumulus that sat like a ghostly sentinel in the night; it seemed highly unlikely that the wind could have rolled the stone across flat ground. "Perhaps you ought to stay on the regular coaching road, Holmes. We aren't in such a hurry to get married that we need have an accident to do so."

"But this is the coach road, my lord."

"Well, try to be a little more careful when we approach the cliffs to the coast."

Holmes glanced back once more at the boulder. "Indeed, I will."

"What was it?" Catriona asked as Knight rejoined her in the carriage, bringing in a breath of cold air.

"Just a boulder in the road." He closed the door against the wind, his face pensive.

"Oh, dear," she whispered.

"It really wasn't anything," he added at her worried look. "The horses weren't injured in any way."

"Of course the horses weren't injured," she said, looking even more distressed. "He always loved animals."

Knight looked down at her, wondering what in the world she was talking about or if he would ever become accustomed to her lapses in conventional behavior. The thing was, he didn't want to change her. He rather liked the mild anxiety of not knowing what she would do next, and he admired the unique passion she brought to life. But this alarm, over a rock in the road?

He frowned, removing his coat to fold beneath her head as a pillow. "'He always loved animals,'" he repeated in a slow, precise voice. "I hope that we are referring to Holmes."

"That's your arrogant English nobleman's voice," she said, biting her lip. "I refuse to answer. You'll shout at me."

He leaned forward, suddenly annoyed. "Do you mean *him?* Do you really believe your little Highland boy just caused a boulder to obstruct our path, out of the blue?"

Her teeth dug into her bottom lip. "He liked to cause trouble, play pranks exactly of this nature."

"Well, so did I, Catriona, but there are some things beyond the realm of possibility." He slipped his arm around her shoulder. "We aren't allowed to quarrel during our elopement, only afterward, and we're almost to the coast road."

She peered around his shoulder. "Are you sure?"

"Yes." He took her face in his hands to kiss her. "And once we reach the—"

She stared up at him anxiously as he stopped, turning his head to one side. "What is it?" she said in concern. "What's the matter?"

"I think—something strange is happening to me." He dropped his head back against the seat. "Is this the sort of thing that occurs when you have one of your visions?"

She leaned over him in alarm. "What are you talking about?"

"Could they be contagious?"

"What?"

"Your visions." He studied her from the corner of his eye. "I think I might be having one right now. What happens to you when they start?"

"Well, I—I feel on edge and irritable—"

"That's me."

"That's always you," she murmured. "But do you feel cold?"

He shivered.

She touched his forehead, suddenly suspicious. "You don't feel cold to me. In fact, your skin is quite warm."

"It is?" He closed his eyes, affecting a loud groan. "The vision is becoming clearer—" He opened one eye. "Is this how they come upon you?"

"No," she said tightly. "Not at all. For one thing, I do not believe I have ever made such an undignified noise in my life as you just did."

The playful twinkle in his eye did not escape her notice. She slid further back against the seat and stared at him. "And what exactly is this vision of yours supposed to mean?"

"Does it have to mean something?"

"Well, there is hardly any point to them if they do not help us to avoid a tragedy."

He pursed his lips. "This vision is not seeming to have tragic connotations."

"Oh, really?" she said coolly. "Describe it to me, then."

"Well. Let me concentrate." He pressed his fingers to his temples. "Ah, yes, there it is again. Oh, my."

All right, she thought. She would play along. "What do you see?"

He sounded astonished. "Why, goodness gracious, it appears to be you."

"Me?"

"Yes." He paused as a grin quirked the corners of his mouth. "It is you, naked in my bed. What a vision."

"You did it again!" she exclaimed.

He rose swiftly to pull her back against him. "Am I forgiven if I allow you to use me as a pillow again?"

She sniffed, refusing to acknowledge him.

"Fine. I will behave myself." He hid another grin as she settled her small body against his. "Come on, now. You can't hold a grudge against your soon-to-be husband."

"Can't I?"

"No, you can't. Now, go back to sleep. I promise to be good."

He dozed off himself only to awaken a half-hour later; he sensed a menace in the moorland stillness long before the carriage slowed. Something did not seem right.

The wind had died to almost nothing. Somewhere in the distant hills, a dog bayed, and Knight was amused at himself for remembering the Devon legends of headless horsemen and demon hounds on the heath sent out to hunt for their dark master. Hunt what precisely? he wondered now. A human soul? His own was a little too damaged to fight for. But what about a fey young woman whose magical touch *he* could not live without?

He rubbed his face. "I'll be making predictions at parties next, I suppose," he muttered.

Catriona stirred, her eyes slowly opening. "What is it?"

"Nothing. Only a dog."

"What dog?" She was suddenly awake, leaning over him.

"It's gone now."

"Perhaps the poor thing is lost," she said. She pulled back the curtain. "We can't just leave a dog wandering on the heath."

"We can't just interrupt our elopement to go chasing after one, either," he said firmly.

Just then, the carriage came to an abrupt halt. From the window, Knight could see moonlight glinting off a circle of standing stones, but he could not understand the reason for this second delay until he heard Holmes cry out, followed by the low murmur of voices.

"Stay here," Knight said over his shoulder, already opening the door, his hand reaching imperceptibly for the pistol inside his coat.

"Do you think we're being robbed?" she asked quietly.

"I don't know." He did not look back. He could see two horses standing behind the stones. Robbery was, of course, a possibility on this desolate road to the coast where travelers, carrying valuables, must pass before embarking from the harbor. Yet Holmes carried a musket and had not used it, unless he was outnumbered or injured himself.

He stepped down onto the road, closing the door carefully behind him. Holmes had left his box and was carrying on an animated conversation with— hell's bells, they had been chased there by Catriona's peculiar little uncle, and beside him a lean younger man in a black cloak, who could only be the fabled tormentor of her girlhood.

Lamont Montgomery.

Their gazes met like a pair of swords connecting in battle. For several moments, the two of them stood assessing each other in silence, until Knight walked forward to express his displeasure. He could not say whether this Lamont was a handsome man or not, although even from there he sensed an ironic awareness in Lamont's gaze, a native intelligence that most people lacked.

And, at the same time, Lamont was thinking: *Ah, yes. Tall, dark, arrogant, and aristocratic, the type who breaks women's hearts with a smile.* So this was the man his wild, wee Cat had selected as her mate. Interesting choice. An impossible pairing of opposites. Could they possibly love each other? he wondered with an unexpected twinge of envy.

"What do you want?" Knight demanded of Murdo, making a point of ignoring the other man.

"An honor to meet you, too," Lamont murmured.

Knight sent him a menacing look. "What is the meaning of this, Murdo? I almost shot you."

"That's exactly what I told him, my lord," Holmes said, clutching his musket. "Good thing my eyesight is keen. I recognized him as the lady's uncle, or he'd have been dead for certain."

"We have come to put a stop to your elopement," Murdo said, looking ridiculously short compared with Knight and Lamont, a gnat between a pair of angry giants.

Knight glanced toward the circle of stones. "On my own horses, I notice."

"One of them is mine," Lamont said, sounding amused. "And I believe the woman in the carriage was meant to be mine also. At least, so I've been told all my life."

He made a move toward the vehicle only to find Knight's hand firmly planted on his chest, holding him in place. "If you take one more step toward that carriage, I will kill you, childhood friend or not," Knight said in an undertone.

Murdo shook his head. "Please, Lord Rutleigh. You do not know the extent of his abilities."

"I suggest he does not question mine," Knight said, not giving an inch.

Lamont allowed himself a smile. "Would you really try to kill me?"

"No." Knight's face looked as if it were chiseled from the moon that shone down on them, cold and remote. "I *would* kill you."

Lamont glanced past him at the silver-washed landscape. "I do believe he is serious, Murdo."

"Aye," the little man said grimly, turning away.

"Then do what you must, Lamont. I canna bear to watch."

"What *is* going on out there?" Catriona called from the carriage. "May I please come out, Knight, and talk to my meddlesome uncle?"

"You've trained her to obey you," Lamont said in astonishment. "I'd never thought I'd live to see the day that anyone tamed her. I am impressed at what you have accomplished."

Knight did not betray his reaction to the words. "If our conversation is done, then we'll be on our way," he said. "Shall I give Catriona your best wishes, or do you want my worst?"

Before Lamont could answer, a dog started to bark from the standing stones. Both men glanced around to look, not noticing the spry feminine figure in a man's coat jump down from the carriage.

"Fergan!" Catriona shouted in heartfelt glee. "Come to me!"

At the familiar voice, the dog burst like a bullet from the stones to launch itself at her. Catriona shrieked in delight, knocked back against the carriage step by the hound's wiry strength.

"Oh, you big, slobbering beast!" she exclaimed. "You've gotten mud all over me, and here I am, almost a bride."

Knight watched her, unaware that his harsh features had softened at the joyful reunion. "That's my coat the monster is ruining," he said gruffly.

She laughed, throwing him a tearful smile. "Do you remember Fergan, from the night I first met you?" she asked as she plunked herself down on the step to hug the dog.

"Yes." He nodded slowly. "I remember him."

"And how is he here, I'm wondering?"

Lamont watched the exchange between his child-hood playmate and the hard-faced Englishman with another surprising pang of envy. The love they shared was obvious, even though Lamont had not yet experienced such an emotion. Perhaps he did not want to. Take this viscount, for instance. Here, Lamont suspected, was a proud man who had been completely undone by a waif like Catriona Grant. Although, to look at her now, the waif had grown into quite a beautiful woman, capable of rendering powerful men helpless.

"Catriona," he called her quietly, only to feel the pressure of Knight's hand on his chest, followed by another curt warning.

"Do not go near her," he said. The muscle that ticked in Knight's jaw was the only sign of the raw emotion underneath.

She stood slowly, the coat engulfing her small frame, the dog at her side. "Oh," she said, wrinkling her nose. "It's you. I should have known."

Lamont laughed in delight.

"I thought I told you to stay in the damned carriage," Knight said in irritation.

"She *almost* obeyed you," Lamont said, still chuckling at her honest greeting. "That's more than anyone else has ever been able to make her do."

"You be quiet, Lamont," she said indignantly, "or I'll be sharing a few of your flaws, too."

"Do you think anyone would care?" he asked with a cheeky grin.

"How did you find my dog?" she asked.

Lamont stared at her. "We met Thomas on his way home. The dog wanted to come with me."

She walked up behind Knight, slipping her hand into his. "I hope you aren't here to cause me trouble, Lamont."

Knight said nothing, his mouth flattened into a grim line. Lamont glanced down at her, studying her face for several moments before he spoke.

"No, Cat," he said, sighing. "I've no wish to cause you pain."

She seemed relieved, studying him closely. "You look different, Lamont."

"Aye," he said. "So do you."

"You weren't nearly as tall the last time I saw you, jumping out at me from the trees."

He grinned again. "And you weren't as short, either, pretending that I hadn't terrified the wits out of you."

"Excuse me, my lord," Holmes said from his box, where he had retreated when it became obvious that his presence was not needed. "But if you want to start across the Channel at first light, we'd best be on our way."

Knight squeezed Cat's hand before turning her toward the carriage. What had he feared? That her uncle's last-minute attempt to influence her would succeed? Or that her reunion with Lamont would spark a dormant flame?

"Get back into the carriage, Catriona," he said sternly, releasing her hand.

"Come with us, Catriona," Lamont said, taking a step toward her.

Knight pushed him aside. "Go back to your birds, little boy."

"Are you threatening me with physical force?" Lamont asked.

Knight pushed him again. "It would appear that I am."

Lamont stumbled back against a boulder. Slowly, almost imperceptibly, mist began to arise from the ground, swirling around the tall, dominant form of the Englishman who stood in front of Catriona.

"Stop it, Lamont," she said over Knight's shoulder. "He's perfectly capable of killing you."

Knight strode forward and grabbed Lamont by the front of his cloak. The mist between them was thickening by the moment. "She's right."

His pride stung, Lamont resorted to every supernatural trick he had been taught to thwart his opponent. He attempted to ignite a ring of fire around Knight, but the flames refused to catch in the soil. He sent bolts of power into the earth to destabilize the Englishman's arrogant stance, but Knight did not even stumble at the underground rumbling, his feet planted firmly apart.

Furious, Lamont summoned rainclouds to swarm overhead, but the heavens would not comply. Only the mist obeyed, an apprentice's trick, and even that was dissipating around the English lord so that he loomed unconquered like an ancient warrior in the tendrils of fog.

Was the force of Knight's love for Catriona so strong that it could defy magic? Lamont wondered in amazement. Never before had he encountered a human with such power of will. Not to mention physical prowess. Knight's well-honed body was a threat in itself.

"Are you finished with your tricks?" Knight asked coldly, arms folded across his chest.

Lamont sighed.

"Let him go," Catriona whispered. "Please, Knight. He isn't worth the trouble."

"I thought I told you to get back into the carriage," he said, annoyed.

She glanced up, clearly so accustomed to his gruffness by now that she did not take offense. "I will, but can we take the dog?"

"On our elopement?" he said, disbelieving.

She smiled up at him. "Since we're going to the castle anyway, he might as well come with us. For the company."

"I thought I was sufficient company," he said dryly.

Lamont gave another sigh of relief as Knight released him.

Knight took firm hold of her arm. "Make your farewells to your uncle," he said impatiently. "I trust there shall be no other delays along the way. And yes, you may bring the dog."

The carriage disappeared down the road at a reckless pace, leaving Lamont and Murdo standing alone on the moonlit heath, the mist dispersing as mysteriously as it had appeared. "Now, that was an interesting meeting," Lamont said with a wistful smile.

Murdo scowled up at him. "I wanted you to save my niece. Anyone can see that she is marrying the wrong man. Even his sister is opposed to their union."

"Why?" Lamont asked, turning toward the stones where his horse waited.

"Why?" Murdo's voice rose in irritation. "Because he is an arrogant beast and a rakehell, that is why."

Lamont shrugged elegantly. "Well, he certainly is not a beast to her, and rakehells can change."

"Bah. *You* just do not understand."

"I understand perfectly," Lamont said, glancing back down at the still road. "True love touches me, Murdo. It always has, and yet there are some things I have been taught to value more."

"But you have the power to stop them, why did you not try harder?"

Lamont shook his head. "The man is willing to die for her. I am not. Besides, I did try. Give them your blessing. You summoned me too late to save her."

Chapter
23

〰️

As the moon disappeared behind a bank of clouds, the carriage cautiously descended the cliffside road to the sea toward the snug harbor of Minehead. There, Wendell's yacht lay at anchor. Darkness engulfed the sleepy seaside, broken only by the light that glowed in the parish church to guide those lost on the moor and ships sailing into the Bristol Channel.

It was dawn when they finally settled in the luxurious rosewood-paneled yacht that Wendell raced every year in Cornwall and used to summer off the coast. They set off under light sail in the experienced hands of a captain, a cook, and three able-bodied seamen. Holmes looked relieved to see them on their way, remarking to himself that he had never seen such a queer wind in all his days, and wasn't it a blessing that it had stopped?

"Lamont was always very devious." Catriona had

turned from Knight to admire the tiger's-head brass moldings on the cabin wall. The flickering candlelight imparted an intimate glow to the confined space.

He came up behind her and drew her back into his arms. "He wasn't devious enough to marry you, was he?"

She half turned, relaxing in his arms. "You aren't angry, or ashamed that my family is so—so—"

She couldn't find the word.

"Unconventional?" he suggested. "Peculiar?"

"Among other things."

He pressed his forehead to hers, his eyes dark with desire. "But they can't be all bad."

"No?"

"No," he said firmly. "They produced you."

He took her face in his hands and kissed her deeply, his hands lifting to untie her pelisse. "I don't care," he said. He scooped her up in his arms and carried her to the comfortable damask sofa that was bolted to the floor. "I don't care if your great-grandfather was Bluebeard or if you were conceived in Newgate gaol. You are mine from this moment forward, and your family really doesn't matter to me at all."

She sighed and abandoned herself to his kisses, thinking that what he said was true. Certainly, she would have loved Knight if *his* great-grandfather were Bluebeard. She stared up at the darkly intent face of her beloved seducer and swallowed a groan. Oh, who was she deceiving? She would have loved this man if *he* were Bluebeard himself.

Then, slowly, her thoughts began to drift away, her senses lulled by Knight's talent for lovemaking and the splash of waves against the hull as the yacht began the three-day voyage up the Channel toward the coast of Wales and the Irish Sea. Within a matter of moments, they were both naked and exploring each other's body, learning the secret ways of sensual torture as if the world did not exist. Several hours later, they still had not moved from the sofa; they were earnestly discussing whether they would have eggs and bacon for breakfast or scones with clotted cream and decided on both.

And in the back of her mind, instead of his comments about her family reassuring her, she felt a tiny prickle of anxiety. He hadn't met James yet. Would the two men make friends? She hoped that introducing them to each other was not an invitation to trouble.

They were married five days later, not at Gretna Green, as they had planned, but in a quiet hamlet away from the bustle of the Border. It was Knight who had insisted on the change. He did not particularly want to take his vows in a place where bounders—Olivia's voice echoed in his mind—wed lovestruck heiresses for their money or where outraged papas chased their pregnant daughters to the altar. No, he wanted to make her his wife in a place untainted by greed or desperation.

Fair skies had accompanied them as they sailed through the Solway Firth into Scotland, and that same mild weather followed them into the Border farmlands, where they rode on hired horses and passed their first night as man and wife in a coaching inn off the Dumfries road. Fergan trailed after, keeping his master and mistress in view.

In the middle of the night, they toasted their marriage with the bottle of smuggled French brandy that the owner of the crowded Georgian stone inn had sent up to their room. Royalty, the man told them proudly, had once lodged in their very chamber.

"Too bad he only remembered to give us one glass," Knight remarked as he sat opposite Cat in the ponderous Jacobean boxwood bed. "Still, I suppose he must know quality when he sees it, or we'd be drinking broth and boiled milk."

"From a skull," Catriona said wryly. She was sitting cross-legged on the bed with a sheet modestly draped over her. He was unabashedly nude in all his muscular glory. "Everyone knows how barbaric we are in the north."

He put the glass on the bedside table and pulled her against him. "I rather like the idea of a barbaric bride," he said, his hands curling around her buttocks to raise her onto his lap. "Would you like to do battle with me?"

"Again?"

"Yes, again," he murmured, easing her down onto the bed, "and again and again. However"—he paused to kiss her, drawing her lower lip between his sharp white teeth—"I should warn you that I can be something of a barbarian myself."

"Oh, aye." Her eyes gleamed in amusement. "You're very good with your spear, for one thing."

He grinned. "Am I?"

"The other barbarians are ablaze with envy."

"I can just imagine," he said. "Wed to you, naked in bed, well, what barbarian could ask for more?"

She wriggled beneath him. "The mattress could be a wee bit more comfortable, for a start."

"A true barbarian would not notice."

"You'll notice if you're covered with flea bites in the morning."

"My heathen hide is too tough to penetrate."

"I thought that was your head." She sat up as he suddenly slid down under the coverlet, his unshaven jaw abrading her belly. "Knight, where—what are you doing?"

"Living up to my reputation," he said in a muffled voice. "And, by the way, the fleas aren't the only things that like to bite in the night."

"You aren't—" Humiliation, underlaid with indescribable pleasure, rendered her helpless. She twisted to escape until he caught her wrists to hold her still as his tongue seared her like a brand. She thought that she might never speak to him again, if she survived to speak at all. But he was her husband, and the things he made her feel, the needs he awakened, brought out a primal instinct that she could only blindly obey.

She was swollen and sore in the places he loved with his mouth. He'd already shown her several nights of shameless passion that had left her weak and trembling, and now, as she was beginning to gain a sense of a woman's power, learning that she could bring this strong man to his knees, she didn't think anything of a sexual nature could shock her again. She was wrong.

He groaned as he tasted her, his big hands forcing her legs wider apart to allow him better access. She was arching off the bed, not to escape him but in reaction to the flickers of white-hot sensations that built in her lower body. And every so often, the rogue would glance up to gauge her reaction or to smile, leaving her suspended in aching pleasure, forcing her to beg him to continue the sweet torture. Then his tongue would stab at her again, teasing the bud of her sex, until she climaxed. Her body was still shivering with aftershocks of pleasure as he slid up beside her. She curled into his chest, breathing the spicy scent of his skin, her arms wrapped around his waist.

"Oh," she whispered, her voice husky.

He closed his eyes in contentment. Several moments passed.

"There is one thing I probably should warn you about, Knight."

His brow lifted. "You have another uncle in Scotland."

"Of course not. I just thought I ought to forewarn you—James is a little odd."

He tugged the ends of her hair that twined around his belly. "And you and your uncle are not?"

"Well, James has a bit of a temper."

"Ah."

"And he shouts."

"Goodness."

"And throws things."

"Oh, dear."

"And he shoots at things."

He drew back slightly to look down at her. "Things? As in deer and grouse?"

"Hmm." She evaded his gaze, hiding her face in the hollow of his neck. "More as in chandeliers and bedposts. And sometimes, well, sometimes he shoots at people."

"At people." He put his forefinger under her chin. "People he doesn't like or just any poor soul in particular?"

"I am not positive," she whispered, "that in his inebriated state James makes the distinction."

"What are you trying to say, Catriona? That your brother might try to kill me?"

"No," she said slowly. "I think it's me that he might be killing."

He sat up, disentangling his hands from her hair. He hadn't known where the conversation was heading, but now he was concerned. "And why would that be?"

She pulled the sheet up to her chin, her eyes luminous in the grainy darkness. "I didn't exactly tell him I was leaving, you see."

He should have appeared more upset, but he had figured this out himself. "So you're saying that you ran away."

"Well, I did leave a note."

"I was under the impression that it was his idea that you find a wealthy husband to enrich the family coffers."

"And so it was," she said earnestly, the words rushing out, "but I couldn't stay and marry the widowed laird with bad teeth and five obnoxious children, now, could I?"

"Your brother had already made a match for you?" he said in astonishment, wishing now that he had made Simmons pursue the matter.

"He was in the process," she admitted miserably. "But I knew I could do better for myself, and I certainly have."

He raised his brow. "I wasn't aware that the condition of my teeth or my childless state rendered me such a catch."

"Among other things."

He shook his head. "Good God, Catriona. I don't quite know what to make of this. If I were your brother, I might do a little shouting myself."

"I couldn't begin our married life with another secret between us. I had to tell you."

He grunted.

"And I couldn't have you walking into that castle expecting a royal welcome. My brother isn't known for his hospitality under the best of circumstances. I can only hope that he finds Gaela soon so he has someone of his own to love."

He glanced around the room, at his clothes thrown over the back of a chair, hers discarded in the corner where he had undressed her, only a foot from the door. They had barely made it up the stairs, stopping to kiss and coax Fergan away from the tavern cat. Gray-violet light had begun to break through the shuttered window and lend an otherworldly undercast to the shadows. From outside drifted a cacophony of muted sounds, the whicker of horses, the creak of wheels, springs, and harnesses, the light patter of rain on the windowsill.

A bunch of heather and broom, twined with trailing ivy, had been placed on the center of the table. "Flowers for the bride," he said to himself. "Well, it's a nice gesture, and I'm sure the innkeeper expects a generous tip for them, and the brandy."

He felt her hand on his back and turned his head to look at her, his muscles tightening in pleasurable anticipation of her touch. So he hoped to awaken every morning for the rest of his life, with her beside him to start the day. He decided that he would like being married more than he'd ever guessed.

"What are you thinking?" she asked.

It was impossible even to pretend that he was upset with her when all he could think about was her enticing body and the intimacies they had shared. "I was wondering how I will react to a brother-in-law who is liable to shoot us on sight."

She laughed softly and tugged him down on top of her, whispering, "He usually misses."

"Now, that's a consolation." He caught his breath as their naked bodies touched, the hard contours of his fitted against her softer curves and hollows. "Do you think we should wave a little white flag when we walk into the castle?" he teased. "Or will writing a letter to alert him of our arrival suffice?"

"He'd raise the drawbridge if he knew a stranger was coming." She sighed as he drew her back against him. "It *is* nice being married to you, Englishman."

It was more than nice, he thought, as two hours later, they dressed between slow, passionate kisses and reluctantly surrendered the pleasures of their marriage bed. Knight kept her close to his side in the crowded taproom, aware of the interested looks his pretty wife drew from the early-morning travelers, the merchants and farmers who had business in the north.

In fact, he was so distracted by her himself that he failed to listen attentively to the innkeeper when he tried to settle the bill. "Excuse me," he said. "How much do I owe?"

"Nothin', my lord. 'Tis all been paid for in advance."

Knight smiled, glancing down at his wife. "That would be Wendell, although how he knew we would end up in this precise place is a mystery." He glanced back at the amicable innkeeper. "The Duke of Meacham is a generous devil. However, allow me to add a generous tip for the extra service we received."

The innkeeper looked a little puzzled. "His grace

might indeed be generous, my lord, but I do not think it was he who settled the account. The name my wife has here is . . ." He squinted to read the ledger book. "Ah, there it is. Lamont Montgomery. Aye, that's the one. And he added a handsome tip."

"Oh, dear," Catriona said quietly, raising her gaze to her husband's face.

Knight lifted his brow and led her outside without a word. Standing in the bustling courtyard, amid the shouts of coachmen and young boys selling hot sausage pies, he said, at last, "I do not know what to think of this."

"Well," she said meekly, stealing another look at his unsmiling face, "it would seem at least that my uncle has forgiven us."

He rolled his eyes at that, then nodded curtly to the boy who was waiting to bring them their horses for the journey through the steep hillside passes. Perhaps it did seem ridiculous, to resent Lamont's "congratu-lations" when Knight had so clearly come out the winner in the contest for Catriona's hand. But some part of his masculine pride still resented another man footing the bill for their honeymoon.

"I suppose," he said as they took the lesser-traveled Annan road in the gray morning mist, "that if you have accepted my family's flaws, I should have to accept yours."

"Lamont isn't really a relative, though," she said quietly, gazing at the verdant hills that rose before them.

"Then that leaves us with your brother."

"Aye." Her face darkened. "It does."

Chapter

24

❦

The road followed the River Nith into a dense conifer forest before ascending the high moor. Three days later, they reached the rugged red-sandstone castle that stood alone in the green foothills of Roxshire. Knight watched his wife as she dismounted and knelt in a patch of golden gorse, suddenly subdued and hesitant to continue.

"What is it? This is your brother's home?"

She nodded, putting her arms around the dog Fergan, who seemed reluctant also to plunge ahead into the quiet that was disturbed only by the gurgling of a small burn.

Knight looked more closely at the castle. The mortar needed repair; the west tower had been damaged during a religious war two centuries ago, she'd explained earlier. But what had happened to his wife's enthusiasm, her eagerness to reconcile with her brother?

"What is it?" he asked again, sliding from the saddle behind her.

She shook her head. "I just thought, what if he refuses to see me? What if he won't forgive me for running away?"

"I'll be there to talk to him."

"She lifted her face to his. "What if something has happened to him?"

"Let's hope that Thomas made it back here to prevent such a thing." He glanced past her to the castle. "Is it always this quiet?"

"No." She frowned and buried her face in the hound's fur. Her voice lowered to a whisper. "The dairy cattle are gone. I think we may have come too late."

He took her hand and pulled her to her feet, his voice firm. "We'll find out. At least he's not shooting at us from the parapets."

"I know," she said with a troubled frown. "That's what has me worried."

They rode through the arched iron gateway into a deserted yard, startling a flock of jackdaws from the rusty pump. A thin plume of smoke rose from the kitchen, but no one came to stable their horses or to escort them into the keep. Catriona took so long brushing down her rented mare that Knight practically had to drag her along the dank, abandoned passageway to the great hall. The air smelled of mildew and burned pitch oil.

It was late afternoon, and no candles had been lit to break the oppressive gloom of the cavernous hall where banquets had once been held and fierce border raids planned. Knight grimaced as the odor of stale salmon and unswept ashes assaulted him. Cobwebs dangled in thick swatches from every corner of the barrel-vaulted ceiling. For a moment, he almost over-looked the tall, blond-haired figure slumped in the carved chair at the head of the table. He seemed as worn and lifeless as the castle itself.

The man slept, a pistol and a bottle in his lap, his lithe frame clad in a filthy hunting shirt and nankeen trousers. Knight glanced away from the fireplace just in time to see Catriona press her forefinger to her lips and creep toward the chair. Before he could stop her, she had grabbed the pistol from the sleeping man's lap to hide it under the table. And none too soon.

The instant she stepped back from the chair, the man awakened, his hand reaching for the gun.

"Hell's bloody bells!" he roared at the top of his voice, half springing from the chair in reaction. "I'm going to rip your head off—"

Knight pulled Catriona back toward the door, his face furious. "Sit down, you damned fool. In your current state, I doubt you are capable of beheading even a fly."

James fell back into his chair, his bewildered gaze swinging from Catriona's downcast face to the angry man who towered over him. "Who—" His voice sounded as raw as a crow's, hoarse from drink. "Catriona, my God, is that you, then? I thought you were—I was afraid you were dead."

"She would have been if you'd gotten your hands on that gun," Knight said coldly.

She took a hesitant step toward the chair. "Did Thomas not tell you that I was safe?"

James shook his head, looking wan and shaken. "The old bastard told me nothing, and I knew he was lying. I'll skin—" He glanced up at Knight and subsided into a brief silence. "Who the bloody blazes is your knight in shining armor?" he asked sourly.

She glanced up at her husband, that infectious grin breaking across her face. "He *is* my Knight. My Knight errant. Oh, James—"

And as Knight watched her with his heart in his throat, she launched herself at her half brother, who hesitated for only a moment before catching her in his lean arms with a sob of emotion.

Knight watched another moment before he turned and walked toward the door, to allow them privacy. James was holding Cat like a lifeline, and she was consoling him, offering comfort as she had probably done on countless past occasions. She was saying something about the daughter who had been stolen from James, and he was absorbing every word like raindrops taken into parched soil.

Family, Knight thought with a sigh as he wandered back out into the shadowy coldness of the connecting hallways. Who but the good Lord could forgive such a multitude of sins? Less than five minutes ago, James had been threatening his sister's life, and now, look at him, a grown man, weeping in her arms.

He turned abruptly in the passageway. On second thought, perhaps it wasn't a good idea to leave his wife alone with the unstable young earl. He quickened his steps, only to find another man obstructing the doorway, watching brother and sister make amends.

At first, he did not recognize Thomas, trim and tidy in a clean white shirt, jacket, and velvet trousers. He glanced at Knight, not in surprise but with admonition. "Ye brought her back."

Knight frowned. "Wasn't I supposed to?"

"I thought ye were going to take care of her," Thomas said.

"I have." He glanced past the man, distracted by the sound of Catriona's laughter. "Damn it, I married her. I intend to spend my entire life taking care of her."

If Thomas was surprised by this announcement, he did not show it. His leathery face reflected only concern as he looked into the hall at Cat and her brother. "Ye might begin by takin' her home, then, if I may speak bluntly."

"Are you capable of anything else?"

Thomas's throaty laughter echoed in the drafty corridor. "So my wee Cat worked her charm on ye, did she?"

"You don't seem surprised," Knight said wryly. "Was that your plan all along?"

"Hell, no," the older man said. "I was hopin' she'd land herself that duke."

"He never had a chance," Knight said quietly, staring at his wife's animated face. "I would have fought a king for her."

Thomas's eyes softened at the affection on the Englishman's austere face, where before there had been only arrogance and anger. "Aye," he said, "love is a power like none other. Yer life is renewed because of it, and my poor laird is drinkin' himself into the grave for the lack of it."

Knight remembered Catriona telling him that James grieved for his young wife and the child she carried who was taken from him. He hadn't given it much thought at the time, but now that he was married himself, the pain was more easily imaginable.

Never before had he felt so vulnerable to heartache, so compelled to protect.

He glanced sharply at Thomas. "Is she truly in danger here? Would her brother really hurt her?"

"Och, no. Nae on purpose. But the longer she stays, the less inclined he is to stand on his own feet and meet his obligations. There are people who depend on him for their verra existence. The estate is in ruins."

"I'll help however I can. That's why I'm here."

Thomas nodded approvingly. "Still, the help he truly needs must come from within him, and I dinna ken whether he has the mettle for it or not."

Knight thought of Olivia, of her battle with her own grief, and wondered why he had felt any hesitation at all over her relationship with Wendell. He ought to be only relieved she had found happiness. It took inner strength to survive the loss of love.

At supper that night, James was subdued; he did not drink once during the meal as he and Knight discussed the problems of maintaining an impoverished estate. But several times, he asked Catriona how long she would stay and if she could remember any more details about the image she'd had of his daughter. It was clear to Knight that James craved her company; she was a glimmer of light in the castle's stagnant gloom.

Knight awakened in bed much later that same night to find her lying on her stomach, staring across their spacious bedchamber at the embers of the dying fire. He touched her shoulder.

"What's the matter?"

She turned, burying herself in his powerful body. "I feel strange," she whispered. "All my life, I wanted to live in this castle, to call it my home. And James brought me here after our father died, but I've never belonged. Do you ken what I mean?"

"Perhaps it's because you belong with me and no one else." He pulled her closer, his voice low and reassuring. "Is there anything else to understand? You won't ever be alone again."

"Not as long as I have you."

"And Olivia."

She gave a quiet laugh. "Don't forget Aunt Marigold. Or Mrs. Evans. Our supernatural adviser."

"And Howard," he said. "Our overly scented, overly amorous, overly annoying footman. You belong with all of us, Cat."

"I have a family." The realization made her heart ache with joy; that was all she had ever wanted. "I have a home."

James stared at the bottle on the table, his gaze remote. For the first time in months, he did not wish to numb his emotions. Was it possible that Catriona had made some kind of supernatural contact with his missing daughter? Dare he allow himself to hope on such evidence? To be honest, Cat's abilities had once both intrigued and embarrassed him, but over time he had come to believe in her powers. And if wee Gaela were in trouble—

He rubbed his face. He needed to find her. She belonged with him, and yet she had vanished from the face of the earth. Without thinking, he reached across the table, then stopped at the shadow in the doorway.

"'Tis late, my lord," Thomas said. "Ye promised to take Rutleigh shootin' tomorrow."

He cursed under his breath, falling back into the chair. "Cat thinks Gaela might be in Sutherland, of all places."

"Sutherland?"

James gave a grim smile. "Unlikely, isn't it?"

"Her mother Ailis had an uncle in Sutherland," Thomas said slowly. "A minister of the kirk."

James leaned forward. "Why did you never tell me?"

"I didna remember until now. I met him decades ago, a fierce, unpleasant man."

"I must go there." James was out of his chair, pacing like a lion. "I'll need men, and the sheriff's depute. As soon as Cat and her husband leave, I will go after Gaela." He came to an abrupt stop, his voice low with fear. "What if she isn't there? What if I travel all the way to Sutherland for nothing? What if I don't find her? A vision is hardly evidence, for Christ's sake."

"It seems to me 'tis a chance ye have to take, my lord. Ye're dyin' day by day in this castle, anyway."

I'm pregnant, Catriona thought sometime during that same night; she was hovering in that hazy state halfway between dreams and awakening. But suddenly, she knew, she *felt*, that Knight's son or daughter was taking form deep inside her. She laced her arms around his strong neck and listened to the rhythm of his breathing. They had fallen asleep after making love, with his leg thrust between hers, her head on his arm, and she'd drifted off, dreaming of children and christenings.

A woman's angry shout awakened her several hours later. Catriona sat up in the curtained bed and stared around the room. Knight had already arisen, dressed, and left her, presumably to find his breakfast. She was starving herself.

"Where did these damn crows come from?" the woman, a servant by the sound of her, shouted from the bailey below. "Be gone, ye ugly things! Go to the devil where ye belong!" Then, "Och, look at the fruit. Pecked to pieces. Nasty creatures."

Catriona frowned, a dark thought crystallizing at the back of her mind only to dissolve as the door opened, and Knight appeared, looking more handsome than ever—and, better yet, bringing her food.

"Oatcakes, early strawberries, and fresh cream," he announced, sitting down beside her on the bed. "James said they were your favorite."

"Are you trying to spoil me?" she asked in delight.

A shadowed form moved across the doorway from the hall. "Your husband," James said cheerfully, "is a very generous man."

"Besides being the most wonderful lover in the world," Knight said in an undertone as he popped a ripe strawberry into her mouth.

"Modest, too," she said.

"Madam, those were your exact words to me only three hours ago."

"What were her exact words?" James asked, poking his head into the intimate atmosphere of the room. "Tell me. There are to be no secrets in my castle."

Catriona and Knight looked at each other, grinning like guilty children.

"The strawberries," Catriona mumbled, her cheeks bright pink.

Knight nodded unconvincingly. "She said they were the most wonderful color in the world."

James stared at the bowl on the tray. "They're red," he said. "Strawberries are always red."

Knight and Catriona looked at each other again. "He's right," Knight said.

She bit her lip. "No. Sometimes they're green, or almost red."

"A red-green," he elaborated, making the situation worse.

James gave them an indulgent smile. "Share your joke. Enjoy each other. God knows that happiness does not always last."

"Oh, James," Catriona said, another berry almost to her mouth. "That is so tragic, I cannot stand it." She thrust her feet through the covers. "I feel a sisterly compulsion to comfort you."

He sighed, rubbing the back of his neck. "Not with your nightclothes half undone and strawberry juice on your chin. Gracious, Cat, you are a viscountess now. You could try to behave a little like one."

She stopped at the foot of the bed, hands on her hips, and looked at her husband. "Did I say I wanted to comfort the monster? Murder him is more like."

Knight grinned at the other man. "I do my best. She doesn't even wear shoes to dance."

"I tried to civilize her," James said, shaking his head. "It's the fairy blood on the other side of the family."

She folded her arms across her chest. "The fairy blood in me is having a hard time deciding which of you to turn into a toad first."

James beckoned Knight to the door. "Mull it over while I take your husband out shooting in the hills. Or ride into the village with Thomas to see your old friends. They're having some kind of heathen festival today."

"Oh, it's May Day," she said, her face brightening.

"Did she bring those awful stones with her?" James asked Knight good-naturedly as he came to the door, his arm draped over Knight's shoulders. He could be a charming host when he managed to rise out of his dark moods.

Knight laughed. "Over sea, over hill, over every bridge, coaching road, and inch of ground from Devon to this castle."

Catriona guided the pony around a tangled path of gorse. The sun was setting in the lavender haze of the hills where her husband and James were enjoying a masculine afternoon of hunting. And making fun of her, no doubt.

Well, let the idiots laugh, she thought. While they were off chasing helpless creatures, she and her stones had healed a case of colic, one of erysipelas, and two of indigestion. Now, all she craved was a good wash and a cup of tea by the fire.

"Everyone was glad to see ye," Thomas remarked as they dismounted in the courtyard and walked together to the keep on the worn flagstone path.

"I missed them, too," she said softly, "but—"

"—ye have a proper home now," he said, nodding in understanding. "Aye, a grand estate to manage, and ye've no need to be worryin' about James. He'll come around."

"Do you really believe that?"

He hesitated. "I dinna know what he'll do. That's fer the likes of yer sort to predict, who can see into the future. As soon as ye leave, he's on his way to Sutherland." He stopped outside the kitchen out-buildings, lowering his voice. "So the visions havena stopped?"

She shook her head. "Not yet."

"I hoped 'twould change when ye left Scotland."

"So did I."

She frowned, refusing to meet his concerned gaze. Had her uncle returned the Earth stone to the holy well? Had the fact that it had been stolen brought her and her mother bad luck? Or should she even have believed Murdo at all? The time had certainly ended for her to go gallivanting off into the hills with him on a mystical pilgrimage, especially since she very possibly was pregnant. Or, at least, she hoped she was.

"Perhaps now that I'm married, I shall become an ordinary woman," she said with a rueful smile.

"Never ordinary," Thomas said fondly.

They fell back into step together only to stop at the sound of arguing in the kitchen. "Cook's in a temper again," he whispered with a grin. "We'd best hie it to the hall before she starts throwin' pots and pans."

Catriona laughed. "Some things never change."

"Aye—" He broke off, pulling her back against the wall as a turnip flew out the window. "What did I tell ye?"

"—and if ye dinna find that key by dark, ye'll not be welcome back in this kitchen!" Cook shouted.

A younger woman's voice, full of indignant woe, replied, "I didna lose the storeroom key. The birds stole it! They're evil things, bewitched—"

Thomas took Catriona's arm and led her away. "The silly bint probably dropped her key in the laundry basket. As if I didna have enough to worry about with yer brother."

Catriona cast an uneasy glance back at the courtyard. Ill-behaved birds made her think of Lamont and his penchant for causing trouble. But he wasn't anywhere near, was he? "Sometimes jackdaws do steal shiny objects to carry to their nests."

"Not this key, my dear. 'Twas as big as yer hand. What sort of bird would wreak such mischief, I ask ye?"

She sat on the edge of the bed and vigorously brushed her hair, resenting the part of the male personality that enjoyed hunting and stomping across muddy ground with a gun.

It was still light outside, the tranquil Borders afternoon broken by birdsong. She wondered whether Cook had ever found the missing key and why it troubled her. As a viscountess, she could hardly go about the castle on a domestic hunt, especially dressed as she was in a delicate silk gown. She had hoped the gown would please her husband, if he decided to return at a reasonable hour.

Her toes and fingertips began to tingle.

At first, she ignored the telltale sensation; it was too soon since the last full-blown experience, her debacle of a debut, and the familiar coldness and mental confusion had not crept over her. But in stages, it began, until the numbness made her feel ill, and it actually hurt to breathe.

Images danced at the edges of her mind, refusing to take recognizable form. She knew only that the vision portrayed two powerful men, their strength seeming equal, who struggled to possess something—or someone.

"Go away," she whispered, kneeling before an old-fashioned chest, one that might even have belonged to her father. Her fingertips pressed the carved wood. *"Go away."*

She heard the door open and sprang to her feet in relief. Knight would be there with her. She would not hide the truth from him this time but would allow him to banish the dark thing.

"Knight, finally, I thought you and James were never coming . . ." Her voice trailed off as the intruder slipped into the room. "Uncle Murdo," she said in astonishment. "Not you again."

"You did not take my warning to heart about returning the stone," he said, going straight to her wardrobe. "The deed is best done by your hand. Where is your cloak? We don't have much time if we're to make the holy well before dark."

She followed him across the room. "All the way to Saint Bridget's well? We'll never make it on foot."

"Which is why we are borrowing your brother's horses. Hurry, Catriona. I fear someone has been trying to steal the stone from me."

She hung back beside the wardrobe, staring at the window. A man's face began to take shape in her mind, his smile mocking. Was it Knight? she wondered anxiously, wanting and not wanting to know at the same time.

Murdo took her hand. "What is it?"

"Nothing."

"The parish allows pilgrims to visit the well only certain times of the year. There is talk that the church will destroy it to discourage paganism."

"Then let them destroy it," she said grumpily, pulling away from the cloak he tried to settle on her shoulders.

"Do you think that is wise?" He stood behind her, his voice full of gentle reproach. "Now that you have a child to consider?"

She spun around. "How did—" Oh, what was the point in asking how he knew? "Where is Lamont?" she asked, resigning herself to the situation.

"Gone off to Italy in search of a darker magic than I care to teach. That young man has grown away from me in ways I do not like."

She followed him to the door. "This had better not take long."

"How difficult can it be to drop a stone into a well, Catriona?"

"At least let me leave a note for my husband so he does not worry."

Chapter
25

❧

James broke the pleasant silence of the ride back to the castle with a compliment to his brother-in-law. "My sister has chosen well in you, Knight."

Knight glanced down at his own shirt and muddied trousers. "She might not agree when she sees me like this."

"A man cannot hunt and hope to—" James slowed his horse to stare up at the flock of corbie crows that darkened the sky. "Odd."

"What?"

James twisted around in his saddle. "They're flying to the loch."

Knight watched the dark cloud disappear over the hills. "Is there anything at the loch that would lure them?"

"Nothing but water, and a small deserted islet where a holy well, as the superstitious believe, is fed by a hidden spring."

A playful breeze stirred the heather that grew along the road. Knight drew back on his horse's reins. "A holy well?"

James shrugged. "I saw it once and was not impressed. It's more a cairn of stones than anything. In past years it was reputed to possess healing powers."

"Did your sister visit this place?" Knight asked, still staring up at the sky.

"Perhaps before she came to live with me."

Knight released his breath. His throat was damp with sweat; to his surprise, he had enjoyed the day with James, but now a sense of apprehension took hold of him, ruining his relaxed frame of mind. "Have you ever heard of a man called Lamont Montgomery?"

"Have I heard of him?" James gave a rueful laugh. "I caught him climbing the tower to Catriona's bedroom a few days after she ran away and banished him on the spot. And do you know what he did to retaliate? He sent a hawk to attack me while I was shooting. A hawk, as if we lived in courtly days. Of course I, haven't seen him since, but the villagers claim he is a wizard." James paused to take a breath, his gaze meeting Knight's. "Do you think—"

"I do." Knight wheeled the horse around, his broad shoulders straightening in a warrior's stance. "No one, wizard or not, is touching my wife."

Olivia looked up into the captivating features of the man who was leaning over her. The letters in her hand had fluttered to the floor, her quill dropped from her fingers a few moments later. "What did you say?" she whispered.

Wendell reached up to loosen his cravat. "I said

that I am in love with you. Insanely so. And that I am going to seduce you on the sofa or die in the attempt."

Olivia closed her eyes, murmuring, "That's what I thought you said. Oh, dear—oh, *oh*—"

She sat up in shock as he began to unbutton her gown, only to subside, sighing, as his strong arms forced her back down. His erection pressed through the layers of their clothing. How could she have forgotten the rumors of his remarkable virility? "Oh, dear," he mocked gently. "Oh, *oh*."

Her eyes flew open. Sensations were bursting inside her like fireworks when for years she had felt only an aching numbness, a grief that had turned her sensual nature to stone. "Oh, no," she said, catching hold of his cravat and twisting it hard. "You aren't going to seduce me, you scoundrel. I am not one of those halfpenny harlots who fall at your feet—"

He laughed helplessly. "What halfpenny harlots? Good God, Olivia, I've never paid for a woman in my life. Well, at least not for one under a shilling—"

He made a choking sound as she tightened her hold on his neckcloth. Unfortunately for Olivia, however, the maneuver only brought him down hard against her, in an intimate position that could not have been planned. She swallowed a gasp of shock as she felt his hand squeezing her breast, cupping its weight in his palm. His warm breath caressed her ear. "You reprehensible rogue. You're every bit as bad as my brother."

He took advantage of her distracted state to deliver a string of kisses over her jaw and throat. She struggled, not so much to avoid his advances as to stop herself from straining against his beautiful male body. "You're tearing my dress, Wendell," she said, trying not to shiver.

"That's a good idea." He nibbled at her ear, giving the hem of her gown an experimental tug. Olivia shrieked softly at the distinct *r-r-rip* that rent the silence.

"You—you dog!" she said, erupting into giggles.

He settled down beside her, laughing again. In fact, that was the best part about being with Olivia, they were always laughing, sometimes, like now, at each other, but usually at the world. They felt comfortable together, old friends who had not so much discovered their sexual compatibility as finally acknowledged it.

"You are a very, very bad duke," she said in a small voice, squeezed against his hard shoulder.

He turned his face to grin at her. "I am as hard as that oak tree outside the window."

"But not as big," she murmured impudently.

"How would you know?" He sounded hurt.

"I saw once," she said, her smile sweetly taunting him. "When you and Lionel went swimming in the lake. I peeked."

He frowned.

"Almost as big," she added, biting the inside of her cheek to suppress a smile.

"Oh, thanks. That's a wonderful thing for my future wife to say."

She lifted her head, shivers going down her back. "Your future what?"

"You heard me." He reached down and took her hand, lacing their fingers together. "We'll get a special license. We'll be married and moved into my house before Knight comes home with his bride. If we work at it, we can even have the first baby of the family."

She sat completely up, thrilled and appalled straight to her toes. "We couldn't. I couldn't. Lionel would—"

"—be delighted for you," he finished gently.

"No."

"Yes."

"Well, not this year," she murmured, the fact barely registering that she had just accepted his marriage proposal, and under very improper circumstances.

He sat up, facing her, and hooked his forefinger under her chin. "Next year," he said firmly, not asking, letting her know. "A huge affair—"

"Not huge." Oh, she had to set a limit somewhere in his wildly romantic plans. "Not for a widow."

He grinned. "Hell, I don't care. We can go to Gretna Green."

"We certainly cannot."

They stared at each other. The temperature in the room grew as steamy as a hothouse, encouraging lush emotions and a passion that made Olivia's body ache in secret places. Strange how she had seen this man practically every week of her life, had taken his peculiar grace and good looks for granted, and now, oh, all she wanted to do was lie naked beneath him and misbehave.

"I wonder," she said, trying to breathe, "what Knight and Catriona are doing this very moment."

He reached behind her and pulled her unbuttoned dress down to her hips. "This."

The wind had come out of nowhere. Catriona's hair whipped around her face, and her cloak hung heavily around her shoulders, drenched by the wavelets that assaulted the small boat. She clutched the stone in her lap as her uncle rode the craft into the rushes that lined the islet shore.

"There's no one else here," she murmured, staring into the thin stand of birches that ringed the tiny island. The space within looked dank and primeval, over-grown with ferns and briars and stinging nettles. She could barely see the path worn by desperate pilgrims.

"Aye," he said, wiping his face on his coatsleeve. "Not in this weather. Hurry, then."

She took his gnarled hand and stepped onto the muddy shore, gazing across the frothy surface of the loch to the other side. The stone seemed to get heav-ier and warmer with every step she took. Truth be told, she wished she had never set her eyes on the thing, and yet half of her hesitated, wondering if she really wanted to surrender that part of herself that was unique, that connected her to her mother and all the women of the family before her. "Will I ever be able to heal again?" she wondered out loud. "Will the visions really stop?"

"I don't know," Murdo said bluntly as he lifted a veil of brambles away with his staff. He glanced around, muttering through his teeth, "He's coming."

She scarcely felt the thorn that snapped against her wrist, leaving a deep scratch. "Lamont? But I thought he went to Italy."

"Aye, or so he tried to deceive me. Give me your hand. I did not dream he would go this far to achieve his ends."

They practically had to crawl through the tunnel of thorns, up a natural staircase hewn in the rocky slope, to the cairn of white stones where the well ran deep and pure. Around them, rags hung from the thin limbs of the trees, fluttering whitely, offerings from petitioners to beseech the saint who guarded the holy waters.

For centuries, the church had forbidden its flock to seek the well's supernatural powers. But in the past two decades the reputation of the well had fallen under a cloud. Fewer and fewer people reported the miraculous healings of yesteryear. Fewer pregnancies were attributed to the fertility-enhancing properties of the cold, bubbling water over which drifted mysterious curls of mist. Catriona could not see clearly five inches in front of her.

"Drop it in," Murdo said, his voice laced with urgency. "Drop the stone into the center."

A deep, taunting voice penetrated the silence. "You will regret it forever," Lamont said, pushing through the bracken ferns to stand before her. "Has he told you exactly what will happen if you release the stone?"

Catriona looked at Murdo. "What will happen?"

"I dinna know," he said in exasperation. "But I do ken what will happen if this bad boy here gets his hands on it. 'Twill be used for all sorts of mischief."

"Me?" Lamont said, looking insulted. "Catriona, listen to me. It is a trick. You cannot trust him. If he had cared about you, would he have abandoned your mother to her cruel life? Look at me, Cat. Look at *me*."

"Don't," Murdo said. "Do not gaze upon his face. Resist. Release the stone." He grabbed her hand, squeezing her delicate fingers. *"Release it."*

The mist was thickening as it had on the moor the night she eloped. *I don't know whom to believe,* she thought, struggling to breathe in the moisture-laden air. *All my life, Mama warned me not to trust Murdo, and yet my heart feels a connection to him.*

"If you drop that stone, you will die," Lamont said fiercely. "Murdo is jealous of your powers."

Her brain seemed to cease functioning, and her vision blurred. The waters of the well bubbled up over the stones, soaking her boots.

"In the name of God," Murdo whispered. "Believe me."

She released the stone and felt a bolt of energy shoot through her entire body. The water hissed and suddenly went still. As if from a distance, she heard Lamont give an angry cry, and then she felt Murdo's arms go around her, his wiry strength giving her support.

It was over, and she felt only a deep sense of peace permeate her mind.

Chapter

26

〰

*B*y the time *Knight located another boat,* having practically promised everything in repayment except his firstborn child to the fisherman who owned it, the wind had disappeared, and an eerie stillness had befallen the loch. He dragged the boat up onto the islet just as a man, face dark above a lace neckcloth, burst out of the overgrowth.

"Where is she?" Knight broke through the rushes to grab Lamont by the throat. "I asked you where my wife is."

Lamont's face paled as Knight propelled him backward over a scattering of boulders into the trees. "Oh, stop," he said, struggling to free himself. "This dramatic coming to the damsel's rescue just isn't the thing. Besides, you're too late. The deed has been done."

Knight's heart stopped for several seconds. "What do you mean?" He tightened his hands around

Lamont's neckcloth, forcing him back into the trees. "What have you done to her?"

"What makes you think I've done anything at all? I was only trying to protect her powers." His mouth twisted into a scornful smile. "You're the one to blame, my fine English lord. You're the one who has turned my wildling playmate into a wife." The last word was pronounced with such a sniff of disdain that Knight found it difficult to believe any violence had been committed.

He gave Lamont a fierce shake. "You didn't hurt her?"

"I only wanted the stone," Lamont said bitterly. "Let me go."

"If you're lying, I'm going to tear you apart and feed you to your damn birds."

"I said I didn't touch her!"

"Then where—"

"Kni-i-i-ght!" Catriona's voice, sounding startlingly cheerful, called to him across the loch. Astonished, Knight turned. He saw her waving at him from the little boat as her uncle plied the oars, cautioning her to sit before she fell and gave them both a good soaking.

"Would somebody care to explain to me exactly what has happened?" he demanded loudly, turning back to the tree only to find that his captor had vanished.

As had the boat which Knight had mortgaged his soul to obtain. Lamont was rowing for his life across the loch, a flock of crows flying in a raucous formation above him.

Cupping her hands to her mouth, Catriona shouted from her receding boat. "Kni-i-i-ght! What are you doing over there? I thought you were shooting with James. Don't tell me you swam across the loch."

He put his hands on his hips. "I'm not telling you anything," he shouted back, "except that somebody had better get me off this islet."

Catriona's shouts were getting weaker. "Murdo said that he'll come back to get you after he puts himself to shore! The boat isn't big enough for you." She hesitated, barely audible now across the water of the loch. "Actually, it is, but he's still a little upset at you for eloping with me."

A few people had gathered on the opposite shore: James, Thomas, the fisherman whose boat had disappeared. There was no sign of Lamont now; Knight decided that the coward had probably rowed to the hill directly behind the holy well and made his escape. The crows were a black blur in the sky.

His wife, at least, appeared safe, even if a body of water separated them—well, only for the few moments. From the distance, it seemed that Catriona was explaining what had happened to her brother, who broke into hoots of laughter, slapping his thigh and pointing to his stranded brother-in-law in great amusement. Then Catriona motioned Murdo out of the boat and took his place at the thwarts. She was grinning as she rowed up into the rushes, grinning and shaking her head as if to ask herself how such a powerful man could have gotten himself into this predicament.

The powerful man climbed into the boat and took the oars from her hands. He rowed with clean, strong strokes that propelled them across the loch in moments. No woman was going to rescue him in front of witnesses.

"Knight." She was chuckling in delight. "May I ask what you are doing here?"

"What do you think?" he said indignantly as they

bumped up onto the opposite shore. "I came to rescue you."

"To rescue me?"

"Yes. James and I noticed the crows flying to the loch and realized that something was wrong. When I reached the shore, I saw Lamont in the act of running away. I assumed this was because he had committed some heinous crime upon your person."

"I see."

"Do you? I doubt it. I grabbed him by the throat and pushed him back against a tree. Unspeakable thoughts about what had happened to you filled my head. I was ready to kill him. And then I heard your voice. I turned and saw you calling to me from the middle of the loch as if I were some sort of idiot Robinson Crusoe who had been cast away."

She smoothed her skirt over her knees. "But you had lost your boat."

"No, I hadn't. Lamont took the opportunity to steal it while I turned around to look at my wife, whom I believed he had probably just murdered, or perhaps worse."

Her eyes widened. "What could be worse than being murdered?"

He shook his head. "You do not want to know. I was a soldier. Believe me, you shouldn't ask."

"All right." Her eyes twinkled with irrepressible mirth. "I won't ask."

He stared at her. "After all that, you aren't even going to tell me?"

"Tell you what?"

He leaned into her. There were a few more people on the shore now, servants who had been summoned from the castle, in the event that serious help was needed to rescue the earl's sister, who had gone and married a Sassenach viscount, who had gone and gotten himself stranded at the holy well.

"Was the Sassenach lord seeking a cure?" someone wondered aloud. "Was he sick?"

"Aye," another answered, "sick in the—"

Knight flashed them a look of annoyance, wondering which of his various body parts they assumed was in need of restoration.

"'Twasn't the headache cure," a maidservant said, as if he were incapable of hearing, along with his other deficits, "'Twas a *family* matter. *Private*, if ye ken what I mean."

"Oh, aye. Ye'd never guess to look at him, though."

"Shame, that. A man his size needin' help to do the manly deed."

Knight lowered his voice. "Do you hear that?" he asked his amused young wife. "They think I was so desperate to perform my male duties that I got myself stranded on this damn loch in search of a cure."

She gave him a winsome smile. "But we both know how untrue that is."

"Do not muddle the issue, madam. Are you going to tell me what happened between you and Lamont or not?"

"Oh, that." She frowned. "Well, he wanted me to give him the stone instead of returning it to the well. He threatened every manner of vile misfortune if I did not comply."

"Which you did."

"I did not!"

He sighed. "Of course you didn't."

"Do you think I'd let a numbskull like Lamont intimidate me?" she asked indignantly.

He studied her in silence, then said, "I thought he terrified you. I thought he inflicted all manner of indignities upon your person when you were a girl."

She hesitated. "I might have exaggerated."

"Do you mean that I almost throttled a man for nothing?"

She sat back, looking a little sheepish. "Well, he did try to trick me into giving him that stone."

"I'd have given him the bloody thing, the whole bucket of them, if he asked me."

She looked stricken. "And doomed our children to the curse I have carried all my life?"

He didn't move, startled by this emotional side of his wife. "What children?" he asked in bewilderment.

James tapped on his shoulder. Knight had completely forgotten that the boat was surrounded by a curious crowd of onlookers. "I think my sister might be trying to tell you something, Knight."

Knight glanced at her, his stern face softening. "Are you—"

She nodded, then whispered, "I think so. Well, I'll be certain in another week."

He leaned forward and drew her into his lap, a catch in his voice. "Oh, Catriona. You must be more careful. Look how wet you are, and riding over all those hills."

James reached down to help her out of the boat. "We should put her straight to bed."

"I am not going to bed," she said.

Knight followed her out of the boat, removing her damp cloak to replace it with his coat. "Come back to the castle and put your feet up."

"I am not putting my feet up."

James frowned at her. "Do as your husband says, Catriona."

"Now, that would be a miracle for the holy well," Murdo said from the edge of the small gathering.

"Come, Catriona." Knight held out his hand to her, studying her in pleasure. "Do you really think it's true?"

She smiled and took his hand, nodding happily.

"I hope that it is true," he said under his breath.

Her fingertips began to tingle, but not from any sense of foreboding. She felt her entire being bubble with profound joy.

"I do, too," she said.

She gave a deep sigh of pleasure as his hand curled around her kneecap, kneading gently at her tender muscles. "Umm. No, not there. It tickles like the devil. Do my feet again."

He leaned over and took her mouth in a deep, deep kiss, until her sighs evolved into little groans of encouragement and her hands came around his shoulders, pulling him lower. They had been trying, unsuccessfully, to dress for almost an hour. "I like you naked, wife," he whispered, bringing his mouth to her soft, full breasts.

She grabbed his shirt at the shoulders and pulled him to her. "I like you naked, too."

He laughed. "You're going to tear the buttons."

"Do you care?" she asked mischievously.

"Not particularly," he said with a devilish smile, sliding his mouth down her belly. "But your brother might not enjoy eating dinner with a man whose shirt is hanging in shreds from his neck."

"Where are your other clothes?"

"Being laundered. I did not bring that many belongings."

"Neither did I." She attempted to sit up, staring at her perfectly flat abdomen. "Oh! All your money wasted on those nice clothes, and I'm going to swell up like a stuffed goose."

He laid his palm down lightly on her belly. "Not for a few more months."

She placed her hand over his, and for several moments they sat in silent wonder, unable to imagine how this unseen being, this speck of life, would change their entire world. Then Knight nudged her back down onto the bed and began to kiss her, his large hand drifting between her legs. Their mouths still touching, she unbuttoned his shirt and pulled it off. He took off his trousers, his penis already stiff.

She was so wet that all he could think about was burying himself inside her and pounding her to the bed. But she was very possibly pregnant, and some part of his brain subdued that primitive male instinct up until the moment she took his shaft in her hands and opened her legs, guiding him without shyness.

"Now."

He straddled her thighs. "I don't need an engraved invitation."

"I didn't think so," she said, moaning as she gripped his lean buttocks to urge him inside her.

"God." He closed his eyes as he sank into her slick heat, praying for control, until, lost in pleasure, he forgot to pray at all.

She lifted her hips to meet his deep thrusts, running her hands up and down the muscular ridges of his back. She loved the animal power of his body. She loved her wicked husband with all her heart.

"Am I hurting you?" he whispered roughly.

"No." She pushed up on her elbows to kiss his firm mouth, her muscles tightening around him. "No. Give me more."

They kissed until neither of them could breathe, and the rhythmic pumping of his body into hers reached a peak. She felt him thrust upward one last time, and the muscles of his upper torso glistened with sweat; uncontrollable shivers of excitement raced through her. A few moments later, he groaned and flooded her with his seed, his powerful forearms bracketing her on the bed.

They lay entangled in hot, pulsing silence until voices from below roused them. The musk of their lovemaking scented the air. He traced the delicate curve of her cheekbone with his thumb. "I think we have just been summoned for supper. Are you hungry?"

"Famished. Knight?"

He reached lazily for the shirt she had practically torn from his shoulders. "What?"

"Thank you for helping James. I know you offered to pay off his debts while you were shooting together."

Their eyes met, his smoky dark with sensuality. For a dangerous moment, Knight did not think he had the willpower to leave the room. "Put on your clothes," he said hoarsely.

She pulled her chemise over her head, shivering as his hands took over the task. For the rest of her life, she would crave his magic touch. "Did you know that Uncle Murdo and I have made amends? It's true. I'm happy, and yet I'm wondering how returning the Earth stone will change my life. What if the visions don't go away?

"We'll buy a gypsy wagon and wander from town

to town, selling fortunes. Aunt Marigold can dance with a tambourine around the campfire."

"And Uncle Murdo can play the fiddle for her."

"Olivia and Wendell could throw knives at each other," he said.

"What about James?" she whispered. "Do you think that he will ever stop drinking? Do you think finding his daughter will change him?"

"I don't know," he said, rising from the bed to hunt for his trousers. "I've seen men go either way when they are given a second chance. In the end, it will depend on how much strength he can summon. But work is a good thing. It will occupy his mind, and perhaps, over time, he can find happiness again." He hesitated, his brow arching. "Why do you have that wicked smile on your face?"

"It's you."

He narrowed his eyes at his seductive young wife. "What about me?"

"You don't look half so intimidating delivering advice when you are wearing only your shirt." Her gaze wandered down his well-muscled torso. "It's quite an impressive sight, nonetheless."

Olivia was busy penning anonymous notes to the newspapers about her brother's wedding. The candlelight caught the dark glints in her hair as she bent over the desk, reading: "'. . . a romantic affair in a Scottish castle with the Earl of Roxshire's sister. The bride wore a gown of Honiton lace and seed pearls created by Madame Malraux, formerly of Paris.'"

"And carried a bucket of stones," Wendell murmured.

"I think we shall omit that detail," Olivia said. "Along with any references to an elopement."

"A good idea."

She peered at him anxiously. "Let the scandal broths stew in their own juices. It sounds respectable enough, don't you think?"

He hesitated. "It does."

She put down her pen. "That is a provocative grin on your face, Wendell."

"Is it?"

"Yes," she said in annoyance. "It is. Does my attempt to put a stamp of respectability on my brother's bad behavior amuse you?"

"Not in the least."

"Then may I ask exactly what is it you find so amusing in my article?"

"It isn't the article itself, Olivia. Not at all. As articles go, it is more than adequate, convincing, superb. No, it is not the article."

"Then—"

"It is the *manner* in which the article was written."

"The manner?"

"In the nude."

"In the—" She glanced down at herself and gasped. "Dear God. I am still—"

"Naked." His grin widening, he rose from the couch and came to the desk to drape his jacket around her bare white shoulders. "I'm not complaining, mind you. It's a lovely thing to watch a woman in the raw write about respectability."

She groaned and dropped her head on the desk. "Oh, Wendell, what have we done?"

"Not nearly as much as I intended to."

Chapter
27
⧂⧂

$\mathcal{K}$ *night and Catriona left the castle* four days later. While she lingered over her farewells, Knight spoke in private to Thomas. "It is a shame that my wife's father did not acknowledge her. He had no idea what was lost to him."

"Stop whispering about me," Catriona said behind them.

Knight smiled down at her, relieved to see her in high spirits. The last thing he wanted was for her to be despondent on the journey home to the happy life that awaited them.

"Wait." James came striding across the courtyard, Fergan trotting at his heels. "I do not believe I gave my formal blessing on your marriage."

Knight saw Catriona study her brother's face, searching anxiously for reassurance that he was still sober. In the morning light, the young blond laird looked melancholy, his hands shook slightly, but he was very much in control. And anxious to make the journey up to Sutherland. He and four men from the castle were leaving in an hour.

"Please, James," she said. "Please don't destroy yourself. You will find joy again in life."

"Silly," he said gently, touching her face. Then he clasped his brother in-law's hand. "Will you bring her back after the baby is born?"

"I might like to fish in that loch," Knight said.

James nodded. "Then come back soon. Do not forget me." He looked into Catriona's eyes. "I'm going to find her. Ailis's parents were old, and it is possible they have died. Even if Gaela is not in Sutherland, I shall not stop until I find her. You've given me hope, Cat."

"You will find her," she said. "I know it in my heart."

The newlyweds had been home at Knight's Devon estate for less than a fortnight when Wendell and Olivia announced their engagement over dinner. Everyone politely pretended to be surprised. Still, it was not a public announcement but a private one, to follow Catriona's news of the night before that she was expecting her first child. And eating everything in sight.

"I have a fancy for cream puffs," she said, having just devoured roast duck, mashed potatoes, green peas, and a raspberry tart.

Wendell smiled across the table at Olivia. "You could still have that summer wedding, after all."

"Not this summer," Olivia said, struggling not to acknowledge that his foot was touching hers under the table. "Next year." Her head spun at the thought of all she had to do.

"Are you planning on returning to your house soon, Aunt Marigold?" Knight politely asked the older woman.

The dinner guests paused for a moment, awaiting her answer.

"Oh, no," Marigold said quickly. "Not with a baby on the way and Olivia a bride." She paused, with a tiny sniff. "Again."

Catriona broke the silence that had fallen. "I wonder if Mrs. Evans can make a cream puff."

"The manufacturing chemist starts to work next month," Wendell said to Knight. "I liked the man."

"A chemist could probably make a cream puff," Catriona said.

"I liked him, too," Knight said to Wendell, then glanced back at Marigold. "Olivia tells me that you will be living with her and Wendell after they are married."

"What?" Wendell said.

Olivia nodded. "Yes. I don't think she should be living alone at her age."

"Of course, I could stay here to help with the baby," Marigold offered sweetly. "I'm tired of my old house. Too many rooms."

Knight nearly choked on his port. "We couldn't ask you to make such a sacrifice."

"Marigold wouldn't mind," Wendell said, sitting back in his chair to enjoy watching his friend wriggle out of this. "She simply loves young children."

Knight stared at him. "Well, you and Olivia could have a child. Or two. Or three."

"In which case, I could divide myself between your

houses," Marigold said thoughtfully. "In the interest of fairness. I wouldn't want you to fight over me."

Catriona clapped her hands. "What a splendid idea. That way, you shall be able to see Uncle Murdo whenever you wish."

Knight blinked. "Excuse me?"

She pushed away her plate with a contented sigh. "Oh, didn't I tell you?"

"Didn't you tell me what?" he said, putting down his glass.

She smiled benignly at his look of astonishment. "I asked Uncle Murdo to come and live with us."

"You did what?" he said weakly.

She nodded. "I asked him to live with us before we left Scotland. Of course, he refused, saying that a wizard needed a supernatural atmosphere, a special place, to be his most effective."

He gave a sigh of relief. "Well, he's absolutely right. Everyone knows—"

"But then I explained that Devon is a supernatural place. I told him the folklore of demon hounds on the moor, about the legends of the headless horseman. And then—" She gave a jubilant grin. "He accepted! Hooray! We shall all be one huge, happy family!"

"Hooray," Knight said in a stunned voice. "I can hardly wait."

Wendell clapped loudly. "What a happy ending."

"What a—" Knight said under his breath, but nobody quite caught the tail end of his thought, except for his wife, who raised one eyebrow at him.

"I will send Ames home tomorrow to supervise the packing," Marigold said, patting her white dinner cap. "I am too thrilled for words."

Knight sighed. That would be the day.

Olivia tapped her spoon against her glass. "A toast. To family."

Knight reached across the table for his wife's hand, raising his glass with the other. One by one, he looked at the guests seated around him before returning his attention to the woman who carried his child, his heir.

"To family," he said. "May we be blessed with one another for all our days."

Chapter
28

❦

Seven months later

*O*livia *stared wistfully at the lacy bridal veil* that lay across her bed. In only a few months now, she would pledge her heart to Wendell, except for the portion that would forever be reserved for Lionel, her first love.

"I won't forget you," she whispered, biting her lip. "I'll love you always."

She left the room. She did not want to turn into a waterworks, not with Catriona's baby due any day now. From her window, she had seen her sister-in-law sitting in the summerhouse reading a book. Because the place reminded her of losing Lionel, Olivia had purposely not set foot inside it to this day. The closest she had come was the night she had caught her brother in the aftermath of seducing Cat.

But something drew her there now, a need for peace.

After all, the summerhouse was where Lionel had proposed to her, and Knight, her awful brother, crouching in the grass to eavesdrop, had burst into whoops of hysterical laughter when he heard her tearful acceptance.

The most wonderful moment of her life subjected to his juvenile mockery. She chuckled, despite herself. The three of them had been forever playing tricks on one another.

I just wish you knew, Lionel, how much we all loved you. And I wish I knew if you were happy, wherever you are. I wish it had been different. I do miss you so.

She climbed the steps to the summerhouse. Catriona was no longer there, but something, that strange feeling, lured her inside.

She stared around the dim interior, faintly embarrassed by her behavior. She knew that Knight and Catriona had been meeting in the summerhouse before their marriage, and sometimes afterwards, too. She smiled as she remembered throwing a shovel at him for ruining the girl. But all's well that ends well. Olivia could hardly complain when her plans had worked out better than she'd hoped.

She stared at the wheelbarrow. She had deliberately avoided looking at it. The garden vehicle sat in the corner where one of the servants had put it, untouched as if in tribute to the young man who had been a constant visitor to the estate. The dead bluebells she had gathered that day sat in the rusty bed, ghosts of their former glory, stalks, really. They looked as if they would disintegrate if you touched them. But in the middle of the dead bouquet, one bluebell lived. It was not possible. Had it somehow taken root in the soil and regenerated?

"Oh," she said, covering her mouth with her hands, and she came forward unthinkingly to rescue the willful bloom.

Someone, most likely Catriona, must have picked the bluebell and tossed the living flower there, not realizing the significance. She plucked it from the surrounding dead stalks just as her sister-in-law returned, stopping in surprise on the steps when she saw Olivia.

"I didn't know you were here," Cat said in hesitation.

"I came to see you." Olivia gestured with the flower. "Is this yours?"

"Mine? No. I didn't even know you grew them in the garden."

"We don't," Olivia said slowly. "They flourish wild in the woods. One of the servants must have picked it on a whim."

"Except that this is winter, and I haven't seen the first snowdrop yet," Catriona said. "Besides, it wasn't there a few moments ago. I know because I was thinking that if I weren't as fat as a partridge, I would use that wheelbarrow myself, but then I saw those dead flowers, and for some reason, they made me sad." She paused, putting her hand to her protruding stomach. "Goodness, what a kick. Do the bluebells make you feel sad, too?"

Olivia examined the delicate flower in her hand. The purple-blue cap was already starting to wilt and needed water. "No. They used to, but not now. They only remind me of good things now."

Knight left his desk as Wendell and the new manufacturing chemist reviewed past designs and future plans for the clay pits in Cornwall. He ought to be paying attention, but his mind was not on business. It was on impending fatherhood and his wife and his wish that she would not flit about the chilly garden like a fairy when the physician had sensibly advised her to take to the couch.

He went to the window. Ah, there she was, in the summerhouse with Olivia, which looked to be a tame enough activity, and—

He stared. Who was that man standing behind Olivia? Not Howard or one of the servants. He looked so familiar, and yet, no, it could not be.

"Wendell. Come here now."

"In a minute."

"Now, please."

Wendell frowned. "What is it?"

"Look at—damn, he's gone. He's gone."

Wendell raised his brow. "Who are you talking about?"

"It was him," Knight said in disbelief. "I think I just saw Lionel."

Olivia stepped out into the crisp morning air. "I'm going to put this flower in water. Be careful coming down. These steps need repair. And—what is it?"

Catriona looked down at her. "What is what?"

"You touched my shoulder."

"No, I didn't."

"Yes, you did. I distinctly felt a hand touching me."

"Well, it wasn't me."

"Of course it was. Who else could it have been?"

"I don't know, Olivia. Perhaps the wind."

"It was not the wind."

"All right." Catriona gave an unconcerned shrug as Olivia turned toward the house, her face preoccupied. "And I thought that we pregnant women were the ones given to fancies."

She took a breath at the queer sensation in her stomach. Mrs. Evans had predicted the baby would come late that night, but Cat assured her it would be a morning birth. She had seen the delivery clearly in her mind.

So the visions had not stopped, that appeared to be an inherited trait that the Earth stone had not affected, but the horrible anxiety and panic that accompanied them had. In fact, Cat discovered that she could will away a vision now if she made an effort to relax. But for the most part, there was no need.

All her glimpses into the future were of good things, of family and children growing old together, of passionate moments and laughter, the gifts of life so often taken for granted that bring hope of heaven to earth.

"Hello," her husband said, suddenly standing before her, her devil of desire, her protector. "I thought you were supposed to be resting today."

"And I thought you were working."

He took her hand. "I was until I saw you from the window."

"And?" she asked, a shiver pulsing through her at his touch.

He drew her gently into his arms. "I never was able to resist you. Come back inside with me."

She glanced up at the house, remembering how it had beckoned her that first night, magical and imposing in the moonlight. She had ached to belong. Now she did, she belonged to this man, and her secret dreams had come true. Lionel's invitation had not been in vain; his kindness had touched so many lives and continued to do so even now.

Somewhere in the distance, a merlin cried, and she

wondered with a wistful smile whether Uncle Murdo was on his way. He was part of her, the link to her mother, to the past. Lamont was, too, gone now to Italy to seek a deeper magic, but even he held a place in her memories.

The man who stood before her was the future. She leaned against him, sighing as she felt his strong arms enfold her and their unborn child. "Could I tempt you into my study, wife?" he asked without an inkling of shame.

She could only laugh. "Are you ever going to stop?"

He grinned. "Actually, I plan to take every advantage of you until your family descends on us. Olivia said you'd had a letter from James warning that he and Gaela are coming to visit soon. Apparently, the girl is, in his words, 'a wee whirligig. '"

"Aye." A frown clouded her face. "To think that Gaela's grandparents died within a month of each other, and she might have grown up with that grim old uncle."

"And now she has the run of her papa's castle," Knight said, kissing her until her frown disappeared. "James has lost his heart to her, and I know exactly how he feels."

She smiled up at him. "And how is that?"

His grasp on her hand tightened. "Happier than I ever thought was possible, because of you, my love. Life is very, very good."